What people are saying about …

Cascade

"A romantic tale that twists and turns with every page, *Cascade* is the ideal sequel to *Waterfall*. A riveting tale to the very end, this adventure follows Gabi back into the arms of the dashing Marcello as the events of history unfold around them in the present. Lisa T. Bergren leaves us with only one question: Can their love transcend time? Read this book—you won't regret it. I could hardly put it down!"

Shannon Primicerio, author of *The Divine Dance, God Called a Girl,* and the TrueLife Bible study series

"While I found *Waterfall* to be thoroughly enjoyable, I thought *Cascade* was completely captivating. It's so refreshing to read teen lit that isn't full of darkness but is still exciting. The characters aren't just more Bella and Edward wannabes—they have a fresh romance all their own, and that love story feels utterly real. I'll be recommending this book to my teen readers every chance I get."

Lindsay Olson, teen specialist for the Pikes Peak Library District

Praise for ...

Waterfall

"I love stories about strong, capable young women—and I love stories set in other countries. Mix in a little time travel and some colorful characters, and Lisa Bergren has stirred up an exciting and memorable tale that teen readers should thoroughly enjoy!"

Melody Carlson, author of the Diary of
a Teenage Girl and TrueColors series

"As the mother of two teens and two preteens, I found *Waterfall* to be a gutsy but clean foray into the young adult genre for Lisa T. Bergren, who handles it with a grace and style all her own. Gabriella Betarrini yanked me out of my time and into a harrowing adventure as she battled knights—and love! I heartily enjoyed Gabriella's travel back into time, and I heartily look forward to *Cascade,* River of Time #2!"

Ronie Kendig, author of *Nightshade*

"I loved every minute of this adventure that took me out of our time and into the fourteenth century, and I marveled at how true to life teenage Gabi remained when facing extraordinary circumstances. Under Bergren's guidance, I look forward to time traveling again in the next book of the River of Time series."

Donita K. Paul, best-selling author
of the DragonKeeper Chronicles
and the Chiril Chronicles

"Diving into *Waterfall* reminded me why Lisa T. Bergren is one of my favorite authors. Unfolding adventures, fascinating characters, and exciting plot twists make this a stellar read. I loved it! Highly recommended!"

Tricia Goyer, award-winning author of twenty-five books, including *The Swiss Courier*

The River of Time Series

Waterfall

Cascade

Torrent (Fall 2011)

CASCADE

The River of Time Series

LISA T. BERGREN

David C Cook

transforming lives together

CASCADE
Published by David C Cook
4050 Lee Vance View
Colorado Springs, CO 80918 U.S.A.

David C Cook Distribution Canada
55 Woodslee Avenue, Paris, Ontario, Canada N3L 3E5

David C Cook U.K., Kingsway Communications
Eastbourne, East Sussex BN23 6NT, England

The website addresses recommended throughout this book are offered as a
resource to you. These websites are not intended in any way to be or imply an
endorsement on the part of David C Cook, nor do we vouch for their content.

This story is a work of fiction. All characters and events are the product of the author's
imagination. Any resemblance to any person, living or dead, is coincidental.

LCCN 2011923883
ISBN 978-1-4347-6431-7
eISBN 978-1-4347-0401-6

The Team: Don Pape, Traci DePree, Amy Kiechlin,
Sarah Schultz, Caitlyn York, Karen Athen
Cover Design: Gearbox Studios
Cover Images: 4495136, 123RF, royalty free
PHP3075584, Veer Images, royalty free

Printed in the United States of America

First Edition 2011

1 2 3 4 5 6 7 8 9 10

032911

There is always one unexpected moment in life when a door opens to let the future in.

–Graham Greene

Dear Reader,

Few of us have a real handle on the medieval time period and Italy's history. So here are a few reminders before you dive back into Gabi and Lia's story.…

In this era, Italy was volatile and divided into lots of city-states. The Vatican had been moved to Avignon, France, because the pope(s) felt safer there. The Vatican would stay away from Rome for almost seventy years total.

City-states were sometimes called communes, or republics, and were run by semidemocratic bodies or groups of elected leaders. In Siena, this group was the Council of Nine. Florence, or *Firenze,* had two councils with more than five hundred men; I've chosen to represent them with the fictional *grandi,* based on a smaller group that actually served as city advisors to the *Fiorentini* (people of Florence).

Other territories were ruled by rich lords with hilltop fortresses or castles—but most had to be in league with others (or had powerful connections) if they hoped to hold their territory for any length of time. Many hired mercenaries or knights to help them fight off anyone attempting to take what was theirs.

Florence and Siena, like all of the big city-states, alternated between peace and a struggle for power and territory. In the thirteenth century, the terms *Guelph* and *Ghibelline* came into use as people fought either for the emperor's imperialistic goals (Ghibelline) or to follow the pope's leadership (Guelph). For the purposes of this fourteenth-century series, Florence/Firenze is referred to as "Guelph" and Siena as "Ghibelline," which is a simplistic generalization of their loyalties. But trust me, if we went deeper, I'd really risk losing you.

I see the backdrop of politics and history as seasoning to the fictional stew; the heart of the meal is the story itself. My hope is that this recap helps you stay with that!

—LTB

CHAPTER 1

Mom freaked out when she saw us, of course.

I couldn't blame her, with Lia in her medieval gown. And me looking like I'd been mauled by a bear. Especially when two meaty guards were hauling us into Dr. Manero's tent. "It's all right, Mom," I said, hands out, as she rushed toward us. Her face was white.

"Lasciateli," she shouted in irritation—*let them go*—brushing the guards' hands off our arms, staring at the blood on me. "Girls, what in the—"

"She's all right, Mom," Lia began. "It's not as bad as it looks."

"It's okay," I said, pushing her hands away as she touched my underdress—a gown made hundreds of years before—and tried to figure out what kind of wound had made me look like I'd been doused in ketchup. "I'm fine, Mom. Really."

But her fingers remained on the raw weave of the silk fabric. Her beautiful blue eyes widened, then her narrow brows lowered as she rubbed it between thumb and forefinger and bent to study the weave. She turned and touched Lia's gown. "Where did you get these clothes?"

"Mom," I whispered, "can we talk about it alone?" Manero—Dr. Manero, my parents' long-time adversary, a bigwig with the *Societa Archeologico dell' Italia*—was staring at us with a smug look on his face, as if he had us all exactly where he wanted us.

"They were found in Tomb Two, Dr. Betarrini," he said, crossing his arms. I pictured him stuffing a cigar into his mouth, leaning back in a chair, and putting his feet up on the desk, hands behind his head. "You know what giving unauthorized persons access can do to one's site approvals."

Mom frowned now and shook her head a little. "Impossible. They'd never…" Her words faded as she saw the sheepish looks in our eyes. "No. Girls, tell me you weren't inside. No. Why?"

"Mom, we need to talk to you alone," I said again.

She stared at me, eye to eye—we're exactly the same height—and then at Lia, and finally at Manero. *"Ci serve un' attimo." We need a minute.*

"What's to say? Yes, your papers are in order, but you clearly need my help here to secure the site. If your own daughters feel free to run roughshod over—"

"We were not 'running roughshod' over the site," I bit back at him. "We were just peeking in."

He raised one dark brow. "Climbing inside hardly constitutes *peeking.*"

Mom looked at us in horror.

"We need a minute, *Mom*," I said for the third time. "We can explain."

She was getting that There's-No-Explanation-for-Trespassing

kind of wild fury look in her eyes. The sort that usually left her sputtering before she found her steam and really let us have it.

Lia saw it too. "Mom," she said, "can we go outside?"

"No need," Manero said, chin in the air. "I shall leave you three to discuss *your* business. I'll return in fifteen minutes to discuss *our* business."

"Thanks for the warning," I muttered. He paused but did not turn, then left the tent.

Mom crossed her arms and took a seat on a folding stool. "Start talking."

Lia and I shared a look. My head and heart were swirling. It was better that Lia told her. I sat down on a stool by the desk, face in my hands, looking at my mother and sister but thinking how lucky I was to be alive, and of Marcello Forelli, the most amazing man on the planet—of all time even. The guy I'd left in the past.

I'm not talking about breaking up yesterday. I'm talking about the past-past—as in the *1300s* past. Lia was telling Mom about it, whispering as fast and as clearly as she could…how we'd put our hands on the prints in the Etruscan tomb—prints that seemed to be our own, they matched so closely—and how it had taken us back in time, to medieval Italy.

Mom's eyes got bigger and bigger, her expression telling us that she thought we'd gone crazy. "Did you hit your head?" she asked, reaching for Lia's blond hair, scanning her scalp for blood.

"No, Mom," Lia said, lurching away in irritation. "Listen to me. I know it sounds crazy, but you have to believe us! Look at my gown. At Gabi's!" Scientific fact, that's what she was bringing it around to. That was something Mom could get her head around.

I turned to Manero's computer, staring at the clock and the date, trying to get my head around the facts too. About a half hour had gone by since we'd first put our hands on the prints. We were probably only gone about twenty to twenty-five minutes. But we'd experienced about twenty days in ancient Tuscany.

My heart skipped a beat. I was no math genius, but if my calculations were right, our ten minutes here meant we'd already been gone from Marcello's time for ten days. Ten days. No wonder I was in agony. I missed him like I was experiencing ten days of pain in ten minutes. I'd left a piece of myself back with him. It was physical, leaving me all empty and achy inside.

I logged on to Manero's laptop and typed "Siena history" into Google's search window.

"Gabi—" Mom began, brows lowered.

"I'll be fast, Mom. I just need to know something." A quick stop at Wikipedia, and I knew two things: Siena would face the plague in five years. But Florence wouldn't conquer her for another couple hundred years. Not that there weren't serious battles before then…

To her credit, Mom seemed to be giving Lia's story half a chance. But her eyes told me she thought it was like a fable that had to have some sort of real basis, a foundation that would make it all make sense. Like grainy Sasquatch film clips that really starred an escaped pet gorilla. Or a UFO sighting that boiled down to a NASA rocket test. She was getting all Science Maven-y on us, trying to put two and two together.

"Mom, there are two castles within two miles of this site. The one we pass every day, on our way in here, and the one over the hill, past the tombs." I reached out and took her hands. "We've been in both. But they were whole—full-on homes for people. Lots of people. Lia could sketch them both for you. One was inhabited by a man who fought for Firenze; the other by a family who was loyal to Siena."

I glanced to the tent doorway, its flap still and hanging, and rose. I lifted the edge of my gown and showed her my wound, now nothing but a white scar on my skin. "Look, Mom. Check out the length of it. How it looks old? Like I got it five years ago, right?"

She blinked rapidly, as if she was seeing things. Trying to make sense of it all.

I dropped my gown and gestured to the bloodstain, directly over my scar. "It's bloody because I was bleeding like crazy, just a half hour ago. I got the wound in that castle," I said, gesturing in the direction of the Paratore ruins, "when Lia and I were fighting for our lives. There's something about the tomb, coming through time, that heals. It healed me."

She bit her lip, still looking at the blood.

I shook my head, irritated at how long it was taking to convince her. "How else could I get that scar? Without you knowing about it?"

Her eyes met mine. "It makes no sense."

"No," I said. "It doesn't. But look at the facts, Mom. Haven't you and Dad always taught students to catalog the facts and then move to theory?" I had her there. I'd heard her say the exact same thing a hundred times.

Her eyes flitted between us and then down at her hands, back and forth, still trying to puzzle it through.

If only Dad were here... He'd always been the more impulsive of the two. He followed his heart. Mom liked to consult her brain first, and there was no way that our story was going to be figured out logically. No way. Hadn't scientists been trying to figure out the whole time/space continuum thing for centuries?

Mom looked up at us then, unblinking. "Show me," she said lowly. "Let's go to the tomb now."

"In front of Manero?" I frowned.

"No," Lia said, shaking her head. "We just got back."

But I was nodding. "I need to go back."

"For what…forever?" Lia spit at me. "There's so much we don't know, Gabi. What if you get sick again, going back?"

"I won't get sick again. I was healed. Time has passed, both here and there."

"You don't know that."

"I do. We 'left' about twenty-five minutes ago. But what'd we experience back in 1342? About twenty days, right? If we go—"

Mom held her hands up, silencing us both. "No one's going anywhere," she said. "I simply want you to show me exactly what happened. On site."

"She thinks she's in love with a dude named Marcello," Lia said accusingly, her distrusting blue eyes on me. "She'll do whatever she has to to get back."

Mom looked at me. "Is that true? You think you're in love with this Marcus person?"

"Marcello Forelli," I corrected, each lilting syllable twisting my gut. "And, uh, yeah. I fell pretty hard for him."

Mom's eyes moved from my face to my clothes again, as if she was trying to remember that there was scientific evidence to support our story. Otherwise, she probably would have dismissed it as some wild dream…like we'd *both* hit our heads or something.

"That's how she got hurt," Lia said, pressing now, sensing she had the upper hand. "I mean, she got hurt in a battle and I had to stitch her up, but she's in love with a guy who already has a girl. And then that chick poisoned Gabi!" She walked over to me, hands on her hips. "You really want to go back? Back to where I almost lost you?" She shook her head. "I can't do it, Gabs. Not after Dad. I can't deal with it. I'll lose it, seriously lose it, if something happens to you."

"Nothing is going to happen to anyone," Mom said, stepping up beside us.

"Mom, just give me a chance. Let me show you the tomb. How it happened." I eyed the computer screen. Another ten minutes. Another ten days, for Marcello, thirty now that I'd been gone. Was he giving up? Giving in to Lady Rossi and the pressure to follow through on their marriage agreement? Had he guessed that she might have been poisoning me?

Mom was still staring at me, at Lia, assessing. "Come on," she said finally, lifting the back of the tent and bending.

She was going to sneak out. My mother never sneaked anywhere. She boldly went where she wished.

I stood up and went to her, looking back to Lia. She hesitated, frowning, and then with an exaggerated roll of her big blue eyes—so like Mom's—followed us. We ducked under the edge and looked around. We could hear voices on the other side and up the hill by the tombs. Just as it looked like we could make a clean escape, a guy in a *Societa Archeologico* hat came around the corner.

Mom froze for a second and then took my arm. "Come on, Gabi," she said, "we'll take care of you."

The man's eyes moved to my bloodstained gown, and he hurried over to us. *"Ti posso aiutare?"* he asked. *Can I help?*

"*Si*, I just need to get her to our car," Mom responded in Italian.

Smart of her, I thought. The parking lot would get us halfway to the tomb.

The man took my arm as if he thought I'd faint at any point, and I accepted his help as if I just might. A couple of other guys were walking up at the far end of the tumuli, but they ignored us. "I can take care of her from here," Mom said to the man.

"You're sure?" He opened the door and settled me onto the seat.

"Yes."

"I can call for an ambulance."

"No. It looks worse than it is."

Still, he hesitated.

"*Lei ha le sue cose,*" I said, turning wise, pained eyes on him, meaning *that time of the month,* or as they said it here, *she has her things.* Whatever. We didn't have time to waste. How long had I been away from Marcello now? A month?

He frowned and immediately began to back away. The blood's location made no sense with the explanation, but I knew it'd send him running.

Mom gave me a little smile and grabbed the medical kit. "In case anybody else starts asking questions," she said, lifting it in my direction. She tucked it under her arm as the man disappeared back among the three tents—Mom's white one, flanked by two khaki peaks from the *Societa Archeologico* team. "Let's go," she said.

Hidden by dense scrub oak, we climbed up the hill. At the clearing, where the twelve tombs rose from the soil in grass-covered domes, we paused and caught our breath, waiting for those two dudes we'd spotted earlier to turn their backs. Any minute now, Manero would go back into the tent and realize we had escaped.

"Now," Lia whispered when we all saw them turn the corner of the tomb.

We hurried over to Tomb Two and scrambled through the narrow igloo-like entrance, Lia and me slower than Mom, since we were in the long gowns. At the end, we stood up, and Mom flicked on the small flashlight she kept in her belt. I pointed to the two handprints.

"I've wondered about those," Mom said. "So unlike any other fresco motif we've ever run across…"

Lia backed up a couple of steps, as if she didn't want us cascading back in time by accident.

"Go on, Mom," I said. "Pull out a glove and touch the prints. See if they're warm." She had a thing about letting the oils of our skin touch ancient frescoes, given that it was her job and all to preserve them.

Mom frowned, then pulled on a pair of cloth gloves from her belt. After a second's hesitation, she touched one, and then the other. "No. Nothing. Cold stone. Why did you expect heat?"

I could tell from her expression that I was losing her. I lifted my hand for a glove. "Let me try."

"Gabi," Lia growled.

"Calm down. I'm just checking. You know that nothing will happen without you," I said. "I tried, remember? We both tried."

I put on the glove and touched her print first, then mine. Even through the fabric I could tell that hers was cold. Mine was hot. Just like last time.

"I know it feels like plain old stone to you," I said to my mother, "but for me and Lia, our prints are hot." Mom stepped forward and touched it again, then turned and then felt my forehead. I laughed under my breath. "I'm not running a fever, Mom. It's real." I put both palms on her face, so she could feel the residual warmth from my right. "Feel that?"

I knew from her expression that she did. She was beginning to believe. Being there, so close to the portal, made my heart pound. I knew I wanted to go back. But I couldn't. Not without Lia. And she was nowhere close to jumping back in.

"What if we don't pull off the wall in the same time period, Gabi?" she asked, reading my look. "What if we end up in Etruscan times?"

"That'd be all right by me," Mom said drily. As an archaeologist specializing in the Etruscan era and populace, she dreamed of seeing everything firsthand.

I frowned. I hadn't thought of that. There was no dial, no program, no way to set the year you wanted to hop into. Last time, I'd pulled my hand away when I finally figured out what was happening. I just happened to end up in 1342.

I looked around the tomb, trying to figure out an answer. "The urn! When it's broken, we'll know we're there."

Mom frowned and bent by the remains of the urn, picking up a piece and staring at its edges under the beam of her flashlight. She looked up at me and I bit my lip, but then seized on the situation, as a means to an end. "Look at that, Mom. The shards, the layer of dust atop them, like it's been there for centuries, right?"

She nodded slowly. "Grave robbers, most likely."

"That would make sense. But I broke it the last time we came through. When I went back to 1342, this place was sealed up tight. There was no hole in the ceiling. It was totally pitch black inside. I couldn't see where I was going, and knocked it over. Sorry," I added quickly, with a grimace. After all, I was an archaeologist's kid, and I'd just admitted to destroying a priceless artifact. I knelt next to her. "But think, Mom. Think hard. When we first got to this site, was the urn broken or whole?"

She paused for several seconds and blinked rapidly. Two memories clearly collided, as I hoped they might. Conflicting memories. One of the urn, whole. One of it broken. "I…I don't think it was broken."

"But look," I said, gesturing again to the shards. "That's like centuries of dust on them, right?" I rose. "Because it happened almost seven hundred years ago. When I was there. Facts, Mom. Facts. They'll lead you to your theory. Is there anything else in here that is different? Different from any other tomb? Any clue to tell us it's a doorway to a different time?" I turned and examined the frescoes in the dim light. "Even better would be anything that tells us how we might control what time we'll land in."

Lia stood in my way, arms folded, shaking her head. "There's no steering wheel for this thing. You remember. We move *fast*, Gabi. You take a breath after it's broken and we might be thirty years off. Besides, we're moving backward. And remember? It's pitch black in there."

She was right. If I waited for the urn, and passed it, I might arrive when Marcello was a baby. That wouldn't be cool. "The light! That's how we'll know. I opened the tomb. At some point, someone rolled that rock back into place. Marcello wouldn't have done that, not if he thought I was coming back. I just have to wait past that…and, well, I don't know exactly how I'll know. But we have to try."

"They might have rolled that stone back a hundred years after we left!"

"We have to try," I repeated.

"You're crazy," she said, eyebrows lifted.

"Please, Lia. Just for a while. I have to go. I have to." I dared to glance at Mom, wondering if she would keep us from the journey.

"I'll come with you," she said. Her tone told me she didn't quite believe us yet but the only way to resolve it was to show us we were chasing some sort of idiotic fantasy.

We heard voices outside and began to whisper.

"I don't know if you can, Mom," I said. "It might be just me and Lia that make the leap."

"We won't know if this is all in your heads if we don't go ahead and attempt it."

I swallowed my frustration over her disbelief. "It's too risky. Last time, I lost hold of Lia, and she arrived days after me. What if you lose hold of us? There'd be no way to get you back—let alone find you."

Mom gave me her There's No Sense Arguing look. "Look, you two aren't going anywhere if I'm not with you. And if this really is a doorway through time, I want to see it for myself."

I don't know why her words surprised me. Wasn't it the dream of every historian or archaeologist to go back in time, see another era for themselves?

Lia was still shaking her head, looking from Mom to me, as if she couldn't believe we were having this conversation. "Are you insane? Gabs, I almost lost you—twice! Please…let's stay here. It's not safe to go back. Think of it as a trip, a wild trip we took once. That's all."

I stared into her eyes, trying to get her to calm down.

"Lia, I have to go back. Marcello—" My voice broke, and I swallowed, hard. "Please." She hesitated, and I pressed her again, sensing that her resolve was slipping. "*Please.*"

Mom shifted from one leg to the other. "Evangelia, you two must be sharing some odd delusion. You have to be. But if…if this is true, if you've possibly stumbled upon some miraculous gateway, allowing us to go back in time and return—again—it would be one of the top scientific discoveries of all time. How could we *not* go?"

"Exactly," I said, leaping on the convenient excuse. Anything to convince Lia.

"Just for a little while, then we come back?" she asked tentatively, looking at me.

"For a little while," I said.

"And what if in returning, you go back to being poisoned? Bleeding?"

"We'll take the med kit," Mom said quietly. "There're shots of morphine and antibiotics in there. A mini-surgical kit. You won't be alone, Lia. We'll take care of her together."

"You think we'll be together."

Mom stared back at her. "To be honest, I'm not quite sure what to think. But you can't accomplish what you can't imagine." Despite the words that told us she believed a measure of what we were saying,

I could still see the trace of skepticism around her eyes. Like a part of her believed she would soon get to the scientific basis of our dream-like story.

Lia heaved a sigh and stepped up to the wall. "We have to pull off at the same moment, this time," she said to me. "Mom, you hold us tight, and whatever happens, don't let go, all right?"

"We're more prepared this round," I said, trying to ease her fears.

Outside, the men's voices came closer. A shout went up.

They'd discovered our escape.

"Girls," Mom said in warning, glancing toward the tomb entrance. "I'm praying you aren't ill, suffering some sort of mental lapse. Because the last thing I need is Manero to find all *three* of us in here."

"If you think Manero's bad," Lia said, "wait till you meet some of the dudes ahead of us."

CHAPTER 2

My plan worked pretty well. The heat beneath our hands intensified until I could barely stand it; I felt caught, like my skin was becoming fused to the stone of the tomb wall, and feared both options—ripping it away or never being able to do so again. The light became our cue. Above us, the hole again showcased a time-lapse video of trees growing and falling, burning, growing again. Everything was heavy, slow motion and yet scary fast, dreamy, like moving through water with ankle weights. The hole above us disappeared, the grave robbers come and gone in a partial breath, and then the entrance stone was gone, letting light rush in from the side.

That's when I saw it.

A pile of clothes, right in the center.

A scroll, rolled and tied.

Marcello.

I looked into Lia's eyes and screamed, "Now," as I pulled my palm from the searing heat. My shout came and went so fast it was impossible for even me to hear, but Lia knew. She'd been watching.

At that point I couldn't feel Mom. But when I fell back, on top of her, I laughed in relief. Seconds later, Lia appeared beside us. We lunged to catch her and managed to break her fall, then laughed in relief and hugged one another.

"That was crazy! I've never experienced anything like it," Mom said, her eyes alight.

"Yeah," I agreed. There was something oddly comforting in having Mom with us. Like she could save us from whatever this time had to dish out. I smiled along with her. Lia rose, face glum.

"Everyone in one piece?" Mom asked, staring at each of us as if she wanted us to count off ten fingers and ten toes.

"Fine, fine," I said. I felt my side. Still all healed, as if I'd had the wound ten years rather than just getting it days ago.

"No ache in your gut?" Lia said. "No poison?"

I shook my head. "Whatever happens in that time tunnel seems to fix whatever is wrong. I'm good." I stood up and made my way to the clothing. Marcello had been thoughtful enough to recall my awkward twenty-first-century clothes from the last time I showed up and had figured out a way for me to avoid the embarrassment again. He'd hoped I'd return—the clothes proved it. Not that I really needed proof. I remembered his intense demand, uttered less than an hour ago for me, weeks for him—"Return to me, and you shall find me waiting."

I handed Mom a gown. "Trust me, you'll want to put that on."

Lia was fortunately still in hers, and since Marcello'd left two, I could slip on the other and be done with the bloody one. I reached for the note and unrolled the parchment scroll, fighting the urge to run all the way to the castle as I read it.

Gabriella, welcome. Please, hasten to the castle at once, but be especially cautious of enemies about. They would consider your capture a sure victory. I await you.—Marcello

"He's waiting for me," I said, letting the scroll roll up again. "At least he was." I looked beside the clothing. My broadsword, with its sheath worn on the back, and a dagger. Beside it, Lia's bow and arrows. I reached for the sword and wiped a fine layer of dust from the hilt. How long had it been lying here? How long had I been gone, really?

"These men know you?" Mom said, picking up and studying the finely crafted bow before handing it to Lia.

"I told you," Lia said grumpily. "This place is rough. We may very well have to fight for our lives."

Mom stared at her for a long moment. Judging from her face, it was all sinking in. "Well, let's make the most of it, shall we?" Her face was exploding as much with anticipation as wariness. "How do we explain ourselves? Surely you had to concoct some sort of story."

I looked at Lia, and we pieced together as much as we could in regard to what we had said. "We're from Normandy. You are a merchantress but have been missing for a while. That's our cover story—it's what brought Lia and me to Toscana, to search for you, where we last heard from you."

"I am a merchant? In what goods do I trade?" Mom paused, and her fingers went to her lips. "And tell me, what sort of Italian is this that is coming out of my mouth?"

"Dante's own, I think," I returned, in the same dialect. "It comes with the leap. You'll find the medieval-speak comes fairly easy too. It's kind of like watching one of Shakespeare's plays—you know, at first, you can barely keep up with what they're saying, and then, boom, you *hear* it coming out of your own mouth. Oh, and you deal in ancient artifacts," I said with a grin. "Although they're fairly superstitious about entering old tombs. You'll have to be careful on that front."

"Yeah, they wouldn't like it if you started excavating," Lia said. "Think like a medieval merchant, Mom."

Lia picked up her arrows, then moved toward the entrance and crawled out to the edge.

"All clear?" I asked. Last time, I'd emerged into the center of a battle between the Forellis and Paratores.

"All clear," she said over her shoulder. Quickly, I put on my deep green gown, and pulled on the matching slippers. I helped Mom with hers, a blue one probably meant for Lia, and then we moved to join her outside.

I sucked in my breath. We'd left in the heat of summer. Now a cold wind blew up through the valley, shaking leaves of autumn from the oaks. "Okay, so I missed our exit point by a few months." Or was my whole time-exchange concept off? Maybe it didn't matter at all.

"Let's hope it's the same year," Lia said, sliding her bow over her shoulder.

My heart paused and then pounded at her words. What if I was off by a year or more? What if Marcello was no longer a guy about my age, but rather a middle-aged man? I shivered.

That would be…awkward.

Mom pulled up short as we came around the bend, staring with wide eyes at the Forelli castle ahead of us—and then back behind us, where the Paratore towers just barely peeked over the hilltop.

"I told you," I said, looping my arm through hers.

"I see it," she said, bringing her hand to her forehead and shading her eyes, still staring at the castles, "but I'm still trying to believe *what* I'm seeing."

I studied them with her, trying to remember that feeling of utter surprise the first time I'd seen both castellos in their original splendor and perfection. But my eyes settled on the flags waving in the brisk fall wind. Both the Paratore and the Forelli castellos were flying the Forelli gold. So they'd managed to hold it, even with the newly drawn border. I wondered if that meant the Sienese forces were constantly under attack. The Fiorentini—the people of Firenze—would not, could not deal with such a shift. No wonder Marcello had left the warning of "enemies about." We moved down the path and soon crossed the narrow river. Cautiously, we picked our way through the woods, telling Mom all we could from our last visit so she'd be prepared, ready for what was ahead.

Lia was telling her about Lord Paratore, and her escape, and of Luca and Marcello, when we reached the creek, barely trickling at this point in the season. "This was the border between the properties when we arrived," I said, balancing on a large rock and hopping to the next. "It changed course at some point, going the opposite way around the hill with the tombs, and suddenly, *bam*, the Paratores thought they could claim it for Firenze. Of course, they weren't really thinking the Forellis would fight 'em for it."

I looked back and saw that Mom was stuck again, her face stricken. I glanced at Lia, and she looked back to me with concern. Yeah, my mom was getting it now, for sure. And apparently, she wasn't into this kind of reality.

"Mom?"

"I'm fine," she said to me, but she sat down awkwardly on a boulder, so distracted that she almost missed it. She looked to the forest ahead—the castles were no longer in sight—and then over to us. "I just realized that if all this is true, then *all* of what you told me is true." Her big eyes found mine. "You almost died."

I held her gaze a moment and then nodded soberly. "Yes. It's true. But I also felt alive, really alive, Mom, for the first time. I *feel* alive here," I amended. "There is something here that we're missing in our own time…something I can't really define."

Lia let out a dismissive sound and jumped across three rocks. "I'll give you your definition. It's spelled M-a-r-c-e-l-l-o."

Cute, I said to her silently with my thank-you-very-little expression. "It's more than that," I said to Mom. "Maybe it's because these people"—I waved around us—"are so close to death all the time that they know something we don't—how to embrace life. Really live. Take every minute for what it's worth. Maybe we've lost something vital in our own time, something—"

"Don't let her get all philosophical on you, Mom," Lia cut in from the other side of the shallow stream. "It's love that made her want to come back. If Marcello wasn't here, *we* wouldn't be here, no matter how bad you wanted to test the theory."

Mom stared at me for a long moment until I shrugged and said, "She's probably right. But still, there's something more. Wait and see. You'll know what I'm talking about." I jumped across the remaining stones and slid back into my slippers as Mom hopped across too.

We heard the horses approaching before we saw them.

"Quick, hide," I said, pulling my sword from its sheath. We separated, Mom hiding behind a boulder, and Lia and me sliding between thick trees. She drew an arrow over her bowstring.

The men came galloping past and broke formation as they crossed the riverbed. Three pairs, heading north toward Firenze. Behind us, at Castello Forelli, bells clanged. They were sounding the alarm. More answered ahead, at Castello Paratore.

A scouting party from Firenze sent to judge the current condition of Siena's hold on this corner of the republic. I was sure of it.

We heard more horses and sank deeper into the foliage.

Twelve men in Forelli gold galloped past in pursuit, so fast I barely caught a glimpse. I edged out, torn between crying out to them and hesitating to interfere in a chase. But as I stepped forward, I knew that the man at the front was Marcello.

Marcello.

The shout died in my throat. I felt suddenly shy, wondering if things were the same between us, or if they'd changed in whatever time had gone by. For him.

The men crossed the riverbed and gathered speed up the road on the other side. I looked around nervously, wondering if there might be enemy knights about, if I was foolishly giving up on the only protection my mom and sister and I really had.

Marcello.

It was then that he raised his hand and pulled up. He cocked his head, like he was listening, while his men streamed past him, belatedly pulling back on their own reins.

Marcello wheeled his horse around and studied the length of the river. At last, his eyes met mine. He was in motion so fast, dismounting, running, it made my heart skip a beat. Luca reached for his reins, frowning, looking toward us, wondering what had drawn his master's attention.

But Marcello's eyes were only on me.

I let out a low cry and ran toward him, too, ignoring the puddles of water that I trudged through to meet him in the middle of the riverbed.

He reached me at last and swept me into his arms, kissing my cheeks, my eyes, my hair. "Gabriella, Gabriella," he moaned. He pulled back and stared at me, as if he thought I was a ghost. "You returned," he said softly, cradling my cheeks in his hands. "You returned," he repeated in a whisper.

"Yes," I said, grinning.

"You are well? Whole? Healed?"

"Completely."

"God on high be praised. I prayed for it, every waking hour of every day." He kissed me then, shortly, his lips lingering on mine for a moment. The men hooted and teased Marcello. Luca was there, then, as were my sister and mother.

But I didn't miss the fact that two men took up a protective stance on their mounts on each side of us, forming a barrier. Danger was clearly all about.

Marcello seemed to remember himself. We stepped apart, and he bowed toward my mother. "Lady Betarrini, I presume. Your daughters favor your beauty. I would've known you anywhere. I am Sir Marcello Forelli. This is my cousin and captain, Luca Forelli."

"Sir Marcello and Sir Luca," she said with a regal nod that made her look every inch a true lady. "My daughters told me of your kind hospitality when they were here last. I am most indebted to you."

"It is I who am indebted to you, m'lady," he said with a bow. "You have allowed Lady Gabriella to return. Kindly accept our escort and shelter at Castello Forelli again. It would honor us greatly."

"You are most kind," she said. "We accept."

"M'lady," Marcello said to Mom. "May I have a moment with Lady Gabriella?"

Mom paused for a second, and her eyes flicked back and forth between us. She gave a long, slow nod, and I had to wonder a bit about her. Since when did she have a dramatic side? Or was she just playing up the whole Mom role because I hadn't asked permission for this Seriously Dating thing?

Marcello smiled and set my hand atop his. We walked down a small deer path and past some trees. When we had a measure of privacy, he pulled me into his arms and kissed me, slowly, then more searchingly. Carefully, as if he suspected I was still injured. Then he pulled me close and asked, "Was it a horrible ordeal, Gabriella? Did your doctors find a way to heal you?"

"Nay," I said, pulling back enough to look up and into his eyes. "There's something about the portal that heals, Marcello. The poison, the wound, the bleeding when I left…it was all as if it had happened years before. As soon as I arrived it was gone. I could still see the blood upon my gown, and there is a scar, but I suffered no longer. All was well."

"'Tis a miracle," he said, stroking my hair. He lifted my hands to his lips and kissed them, staring into my eyes. "You are a miracle. Here. Now. God has been gracious to return you to me."

I smiled and nodded. How else could I explain it?

"You are here for good, Gabriella?" he asked. His brown eyes, so warm, so searching, begged me to make the promise. I wanted to. Everything in me said I had to stay with this man forever, every minute of every day I could spare. There was no other place I wanted to be.

"I do not know," I said, forcing the words from my lips.

He frowned. "How can you not know? You have your sister, your mother. Me. What else do you need?"

"It is not I who would need anything more," I said. "But Mom—my mother—and Lia…Marcello, it's a lot to ask of them."

"We will simply have to convince them that the Ladies Betarrini belong here."

I felt a smile tugging at the corners of my lips again. "And you think that an easy task, then? Choosing to move to another era?"

"I can be quite charming," he said smugly. His eyes narrowed. "Mayhap you've missed that."

I laughed under my breath. *Hardly.* "Nay, m'lord. I have not."

"Excellent. Then we shall simply turn our efforts toward your sister and mother. Together, we shall convince them that this is where you belong."

He wasn't going to get an argument from me. He leaned down and closed his eyes, gently kissing me, then broke it off just when I wanted to pull him closer. "Come, m'lady. We must get to the castello. I have neglected your security in a selfish desire to have you to myself."

"Those men we saw…"

"Spies from Firenze. They've been relentless since you've been gone. We've caught several of them. But still they come, seeking to find the weakness that will bring us down. Our days of battle are far from over. And you, my love, are at the heart of it. I've heard that men of Firenze have searched from Napoli to Venezia for the Ladies Betarrini."

"Us?" I said. "What do they want from us?" I glanced toward my mom and sister as they came into view, taking comfort in the sight of Marcello's men still acting all commando around them.

"Nothing good, I can assure you," he said, pulling me into an embrace that spoke of shielding, shelter.

Nothing good. "I'm fairly adept at making friends, but it seems even better at making mortal enemies, no?"

Marcello pulled back and smiled at me with that grin I loved, his eyes glinting. "All fine leaders tend to have such effect. But now I must insist we take our conversation to the safety of the castello."

I stifled a sigh as we moved back to the path and rejoined the group on the road. Luca was making Lia giggle.

"Mayhap we shall have assistance in our quest to convince your family to remain," Marcello said in my ear.

"Mayhap," I said. But I knew it'd be tough to sell either of them on the idea. Mom would probably want to try to reach Etruscan times. Seriously, how could she pass it up? My only hope was to get her all intrigued with medieval society and the history on the verge of the Renaissance, a tall order. But my sister? She wanted life as we'd always known it. Safe, secure, easy. And if Mom or I were in danger…if we neared death again? It'd be all over. She'd lose it, totally lose it.

He gestured to his men, and two brought horses forward. Luca reluctantly lifted Lia up behind Giovanni, looking like he wished he was to be the one to bring her to the castello. Another knight lifted my mother atop of Pietro's mount as Marcello helped me to the back of his and then carefully rose to his own saddle so as to not unseat me. I wrapped my arms around his waist, inhaling the scent of him—all forest and spice and everything nice.…

I wasn't dreaming. We'd made it. "How long have we been gone?" I whispered, remembering that I'd need to know such facts.

"Almost three months," he said lowly over his shoulder. "Every hour seemed like a day to me." We rode in silence for a bit. "It is good you returned with your mother in tow. We told everyone that after seeking out a doctor, you had gone in search of her. Which, of course, was what sent our enemy to seeking you as well."

"*Perfetto*," I said, pulling a bit closer to him and resting my cheek against the breadth of his back. "At least it kept a few of them busy and away from you."

Too soon for my taste we arrived at the castle. It felt too good to be holding onto Marcello to let go just yet.

Guards, twice the number as there had been when we left, lowered their bows when they saw the Forelli gold. One shouted his greeting: "Caught yourself some pretty Ghibellines, m'lord?"

"Nay, even better," Marcello shouted back. "Guelph, through and through."

One shouted our names when he recognized us. "The Ladies Betarrini!"

"None other," Marcello said. "Open the gates!"

"Open the gates!" repeated the guard.

We heard the metallic slide of the giant reinforced crossbeam. Marcello, out on patrol. Gates, sealed up tight. Double the normal guards at the parapets. I shivered. "You are expecting a battle today, even after chasing those spies out?"

"The Fiorentini do not mount an all-out war, but they poke at us, constantly. We have to be ever at the ready. We've lost five men."

"And the Fiorentini?"

I could feel the laughter rumble in his chest. "Far more."

"What of Siena? They are coming to your aid?"

"There is a contingent in Castello Paratore and another beyond Castello Forelli. Truly, we are on the brink of war if this continues. But rest assured—we are far from alone."

That comforted me. The night we'd taken Castello Paratore and freed Lia had been a brutal one. I'd hate to encounter twice the number of enemies without twice the number of allies.

I smiled as the courtyard came into my view, bustling with activity. Clearly, there were many visitors from Siena and beyond. As one of the most northernmost outposts for the Commune of Siena, Castello Forelli was destined to be a hub for politicians, soldiers, and merchants alike. Far more than when I first arrived. *But it's been three months.*

We pulled to a stop. Marcello dismounted, then reached for me. I took his arm, barely able to keep myself from grinning.

And then I saw her, across the clearing, on the arm of another, dimly familiar man. Heading our way.

Lady Romana Rossi.

Marcello's intended. Possible assassin. Had she tried to poison me?

I stopped and glanced at Marcello.

His brows lowered over his handsome brown eyes. "I shall explain." He shook his head. "Please. Tread carefully. Our betrothal pledge has been broken. But other alliances had to be considered."

I looked from him to the diminutive woman approaching. What did he mean, it was broken? Then why was she still here?

"Lady Betarrini," she said, smiling just a bit too sweetly. "What a lovely surprise."

"Lady Rossi," I said, trying my best to give her a civil nod. Had she known? Given the doctor the directive to poison me? Or had she been an innocent pawn?

"We welcome your return," said the man beside her.

My eyes shifted to him and then widened. "Fortino!" I grinned. He'd changed so much, I hadn't recognized him. He'd gained a good twenty pounds and had a healthy pink tinge to his cheeks. Now he was clearly Marcello's brother, similar in stature, although Marcello was taller and slightly broader. "It is good to see you so well, m'lord."

"It is good to *be* so well," he returned with a nod. "We have continued the treatments you prescribed, and I have enjoyed far better health."

"I am so glad," I said. I wished I could go to him and hug him. It was a miracle, to leave him sicker than I'd ever seen anyone and find him well just hours later.

"You were reunited with your mother?" he asked, looking beyond me to Lia and Mom, who came up behind us.

"Indeed. M'lord, may I present Lady Betarrini?"

"M'lady, it is a distinct pleasure," Fortino said, bowing. On his arm, Romana curtsied prettily, the very picture of femininity. "This is my wife-to-be, Lady Romana Rossi."

I stiffened.

Fortino? With Romana? *Other alliances had to be considered.*

Lady Rossi turned her catlike eyes to me. "Lord Marcello was quite taken with you, Lady Betarrini," she said, barely covering the jealousy in her tone. "It left us at significant odds, as you can imagine, with both houses so intent upon our union. Thank the saints that you proved to be as adept a healer as you were a…" She smiled demurely, apparently catching herself from saying something nasty. "Figurehead," she finished. "Fortino made such excellent gains on his health." She smiled up at him, and he smiled down at her. "We'd always been fond of each other. It wasn't long before Fortino arrived at the perfect solution."

Fortino. Yeah, right, it was all his idea. Sure. The chick had seen that Fortino was going to recover and become lord of the castle so she went for him instead. It probably would've happened even if I had never showed up, if Fortino had improved. This girl was all about the power.

My mom and I shared a look, and that second of silent understanding, connection, took me back. How long had it been since we'd done that? For years, the most I'd seen of my mother's eyes was in the rearview mirror on the way to a dig site. Well, except for when my dad died. That'd brought all three of us together in a new way. Not *close*, exactly. But closer. For the worst reasons I could've imagined.

Thoughts of Dad made me think of Lord Forelli. I hadn't seen him since we arrived. "And what of your father, Marcello?" I asked carefully, already guessing the answer.

"His weak heart gave way a fortnight after you departed," he said.

Everyone crossed themselves, like they were warding off evil spirits or something. Awkwardly, my mom, sister, and I did the same, a second too late to really blend in.

"What of Lady Rossi's trusted doctor?" I asked lightly, speaking my true intent—*you know, the guy who poisoned me?*—to him with my eyes. "Was he ever found?"

"He was a blackguard. An agent of the Fiorentini," Marcello said levelly, silently asking me with slightly widened eyes to let it go. *I'll fill you in later,* he seemed to be saying.

"My father discovered the treachery," Lady Rossi said. "He went to Marcello, and they captured both the doctor and Lord Foraboschi as they tried to escape to Firenze."

"Trust me when I say that they paid for their crimes," Fortino said. "Men shall think twice before aiding our enemy."

But the doctor and Lord Foraboschi had been close to the Rossis for years. My eyes flicked over Romana, who was adoringly looking up at Fortino. How could her father, one of the ruling Nine, be so duped?

I wasn't buying it, but Fortino seemed earnest, like he was trying to reassure me with this news. Perhaps Romana was innocent after all…and I was being overly suspicious. "I am glad to hear that they faced justice and are dead," I said to Fortino. "I confess, I worried they might still be about."

Mom tucked her head, frowning at my radical words. It'd take her a little while to get into this *It's Us or Them* mind-set. Not that I was eager for her to know that the Fiorentini were on an all-out search for me and Lia. Marcello's odd hesitation, and the look I'd caught the brothers sharing, made me return my attention to him.

Marcello edged closer. He shook his head a little. "Gabriella, they were tortured and imprisoned. But they were recently traded for Sienese prisoners."

He took my hand, and out of the corner of my eye, I caught Romana stiffening. "They are far from here, Gabriella. No one shall harm you again. Not if I can help it."

They were beautiful, warm words. But I knew that no person could protect another from death. Life was life—temporary, a blip on the screen. The doctor had poisoned me while Marcello danced with Romana in the same room! And Dad had died on a road not two miles from our apartment, maybe ten minutes after talking to Mom on the phone.

My eyes moved to Romana. Castello Forelli still might have a devil within her gates, a serious threat. Staring at her—pretty, demure, all Girl in Love—I knew I had to be right.

Or was I just jealous, wanting her gone from my life? This woman who almost became Marcello's wife?

CHAPTER 3

Fortino called for a feast that evening, and within hours, we were sitting down to a table laden with roasted hens, roast pig, figs, currants, pears in Greek-wine syrup, meat pies, and generous loaves of bread. I spread a dollop of churned butter on my bread and eyed my mother as Fortino asked where we had finally been reunited.

"I was in Piacenza, convalescing from a fall," she said. I had never known my mother to lie, but she did so with convincing authority. "My hired men turned on me, stole everything I had, and fled." She shook her head in dismay.

"How horrid," Romana said. "'Tis not safe for a woman to travel alone. Who might we thank for preserving you?"

Fortino coughed, and Romana immediately stood to pour more water into his goblet.

I stared for a moment. Since when did Romana play the servant? That was a new one. But even as she was pouring, she returned her gaze to my mother, not letting her off the hook.

"If it had not been for the kindness of pilgrims on the Via Francigena, I might have perished." Smart, my mother was. Brilliant, really. Pilgrims on a holy road would be impossible to find and question. Gone come sunrise. Scattered.

Romana's eyebrows came together in confusion. "Wherever did you stay, m'lady? With what funds?"

Mom stared back at her, the hint of a smile on her lips. "The pilgrims paid for my lodging, leaving me enough to see me to health."

"Just like the good Samaritan," Fortino said, patting Romana's hand as if to say, *That's enough now. Let it go.*

"Indeed," said my mother. "My daughters found me just before I would have been cast out."

"Saints be praised," Fortino said.

"Saints be praised," said the rest of the table.

But Romana's voice was little more than a whisper.

"When word reaches Siena that the Ladies Betarrini have returned," Fortino said, "oh, the feasting shall be grand indeed."

"Add to that the union of the house of Rossi with the house of Forelli," Romana added, "and there won't be a wine cask left corked."

My smile faded when I saw Marcello. He looked grim and was shaking his head. "We cannot take them to Siena," he said to his brother, carefully avoiding looking my way.

"We can do nothing but," Fortino replied. He was much more forceful in his speech than I remembered. A new man, really. Was it his health? Love? The promise of a future? He gestured over to us. "They'll drive us home at the point of pitchfork and sword if we do not bring the She-Wolves of Siena to be properly honored. What happened here, on their last eve—we all bear the burden of responsibility to right such wrongs. And mark my words, Lord Rossi shall be the most insistent of all."

Marcello leaned forward, eyebrows furrowed. He shook his head again. "Brother, it is best that the Ladies Betarrini stay here."

Fortino made a dismissive sound and threw up his hands. "Who is the lord of this house?" He smiled as if trying to reassure us, but the look he sent his brother was unmistakable. It said, *Back off, baby brother.* "Put your faith in me, m'ladies," he said. "I will see to it that the road from Castello Forelli to Siena has never been safer than the day we make our way there." He picked up Romana's hand and kissed it.

But my eyes were on Luca and Marcello. They were sharing one of Those Looks.

It was never good when they were sharing one of Those Looks.

Fortino went on, "Truly, Gabriella. If any Fiorentini wishes to try to capture you, they'll have to get through hundreds of men. They'd have to bring an army capable of full-fledged war. Our scouts would see them coming from miles away. We'll have ample opportunity to get you to safety. Good?" His eyebrows lifted.

I studied him, so full of life, bravado, hope. All the things I'd wished for him but never thought he'd see. Not really. And now, here he was before me. Lord Forelli, and relishing every bit of the part. I even had a brief thankful thought toward Romana for giving him a glimpse of love, happiness, a future. Who was I to stand in the way of this man and…life, lived to the full? Wasn't that exactly what I had to convince my mom and sister to allow me to do? If he wanted to take us to a party, what harm could there be in it?

I dared to glance in Marcello's direction and read the warning there. But what was I to do? I mean, really? "Whatever you believe is best, m'lord," I mumbled in Fortino's direction.

"Excellent!" cried Fortino with a broad grin. He rose. "I propose we begin the celebration this very night. The Ladies Betarrini have returned! To their return!" he said, lifting his goblet.

"To their return!" thundered all in the room.

But Marcello did not raise his goblet with the rest.

Fortino—who'd apparently discovered his inner wild child—ordered musicians into the hall and led everyone in dancing, though he never danced with anyone but Romana. The party finally died down in the Great Hall a couple of hours later. Lia and I slipped out to show Mom around, pointing out the pentagon shape of Castello Forelli and where the kitchen and stables were. As we walked back down the corridors toward our room, I said, "Up here is Lord Fortino's den, where he spends a large part of his leisure time." I peeked around the corner and then abruptly pulled back, bumping into my mom and Lia.

"Ow," Mom complained.

"Sorry," I whispered. They were in there. Fortino and Romana. Grinning across a chessboard like they were any old dating couple. I frowned, thinking. Dancing and now chess. Could it be? Had they really fallen in love? Just like that?

A heavy door shut behind us, making me jump. From the

shadows, Marcello emerged. "M'ladies," he said. "On whom are we spying?" His eyes twinkled in the candlelight.

"We are not *spying*," I hissed back. "We are simply having difficulty; rather, we are feeling awkward—" I let out a sigh of frustration. "We do not wish to intrude."

"Nonsense," he said, putting a hand at my lower back and propelling me forward. "The sooner we ease this tension, the better off we'll all be," he said. He looked back at my mom and sister. "Would you care to join us, m'ladies?" he asked in a normal voice. "Mayhap we can convince Fortino and Romana 'tis time for a round of Tric-Trac. We can play in rounds."

I forced a smile to my face and nodded at the couple on either side of the chessboard. Two maids-in-waiting looked up from their needlework in the corner. Of course. Chaperones. I'd probably have to get used to the idea, if I wanted to come off as a real lady, worthy of someone like Marcello.

But as Marcello brought more chairs to the table, Mom leaned toward me. Lia did the same. "I need to turn in, Gabs," Mom said, lifting a hand to her temple. "I have quite the headache." Lia nodded, as if she felt the same. I knew what they meant. I had one too; maybe a side effect of traversing six hundred–plus years? It didn't really matter to me; I wasn't about to miss a second with Marcello, headache or not. "Go on," I said. "I'll join you in a little while."

Mom nodded, and Marcello neared. "Lady Evangelia and I must return to our quarters," she said to him. "We are weary beyond measure from our journey, but my eldest seems to have more energy than we. Might you look after her and see her to our door when your game is complete?" So, yeah, Mom was ahead of me on the whole escort deal.

"It would be my honor," he said with a small bow.

She glanced from him to me, a smile alight in her eyes. She looked as proud as if she were pinning a corsage on my prom dress, and I shifted, embarrassed. "Good night, Mother," I said, wanting them outta there, like *now*.

They turned, and in spite of myself, I stared after them until they disappeared into the dimly lit corridor. They totally looked like the real deal. Seriously. Like they'd always lived in 1342, rather than popping in for a visit from the twenty-first century. There was no way I looked that good. It was no wonder Romana suspected me as much as I suspected her.

She rolled the dice. "You shall have to teach me this game," I said, staring at the board—which looked a bit like a backgammon board—and pegs.

All three of them stared at me. "You have never played Tric-Trac?" Romana asked. "How can that be? 'Tis a game of the Normans."

I gave her a slight lift of my shoulders. "It is not popular in our circles at home." *Lay off, chick. It can't be that crazy.*

"Mayhap we should begin an import business," Marcello casually said to his brother. "Sets of Tric-Trac. We could make a fair fortune, since it seems the Normans have yet to capitalize on it."

Fortino cocked a brow and nodded, and I smiled again, taking in the sheer health of him. So different from the last time I'd seen him. I had wondered if I'd see him or his father again. While Lord Forelli had passed on, Fortino appeared to be on the brink of a new life. As he patiently explained the rules of the game to me, he and

Romana shared several secretive, lingering glances. It was as if her relationship with Marcello had long been forgotten—as if she had never had eyes for anyone but the eldest Forelli.

I stared hard at her, trying to see if I detected any bit of fakey-ness, but could see nothing but honest, girly love in her eyes. Maybe I'd done them all the ultimate favor, splitting Marcello and Romana up, so she could get together with his brother. As we began to play, my eyes fell on a leather-bound copy of *The Golden Legend* on the table between two wooden chairs. "Have you moved on from your readings of Dante, m'lord?" I asked casually, moving my peg two notches along the board.

"Nay, 'tis Lady Romana who has taken to reading of the saints," Fortino said, shaking the dice in his hand. He paused to smile over at her. "An early wedding present from me."

I imagined the two of them in a Sienese bookshop. Books in these days cost a fortune. "You have suffered no relapse in your health, m'lord?"

He pursed his lips and laid down a card, and then his brown eyes met mine. "There are good days and there are bad. But most are good, now that Romana has agreed to be my bride." He lifted her hand again and kissed it. She smiled indulgently in his direction. I sighed inwardly. The two of them were a bit disgusting with all the lovey-dovey stuff. Were Marcello and I that bad?

I looked his way, and he smiled gently back at me. We really hadn't had a chance to be together, day by day. To just *be*. It had been crazy, the last time I was here, dashing from one battle to the next. Would we settle into plain old boring life as these two had? I hoped not. And then I changed my mind. It wouldn't be *all* bad, always being together, sharing covert glances, stolen kisses.

I sneaked another glance at Romana and Fortino. They seemed good. Solid. Real. As long as Romana was not an assassin, and she wasn't trying to steal back Marcello, who was I to get in the way of love? I looked back at Marcello. Was he really over her? Was he truly mine, through and through? A warm sensation flooded through me, so sudden it stole my breath for a moment.

We finished the game, Marcello, Fortino, and Romana bantering all the while, as I struggled to keep track of the rules.

"Friends," I said when Romana emerged as the victor. "I can see that I shall enjoy this game very much, but I must beg your leave and retire to my quarters. I am suddenly so weary I fear I might nod off right here and now."

"May your sleep be sure and sweet," Fortino said. He and Marcello rose with me. "I'll return in a little while," Marcello said to them. "I shall not rest until I have beaten you both."

"It shall be a long evening, then," Romana said, daring him with a cocked brow. Fortino laughed, and I forced another smile, pretending that it didn't matter at all to me that Marcello intended to return here, near *her*. I had to get over this suspicion and fear and jealousy. *Get a grip, Gabi. He left her for you.*

We headed to the next corridor, but at the turret stairs, Marcello paused and gestured upward with his chin. "Shall we? For but a moment?"

Going anywhere with him sounded perfect to me. Outside for a breath of fresh air, under a blanket of celestial stars? Better than Black Friday and a wallet full of cash.

I smiled as Marcello took my hand and led me up the curving staircase. I loved the feeling of his warm fingers and palm covering mine! I shivered in excitement, still trying to convince myself that this was all totally real.

We emerged through the small door that led to the parapet—the castle walkway, at the top of the walls, beyond the crenellated barrier. Ahead of us was a man, hand on the hilt of his sword, staring outward and walking away from us. Marcello put a finger to his lips—*shh!*—and pulled me around the corner, out of the guard's view, and then into his arms. He bent and kissed my lips, softly at first, then more insistently. "Much better than Tric-Trac," he said, stroking my hair, and then, cradling my cheek, kissed me again, more eagerly.

He pulled back after a moment, eyes closed, as if wanting to memorize this moment. I knew the feeling. "How I've longed for you, Gabriella," he said.

"I was gone but hours," I said with a smile.

"For you," he said, shaking his head. "'Tis still nearly impossible for me to believe. If I hadn't carried you in there, so close to perishing, seen you disappear…Indeed, if Luca had not been beside me to witness it, I might've thought you were nothing but a figment of my imagination."

"Have you told no one?" I asked, wrapping my arms around him.

"Not a word, to a single soul," he said, tucking a strand of my hair over my ear and kissing the top of my head. "We'd all be tried for madness and found guilty. They'd call us wicked, turn us out."

That sounded pretty un-fun. "Marcello…what of Romana? Did you…were you not…"

He waited until I looked into his eyes, then shook his head. "What I feel for you, Gabriella, is nothing like what I shared with her. I feel kinship with her. Responsibility. A general fondness. Not love."

"And Fortino? Does he love her?"

"Fortino is glad to be embracing life. He is happy to have a pretty woman on his arm, a future ahead of him. He is content to fulfill our family's duty to Siena. But you saw them for yourself—there seems to be more between them than there ever was between me and Romana."

"I'm not certain I could marry anyone out of a sense of duty." I pulled him closer, so glad there was more between us than that.

"I very nearly did. Is it so different in your age?"

Uhh, yeah. In a hundred different ways. "People rarely marry for anything but love. Some live together and forgo marriage."

He pulled back, looking at me as if I was joking.

"Truly," I said.

"And what does the Church say of this?"

I cocked my head and thought about that. "I think they don't like it, but I really don't know."

"You do not know? What of your priest?"

"I…I have no priest."

"You mean your church is waiting on a new priest to be sent?" He pulled back a little farther, looking hard at me.

My mouth felt dry. Why was I suddenly feeling separated from him? Why was he making such a big deal of it?

"No, I mean, we don't attend mass. Christmas, Easter, we go. But beyond that…"

He stared at me, hard. I shifted, uncomfortable when he remained silent.

"Gabriella, you are baptized? You believe in God?"

"Well, yes. Of course." Most people I knew believed in the Big Guy. Or at least some sort of Good Force. A Creator. I knew a few agnostics and atheists, too, but most of them took the title to get attention.

He seemed relieved by my answer, and I was more than ready to move on to another subject. I took a step away. "Marcello, are you certain Romana had no idea that the doctor was poisoning me?"

"Would I allow my brother to marry her if I thought her capable of such duplicity?"

I let his question go unanswered. He had good reason to give her a second chance, with all of Siena lobbying for a union between the house of Rossi and the house of Forelli. But even with that pressure, Marcello obviously thought her innocent. But that didn't mean she was. Was he simply so happy to be relieved of his duty that he was willing to overlook any lingering questions? This whole dumping one brother for another was new to me—I couldn't imagine Lia dating someone who'd broken up with me. But for these guys, it seemed as if it was totally fine. I didn't get it. Maybe you had to be born here, in this time period, to understand.

But as relieved as I was that Marcello was free, I was worried about Fortino. The guy had barely escaped death. I couldn't stand the idea of his life being anything less than perfect from here on out. I'd have to find out more.

We walked the wall. The castle had five segments, with a turret at each corner. She was so highly defensible that she'd never been attacked, other than the night I had persuaded Paratore to do so, therefore leaving his own castle compromised. On the far end, we paused and looked out over the rolling hills, golden and velvety with the last bit of sunset.

There, I could see fifty pitched tents, the clouds of dust rising behind troops' horses in the light of dusk. I paused, surprised. "The Sienese?"

Marcello nodded. He was so crazy handsome, I didn't want to look where he was pointing. Gradually, he realized I was staring at him, and he looked down into my eyes. He squeezed my hand, and my skin sparked with pleasure. "I missed you so, Gabriella," he whispered.

"I missed you, too."

I wished he'd kiss me again, but we were too visible here, at the center of the wall. Below us, in the bailey, or courtyard, servants milled in and out of the kitchen and stables. I stepped forward, continuing our walk, self-conscious. Of course they'd be interested. Marcello had broken his engagement to Romana…for me.

For me.

I took a deep breath. Where the heck did that leave us? I was all of seventeen. My eighteenth birthday was still six months away. Not that I was ready to get married at eighteen. Mom would totally freak if I even mentioned that I was thinking about it.

Totally. Freak.

"How long until Fortino and Romana wed?" I asked.

Marcello glanced at me and then helped me up the narrow steps around the next turret. "A fortnight."

"Fortnight?" I asked, racking my brain, trying to remember how many days that would be.

"Fourteen days," he said, a tiny smile on his lush lips. At least now he understood why I didn't always get those sorts of references.

I tried to cover my hesitation. "Will that be odd for you? To see someone long promised to you marry your brother?"

Marcello shrugged and said, "I am happy for Fortino. And glad for Romana. It is actually better for her. She always wanted to be Lady Forelli, mistress of the castello."

Yeah, there you have it. Marcello was too good, too willing to see the best in everyone. He'd obviously never dated around. How could he? In many ways, he'd been hitched when he was just a boy. It had always been Romana. And being the loyal kind of guy he was, he'd apparently never considered anyone else.

Until me. Somehow, some way, this dude was crazy into me, from the get-go. Enough that he'd opted to break his engagement to Romana, on the off chance that I might come back someday. Or maybe because he knew there was something more. It still made me almost dizzy with excitement. Is this what people were talking about when they spoke of love?

Love. I nodded, answering my own unspoken question. Being here, again with Marcello, after wondering if I could ever get back, I knew it to be true. I was in love with him. In love with a dude who, in my time, had been dead for almost seven hundred years.

He pulled me to a stop and looked out over the forest. From here, there was a peekaboo view of Castello Paratore. "How is it possible, Gabriella?" he asked. "How is it that you can travel from your time to my own?"

"I know not," I said. "'Twill drive my mother to distraction. In our time, she's a scientist."

"Scientist? I do not know that word."

"A doctor, of facts, of the way things work. A scholar. There's always a logical reason for everything. Every mystery can be unraveled, with effort. But this one, this time portal…" I looked out over the trees melding as a mass in the growing darkness. "I don't believe anyone can figure it out."

He lifted my hand to his lips and kissed the knuckles. Delightful shivers ran up my arm and down my back. "'Tis a miracle of God. A gateway that only He could open."

I stared into his eyes. I felt the same. Something this good, this sweet, could only come from Someone beyond my comprehension.

"Will you stay this time, Gabriella? Stay here, with me?"

My breath caught. Really, there was no other place I wanted to be. But forever sort of promises? *Whoa, that's a biggie.* Never go to college, figure out what kind of job I'd be good at? Never see my friends again or even speak to them? Never vote? Never again touch a computer, listen to a radio, watch a movie?

But then, living here, with him, would sort of be like entering the most romantic movie possible and never leaving, right?

"It is much to consider, Marcello," I said. His face fell a fraction, and I rushed on, "It is not you I doubt. It's my life…My own time has much to offer. It is so vastly different…As strongly as I feel for you, it is not a decision that can be made lightly. Do you understand?"

"I do," he said carefully. But I could tell I'd hurt his feelings. He dropped my hand and put both his hands on the wall, leaning over it, looking out. He glanced over his shoulder at me. "But what I feel…Am I alone in believing that we are in love?"

I touched his shoulder, not caring that we were the evening's entertainment for the people below. "Marcello."

He straightened and faced me, the muscles in his jaw clenching. But as I stared into his eyes, he began to smile, reading my answer in my expression. "Would I have returned if I did not feel for you what you feel for me?" I asked. I felt shy, suddenly. Afraid to use the *L* word.

"And what is it you feel for me, Gabriella?" he asked, tucking that constantly escaping strand of hair behind my ear. "I've been waiting months to hear it."

There was no getting around it. I was as sunk as he was. Buried. Delightfully, deliciously captured. "Love," I said, staring into his eyes, feeling every letter of the *L* word, owning it. And feeling that somehow, some way, this thing had to work.

Because it was too right to be wrong.

Wasn't it?

CHAPTER 4

Castello Forelli was slammed with people. Judging by the packed house in the Great Hall that first night, and because they put the three of us in one room, I realized Castello Forelli had become The Place to Be. There were constant bigwigs visiting, including five of the Nine and their peeps—I swear, you'd think they were like reality TV stars or something—and I soon figured out that Marcello and Fortino were the leaders of this entire front in the ongoing battle between Firenze and Siena.

When we walked toward the Great Hall on our second morning, intending to nab some breakfast—which was usually a sad, pasty kind of oatmeal or dry, day-old bread—we found the courtyard alive with activity. Marcello heaved a wooden case up to Luca, in the back of a wagon, who turned and placed it on top of several others. As much as I liked seeing Marcello slightly sweaty, with his shirt sleeves rolled up and collar untied and open, I frowned at what clearly looked like a group of men preparing to head out.

I swallowed the indignant *Where're you goin'?* that I wanted to let out and instead pretended to be the lady I was supposed to be. "Good morning, m'lord," I said to Marcello, stopping beside him.

He grinned and wiped his forehead with his shirtsleeve. "M'ladies," he said, dragging his eyes from me to my mother and sister and back again.

"You prepare to depart?" I asked carefully.

"The autumn harvest is upon us," he said, "and yet many farmers are off serving Siena and Castello Forelli, guarding our borders or languishing in Firenze's prisons, unable to bring their crops in. Some shall never return, buried in shallow graves. Their women and children struggle, trying to bring in the harvest on their own. My men and I shall not stand idly by." His eyes moved to the dignitaries of Siena, who walked in groups around the courtyard, watching the knights as if they'd gone crazy.

I smiled. Man, I was wild for this guy. Aiming to go out and help women and children in need. Could he get any hotter? "We shall accompany you," I said.

"Yes, please," Lia said. She was already as sick of the castle as I was.

But Marcello was shaking his head. "Nay. 'Tis safest for you here, inside the gates."

"We shall work beside you and your men," I returned. "There are more than a hundred of you assembling." I leaned closer. "How could we be any safer? And I assume we won't be far from the castle's reach."

"Please, sir," Mom chimed in. "I myself am anxious for a ride out into your pretty countryside. You'll find both I and my daughters are able workers, ready to set our hands to any task you give us."

Marcello leaned back and looked at all three of us, then let out a long sigh. "I assume that if I decline your request, you shall continue to pester me?"

"Most likely," I said with a nod.

"Very well." He shook his head and rubbed his neck. "You'll want to change into suitable clothing. It will aid us in disguising your identity, in some measure." He cocked a brow. "'Tis dirty work ahead of us."

"You shall find we do not fear dirt, m'lord," Mom said with a sly smile. She'd always been the first one into a dig site and usually left covered in dust from the roots of her hair to the tops of her dingy brown socks at day's end.

And so began our daily journey to the fields and vineyards to help out, before returning, exhausted, to Castello Forelli. We met wives of prisoners and widows of soldiers slain in the battle against Firenze. We struggled alongside them to bring in the wheat on narrow farms carved among the hills or the bounty of grapes that clung to vines.

Marcello tolerated us accompanying them, but only because of the soldiers who worked alongside us, and only with ten times the scouts on duty that I knew he'd usually post. We worked hard, but the afternoons felt long and leisurely as we learned to cut wheat from their shocks with large, fearsome scythes and bind them into sheaves. I figured that even if I were with Marcello in the middle of the desert, I'd feel like it was a resort. I was feeling *that* kind of Serious Happy.

Today they'd brought us to a vineyard. We were cutting grapes from their thick, winding vines and placing them on flat carts.

Mom had elected to stay back at the castle, busy hand-copying a botanical volume in Fortino's library, recognizing that it contained many references to specimens long lost to the modern world. She was like a kid with a jar full of coins in a candy store, delirious with the options of study before her. It was a little irritating, really. I had finally felt like I was connecting with her in some way, and *bam,* there she was again, on to something else. I sighed. It was all right; I was more into the guy beside me, even if he was laughing at my meager contribution of grapes to the wheelbarrow.

Luca stood up, hands on hips, and looked at the flat wagon between Lia and me. He cocked one brow and nodded over at us. "While these two would be the prettiest peasant girls within miles, they'd make poor wives for a hopeful vintner. Look at that," he said, gesturing toward our wagon, mocking us. "It's downright pitiful."

"Hey," Lia said, pretending to be outraged. "Just because we did not grow up cutting grapes doesn't mean we cannot keep up with the best of them." She waved toward the guys' wagon. "Certainly, you have a pile there. But *look* at them," she said. She walked over to it and picked up a bunch. "These are terribly small and some are not yet ripe. You are *fast,* but alas, you are not *careful,*" she said to Luca.

She was gorgeous in the warm afternoon light. Her blond hair was coming out from its knot, curling in soft tendrils around her neck. I looked to Luca as he tossed back his head and laughed with delight, gesturing toward her as he met Marcello's eye. "I must confess, I do enjoy these Norman girls."

It had become their secret word for us. *Norman.* Our cover story—that we were from Normandy. But he meant it as "these girls from that other time." He looked back to Lia and considered her while wiping sweat from his lip with the back of his hand. "Let us agree upon a little wager," he said. "We will race to the end of this row. But Signora Giannini shall decide who has the better bounty upon their wagon."

Lia considered him. "And the winner receives…"

"A rest," he said, folding his arms in front of him, jutting his chin out. "Underneath that fat oak on the hill, upon a blanket. The losers shall serve the victors by pouring wine and cutting slices of cheese and bread for them. Better yet, the losers shall *feed* the winners."

Marcello smiled and looked over Luca's shoulder at Lia, then at me, a similar taunt in his eyes.

Oh, it's on, I thought. I grinned at Lia. We'd spent the morning getting the hang of using the knife, the feel of cutting through the stiff vine, the rhythm of tossing the bunches upon the wagon. The guys had no idea what was ahead of them. Our dad had passed on his competitive spirit. He'd beaten us at cards and Scrabble and swordplay and with bow and arrow until we could beat him, fair and square. *No wimpy Betarrini girls,* he'd always said, *not a one. That's what I loved first about your mom. Her strength. Her savvy. Her smarts. Her spirit. I want daughters just like her.*

So I was thinking about that as Marcello casually counted down and began cutting and tossing as if he had all the time in the world. We'd always tried to be like Mom. Strong, smart, and spirited. And as much as she was a little distant, always in her own little mental world, Lia and I both wanted to be like her.

I glanced over at the guys. Luca was milking it, clowning around, eating a bitter grape from the bottom as if someone were feeding it to him. He waggled his eyebrows at Lia, as if he was visualizing her as his servant.

She laughed under her breath. Her blue eyes met mine. "Ready?"

"Oh, yeah," I said in a low tone, not wanting to tip off the guys. "Let's show 'em what Norman girls are made of."

We moved quietly forward, gaining momentum. It took the guys about five minutes before they realized we were pulling ahead. They surged into motion, matching us in speed, gradually a step in front of us. But we kept our heads down, reaching for the next bunch of purple grapes, even as we set the last upon the cart. Lia stopped at one point, reached for the skin of water and casually took a drink. "Care for a sip, Gabi?" she asked, as if we were sitting by the beach and not in the heat of competition.

"That sounds divine," I said, standing and taking a long swig.

The guys rolled their eyes and kept working, intent upon winning now. We moved back to the vines as if there was no race at all and then went to it, utterly focused, ignoring the taunting calls of the guys, hearing nothing but each other's whispers in English. *Keep it up. Come on, a bit faster. We can do this.*

We were nearing the end of the row when I looked up. Marcello and Luca were just rising, tossing the last of their grapes upon their heaping cart. They were three paces ahead of us. They grasped each other's arms in that medieval form of a handshake, or like modern-day boys giving each other a high five or a chest bump. My heart sank a little, but then I looked from their cart to ours. Despite their being ahead of us, our mound was a bit higher.

Marcello, confident in their victory, hurried over to Signora Giannini, three rows beyond us. He brought her back, and I realized, for the first time, that she couldn't be much older than twenty-five, with a wide face and small, squinty eyes. Two little girls clung to her skirts and a boy, about seven, hovered behind her. What would it be like, to be a widow in these times? Who knew if her husband would ever return to her from Firenze. She could be alone, forever. A shiver went down my back.

What if Marcello was killed? I glanced over at him, so alive, laughing with Luca, who was thumping him on the back. But I knew he was as much a target of Firenze's spies as Lia and I. We had gotten into a routine, felt lulled by the peace these last couple of days. I scanned the fields and valley, seeing nothing but Forelli men, either at work or on guard. We were safe. Marcello was safe. For now.

I put the awful thought out of my mind as they came closer and the woman clapped over the literal fruits of our labor. "I can't thank you well enough, m'lords, m'ladies. To think that you'd take time to assist me—" She brought a hand to her throat, apparently too choked up to continue.

"We shall do another row after we break to take our noon meal," Marcello said, smiling at her kindly. "But first, Signora, I beg you to be a judge of these two pallets of grapes. Which is best? Which will fill the most jugs with your best wine?"

The woman looked from him to the wagons. She walked around each and began to pull bunches from one—because the grapes were too small or not yet ripe—and set them aside. She worked with the calm assurance of years of experience, sorting. In three minutes, she had gone through the guys' entire pile. In a few more, she had sorted ours.

Sweetly, with hands folded, she bowed in our direction as the guys sputtered in disbelief and mock outrage.

I smiled at Marcello as Lia folded her arms and jutted out her chin, mimicking Luca's prematurely victorious stance. "I think we shall enjoy our meal this day," she said, "more than any other."

Luca frowned and gestured toward Signora Giannini as if she had surely misjudged. Marcello laughed under his breath, a low, rumbly, warm sound that made me smile even more broadly. We pranced past them, heading toward the hill, anticipating a leisurely hour ahead of us. When I glanced back, Luca lifted his head, sighed in defeat, and followed behind Marcello.

We were halfway through our meal, accepting another cup of watered wine, which tasted only vaguely of fermented grapes, when Marcello and Luca leaped to their feet, sensing the approaching riders before we did. Their hands went to the hilts of the swords they wore at their sides as Lia and I rose, standing slightly behind them.

I only took a full breath when I realized it was Sienese soldiers that approached. But they were riding hard. It was the handsome captain from Siena, Romana Rossi's cousin, at the front. His eyes moved from me to Marcello and back again. There was none of the interest I'd felt from him before, at the city wall, then at the dance. *Probably crossed some line when I stole his cousin's man,* I decided. Family loyalty was huge in modern Italy. In this era it was practically a religion.

"Sir Marcello, do you think it wise to be so distant from the castle's gates?" he asked, his horse dancing beneath him. "Especially with the Ladies Betarrini alongside you?"

Luca and Marcello took a step closer, as if they were protecting us. I shared a look with Lia.

"We shall not be prisoners in our own home," Marcello said. There was an edge to his voice, and he was suddenly all I'm-the-Boss-Here in his stance. He clearly didn't like it that Captain Rossi was slow to dismount and show deference. Neither did Luca.

"Better to be a prisoner in your own castle than in the dungeon of your enemy." His eyes flicked to Lia.

Luca took a step, but Marcello reached out a hand, cautioning him to stand down. *More weird family politics?*

"Our people are in need," Marcello said. "We will not stand by, idle. I suggest you encourage your men, as have I, to assist them. We do the greatest damage to our enemies by drawing together, bringing in the harvest, storing up for the winter ahead."

Captain Rossi glanced away from him dismissively. *Again with the attitude.* I didn't know why I ever thought the dude was cute. He was as caught up in himself as his cousin was. He dragged his eyes over me and Lia before meeting Marcello's gaze. "I suppose you are right, m'lord," he said with a slight nod he clearly wasn't feeling. "Siena's people will soon demand that you present the ladies to their republic. They've gone too long, wondering about them. And when they hear that they were out beside you, assisting the needy…Why, their legend will merely grow."

Marcello and Luca were really ticked now. I could see the tension in their shoulders. A muscle twitched in Luca's cheek.

"Is there a purpose for your visit, Captain Rossi?" Marcello asked, every word clipped.

"Indeed," he said, cocking his head and glancing at me. "My uncle would like you to attend a meeting in Siena, in three days' time. And he, of course, insists you bring Romana and Lord Fortino—if his lordship's health can tolerate the journey—as well as the Ladies Betarrini."

"For what purpose?" Marcello asked.

"If you accept the invitation, my uncle shall host a festive ball, ostensibly prenuptial goings-on. But there is a rumor," he said in a confidential manner, leaning forward, "that diplomats from Firenze shall be in attendance. He would like your brother and you to be there to listen to what they have to say. It is my uncle's hope that we can again establish peace between Firenze and Siena. This unrest accomplishes little."

Marcello straightened. "I shall be there at the appointed time. We shall send word as to whether the Ladies Betarrini will join us."

Captain Rossi hesitated. His horse took a step back, then forward. "Mayhap I did not make myself clear. Lord Rossi prepares a feast to celebrate the Ladies Betarrini's return. The meeting is merely providential timing, when all shall be in the city together. But he shall not abide anything but an affirmative answer."

Marcello's mouth was a steady, grim line. "Mayhap *I* did not make myself clear. I shall consult with my brother and then decide if the ladies might risk the journey."

Captain Rossi cocked a brow. "You have left them vulnerable here," he said, gesturing toward the countryside. "Would they not be far safer within the protective wings of Siena?" He turned away, not waiting to be excused. Even I knew it was a total diss. Luca stepped after the captain, as if he were ready to haul him off his horse, but Marcello grabbed his arm and stopped him.

The blond captain wheeled his horse around and looked down at them, a small smile tugging at the corner of his lips. "M'lord," he said to Marcello with a tiny dip of his head. "We shall be honored by the presence of your household. For Siena."

"For Siena," Marcello muttered. He stood there, watching Captain Rossi and his men thunder away in pairs, but his eyes shifted to the woods around us. He looked at Luca. "He's right. I've been foolish, exposing the women as I have."

"No, Marcello," I tried. "We must be able to be out and about. As you said, to be confined to Castello Forelli would be like being prisoners in our own home. And you've taken more than enough precautions to ensure our safety."

He turned and took my arm, and the four of us formed a small circle. "It may be different in *Normandy*," Marcello said. "But here, everyone thinks of you two when they consider our victory, even more than they think of my brother or me. The republic is transfixed with the idea of two female warriors. You caught a glimpse of it at our own little feast, inside the castle's walls, before you left. But in Siena..." He shook his head, deciding. "It shall be utter mayhem."

I stared at him for a long moment. From what I could see, there really was no way around it. I looked at Lia, asking her permission. She gave me a little smile. "I always thought it'd be cool to be homecoming queen, didn't you?"

"Talk about an anthropological gold mine. Mom would flip." She had a secondary degree in anthropology to back up her doctorate in archaeology. Lia and I'd always wished she'd put half the effort into contemporary relationships as she had with those in the past.

The guys were looking at us as if we really were speaking French.

"We shall attend the festivities with you," I said to Marcello.

He frowned and glanced at Luca.

Luca laughed under his breath. "You know what these Normans are like, m'lord. If we leave them behind in the castle, they'll take it upon themselves to climb over the wall. May as well keep them where we can watch over them."

"Indeed," I said. "Will it not soothe Lord Rossi's ruffled feathers to have us join the festivities? Give him a semblance of deference and power, to have us all there? Reorient things?"

Chin in hand, he studied me. "It has not taken you long to absorb our politics, m'lady."

I smiled, basking in his praise. So I was right. It was important we be there. For his long-term security, if not our own. We needed to win Lord Rossi's support again, despite what had transpired for Romana. Politics trumped pride, even in the twenty-first century.

And while I was there, I could do some digging, surveillance of my own. I wanted to know if Romana was really okay being with Fortino, make certain I was just being a paranoid chick.

I looked down the road, to Captain Rossi, now a half-mile away with his troops. A shiver of foreboding ran down my back. Just what was up with the Rossi family? I remembered the doctor talking in hushed tones with Lord Rossi, even as he was poisoning me. Lord Rossi was frightfully clever. A leader of all of Siena. So how had such a man—and Foraboschi, too—wormed his way into Rossi's circle of confidence?

Maybe everyone else was ready to dismiss the connection. But I wasn't. My hand went to my belly. Maybe it was because I had almost died. The pain was not too old—stitched up just days ago, from my perspective—for me to remember it well.

And I was determined that none of my loved ones would be touched by such treachery again.

CHAPTER 5

We made the journey to Siena with none of the drama that had accompanied us before. No one attacked our heavily fortified troops. No swords were even drawn. But Lia and I both traveled with our weapons at our backs and our mother between us. We'd gained enough knowledge of this territory to know we were best served to be always at the ready.

Little girls at the city entrance were our first hint of what was to come. Dressed in flowing gowns, with crowns of daisies on their heads, they threw sunflowers before us. The horses trampled them, leaving the sweet smell of sunflower oil wafting up behind us. The boys were next, heralding the heroines of Siena, the She-Wolves. They cried out, howling with great smiles on their faces and waving wildly. They scurried ahead of us and behind us, as if beside themselves, they were so excited. Ultimately, the villagers on the outskirts of the city gathered, waving and throwing more flowers before us.

"Can you believe this?" Lia asked me, eyes wide. Mom looked similarly stunned, shaking her head and smiling. I liked it that she

was seeing us—really *seeing* us—anew. Capable. Strong. Honored.
I glanced at Marcello, but neither he nor Luca seemed to be sharing our glory. Their eyes were constantly scanning the crowds, their
brows furrowed.

The guys flanked us when the road was wide enough, politely
bending to accept the proffered flowers for their charges but grimly
aware of the danger that the people brought us. Might there be an
assassin within their ranks, waiting for just such an opportunity as
this to close in and attack, then disappear?

"We must hasten to the Rossis' as quickly as possible," Luca said
to Marcello.

Marcello nodded once, fast.

I hated that their paranoia was making me paranoid too.
Suddenly I was all air-marshall-on-a-risky-flight, checking everyone
out, watching to see if people were acting weird, moving in a way
that stood out. A shiver ran down my back. "So much for our homecoming queen glory," I whispered to Lia.

"Yeah, that's over before it began," she returned. "We get to pretend we're the homecoming queens and worry someone will stab us
at any moment."

"Or shoot us with an arrow."

"Or poison us. We've seen, firsthand, how well that works."

Marcello reached over and touched my elbow. "Please. Do not
jest. It is quite serious."

Yeah, I get that. I heaved a sigh. "Just trying to ease the moment
with a little humor. You never do that?"

"Rarely," Luca said, one eyebrow raised. "Not for wont of trying,
on my part."

Marcello's lips curved a bit, but he stayed on his own track. "We must be vigilant."

"Vigilant, ever vigilant. Is it to be thus the rest of our lives?" I asked. What I wanted to know, really, was *Is this what I'm signing on for if I stay?*

He read the question in my eyes. "There are times of war and times of peace, Gabriella. We shall pray for peace. For now, enjoy your fair measure of glory. Luca and I shall ensure you remain secure."

I shifted my eyes forward and smiled at a tiny girl reaching up on her tiptoes to hand Marcello a flower. She smiled shyly at me. He reached for it, and I looked back at her as we passed, giving her a wave. She ran off, screeching to her mother as if the latest Disney princess had just given her an autograph.

Marcello was studying me. "You and your sister have given our people hope. If Siena can produce such strength, invoke such passion as you two embody, no one can defeat us."

"Why us? You and Luca, you did as much to turn the tide of that battle and capture Castello Paratore. You're the ones that bear the famed Forelli name."

He shrugged. "You are female." He allowed a smile then, a real smile. Oh, how I loved the way his brown eyes sparkled....

But the equal-rights chick in me bristled at his words. He only meant them as admiration, I told myself. In this time, in this place, women weren't ready to fight beside their men. They were back at home, baking the bread, raising the babies. So, for them, we were basically...foreign. And fascinating.

I'd never really fascinated anyone. And I, in turn, found that oddly irresistible.

"So if Siena is full of adoration for my girls," Mom said, leaning closer, "why are you concerned?"

"Because for every thousand members of their adoring people, there are bound to be a hundred dissenters. Those who are proponents of peace with Firenze and object to our taking Castello Paratore. Others who wish to sow outright discontent. Spies, even."

"How many total citizens abide in Siena now?" Mom asked.

"More than two hundred thousand."

Fantastic. Then if we only had a hundred bad guys for every thousand, there might only be two thousand who wanted to take us down.

"Let's just hope they don't all rally together," Lia said softly, blue eyes wide, doing the math too.

Luca sat straighter. "I shall never let you out of my sight."

She seemed to take comfort in that. Was that more than just a casual connection between them? My eyes met my mom's.

"If we are attacked, I shall need to take the girls home," she said, speaking to the men, but looking at us, warning us.

The guys stayed silent.

So did we.

I think we all knew it was just a matter of time. But I figured we'd argue that out when we really had to deal with it.

The men had to bodily push the crowds back down the narrow, curving streets with their horses in order for us to make it into the Rossi palace. The palazzo was one of many that ringed Siena's beautiful central piazza, where I figured much of the celebration would happen in the days to come.

Lord Rossi was nice enough, greeting us with kisses to both cheeks. I couldn't tell if he was ticked off inside—on the outside, he was nothing but a gracious host, fawning over my mother, who was six inches taller than him, praising God for our reunion.

"Guess the rock-star status fixes the stolen fiancé issue," Lia whispered, leaning toward me.

"Guess one Forelli is as good as another," I muttered sarcastically. My eyes followed Romana, who hung on Fortino's arm. She never left him alone. In the six days I'd been back, I hadn't had one opportunity to talk to him, find out if he was all good with how things had come down. Was she purposely trying to keep him from talking to me? Or was it all in my head? Why couldn't I just let it go? I had my guy. Pushing the Fortino-Romana issue might wreck things, especially if I was wrong. *Let it go, Gabi. Everything's fine.*

But it didn't feel fine. Remembering the doctor and Lord Rossi whispering secretively, I set my lips in a grim line. I just couldn't believe the Rossis had been as duped as I had been. Used. Both Romana and her father were far too clever to allow it.

One thing comforted me: If the Rossis had been in on my poisoning, it was more likely they'd have done it to get me out of the way and seal the deal with the Forelli-Rossi union, not because they were working on the enemy's behalf. I mean, Romana's dad was one of the Nine. A head honcho. King of the hill. Why would he be willing to sell out his fellow Sienese and risk the republic's security?

Unless he had been promised far more in a new republic, run by those in Firenze.

I glanced around the ritzy palace the Rossis called home. Servants bustled across polished marble floors. Thick tapestries lined the hallway. Everyone was dressed in fantastic gowns and tunics. I knew dinner would be a minifeast before the big feasts began.

What else did he need?

Money. Man is always motivated by money, my dad said to me once. *It can work for us, or it can enslave us. Even when we have much, we feel like we need more. No matter how much we have.*

I'd been whining last summer about not having a car, about how other girls back at home were driving around. Begging to the point of bugging my parents, really. I thought if we had our own car, Lia and I could escape the summer dig, drive around, find some fun for once. But there hadn't been cash for that, of course. The Big Dig, the big payoff, was always around the corner for my 'rents.

Even now, Mom had discovered the Big Dig at last, and where was she? Six hundred years away. No, we Betarrinis were smart but never rich.

"I shall not be far," Marcello said lowly, nodding at Lord Rossi's wave of invitation to him to join the others.

"Do not be troubled," I said. We turned to go, but I glanced over my shoulder to the group of nobles in the corner, the only ones we had not been introduced to. One, a tall, handsome young man with jet-black hair that waved over one eye, studied me without hesitation.

The Fiorentini, I thought. *Enemies.*

Or soon to be brothers, friends? I wasn't trying to get in the way of the Medieval Peace Process. Life would be far more pleasant at

Marcello's side if I weren't constantly worried that one or both of us would be killed.

But the question remained…was there a possibility the Rossis would sell out? Abandon Siena in exchange for a fat Fiorentini bank account?

And why were they so anxious to place a daughter within Castello Forelli's walls if that was their aim?

I shook my head, totally confused.

"What?" Lia asked, looking at me from the corners of her eyes as we walked down the hall.

"I don't know. Something's off. Wrong. And I gotta figure out what it is before it's too late."

CHAPTER 6

As I suspected, the Rossi feast began down in the Palazzo Pubblico, the public palace, at the bottom of the clamshell-shaped plaza. I shoved back dark memories of the last time I'd feasted and danced in the hall—the place where Lord Vanucci had approached me and I first learned that Lord Paratore had captured Lia. For this night, I wanted to enjoy the feel of being in my new, gorgeous golden gown—a symbolic gift from Lord Rossi—on Marcello's arm, dancing with him.

I mean, I'd waited seventeen years to have a boyfriend, and now I had one. At last. I wanted to just enjoy the day, the evening. Back home in Colorado, I'd only been to one dance, and it was with a guy I asked out.

Guys are just scared of beautiful girls, Dad said.

Sure, Dad, I said. *Only ugly girls go to dances.*

The right one will come around, he promised. *You'll see.*

And Oh. My. Gosh. He had. I wished Dad were here to meet him. To do that Dad-Boyfriend thing he would've been so bad at…

but would've figured out soon enough. I think he would've liked Marcello. Liked how he got all protective around me. And listened to me. And looked at me like he thought I was fascinating.

When I caught sight of Marcello waiting for me in the main hall, I couldn't stop staring at him. His curly hair was neatly tied back. He wore a white silk shirt that was kind of loose, but over it was a finely woven tunic with a fair amount of gold thread in it, obviously to represent the house of Forelli. It made him look all the more buff. Leggings encased his thighs and were tucked into new leather boots.

He smiled at me with that grin…and I floated across the floor to him, my handsome prince.

He met me halfway and took my hand, bent, and tenderly kissed my knuckles, sending shivers of delight up my arm and neck. He straightened but still held my hand in his. "You, m'lady, look more beautiful than ever in Forelli gold."

"Thank you," I said. I was sure I was blushing. But I didn't feel like an idiot. I felt all giddy-ish. Light. Like my lungs were full of perfectly clean air. It was like I could breathe, really breathe, and it made everything sharper, clearer around me. See every detail with better than my normal twenty-twenty vision.

Like I told Mom. I was living fully, for the first time or something.

I'm down with this love thing, I thought, sneaking another look at my man.

I tried out that *L* word again, silently in my mind, as we paraded as a group through the piazza and down to the larger building. Men and women, commoners and nobles, bowed and curtsied when we passed as if we were royalty.

It was cool. But I hoped the whole heroine-worship thing wouldn't last forever. We were just two girls in the right time, at the right place. I chuckled to myself over my lame joke. *Right time, right place.*

"What is humorous?" Marcello asked, leaning toward me.

"It is nothing," I said. "I simply amuse myself at times."

"It is so good to see you smile, beloved," he whispered in my ear, and his warm breath and sweet words made me want to haul him into a dark, secluded corner and kiss him like crazy.

I managed to squelch that desire—I swear, it was like when you want to pull a fire alarm—but just barely. "I can't stop smiling, m'lord," I returned, staring into his eyes. "Not when I'm with you."

We stood there for a moment, people swirling around us, laughing, greeting one another, kissing on both cheeks in Italian fashion. And our deep stare into each other's eyes was as intense as a kiss of our own. It was like he was speaking to me, singing to me, all through that long, silent, sexy-as-all-get-out look.

"Sir Forelli," said a man—maybe for the second time—and we both started and looked in his direction. Mr. Tall, Dark, and Handsome. I felt Marcello's arm tense beneath my hand.

"Lord Rodolfo Greco," he said, his tone careful, curious. He paused for a second and then said, "May I present to you Lady Gabriella Betarrini?"

I sensed other men moving in our direction, caught sight of Luca, his mouth grim, when Marcello lifted one hand.

Lord Greco clearly sensed their presence, but his eyes remained on me. He took my hand and leaned down to slowly, elegantly kiss it. "As beautiful as it has been rumored," he said, still holding my fingers in his.

"Agreed," Marcello said, sliding his hand into mine, making Greco release me.

"May you know that not all in Firenze are your mortal enemy," Lord Greco said softly. Then, with a slight bow, he moved away, cutting through Marcello's men, who now had formed a double circle around us.

"M'lord," said a servant, nervously clearing his throat—and we all looked in his direction. He was standing on his tiptoes, trying to see us over the shoulders of Marcello's men. Marcello waved them away. "Yes?"

The small servant bowed, and the corners of his mouth curved in a knowing smile. "I am to escort you and Lady Betarrini to your table."

I looked around, suddenly remembering I had a sister and mother—and feeling a bit guilty for forgetting them for a moment— but saw they were already ahead of us, seated at a table that was elevated above the rest. Lord Rossi was at one end, with Romana and Fortino—also in shades of gold—to his right, along with other friends of his I recognized from last time I'd been here. Two were numbered among the Nine—I remembered that much— but I racked my brain for their names. I'd always been lame with names.

The Fiorentini, I saw, were seated at a table of their own. Apparently, negotiations had only gone so well. Well enough to be invited to the party, but not well enough to make it to the inner circle.

"You'll remember Lord Lombardi and Lord Esposito," Marcello whispered in my ear, studying me. *Man, was I that easy to figure out? Or was it just that this guy knew me so well already?*

Meeting Greco, a potential enemy, stirred up memories of meeting the creepy Vanucci. "You'll be close to me all evening?" I asked Marcello as we reached the dais.

"Never out of reach," he said. "It's all right, Gabriella. This will be an entirely different evening from the last time we were here. Even with our Fiorentini *friends* nearby."

I smiled at him, liking how he'd read into my fears and so easily comforted me. It was a bit awkward still, with Romana sneaking looks at us through dinner, just as she had back at Castello Forelli. There were several toasts to the "Ladies Betarrini," and some sly comments that connected me and Marcello. Nah, no real secret there…

I felt a little sorry for Romana. I really did. It wasn't hard for me to remember sneaking looks at Marcello and her, feeling totally jealous. I took a bite of perfectly roasted chicken and stared at my plate. I wished we could just talk, like girls back home did.

Hey, I know this is awkward. Weird. But are you—we—okay? You're all good with it? You have your guy, I have mine? Because, we have to, you know, figure it out since we'll see each other every day and stuff….

I swallowed hard. Maybe he hadn't felt love for her, but that didn't mean she didn't have it goin' on for him. And now she'd been tossed to Bachelor Number One, back from death's door, suddenly on the market. That worked out for local politics, but what about Romana? What if she was no evil poisoner but just a pawn?

I looked across the table at her; she caught my eye and then hurriedly turned to Fortino, all light and charm. She'd been avoiding me all week. Apparently she wasn't ready for any heart-to-hearts.

Thankfully, we were soon finished with our meal and moved to the other hall for the dancing. Again and again, Marcello intervened when men inquired if they could dance with me, as did Luca, beside Lia. "For reasons of security, we must decline your kind offer," he said. "Only the Nine get a chance to dance with these women."

Belatedly, I remembered Mom and Lia might not know any of the steps. "Lia," I whispered, "what about the *dancing?*" I looked over her shoulder to our mother, who was totally acting the part of the charming, medieval merchant, chatting with one of the Nine, her face animated with interest. I bet she was missing her video recorder and notepad. We'd barely been able to get her to sleep since she arrived.

"It's all right," Lia said. "Luca gave us both lessons back at the castello. We're ready."

I smiled and raised a brow. "Ahh, right. Dancing lessons. Spill it. How much did *you* like *your* lessons?"

"He did a fine job of instruction," she said lightly, cutting me off. But she didn't move away fast enough for me to miss the smile. *Oh yeah,* I thought, *you're falling for the funny dude. You always fall for the funny, charming dude.*

I looked after her in satisfaction. It was all going to work out, somehow. I felt it, deep inside. As crazy as it seemed, I had hope, real hope, that I might be able to stay here, with Marcello, long-term. Like, forever.

"M'lady," he said, his low voice rumbling in my ear. I looked over to him. "May I claim the first dance?"

I forced myself to remember my place. "Dancing with anyone other than you, m'lord, would be the most terrible form of torture," I said.

"But it will make our dances all the more sweet," he said with a smile, and I laid my arm atop his as he led me to the center of the ballroom. The strings played and the group moved, in perfect, elegant timing, as one.

But with the way Marcello looked at me, touched me, held me in his arms, we may as well have been the only couple in the room.

CHAPTER 7

I was bummed when the dancing ended, just as I finished doing my duty in dancing with the last of the Nine, and only got one more with Marcello.

"The people are calling for you," Marcello said. Luca and Lia and Mom drew near, and that was when I heard it. *"Lu-pe! Lu-pe! Lu-pe!"* She-wolves, She-wolves, She-wolves. They were chanting for the She-Wolves. Us.

"Now I really do feel like rock stars hittin' the stage," I muttered, still shoving down my frustration at not having one more turn on the dance floor with my man.

"My, aren't we ungrateful?" Mom chided me gently.

"All right, all right," I said, then looked to Marcello. "Let us see this eve to its end so that I might be alone with you at last."

His eyes widened in a mixture of shock and delight. He glanced around, suddenly all nervous that someone might've heard me.

"Hmm, that was a bit too forward," Mom said in my ear before giving me a small scowl.

Ya think? I wanted to bite back. "Forgive me, m'lord," I said quickly. "I confess that the evening has already severely taxed me."

His small smile faded into concern. "You are ill, m'lady? Must I get you back to your quarters to rest?"

"Nay, nay," I said. I stood taller, throwing back my shoulders. "We shall see this through." Memories of his words of warning went through my mind. "But Marcello, your men—"

"Will be surrounding you. Some are disguised as commoners. But I swear on my life, Gabriella, no one will get to you, your sister, or your mother."

Man, I had to admit that I loved it when he got all Tough Protector Warrior on me. "Lead on, m'lord," I said. *'Cause anywhere you're goin', I am too.*

We proceeded outside and they escorted us to three high-backed chairs, this time, set on a raised platform under a canopy. It was dark out, so I guessed it was just to show everyone that we were the Girls of the Hour. The crowd erupted with cheers and applause. *She-Wolves, She-Wolves, She-Wolves* became the chant again.

"Heavens," Mom said. "You're really going to have to tell me more about what brought all of this on."

I'd been brief with her, not wanting her to stress over me and Lia. I mean, she knew I'd narrowly escaped death in freeing Lia from Castello Paratore, but she didn't know *all* of the details. That, like, I'd almost been killed a *dozen* times. You just didn't tell your mom that kind of thing—not if you were trying to keep her from rushing you off to some safe tower. Which they had around here. Dozens of 'em. I glanced over the crowd and above to the skyline. Nearly every palazzo of note had a tower, each seeking to be taller than its neighbor's. Yeah, these people seemed unified. But the towers said something different. They said, *Don't mess with me or I'll take you down, neighbor or not.*

Lord Rossi rose from his chair, one of nine seated in an arc in front of us, and raised his hands. "My people, I give you the Ladies Betarrini."

A roar went up in response, reverberating in my chest as if we were at a concert right beside the speakers. Torches rose to the sky and then dropped to light massive bonfires all around the square. The choir of wolf howls became deafening. I didn't dare look at Lia. We might've burst out in nervous, hysterical laughter. I still couldn't quite believe it was happening.

When they finally quieted, Lord Rossi said, "As you know, the Ladies Betarrini have done a great service for our fair commune."

Again, the crowd cheered.

"And while these women are from a distant land, they are forever daughters of Siena."

The people went crazy for that.

"But Toscana has not always treated them as the prizes they are. Prior to fighting for our cause, they were robbed and left with naught but the clothes upon their backs."

I hadn't ever heard real people say things like "boo" much and actually hiss, but I did at that moment.

"So the Nine have taken it upon themselves to rectify that problem. As of this evening, the Ladies Betarrini are as wealthy as they are beautiful and heroic!"

With that, all nine men rose, with small chests in their hands. One by one, they bowed before us, and then with Las Vegas splash, dumped the golden florins at our feet.

The crowd gasped and shouted and pressed in, eager to see, passing back word behind them. I looked from the pile to my mother and sister, stunned. We'd never had a penny to our name here. Now the Nine had done what they proclaimed—made us rich. What we had before us was more than enough to buy land, build a home. Whatever we wanted.

"Gabriella," Marcello said in my ear, "You must speak."

"Me?"

"Yes, you, She-Wolf," he returned with a slight smile.

I rose, on shaking legs. I'd never been good at speaking in front of a crowd. I always gave in to such admirable traits as blushing and hyperventilating. Seriously uncool on the stage, that's what I was. *It should be Lia…she's the stage person…the one good at this…*

She rose beside me, but she was nodding, urging me on. As eldest, apparently this was my gig alone.

"M'lords, people of Siena," I began, "we are overcome by your generosity. From the moment I arrived, the house of Forelli, and behind her, Siena, has done nothing but protect me." I looked over to Marcello, remembering how he saved me the second I stepped out of the tomb. "I could do nothing less for her." *Or him.*

The crowd cheered.

"You have our undying allegiance," I said. "You have stolen our hearts, even before your leaders bestowed such riches upon us. We are forever proud to be called daughters of Siena."

"There is more," shouted Lord Rossi, waving the crowds to silence. He turned to the side and made a gesture of invitation.

Captain Rossi, Romana's handsome blond cousin, came in, and behind him, pairs of his troops, with men in chains between them.

The crowd's hissing, shouting out hateful things, was my first hint that something bad was coming our way.

When the knights separated, I gasped and took a step back. So did Lia. Luca and Marcello both took our arms, willing strength into us. Behind me, I sensed Mom step closer, hovering.

Bloody, beaten, before us was Lord Paratore. The slimeball who'd held Lia captive.

I'd assumed he was dead, killed the night of the great battle.

Two knights pushed him forward, and the Nine separated, staring at him, then up to us. Paratore rose, throwing back his shoulders. Blood crusted over a ragged gash through one eyebrow, and the eye was swollen shut. His other cheek was scraped, as if he'd been dragged over stone. He was missing teeth. They'd clearly been torturing him for months. But still, he stared defiantly at me with hatred, his one good eye looking me over from head to toe before he spit at me.

Marcello moved slightly in front of me, almost subconsciously. He radiated tension and fury.

"Lady Gabriella, Lady Evangelia," Lord Rossi said, walking around Lord Paratore as if he owned him. It reminded me of the day Lord Paratore did the same with me. I shoved back a shiver. "The fate of this man, and those who wear his colors, are in your hands," he said. "Our new friends of Firenze, forward-thinking men who seek to regain peace between two cities that once considered themselves sisters, would like to offer you a trade."

Lord Greco stepped forward alongside his friends, surrounded by knights of Siena, apparently there to keep the crowds from seizing them. "Ladies Betarrini," Lord Greco said, carefully keeping his eyes on our feet. "Despite Lord Paratore's dishonor, he is still one of our own. Release him, and we shall send you a hundred of Siena's fighting men languishing in our prisons."

The crowd booed, calling for death, hanging, drawing and quartering Paratore, along with these men from Firenze.

When they quieted, I said to Greco, "By his hands, Lady Evangelia suffered mightily. After suffering most grievous wounds, inflicted by Paratore men, I myself very nearly died. There is nothing I'd like more, Lord Greco, than to see Lord Paratore hang, to know he is no longer a danger to the good citizens of Siena."

The crowd ate up my words, cheering, shoving.

Lord Rossi said, "You, Lady Gabriella, have a most difficult choice to make. The Nine now grant you the authority to send him to Firenze, on the grounds that we could win the freedom of so many of our own. Or"—he took a few steps to the other side of Paratore and then looked back to us in dramatic fashion—"you may send him to the gallows and watch him hanged this very night."

I heard Mom suck in her breath behind me and remembered that early evening within the walls of Castello Forelli when I tried to save two prisoners. She didn't get it, yet. The violence of this place. The *Us or Them* thing. Just as I hadn't then.

I looked to Lia, then to Marcello. "What is best for Siena?"

"Gabi, you can't mean you would actually send that man—" Mom began.

"Mom, you have to stay out of this," I returned. If the crowd got wind that she was defending Paratore, in any way—

"Look at how he's been beaten. Is that not enough?"

"*Mom*," Lia whispered, eyes wide. "We'll explain later. It's *complicated*."

I glanced down below us. Two of the Nine had clearly heard and frowned in confusion. So had Greco and Paratore. The prisoner was smiling a little, looking at me with a sick, ghoulish expression.

Quickly, I looked to Marcello, taking comfort in his eyes—calm, steady, warm. "I will abide by your decision, m'lady," he said lowly. "It is yours to make. But I personally know of ten men who should be home with their wives and children. One of them, Giannini." He glanced at Paratore. "I would not lose a night's sleep, knowing he was dead. He has killed and tortured many, so many." His brown eyes moved over to Lia, behind me. "But is not the greater good served in trading him out?" He shook his head. "His life will not be easy, in Firenze. He will suffer."

I looked back to Paratore. His smile had faded.

"They are not who they say they are!" he erupted. "They are not Normans, I swear! You give my life over to impostors! Spies!"

I froze.

The knights tackled him, gagged him, and raised him back to his feet, but the damage had already been done. I felt physically sick as I felt the whispers spread through the crowd.

I could almost see the love of the crowd fade at the staining of his words.

In that moment, more than ever, I wanted him dead.

Gone from my life forever, never to hurt any of us again.

I looked to Lia, wondering if she agreed. "There goes our gig as the glory girls," she said so only I could hear. She waited a moment, until I shared her sickly smile. Her own faded, then. We were both up for fighting to the death, but ordering him killed? That was a different deal. "Do the right thing, Gabi."

The right thing. For Siena, not me. *Trade him out.*

I looked to the crowd. They were still whispering, repeating Paratore's words. Would they believe what he said, that we weren't who we said we were, that we were spies?

They'd believe this *slime,* this total jerk who had threatened Lia in the dungeon of Castello Paratore? Hauled her up in chains? Used her to manipulate me?

In several different spots, men were shoving against one another, punching, fighting over the comment. Daring to question. Or leaping to our defense. How soon until it was happening throughout the thousands that were gathered here, in the piazza? The Sienese posse assigned to protect Lord Greco and crew were already rushing them out, aware that the mob was on the verge of eruption.

I had to rob his words of their power. Or we might be driven out, back to our own time. Before I was ready. If I was ever to be ready again.

"Marcello," I said over my shoulder. "Please. Take my mother back into the building." I stepped forward as he ushered her away. I faced Lord Paratore alone, chin raised. I pointed at him. "Lord Paratore has listened to lies and dared to repeat them here. His ears have deceived him, leading him to false proclamations! He shall be released to Firenze and traded for a hundred of our own," I cried, all Princess It-Shall-Be-So in my tone. "But I demand he be sent with a reminder that he should never again listen to lies against *any* daughter of Siena."

Slowly, sensing I'd taken back the crowd with my regal air of authority, I looked to the knights on either side of Paratore, wondering if I had it in me to do what I had to.

"Send him back," were my words, sounding like they belonged to someone else. "But first, cut off his ears."

CHAPTER 8

"Kneel!" the knight shouted.

Yeah, I sounded all high and mighty and bravelike, but I closed my eyes as Paratore bent and received the swift strokes of the knight's sharp blade. Vomit rose in the back of my throat. Had I really just ordered someone's ears cut off?

Lia took my arm and rushed me down the steps and back toward the Palazzo Pubblico, Luca behind us, Giovanni and Pietro on either side of us. "You did what you had to, Gabs," she said lowly. "I wouldn't've had the courage, I think. It was us or him. If you'd killed him, we wouldn't get the prisoners in exchange for him. And if you hadn't shut him up, the whole city might've turned against us."

The whole *Us or Them* thing again. "What's happening to us?" I asked Lia, turning to face her in the dark hallway. Luca waved the men away to take up stations as guards a few paces distant. "When did we become capable of such things? Killing others? Maiming them?"

"When you dragged us back to this place that only understands that sort of justice," she hissed.

I pulled up short in the face of her anger. She was right. We wouldn't be in this mess if I hadn't made her come back. I glanced at Luca, expecting him to be saddened by her harsh words, but he just looked caught between curiosity and protection. "Will they inquire further about Paratore's accusations?" I was having visions of interrogation under a single bulb in a dark room, questions barked from the corners. Hands tied behind me. Waterboarding.

"No, you were wise, Gabriella," Luca said softly. "Had you not acted, they might have. But you made questioning your story akin to an act of treason, one due swift punishment."

Marcello came up then with Mom, and I rushed into his arms, not hers. He kissed my forehead, and I wished I could stay there, in his arms, forever. "Be at ease, Gabriella. You are well?"

"Now. I think."

Mom studied us and Marcello immediately dropped his arms, looking like he'd just been caught with his hand in the cookie jar. In this day and age, kids didn't hang all over each other. In plain sight, anyway. "What happened?" she asked stiffly, bracing herself.

Voices were approaching. "I sent Paratore back to Firenze," I said, turning away, not ready to see her How-Could-You look if I told her all of it. No one could give that look like my mom. The only expression that could kill me more was her I'm-So-Disappointed-in-Your-Decision.

I'd deal with her confusion, her anger, tomorrow. Tonight, I was spent. All I could think of was getting out of the gorgeous gown and climbing between my sheets. I wanted to shut out the day, all of it, even its high points. Even Marcello. I wanted to forget Lord

Paratore's cries and the sickening sound of the blade, his severed flesh falling to the ground.

I wanted my mind to be blank for a few hours, at rest. Not thinking of anything at all.

"Gabriella," Marcello said, putting his index knuckle beneath my chin and making me look at him. He read my look in an instant. "I shall have you to your quarters momentarily. Stay with me."

Stay with me. I wasn't about to faint. Every sense seemed heightened, like I was feeling everything to the tenth power. At that thought, my knees got wobbly, and I started to falter.

"Gabi!" Mom cried, reaching out.

But Marcello already had an arm wrapped around my waist. He glanced back at her, giving her a look of encouragement, then back to me. "Come, beloved," he murmured. "I shall get you to safety. All will be well." He ushered me forward, down some stairs, then through a dark, narrow passageway.

Before us went Luca, lighting torches along the way. It seemed to be a secret passageway of some sort, beneath the piazza. I was embarrassed now. *Look at the She-Wolves of Siena, sneaking about in the night. Hiding away.* The deeper we went, the more we could hear above us. Muffled shouts and singing.

"They're singing," I said to Marcello. I liked that even though we had to walk single file now, he was holding my hand, pulling me forward.

"Singing? Yes. Over our victory."

"A victory over a foe narrowly vanquished." It was out before I had time to really think about it, and Marcello stopped and turned toward me.

"Narrowly?"

"Well, yes," I said, shifting my weight to the other foot. He was frowning, searching my eyes. "Could not it have gone in the enemy's favor if *they* had been the ones to have an army in hiding, waiting for their own signal?" I was hedging. I had no idea about what would happen if I told him something about the future. Like that Siena would face a plague within a few years. And that Florence would eventually rule them. What would happen if I let such things slip? All sorts of time/space continuum stuff might come crashing down. Or maybe it wouldn't.

I should've watched more Star Trek *as a kid.*

I really needed to talk to Mom, really talk. Find out what she thought. She'd have scientific answers, logical answers, direction. I'd been so caught up in Marcello since we returned, and Mom had been so absorbed in taking in all she could of this forgotten world, that we'd barely been together.

But right now, I was weary beyond belief. We reached the end of the tunnel at last, then climbed curving, narrow stairs to the top. There, Marcello knocked three times, and after a short wait we heard a crossbar lift, and the door opened, spilling golden candlelight onto our path.

Marcello pulled me forward, through a narrow guardhouse— manned by a couple of knights—and beyond it, a tiny apartment, with a couple of other knights snoring in their beds. Pretty clever, I thought, hiding it behind a teeny house. No one would ever suspect.

Luca paused, with his ear at the door, and waited for a group to pass by, then opened the door and peeked out. We were along the Via di Banchi, just steps away from the Palazzo Rossi's stables. In moments, we'd entered the palace. Marcello reluctantly kissed my hand and bade me good-night. Then I quickly hugged my mother and sister, and we parted, separating to our private rooms. There were far more rooms and servants in Palazzo Rossi than in Castello Forelli. Here maids waited to help us undress, take down our hair, wash our faces, and help us slip beneath the covers.

It couldn't happen fast enough for me. I barely spoke to the maid and was so glad to feel the rough silk of the sheet beneath my cheek and the feather-filled comforter over me. It felt clean and new. Safe. I closed my eyes and was asleep before my maid left the room.

I awakened, fully aware that I was not alone in the room.

I sat up fast, clutching my blanket to my chest and staring, trying to make out the dim figure barely visible in silhouette against the window. I cast an eye to where I'd left my sword, beside my bed, but now it was fifteen feet away, leaning against the door.

He looked over his shoulder. "You didn't think I would be so foolish as to leave your weapon beside you, did you?"

Lord Rossi. Shorter than I, but powerful in his own way. I took a better grip on my blanket.

He turned toward me but remained at the windowsill. "Who are you, Lady Betarrini? Truly?"

His voice was deadly calm, light even. But I could hear the tone of threat behind it. He hadn't liked that Lord Paratore's accusation had caught him unawares. He was here to see if there was any truth to it.

"It is as I said. We are from Normandy. We came to find our mother and did so at last."

He waited for five, six seconds. "A mother that not one of my men or contacts could find."

"It was God Himself that finally brought us back together," I said, invoking the Almighty in my desperation. "M'lord, your presence here is hardly appropriate—"

He strode over to me, faster than I'd thought possible. "Nay. What is inappropriate is you unseating my daughter as Marcello's betrothed. Such humiliation has never been borne by a daughter of the Nine."

"But Fortino—"

"It is fortunate for you that he regained his health and is the rightful Lord Forelli."

I paused. "I am well aware of that fact. I never meant to come between—"

"But you did. A union that was decades in the making. Only Fortino could save my daughter's reputation."

"As I said…I never intended for it to happen, m'lord."

It was his turn to pause. He raised his chin and strode back to the window. Not playing the tough guy. Giving me some space. I glanced to the door. Could I make it out? And call out to who, exactly? The lord of the place, one of the Nine, was in my room. Anyone that came to my aid would turn and run, pretending they'd seen nothing. Except Marcello. Or Luca.

But that'd just make matters worse.

"You shall tell me who you are," Lord Rossi said, looking out across the vast, empty plaza, the bonfires dead and smoldering by now—I could smell the smoke on the slight breeze. "Out with it. The truth, please."

I remained silent, for a time, considering my response. Wasn't silence the best defense? At least, that was what I always heard in reruns of *Law and Order.*

"Lord Rossi, I am no threat to you," I said, as gently as I could. "I only wish the best for your house, the house of Forelli, and Siena. I beg you to believe that."

He eyed me over his shoulder for a long moment. "You shall not tell me, then? The truth?"

I swallowed. "I have told you all I can."

"You shall tell me all of it, Lady Gabriella. Someday. When you are desperate. I shall refuse you aid until you give me what I wish to know. And if I discover anything"—he turned and shook his splayed hands—"*anything* that makes me believe you are a threat to me or mine, I will not hesitate to order your death." He paused, and his lethal words hung in the air, taking form like subtitles in a foreign flick. "Do we understand each other, Lady Betarrini?"

"We do," I said, hating the slight shake in my voice.

A knock came at the door, quiet but insistent. "Gabriella?"

It was Marcello, checking on me. Had he heard us?

"And you do understand," Lord Rossi said, ignoring Marcello, sliding back to the edge of my bed and leaning over me, "that if you do anything to damage this new union between Fortino and Romana, that I shall also have no choice but to…move against you?"

Marcello was knocking again, becoming more insistent. "*Gabriella.*"

"I do," I said quickly, wanting Rossi out, away. How did I ever see him as some sort of father figure, last time I was here? A guy that I now knew had to have been in on my poisoning? Who was threatening me now, to my face? *Man, Gabi, you really must've been missing Dad.*

He sauntered to the door, unlocked it, then glanced back at me as the candlelight from the hallway spilled inward and Marcello burst through, looking in confusion from me to Lord Rossi. Seeing me in my nightdress, in bed, he looked to the ground, then furiously at Lord Rossi.

"Highly unorthodox, I know, Sir Forelli," Lord Rossi said stiffly. "But then so is this girl who has so captured you," he said, looking over at me. "Tread carefully, sir. I fear this one is most…bewitching."

With that, he left. Marcello rushed to my side and wrapped me in his arms. I clung to him, still trembling at Lord Rossi's threat. I could see Luca's shadow, shifting in the doorway as he stood guard.

"Gabriella, did he hurt you?"

"Hurt me? Lord Rossi? Nay. He merely threatened me," I said with a humorless laugh. I pulled away and wiped my eyes. "I do not know why I am crying."

"You've been through a great deal." He knelt down beside the bed and wiped yet another tear, streaming down my cheek.

"Marcello, you shouldn't be in here. If someone were to see—"

"Shh. Leave the palace gossip to me. I've lived with it all my life, remember?" He took my face with both of his hands and waited for me to look into his eyes. "What did he want, Gabriella?"

"He wanted to know who I was. Really," I whispered. "After Lord Paratore's outburst, he won't be the last who wonders."

Marcello shook his head. "Paratore is an enemy of the republic. And no one but one of the Nine would dare to ask you. Lord Rossi— he has other reasons."

I nodded. Romana. Fortino.

"What did you tell him?"

"Nothing," I said. "I tried to reassure him. But he's concerned I might intervene between Fortino and Romana."

Marcello let out a scoffing laugh. "With but a week before their nuptials? Why would you?"

I remained silent.

"Gabriella."

"I do not trust her, Marcello." I turned to meet his eyes, adding, "Do you?"

"Romana? Yes. *Yes*."

"Even with the Fiorentini? Here? In this very house?"

He set his lips in a grim line. "It is the way of the Nine to seek peace as well as to fight for what is ours. It is what we need in our leadership."

"At what cost?" I muttered. "Your brother's happiness?"

I knew I was out of line to say it. The expression on Marcello's face confirmed it. "It's only that…" I paused, then went on. "After all he's been through, Fortino deserves"—I gestured between Marcello and me—"this. What we have. Love. Not some sort of hand-me-down relationship, forged because it strengthens an alliance."

Marcello leaned back and sighed. "Marriage is a sacrament, a blessed union. And I admit, it has become more a method of securing political gain than ensuring happiness for either bride or groom." He shrugged his shoulders. "But it is what it is. Our parents' marriage was much the same. In time, my mother and father grew fond of each other. Already, Fortino and Romana share such fondness. You've seen it for yourself, no? Might we not hope and pray that love might grow from those tender seeds?"

I gave him a sad, weary smile. "Mayhap. I suppose the perils of my own world," I said lowly, "have made me suspect all. Half of our marriages end in divorce."

"Divorce?" he said, bringing a hand to his chest as if I'd wounded him. "Half? Impossible."

"Half."

He paused, considering. "Your mother? Your father…"

"No, they loved each other. Really loved. More than I'd seen in most other couples. But my father died six months ago in an accident."

"I grieve with you, beloved," he said, drawing near again, touching the side of my head tenderly, then cupping my chin. "Do you think he would have blessed our union?"

"I don't know," I said. Then, "Believe me, m'lord, my mother will be far more difficult."

His eyes narrowed, and he dropped his hand. "Why? Does she find me somehow…wanting?"

I snorted and shook my head. "Nay, m'lord. How could anyone find you wanting?" I sighed, not wanting to get into the whole mess of whether Mom would agree to leave everything behind so I could get hitched to Mr. Medieval. "Might we speak of it later? You really must steal out of here before someone sees you."

He smiled into my eyes. "You are as wise as you are beautiful, Gabriella Betarrini. Come to the door after I am gone," he said, kissing the top of my head. "Lock it behind me. No other visits shall you have before your maid, come morn. I shall stand guard myself."

CHAPTER 9

I didn't know how I was going to get to sleep after all that, but I did, just like someone had given me warm milk and a bedtime story and tucked me in. I awakened to my maid's knocking. She came in chattering on and on about all the invitations we ladies had received. Thankfully, she also reported that Marcello had declared that we would leave the city promptly and return just in time for the wedding. She said he had business to tend to at the castello, while Fortino was "otherwise engaged," but I knew he really wanted me and my sister and mom out from under the squinting eyes of the Nine and back home.

Home. Was I really thinking of it as that?

It was more home than this place, in Siena, especially with Lord Rossi set on watching me more closely than ever. If Marcello was hittin' the road, I was goin' with him. And if my mom and sis were with me, even better.

At least that was what I thought.

But when we exited the gates and set into the pace that would get us to Castello Forelli by nightfall, I realized that Mom was thinking this was the perfect opportunity for a heart-to-heart. We were moving along, two by two, and Marcello had just ridden to the front of the pack when she glanced back at me. "Gabi, can I have a moment?" she asked lowly, glancing at Lia meaningfully.

"Uh oh," Lia whispered. "Day Seven."

Our mom wasn't one of your average, cozy, hovering, wanna-know-it-all kind of moms. She was more of a communicator on an as-needed basis. She had discussions with me and Lia. And sure, we knew she loved us with a crazy kind of passion. But we'd grown up with her mostly distracted, six out of seven days a week. She had an intensity of focus that I hadn't really seen in many others; maybe it was the scholar in her. But once in a while, she'd pop into what we called Day Seven—even if it was literally Day Five or Day Ten—and act like she was trying to make up for lost time.

Lia pulled back and rode beside Luca for a while, while Mom pulled up next to me. She glanced around at the hills, the grass brown and fading but still holding a thick sheen, like a doeskin-colored velvet. "Think we're safe, Gabriella?"

I glanced around and shrugged. "As safe as we can be with a hundred men ready to lay down their lives for us."

"That's pretty cavalier."

I wasn't really sure what *cavalier* meant, but I could guess from her tone. A *Whatever* sort of mode. "Yeah, go through a few battles where you almost lose your life and this seems like a vacation," I said. "Or just like every other time we've been in Toscana. I mean, beyond…well, you know."

Her eyes grew distant, and she bent to pat her horse's neck.

I felt a pang of guilt. She was thinking of Dad. I knew she was. Of him dying. And I'd made her think about it. Nothing this year felt like "any other," even before we were leaping through time. Maybe it was uncool of me, acting like I didn't really care. "I, uh, can't really think about it, much. I mean, I stay ready all the time. But if I obsess about death, then I can't enjoy being here, now." My eyes flicked toward Marcello, and she followed my gaze.

"Is that what this really is, Gabi? The ultimate opportunity to run away?"

"No," I said. "I didn't do this to get away. It just happened. But now that I'm here…now that Marcello is a part of my life…It's hard to describe. But I'd say it's more like running *to* something than running *away*." I glanced at her. "Would I have brought you and Lia along if I wanted to run away?"

"Not that you had much of a choice."

I smiled with her. "That's true. But Mom, even if I didn't need Lia to get here, if I had a choice, I'd never choose to leave you guys behind."

She looked out across the countryside, and we rode in silence for a bit. "Your dad lived in the moment," she said, her tone heavy with an unexpressed sigh. "He'd be proud of you, Gabriella. You know that, right?"

I thought of him and choked up unexpectedly. I blinked fast, not wanting to cry. But it hit me then. I wished he were here. With us. Just as I had wished a thousand times, back in our own age. It was just that…for a while, I'd been able to put him aside. Put the sadness aside. It was all so different…and now, suddenly, it was back, that freakin' heavy blanket of grief.

She reached out and touched my arm, making it worse. It was always worse when I was feeling vulnerable and then someone showed me compassion. I had to look away, focus on the horizon, think of anything but Dad for a minute. Then, when I knew she wasn't letting me off the hook, I managed, "I know, Mom."

She seemed eager to lift my tension. "He'd be especially pleased to see your skill with the sword."

I smirked in response. Never in all my training had Dad considered I might need a sword as an actual weapon of defense—

"Although I'm not certain he'd approve of what you did last night."

So…she'd heard. From Marcello? I let that sit a moment. "And you?"

"I think you did what you had to."

I nodded. "You should know, Mom…that man would not have hesitated to slit my throat or Lia's, if he'd had the chance." I shivered, remembering how he'd leered at Lia when she'd been his prisoner.

"Marcello told me."

I nodded, swallowing hateful, angry words. Just the thought of Lord Paratore made me want to throw up.

"And he won't be a threat to you now that he's free?" she asked.

"Marcello thinks he'll be banished, sent away from Firenze forever. He's as good as dead."

She paused. "I hope so." I could see that she was again looking at Marcello. "Tell me of Marcello, Gabi. What you know of him."

I lifted a brow and then smiled, feeling suddenly shy. "He's pretty amazing, Mom."

"I can see that. From what I've gathered in a week, anyway. But tell me, Gabi. Why do you think you might be in love?"

I blinked a few times, a little taken back by her direct question. She didn't say it in the dismissive way Lia said it. She was taking it seriously. I knew she was thinking, *She's too young...How can she know?* But day by day, it became clearer and clearer to me. I loved Marcello.

"Because he's...*Marcello Forelli,*" I said lamely, as if that explained everything.

A small smile turned my pretty mother's lips upward. "And who is Marcello Forelli? Tell me. Pretend I've never met him."

I looked at him again and sighed. "He's...so much, Mom. Brave. Strong. Dedicated. Smart. Tender, sometimes, in a way that always surprises me. Loving. And this is the wild thing..." I waited until she met my eyes again. "He's totally into me."

Her smile grew wider, and she nodded. "It was only a matter of time. Before a guy finally worthy of my girl came her way."

My heart lurched. "So you're okay with it?"

She paused, and her smile faded a little. "I'm okay with it, Gabi. But in this place, they take romance very seriously." She looked into my eyes. "Marcello has intimated...clearly, he assumes this romance is leading toward something very serious. Very permanent."

Marriage, she meant. "Yeah," I said. "I know." *He kinda risked political suicide, opting for me over Romana.*

"Marriage," she said with a sigh. "That, I'm not ready for." She looked my way again. "You're seventeen, Gabi—"

"Almost eighteen," I said. "In a few months."

"Even at eighteen," she said, shaking her head. "Far too young to make a forever kind of promise."

My mouth got all dry. Half of me hoped she would block Marcello's we-gotta-get-married pursuit. Or at least slow him down.

The other half of me shook at the thought. Nothing, nothing could stand between me and Marcello! Not here. Not now. I couldn't tolerate the thought of not being with him, every day, for as long as I could.

"Just, please. Think about it," Mom said. "We can't stay here forever."

I remained silent. I was not so convinced. In fact, with every morning I awakened here, now, I wanted to stay more. But making my mom and Lia stay too? That wasn't very fair.

She studied me. "He means that much to you?"

"Yeah. Pretty much," I said miserably, feeling totally caught.

"Then…at least take it slow, kiddo, okay?"

"I'll do my best," I said, eyebrows raised. "People around here seem to be all-in when it comes to settling down young." It didn't take an anthropologist to figure out that a lotta girls my age already had a kid or two at their hips. The castle and countryside were riddled with them. Giacinta, my redheaded maid, was already a young mother herself.

"Well, with an average life span of forty years," she mused, to herself mostly, slipping back into scientist mode, "they have to."

Forty years. That meant that Marcello's life might almost be half over. He might only have twenty years left, if that. It made my heart pound a little. Twenty years used to seem like forever to me. This time-travel business was messing with my head.

But one thing was clear to me: Any day I had with Marcello was something I was willing to fight for.

The scouts told Marcello that there were no enemy troops about, and with a temporary peace treaty in place and a contingent of the Sienese between us and Florence, we again set out to check on Signora Giannini. Luca and Lia traveled with us, but Mom elected to ensconce herself in Fortino's library, reading the texts in Latin as if she was committing each one to memory. It kind of irritated me, that she'd choose the books over us. But I was thankful for the reprieve, too. Already, my mom and I had spent more concentrated time together here in the last week than we had in the last three months at home. A little space felt good.

Not that we had a lot of privacy. Even with the temporary peace agreement negotiated by Lord Greco and the men of Firenze who had been with Lord Rossi, twenty soldiers still rode beside us. My man was careful, vigilant, if a little over the top on that front. I took off on my mare, teasing him with a smile as I passed by. He urged his gelding into motion and soon was beside me, head down, pounding down the lane, keeping time with me. I looked over my shoulder; ten men were right behind us, the rest with Lia and Luca, who seemed intent on keeping their leisurely pace.

Marcello's grin made me smile too. In minutes, we reached the hilly farm and pulled up, panting, in a cloud of dust. I saw Signora Giannini outside her cottage, the children playing at her feet, and raised my arm in greeting. But she did not look our way. She was staring intently to the north.

I followed the direction of her gaze down the hill. A man was dismounting, hobbling toward the cottage.

Signora Giannini cried out. I frowned and gripped Marcello's arm. "Marcello—"

"No," he said, his voice alight. "It's all right. It's Signore Giannini, her husband."

The woman cried out again and then broke free of the children and ran down the hill, skirts flying. Her husband made his way toward her, grappling with a crutch but hurrying as best he could. They met midway, and he reached out his arms as she slammed against him. They turned and turned, kissing, embracing, crying.

The men around us cheered and called out bawdy things I thought only pirates in movies said. But they meant well.

"You did that," Marcello said.

"What?"

"That," he said, slipping an arm around my waist, nodding toward the Gianninis. "You reunited them."

I remembered then. Figured out what he was saying. This man was one of the hundred that had been traded for Paratore. I grinned, thinking of this scene being replayed in ninety-nine other villages. How had I considered anything *but* this option?

The children ran up to him, and he embraced them, lifting the smallest above his head, laughing. After a few moments, they looked our way, waving us forward as Lia and Luca and the other ten soldiers arrived. We went, eager to hear his story.

But as soon as we drew near, I knew something was dreadfully wrong. The man's eyes were ringed with purple and his leg was clearly injured. He was so bruised and swollen under his jaw, it looked like someone had tried to choke him. What suffering had the men endured in Firenze's prisons?

"M'lady, I owe you my life," he said, bending to kiss my hand.

I tried to be polite, smile and look into his eyes, but I had to fight the urge to pull my hand from his. His fingers looked liked they'd been dipped in oil, black from the last joint down. Stained, almost. As he moved away, I studied his neck. He hadn't been choked—he had massive, discolored, swollen glands, one of which looked like it had burst. Marcello was shaking his hand, introducing him to Lia and Luca, when I finally figured it out.

"Nay! Stop! Hasten away from him!" I cried. I bodily pulled Marcello several steps backward.

The Gianninis stared at me, confused.

"He's ill! You're ill, aren't you?" I asked, forcing the edge of totally-freaking-out-ness from my voice. *Calm down, Gabi. Calm down. Maybe it's not what you think.*

"I have been through a great deal, m'lady. Certainly, I am not at my best—"

I glanced at Lia and saw that she was worried too. "Mr. Giannini, what ails you?" she asked gently.

"A fever," he said reluctantly, reaching up to wipe his forehead with a filthy handkerchief. "But it comes and goes. Only the night sweats can be counted upon daily." He forced a smile. "I simply need to be home, eating my wife's good soup, cuddling with the children. I'll be well and among the vines in a few days' time, you'll see."

But he was wrong, seriously wrong. Frowning, I looked to Marcello.

"What is it, Gabriella?" he asked, his brown eyes hooded by his worried brow.

"Plague," I said.

CHAPTER 10

A knight near me overheard. "He has the plague?"

"Plague?" cried another.

The first knight backed up, and others moved back with him. There were certainly no more deadly words than those in this day and age.

It was far worse than war.

I looked to Lia and whispered, "I thought we had some years, yet."

"It probably didn't all happen at once," she whispered back. "Maybe an early strain that died out?"

Waves of it. *Right.* Like colds and flu at school—you just got over one bug, and another came around.

"Nay, nay," said Signora Giannini, bringing a fist to her mouth and taking her husband's arm. "He has no such thing. No such thing," she repeated angrily, as if it would make it true. Like *No. Such. Thing.*

The children sensed the mood shift, and one begged to be taken up into his father's arms. Automatically, the man bent and lifted her.

"You must not touch them!" I shouted, figuring out I had to see this through, as much as I hated to. How much had we all been exposed, already? I shoved away the memory of him kissing my hand. "Forgive me," I said sorrowfully, trying to quit shouting and adding to the chaos. "I loathe this more than you can imagine. I know how you've longed to be reunited, but Signore Giannini," I said appealing to him, "your illness, if it is not plague, will still need to be treated as such. Consider your family. You do not want to endanger them, do you?"

He paused and then shook his head as if it pained him.

"Nay!" his wife cried, looking like she wanted to claw my eyes out for suggesting it. "I shall not leave him!"

I wished I knew more about the plague…was there any sort of treatment other than treating the symptoms? Anything in our medical kit that might help? Were we all exposed already? Or only those of us who'd neared the man? If only Mom had come along…But then she'd have been exposed too. *Thank You, God,* I said to Him, in my head. *Keep her safe. Please, please keep her safe.*

I looked to Lia, and she understood my unspoken question. "I read once," she said, "that it is best to quarantine. And burn all the clothes. It takes seven to ten days to find out if those exposed will… exhibit the symptoms."

I glanced at Marcello.

We were in a world of hurt.

Trapped outside the castello.

Needing to be quarantined ourselves.

A target for enemies.

And unable to attend the wedding festivities of Fortino and Romana.

Lots and lots of people were going to be seriously cranky.

Three knights had mounted up. "M'lord, we must retreat, back to the castello," said one.

"Marcello," I hissed, "they must remain."

He turned to them and barked, "Dismount! At once!"

Reluctantly, they returned to the ground, holding their reins in their hands.

Marcello turned to face me and Lia and Luca. "What is our best course?"

All three of them looked at me. "I know only a little. Lia's the one that's read something on this—"

"A novel, Gabi. Fiction. I know not how to treat the plague."

"If it is plague. We're guessing." I looked at Marcello. "Have you heard reports of it, out of Firenze?"

He shook his head. "But few cities would be apt to herald such news. All commerce stops for a city battling such illness."

"So instead they simply export the pestilence," I said bitterly. "The men of Firenze must have laughed under their breath when they sent sick Sienese soldiers home."

"Might not the knights that arrived with me and Lia return to the castello?" Luca asked, glancing back. "They were a good distance apart from us."

I shook my head. "Others have mingled with them." I splayed out my hands, then checked out a fleck of black on my pinkie. Only dirt. "*We've* intermingled. That is the difficulty of this disease. It's so rapidly passed along…we have to be certain."

"But if they remain with us, they risk exposure again," Marcello said.

"We can try—keep them separated. Tell them, quickly."

Luca turned and shouted to the men, "Those who arrived with me, separate yourselves. Go down to that oak at the bottom of the field until we give you further direction." He lifted a warning finger. "No one, *no one* is to depart without my leave."

He looked fierce, like he'd hunt down and kill anyone who tried to escape. There was none of the customary happy glimmer in his eye.

"We need seven days, mayhap more," I said to Marcello. "There are twenty-eight of us. Where can we go? Someplace where few others travel. We'll need shelter, food, access to some supplies."

Luca eyed Marcello. "We could go to the old Orci villa."

Marcello shook his head. "We cannot defend her."

Luca cocked a brow. "It's as defensible as we'll find. Off the main roads. And only ten or so servants to displace."

Marcello studied him a moment and then looked to me. "He may be right. It's an old walled villa on a hill. It once belonged to my mother's parents and has been somewhat maintained by my father. But it takes us closer to the border. And it's hardly the castello. We would not be able to repel an outright attack."

"If we all become ill, it will hardly matter," Luca said.

"Might we wait until dusk and make our way under cover of darkness?" I said, shoving down the thought of us all stricken with plague, with no one to care for us. It was enough to send the hypochondriac in me into full-on panic. I was already fighting the urge to go running to the tiny Giannini cottage and dip my hands into a cauldron of scalding water. "If we reach the Orci villa with no one seeing us, we can swear the ten servants we displace to silence."

"Or we may have to insist they remain," Marcello said grimly.

I frowned. If we were to become ill, we would be condemning ten more to a similar fate. "Our secret will not remain one for long. We cannot miss the nuptials in Siena without everyone in Toscana asking where we are. It will have to be known that we were exposed and have separated ourselves to keep the disease from spreading."

"And anyone with any knowledge of your family will soon figure out where we've gone," Luca said.

Marcello heaved a sigh and paced back and forth a moment, thinking. "It will take them a few days. We will ask Lord Rossi to not make it public until the day of the festivities. That's yet five days away. Then we only have five more days to wait it out, see if any of us becomes ill, right?"

I stared back at him. "It's worse than that. If any of us becomes ill, then we all must be considered exposed again. We essentially have to remain apart until all illness has been stamped out for ten days."

"Or we're all dead," he said, voice low.

I nodded, grimly. "Or we're all dead," I repeated. I couldn't believe such words were coming out of my mouth like it was no big deal. It seemed impossible.

"Gabriella. You, Evangelia could...*return*," Marcello said carefully, staring into my eyes. "In *Normandy*, they have a cure for this illness?"

A cure for the bubonic plague? I didn't really remember, though I had done a school report on ground squirrels and skunks that occasionally showed up with it. But few humans seemed to get it in the Western hemisphere. Was it like HIV, passed by blood?

"Do you remember, Lia? Is it passed by blood? Saliva? Touch?"

She looked up to the sky, trying to remember, and my heart skipped a beat. Her blue eyes matched the skies. What if those eyes became still, in death? I could not tolerate losing her. After a moment, she shook her head. "I cannot remember. Was it not fleas or ticks or the like?"

That jarred a memory, and I nodded. "Mayhap. We need Signore Giannini and everyone he's touched to be bathed in hot water, their clothing burned." I looked to Marcello. "Send Pietro to the castello to fetch us all several changes of clothes—clothes we won't mind seeing burned. And he must remain a hundred paces from the castello."

"He can tell them what has transpired," Marcello returned. "But Gabriella, you did not respond. You and Evangelia—"

"We shall remain," Lia said, surprising all three of us. She glanced at Luca, blushed, and then hurriedly to me. "Gabi will be impossible at home. She'll only fret on and on about your health," she said, nodding in Marcello's direction.

But was she covering? Using me as an excuse when perhaps she'd be worrying over Luca? I thought so. By the tiny grin on Luca's lips, I believed he did too.

The messenger—and two others to help him transport the clothing—departed, and we all moved up the hill to the Gianninis' tiny house. Signore Giannini was settled onto a mat and given a blanket under the trees, a hundred paces away, to keep us all from further exposure. In the house, we placed several pots of water over the crackling fire, and began the process of bathing ourselves and burning our clothes. Too tall and broad-shouldered to fit in one of Mrs. Giannini's dresses, I was one of the last to bathe behind the screen, after the messenger had returned.

I put on a simple day dress, feeling a pang at the loss of the lovely green gown that was about to go up in flames, and Lia helped comb out my hair. Neither of us were much good with the pins, so after a few tries, we bailed and just left it down. When we came outside, Luca rose, mouth half open, eyes solely on Lia, then rapidly knelt at her feet and took her hand. "M'lady, you look like a bride on her wedding day. Since we might not live through a fortnight, shall we marry this very eve?"

She laughed at him and tried to pull her hand from his, shaking her head. She was blushing though, not angry. "Luca. Must you always be the court jester?"

He cocked one brow and rose. "Ahh, but I do not jest." He still held on to her hand and stared down at her, as if they were the only two in the clearing. Some of the knights caught sight and laughed, welcoming the break from the gloom and doom that had settled over us.

Eyes bright, she pulled away and looked to me, the pretty tinge of pink still at her cheeks. "Get me outta here."

"You've got it," I said, and walked toward Marcello. For a few minutes, I was able to forget that we were on the brink of death, and it felt good. But the look on his face brought it all back. He strode over to me.

"Gabriella," he said, leading me a few steps away. "I will say it again. I wish to send you and your sister home, away from harm."

I reached up and touched his face, feeling the appealingly masculine stubble there. "Marcello, I am not going anywhere without you. We will face this together."

His lips clamped shut as if he was upset, but he held my hand as he turned to address the two groups, each a hundred feet from the other. "Come dusk, we shall ride to Villa Orci, leaving the road just past Castello Pisi and moving through the trees. With the Ladies Betarrini in our company, our goal is to remain unseen. To be less obvious, we will travel in groups of fourteen. As I'm certain you all know, outside the protection of the castello, we will become a prime target for every one of Firenze's sons."

"What of the peace treaty?" Luca asked.

"It is due to run out the day after my brother's nuptials; it is a nod to Lord Rossi, nothing more. And no loyal Fiorentini would skip such an opportunity as this," he said, eyeing me and my sister. I shivered.

"By morning, Sienese forces shall assuredly move to our side to help protect our flanks."

Right then, morning seemed a long, long time away.

"Our intention is to remain ten days," he continued. "By God's grace, no one else will take ill in those days and we'll be free to return home." His eyes slid to Signore Giannini, standing on his own, up the hill. "Signora Giannini refuses to come with us, not without Signore Giannini along."

"But—" I began.

He raised up a hand to shush me. "There is no dissuading her, Gabriella," he said softly. "She feels God has answered her prayers, that he is here at all…She feels it is her place to remain with him, either to a place of health or death."

I shook my head. "She's condemning herself," I sputtered, "her children."

"Speak not of what you do not know for certain. We shall pray that God will have mercy on all of them." He turned back to the others. "Luca's knights will take the lead. Once at the villa, you shall evacuate those inside and send them to Castello Forelli, under strict orders to tell no one where we have gone. Word must not get out. The Gianninis have been sworn to silence. But it's all a game, really. A slim chance that we can keep this secret for long. And once it's out…battle is bound to be upon us, peace treaty or not."

We moved between the trees, a hundred yards from the main road, but it was pretty hard to hide twenty-eight people on horseback, even if we were in two groups. The deep shadows of dusk were creepy, making me jump every time I heard a woodpecker at a tree or the wind washing through the leaves. Marcello was on guard too, his big brown eyes wide and sober as his gaze swept from one side of us to the other.

He heard it before any of us did. "Riders coming, hard," he growled over his shoulder. The word was passed along, and we all pulled our horses to a stop.

It was another couple of seconds before I heard the hoofbeats. It sounded like twenty horses. Along the road. Would they simply pass by? Were we deep enough in the woods that we wouldn't be seen?

I held my breath and tried to listen over my heartbeat thundering in my ears. We couldn't see them. We could only hear them.

And then the sound divided, clearly coming from two directions, swooping in at our front and back. Marcello's scout arrived then, hunched over in his saddle, an arrow through his shoulder.

"Move into formation!" Marcello cried out to Luca. "Get the women to our center! Weapons at the ready!"

We had seconds at most. There was no time to flee. Besides, where were we to go where we wouldn't be exposed? I just knew one thing: There was no way I was going to hang out behind the guys. If someone was taking us on, I was all in.

"Quickly, Lia, up into the trees with you," I said, pulling at her elbow. From up above, her arrows would be most helpful against our attackers. And the tree limbs would give her a bit of protection....

I leaned down, my fingers laced together in a makeshift stirrup. She put one slippered foot into my hands and braced against my shoulders. I lifted her up until she could reach the first branch, then she scurried upward, shifting her bow and arrows so they'd be out of her way.

"Gabriella!" Marcello barked. "Return at once to my side!"

I would've given him some sort of smart-aleck response, but the horses sounded like they were directly behind me as I ran to the circle of knights. A shiver ran down my back.

"They'll know who we are as soon as they see the Forelli gold on our horses," I said to him, as his eyes shifted to the expanse of wood before us and back to me.

"They know who we are already," he said grimly, nodding to the fallen scout in his golden tunic. "You must not be captured. Do you understand me? Fight. To the death if you must."

I tried to swallow, but my mouth was dry. This was not the kind of thing Marcello usually said to me. I knew he'd be beside me every moment. But it was what he *wasn't* saying that bothered me most—that if it was Firenze coming our way and they captured me and Lia, we'd *wish* we were dead.

"You help take down one castle," I muttered to myself, "and suddenly you're on a hit list. Can't these dudes just move on with their lives?"

"Gabriella," Luca called to me, frowning at me over his shoulder. "Where is your sister?"

I pointed with my chin, up into the trees, and the worry on his face gave way to glee. "Well, if that is not the most beautiful squirrel in the wood, I know not—"

His words died as our enemies arrived. I lifted my sword higher, at the ready.

"Gabriella, get back," Marcello said.

"Nay, you have need of every sword—"

They pounded out of the woods then, streaming toward us from three different directions. By the sound of it, I was sure they did the same on the other side. The first of them swept by us, striking at the six knights in front. Four knights moved forward to protect their fallen brothers as the next wave came by. I glanced up and swallowed hard. Still, they were arriving. How many? Thirty? Fifty?

They clearly knew who we were. Had they been hunting for just this opportunity to pounce on us? How far away were the Sienese? A tall, broad-shouldered knight with black hair pulled up on his reins, and his agitated horse circled. He stared hard at Marcello before digging his heels into the flanks of his horse and charging toward me.

Lord Greco. *What?* I thought angrily. *You trying to make a name for yourself, Big Boy? Attacking a group in search of refuge? Think that makes you a man? So much for your peace-seeking gig, huh?*

But then I had another guy to contend with, coming at me from the left. He swung one of those horrific spiked metal balls above his head and grinned at me as he moved closer.

The ball made a *whoop-whoop* sound as it passed by once, twice, missing me by inches. Marcello raised his sword in the air at just the right moment and the chain caught, wrapped, curled around it, and then Marcello yanked the handle from the man's hand. With a roar, the man rammed into him. One of Lia's arrows sank into his back, but he kept moving forward as if he didn't feel it. He only wanted Marcello.

I returned my attention to Greco. He was similar in stature to Lord Paratore. But he had the face of a politician, not a soldier. He would've found easy work in Hollywood in seven hundred years, but right now, he seemed entirely focused on me. Like he couldn't see any of the twenty-some skirmishes around us.

I took a few steps back and looked to my right, where Marcello was rolling atop his adversary, punching him, and to my left, where Giovanni's foe fell forward, two arrows in his back.

Lord Greco followed my gaze and then looked to the trees and spotted Lia, who was aiming her arrow at a man on horseback who was attempting to pick her off with the same weapon.

He smiled over his shoulder and then at me. "The She-Wolves of Siena. At last I get to see if the stories are truth or fable."

He bowed as if we were back in the Rossis' palazzo, and I took the opportunity to swing my sword around, not in any mood to observe polite niceties.

But he saw my movement and bent backward at the last moment, surprisingly agile for his tall stature. The sword whipped by an inch from his chest.

I grunted and turned, using the momentum of the sword rather than expending energy to stop it. When I brought it down and around, he stopped it with his own. His face was a foot from mine. "Come now. Might we not go about this conversation in a more civilized fashion?" He raised one dark eyebrow and gave me a crooked, flirty smile.

I didn't bother to answer. I lifted my sword and struck again, but he easily parried every stroke. Still, I drove forward, again and again.

He caught my sixth strike above his head, his own sword crossing mine like a barrier again. "Cease this at once. Surrender, and I swear I will inflict no further harm upon you. Moreover, the peace treaty shall be preserved."

I laughed under my breath, Marcello's demand that I fight to the death ringing through my head. *Nah. You won't hurt me. But your people will.*

"You broke the treaty when you attacked us, Lord Greco," I said, panting, turning, and lunging again. "You intend to take me back to your city? For what purpose?"

He blocked my next strike, frustratingly good at anticipating the angle of my blows. "You might find that Firenze is to your liking."

"Until your people draw and quarter me."

"Nay. My people are not animals." A small smile edged up to the corners of his lips. "Swear your allegiance to Firenze and turn your back on these Sienese, and you shall be treated like royalty. They are as new to you as we are, right? Three women from Normandy?" He looked beyond me, over the others. "Your mother is not with you?"

I ignored his question and pushed forward again, but he batted away my next two strikes as if he were shooing away a fly.

I was getting tired. And he sensed it. He immediately pressed his attack, driving me backward. An arrow came whizzing by his head and rammed into the ground, then another. But he was no fool. He moved to the left, and then right, herding me while avoiding Lia's strikes. Using me as his shield.

Desperate, I jabbed my sword at him. He dodged it, then grabbed hold of it, wrenching it from my hands, ignoring the blood on his own. He tossed it aside, pulled out a handkerchief—tucked inside his breastplate—and calmly wrapped his bloody palm as he moved toward me. I glanced toward Marcello, but he was fighting two others. His eyes paused on Lord Greco and then flitted over to me under a concerned brow.

Lord Greco looked from me to Marcello. "'Tis a pity that it had to be you who captured Sir Marcello's heart. I wish him no harm. But alas, a duty is a duty."

I pulled my eight-inch dagger from my belt and held it in front of me.

"Come now, She-Wolf," he said, like I was a silly five-year-old. "Do you wish me to take off your entire arm with my sword? Put that down."

The blade felt light and nimble in my hands. But he was right; it was no match for his powerful sword.

He lunged forward, surprisingly fast, grabbed hold of my forearm and turned, sending me flying over his back and onto my own, in the dirt, disarmed. He immediately was on me, pinning my arms to the ground, barely allowing me to breathe with his weight on my belly. He grinned exultantly at me, then over at Marcello.

"Gabriella!" Marcello screamed. But he could not get past the two knights that held him at bay.

From what I could see, five Forelli knights lay dead on the ground. Only three of this man's mercenaries were beside them. And I knew they came with far greater numbers.

Lord Greco lifted a fallen soldier's shield and casually set it behind him to protect his head and upper torso from Lia's arrows. "So…Lady Gabriella, I say it once again. Come with me, as my willing hostage. Mayhap, in time, we can work out an exchange with Sir Forelli."

"Never," I said, wanting to spit in his face, but judging from how things were going, I was fairly certain it would just lob up and fall back on me. I cast around for any reason to get us out of this predicament.

Plague.

I tried to laugh but found it hard with him sitting on my diaphragm.

"What amuses you?" he asked, his handsome eyes squinting.

"You are already dead."

He raised a brow and glanced around. "On the contrary, it is Sir Forelli's men who seem to be anxious to meet their Maker."

"You will too, soon enough."

He shook his head a little, as if I was merely wasting time. My fingers were going numb, the circulation cut off beneath his knees.

"Do you not wonder why we were out here? So close to Firenze's border, with so few?" I asked, a note of triumph in my voice. "Did you not wonder why you suddenly had a chance to attack?"

He paused, waiting for it.

"Because we have plague among us, you fool. *Plague.*" P-L-A-G-U-E. My grin widened.

It took me a moment to understand that he was off of me. I could breathe again. I coughed and rolled to my side, then hurried to my feet, crouched, ready for another attack. But Lord Greco's eyes were scanning our group.

"You dogs sent home a prisoner—in exchange for Lord Paratore—infected with plague. We went to assist his wife this day, in her vineyard, when he returned. Was he the only one?" I advanced upon him, shaking with fury, sensing my advantage, his fear. "Or did you send every ill man you could find home to our people? Is there no sense of decency about you? No shred of morality?"

He stared back at me, hard. And then I knew. They *had* sent back prisoners who were suffering from illness, of one sort or another. Of all the underhanded, horrible war tactics…

"Signore Giannini kissed my hand, embraced our men in greeting," I spit out. "There is plague among us, and now, mayhap, among you, too."

Finally he read my righteous anger as truth. "Cease your attack!" he cried, backing up. "Retreat! There is plague among them!"

I didn't bother to tell him that it was too late, that they were probably already exposed. *Run home and infect all your people. Go!* I felt mean for a sec, but I was definitely in that eye-for-an-eye mode.

Marcello arrived beside me, panting, bleeding at his brow. But he seemed okay. He edged in front of me as Lord Greco mounted his horse and looked over to us. He wiped his upper lip of sweat, crossed himself as if to ward off evil spirits, gave Marcello a long look, and without another word, galloped away, his troops behind him.

"He seemed…reluctant to fight you and your men," I said to Marcello. "Though it didn't keep him from coming after *me*."

"At one time, during more peaceful times, our fathers traded. They were with us every year."

"So he knows your land well."

Marcello nodded grimly. "I doubt they ever returned to Firenze, since their time in Siena. They simply were lying in wait for us, for the opportunity to try and kidnap you."

"Will he know where we're heading?"

"It will not be difficult to guess," he said. "But we have little choice." His eyes moved to the men, gathering together around the bodies of their fallen comrades. We'd managed to take down five of Greco's men. But they'd left us with eleven dead. Only thirteen knights left. My heart pounded.

"Bury them," Marcello said to the men. "We cannot take their bodies back to Castello Forelli anyway." There was a note of defeat in his voice, the first I'd ever heard there. I knew he considered all of the men friends, brothers. I could only find some gladness in the fact that Luca, Pietro, and Giovanni, his closest friends, were not among the dead. But I, too, knew all of the dead by name.

I placed a hand on his arm, waited for his sad eyes to meet mine for a moment, and said, "I am sorry for your pain."

"Far greater would my pain be had they captured you," he said, touching my chin.

I returned his sad, somber smile and looked to Luca, who was helping Lia from the tree. I hurried over to her, and we embraced, with Luca awkwardly standing to the side, as if he wished he were in on our hug-fest.

"Your arrows flew straight and true," he said, smiling down at her.

"If only my aim had been as straight and true," she returned ruefully. "It was most difficult, with the branches."

"And yet those branches kept you safe from our enemy's strikes," he said.

All three of us looked up. I swallowed hard when I saw the fifty or more arrows lodged in the trunk and branches all around Lia's position. I hugged her again. "Oh, Lia."

"I'll be fine," she said, through teeth chattering from nerves. Her blue eyes met mine. "We should go, Gabi. Grab Mom and get out of here."

She spoke in English, but Luca obviously understood. His face fell from concern to hurt. He turned and edged away. Lia glanced his way, and a tinge of sorrow crossed her face, but then she looked back to me. "We should go," she repeated, pulling me a few paces away, where we could speak in privacy. "Before we're all dead."

"But you were the one who said we should stay," I returned fiercely.

"Yeah, well, *that* was a serious dose of reality," she said, gesturing toward the men, hauling the dead bodies away.

"We're miles from the tombs and the castello now," I said, piecing together my argument as I went. "We need to get to safety, see to the sick, before we think of home again."

She shook her head. "If we get the plague, we'll never make it to the tombs. In the dark, we could make our way—"

"Did you hear what Marcello said to me? As the men attacked? *Fight to the death.* Clearly, if we're caught and hauled off to Firenze, it won't be pretty. Our only chance is to stay with the men."

She shrugged. "We won't get caught."

"You think."

"I think."

Marcello neared, obviously wondering what was up. But Lia and I were only looking at each other.

"Even if we were able to get back there," I said, "grab Mom, and make it to the tombs. Then what? We arrive back in our time to what? To spread the next round of the bubonic plague in the twenty-first century?"

"No," she said. "The tunnel would heal us, just as it healed you of the poison and your wound."

She was right, of course. But I couldn't let on that I agreed with her. I couldn't leave. Not now. I would always wonder if Marcello had died of the plague, whispering my name, wishing I were there. I didn't know if I could live with that on my conscience—that I'd taken care of myself and left him to face it alone.

I glanced at him, standing there, watching us argue in English, arms folded, then looked back to my sister. "What if the tomb doorway doesn't heal us this time, Lia? What if that was just a one-time deal?"

"They have medicine for the plague, in our time," she said, delicate brows lowering over her eyes.

"Medicine for the twenty-first century version of the plague. What if it's evolved? Different? You know, like H1N1? Or the flu? How it's always different, every year? What if they can't stop it? What if we're responsible for bringing back the greatest horror the world's seen in some time?"

Her pretty lips clamped shut.

"You know how many people died in the Spanish flu epidemic of 1918?" I asked, pressing her now, knowing I was gaining some ground.

She rolled her eyes. She always loved it when I pulled out health stats.

"Fifty million. A third of the world's population got it." I shook my head. "No, we fight this bug *here*. We're not taking it home."

"Whatever, Gabi," she said, edging past me. "You're making an excuse. You know it as well as I." She walked toward her horse. Luca silently helped her mount and then turned to his own.

I sighed and followed, Marcello right behind me.

It was almost completely dark now.

I hoped no other loyal Fiorentini or mercenaries lurked, willing to risk illness in order to capture the handsome price on our heads.

Because right then, I was running low on the will to fight.

CHAPTER 11

When we arrived, the people from the large manor had scurried out as if warring tribes would soon be upon them, rather than their own protector, Sir Forelli. They looked frightened and stayed well clear of us as they left on wagon and horse for the safety of the castello. We huddled together in the main room of the house, weapons at the ready, guards at the perilously short walls, all night. And we'd given up on keeping the "most exposed" away from the rest, since in the battle, we'd all intermingled in order to survive.

I was just dozing off at sunrise, my head dropping to Marcello's shoulder like a thousand-pound weight, when a guard banged open the door. Marcello and Luca and a couple of others were immediately on their feet but eased when they saw Pietro's face. "M'lord, a thousand pardons," he said, "but the Sienese contingent has arrived. They ask to speak to you."

"Good," Marcello grunted, following him out. I could hear the relief in his voice. He motioned to me and took my hand, but we left Lia where she was, sleeping in the corner.

We climbed narrow steps—short half timbers stuck in the mud of the wall—to the top and looked out upon a brilliant Tuscan morning. Warm light glowed across the thick forest and grasses of the hill before us. The Sienese knights were a hundred feet away, keeping their distance.

"M'lord," one called, lifting a hand toward Marcello. "I am Captain Alberto Bicchieri. The Nine have sent us here to provide protection as you and your company regain your health."

"Thank you, Captain," Marcello called back. "We are greatly relieved you are here. We suffered an attack by Lord Greco of Firenze en route here. He may linger yet."

"We shall make certain he returns to his side of the border," the captain pledged with a cocky grin as his horse danced beneath him. "You are in good health, m'lord?"

"Indeed," Marcello returned. "As of yet, none of us show any symptoms. We were forced to leave Signore Giannini, from the vineyard south of the castello."

"May God protect you all. We shall set our ranks in groups of thirty men, on all four sides of the manor, sir, with scouts on all sides as well. If anyone is coming our way, we'll know of it."

"Thank you, Captain," Marcello called. "There are more reinforcements on their way?"

"Fret not, m'lord," the captain returned. "We are well aware of your…vulnerabilities." He gazed at me for a second. "Reinforcements have been sent for and should arrive by sundown."

"Very well," Marcello said. "Thank you, Captain."

We left after the captain pledged to get us any supplies we found lacking, and returned to the main hall of the manor. Now that our meager walls were guarded, we felt safe enough to retire to separate quarters instead of huddling together like a bunch of refugees. I was just thinking longingly of settling atop a straw tick—I was so tired that I thought I might be able to catch a few z's, even on a bed of nails—when Lia appeared at my door. "Gabi! *Come.*"

I followed her to a room on the first floor. She was going too fast for conversation. When we reached the doorway, she glanced back at me, and the terror in her eyes filled me with a deep dread.

Oh no. No, no. NO.

Luca was by the fire, shivering, sweating profusely, Marcello by his side.

Lia shook her head worriedly in my direction, daring to hold his hand in hers after feeling his pulse. "It's fast," she said. "So fast, Gabi." She looked like she was about to faint herself.

"You really shouldn't be in here, Lia."

"None of us should," she muttered, looking at Luca. "What's the point?" she said. "We've clearly all been exposed." One maid had refused to leave with the others, claiming she was too old to die anyplace but Villa Orci. She arrived with a bowl of water and rags but then stepped back.

I knelt beside Luca and wondered what I could do. I didn't really know about treatments for bubonic plague, though I'd stumbled upon information about it once when my lymph nodes had been swollen. The size of his nodes had tripled in hours, making his neck look gross, bulbous. I reached for his hand; at least there was no sign of the gangrene that Signore Giovanni had suffered. Yet.

He was panting, his eyes unfocused. Delirious. There was no trace of the Luca I knew.

"Marcello, can you remove his shirt?" I asked. But as soon as we saw his bare chest, I wished I hadn't.

Lia gasped. All around his armpits were spiderwebs of broken blood vessels.

"Water," I muttered to a knight behind me, who was hovering in the doorway, though I asked more to appease my dry throat than to force any down Luca's. I knew why I was freaking. This plague was as horrible as the stories said, taking down one after another. *Luca. Not Luca, Lord. Please…*

He was beautiful. His chest was well muscled, perfectly formed. But I could not keep my eyes from the purple webs. "Please, Marcello, raise his arms," I said.

"Are you certain?"

I nodded, and he moved to reluctantly do as I bade.

Lia and I leaned back when we saw it. Lymph nodes, the size of grapes when they were normal, were now as big as eggs, one beside the other. And the *smell*—one of the nodes had burst, leaving an odd pit beneath the skin where it once had been.

I shook my head, trying to get my mind around it. "He was perfectly fine just hours ago, right?" I looked to Marcello, then Lia, and they both nodded back at me.

How would we fight such an aggressive monster? *How, God, how?*

Luca's belly was not distended, but below his belly button, there was more discoloration. Lymph nodes in the groin, too, I dimly remembered.

Wincing, Lia turned away from Luca. Tears ran down her cheeks.

"We must bleed him, m'lady," the maid said to me. Over her shoulder, a knight arrived with the requested water pitcher and clay goblet.

"Bleed him?" I asked, hoping I'd misheard her.

"The buboes," she said, nodding toward Luca, referring to the swollen lymph nodes. "We must cut them open, let them bleed out, then stuff them with eggshells and lily root."

"Eggshells and lily root," I repeated.

"Mischiato con uno stronzo," she added, as if I should know this.

Stronzo. Great. Fan-freaking-tastic. The woman actually wanted me to mix eggshells, lily root, and some of our business from the chamber pot, and pat it into his open wounds. I was no doctor, but I was as good as they were going to get. And I was pretty sure that putting poop on a wound was a bad idea. In fact, I was pretty sure that cutting open the buboes was a bad idea to begin with.

"Some say that if you put a red hen beside the buboes at night," the maid added, "that it'll drag out the poison."

I stared at her. She was serious. I remembered a story my dad had told me. About the priests in Siena taking down the statues of Venus and other goddesses and gods in the piazza, certain that the plague was the result of God's condemnation. They chopped up old Venus and then sneaked bits of her into the mud of Firenze's new wall, hoping it'd transfer the Divine's attention from Siena to their enemies.

Even the educated had become desperate, steeped in superstition.

This is gonna get really, really ugly.

At that moment, I wished I'd said yes to Lia. That we'd made a run for it. Grabbed Mom. Hightailed it home.

But with one look at Marcello, patiently waiting on my direction, then Luca, so bravely fighting this dreaded disease, I knew I had to stay here, with them, to the bitter end. Fight it out.

For them. For us, somehow, too.

I knew it looked grim for Luca. Bursting buboes couldn't be a good sign. Or could it? Was it like a blister busting open, the skin tearing away and then healing?

I scratched a tiny bite on my arm and wondered if I'd been bitten, if a tick or flea had infected me, too. But I knew that was silly—that I was more likely to have gotten it from Signore Giannini when he kissed my hand.

I'd once happened upon a medical show where they demonstrated how far spit flew when someone coughed with their mouths uncovered. During a particularly gross-out segment, they had a child blow out candles on a birthday cake, and then they shined a blue light on it. It was covered. I mean *covered*. I hadn't eaten a piece of birthday cake since.

"Vinegar," I said to the maid in the corner. "See how much you can find and bring it here, to this room."

I turned to a knight. "Hot water and rags. We'll need a lot of it."

There was little we could do for Luca, other than try to make him as comfortable as possible. But my mind was turning to the rest of us. And vinegar and hot water—the only means we really had toward cleaning up the germ-coated room around us—was as good as we were going to get.

Luca stayed out-there, not-with-us, and I was relieved. Every minute he was in la-la land was a minute he wasn't in misery. Five guys arrived, heavy jugs of vinegar in their arms. "They are heating water in the kitchen, m'lady."

I nodded. "Is that all of it?" I asked, gesturing toward the jugs.

"There are six more in the kitchen."

"Good," I said. I turned to Marcello. "Might you assemble our people, m'lord?"

He ducked his head and called out to everyone to gather. I met them in the main hall.

When they were close, I said, "I do not know how to treat the plague any more than you do, but in Normandy, our doctors maintain that it is passed in several ways—fleas, coughing, and touch." I glanced back at Marcello, who offered me a tentative smile. "It is likely that we all already carry the disease. Please..." I looked each of them in the eye. "If you are feeling symptoms—fever, headache, the runs, the sweats—you must not hide it."

"Has anyone felt any of those symptoms?" Marcello asked.

No one had. Or at least, no one admitted to it. I sighed and assigned another round of baths and our clothes to the fire pit. "There is clothing in the wardrobes and chests of the people who live here." After we were washed, we'd scrub down the main hall.

"I will go to the chapel," the maid said to me, referring to a tiny grotto in the corner of the mansion's courtyard. "I will pray to God that He will have mercy on us all."

She looked to me for, what? Confirmation that that was a good call? I knew for a fact that in a few years, God would stand by watching while a third of Siena's population died. Would He be looking out for Luca and us now?

I had no idea. I hoped He would.

The maid's lips clamped shut as she read the fear in my eyes. She wiped her cheeks and nose with the back of her hand. "God will not abandon that knight or us. Mark my words. We shall not be abandoned."

Lia, freshly scrubbed, came near, a pile of clothes in her arms, and looked over her shoulder at the departing maid. "Making more friends, I see."

"Whatever."

"I found a couple of gowns for us to wear," she said, handing me one. "Yours will be short, but at least it's clean."

"Thank you," I said.

"Do *you* feel all right?" she asked, all concerned.

"Fine, fine. Just depressed. I wasn't cut out to be a nurse. I'm no good at it."

She squeezed my hand. "Neither was I," she said. "But at least we're together. We'll get through it, Gabi. Somehow. And Luca…" She numbly gazed toward his shut door. "Gabi, do you think he'll make it?"

"I hope so, Lia. I hope so."

"M'lady?" said a knight, ducking out of Luca's room. The men were determined to be by his side, in turns, regardless of how I pleaded with them to steer clear. "Come. He's lucid."

CHAPTER 12

Lia reached him first, three strides ahead of me and Marcello.

Luca was shaking off the hands of the other knights, evidently having just fought to regain his feet.

"Luca, lie down," I said.

Lia reached up and touched his cheek, then drew back as if she'd been scalded. Worried, she looked my way. "Still burning up."

"Nonsense. I'm well enough. But I still might need a pretty, blue-eyed nurse to tend me, day and night, to make certain I stay that way." He smiled over at Lia.

His smile quickly faded as his legs folded beneath him. Luckily, the knights were close enough to catch him and gently help him to the bed.

He was trembling, giving in to the fever's tremors again. We pulled a blanket across him.

"Surely we can do something for him," Marcello said.

"Please, Gabi," Lia said, looking down at Luca. "Tell us."

I widened my eyes in her direction, totally exasperated. She knew as much as I did! But her helpless, desperate look made me act.

"Hot, clear, broth," I muttered. Was it feed a cold, starve a fever? Or feed a fever, starve a cold? I couldn't remember. Or if it even applied to *plague*. I just wanted to try something. "More clean water, cold and hot. Rags, vinegar."

Marcello nodded once and rose to repeat the requests to those outside.

"Yes, a sponge bath," Luca teased, a smile on his lips even as he winced and panted for breath against some unseen pain. "I simply cannot tend myself. I need you ladies to assist."

"In his dreams," Lia said in English, rolling her eyes at me.

In minutes, servants returned, with two knights behind them, carrying water and vinegar and rags.

Lia poured some cold water into a basin, dunked a rag into it, and carried it over to a small table beside the bed. She sat on the edge, wrung out the cloth, and placed it on Luca's forehead. He was trembling, but he caught her hand and held it a moment. "Mayhap you and your sister should be as far from this room as possible," he said.

"Nay," she said. "We are likely as infected as you. The disease is spread through fleas, but also coughing. Blood. Touch."

He hastily released her hand. "But you show no signs of it?"

"It is because of our superior strength," Lia teased. "You pretend to be a mighty knight. But it takes an enemy smaller than a speck to take you down."

Luca grinned, but he let his eyes close as if the irises themselves burned with the fever.

She wrung out the cloth again and put it back on his head. Then, as his breathing became more even, as if he was giving into sleep or unconsciousness, she added vinegar to the water and washed his hands and forearms and then, carefully, the swollen nodes beneath his armpits.

"In some cultures, vinegar is considered an aphrodisiac," he said suddenly, still with his eyes closed.

"In my culture," Lia returned, "it's the smell of old, fat ladies laboring to clean foul places."

Luca chuckled, and then trembled so hard the whole bed shook.

"Shush now," Marcello said sternly. "Save your strength, cousin, to fight this battle within you."

A knight returned to the door. "Sir Marcello, may I have a word?"

"Certainly," he said, moving from his sentry position beside Luca. He squeezed my shoulder and gave Lia an encouraging smile. "I'll return shortly. Watch over my cousin. He could ask for no better nurses than you two."

"Not sure about that," I muttered to Lia in English, as he disappeared.

"Yeah, if only I could drop back home and find out what to do. For sure, you know?" She folded her arms in front of her.

"I know," I said. I gave her a close-lipped smile, then said, "He's strong, Lia. Inside and out. If anyone can fight this off, it's Luca. Right?"

She nodded, but I could see the fear in her eyes. She cared for him. Really cared. It made my heart skip a beat.

What if she watched him die?

A massive creaking sound outside made me move to the window—not glass, but rather nine panes of thinly sliced, almost transparent, ivory stone. I unhinged the lock, and the entire thing swung inward.

From here, I could just see the front gate. Marcello was standing in front of it as his men opened both sides. "What is he doing?" I muttered. Did he not fully get what a quarantine should be like?

As the gate doors were opened, I caught sight of a patrol of about twelve men, their captain leaning forward, a bright red stain at his shoulder. Injured.

I lifted a hand to the wall and my other hand to my mouth. Beyond the patrol, a contingent of Sienese seemed to be on the move, with great clouds of dust rising in the sky. What was happening? Weren't our reinforcements due about now?

Marcello abruptly turned, the gates were shut, and with a few hand motions, he had knights on the run.

Whatever it was, it was bad.

I glanced to Lia. Luca's eyes blinked open. "Stay with him," I muttered. "I'll be right back."

Marcello met me outside, took my hand, and led me back into the main room. It registered then, in my cloudy brain. The knights were arming themselves, taking stock of the meager weaponry available in the cabinets beside the front door.

"Gabriella," Marcello said, pulling me into a private corner. "Firenze is on the attack. They've cut off the reinforcements. They march on us now."

"Firenze?" I asked blankly. "But Lord Greco, he knows we have plague among us. He wouldn't…he was—"

"His intent must be to kill us, claim victory from afar, while containing the illness. But there is more. Gabriella," he said, taking my hands in his, "they very nearly captured your mother."

"My mother?" I frowned, trying to make sense of what he was saying. I shook my head. "Nay, she is back at the castello. Safe. She would never have—"

"She insisted. Threatened to go without the men if they did not bring her here. She was coming.... Gabriella, she told my men she wanted to come and take her daughters to safety."

The tombs. She had intended to get to us and escape. Return home. "But she is all right? She made it back to the castello?"

"I do not know. The men that came here split from a group of twelve others who were to see her back to safety. We'll know soon enough. If we can survive the night ourselves."

He ran a hand through his hair in agitation, then leaned closer to my ear. "They intend to destroy this mansion, and all within it. Burn us out or to cinders. More men from Siena will ride to our defense, of course, but even if they get here in time, we are about to be at the center of a long and difficult battle."

I took a deep breath and stood straighter. "They will find we are not easily vanquished."

"Nay," he said soberly. He cradled my cheek in his hand. "They shall not find *you* at all."

CHAPTER 13

"What?"

"You, your sister, shall exit here," he said, nodding to the corner behind me. I turned and then edged away. He pulled on a wall sconce—a holder for two candles—and it tilted outward. I heard the dull sound of a metal latch unhooking, and a door opening behind a moth-eaten tapestry in front of me.

Dude. This is SO Nancy Drew. And Harry Potter. Nancy Potter.

I pulled aside the cloth and glanced from the small door in the wall beyond it, back to Marcello. "A hidden passageway?"

Marcello nodded. "Luca and I found it when we were just boys. 'Tis a tunnel that runs a mile north. It emerges in a cave by the river. Unfortunately, it comes out in a wood on Firenze's side of the border."

"Great," I muttered.

He gave me a rueful smile and a small shrug. "At least we have an option for escape. If they manage to attack the manor, they would not expect you to flee into their own territory."

"But what if they know about the tunnel? What if they're lying in wait?"

"They do not know of it. I'm certain of it. My grandparents disguised the exit more carefully after they found out we had discovered it. Had our enemies found it, they would have used it to attack the manor long ago. Nay, they do not know. Besides, they will be hunting us on the Sienese side, where I will be leading them, making it look as if we are fleeing."

My eyes met his. "I will not allow you to sacrifice yourself for me."

He smiled and rubbed my lower lip with his thumb, then leaned in to kiss me—slowly, softly—then lifted his head and stared into my eyes. "I did not say I would sacrifice myself, Gabriella. Only lead them astray."

"Nay," I insisted, pushing him a step away, refusing to be swayed by his charms. "It is still far too dangerous. We shall remain together."

He shook his head and looked to the main room, where the men conferred, then back to me. "We shall be far more identifiable together. We must part for a time, beloved, until we can again be safe at the castello, or in Siena herself. And with the illness among us...I cannot see you to safety. We *must* separate."

I sighed, knowing he was right.

He touched my chin with his finger. "You must hide in the wood, until you're certain you or your sister do not carry this plague. Then travel by moonlight, back to our land. I shall meet you at the castello in ten days' time."

I shook my head, not liking his plan. Yet I could not find a way to stop it, argue against it. And what of my mother? How was I to find her, make sure she was okay, if I was hiding somewhere deep within Firenze?

"You must depart now. As soon as you gather supplies, you must be off. Even now, the woods to the north gather with those faithful to Firenze. The longer you tarry, the more resistance you are apt to encounter."

"But they fear the plague," I said weakly.

"Lord Greco feared the plague. He has much to live for." He looked away, as if lost in thought. "But there are many peasants and even knights who are willing to sacrifice themselves. Lord Greco and his fellow noblemen have likely placed a price on our heads that would be a fortune to a hundred families. In this case, the reward is not only glory for a man's lord—it is also gold for his own pockets."

Kamikazes, I thought. The Japanese fighter pilots who sacrificed themselves during World War II, flying into battleships, with the intent of bringing the great carriers down.

I didn't know what to do with that kind of insane loyalty. Had I felt that kind of dedication…ever?

Only to family.

And to Marcello. My eyes met his. "Please—" I whispered, as his lips covered mine for a moment. "Please come with me," I continued, when he released me.

He faltered. Sensing that he was thinking twice about it, I pressed. "Please, Marcello. Your plan is good in that it gives us an opportunity to get farther away. But without you, without Luca, if we encounter the enemy, what shall become of us?"

A slow smile softened his features. "The She-Wolves of Siena? Woe to the man who encounters them and stands in their way."

"Indeed," I said with a small grin. "But I admit that even the She-Wolves of Siena do best with the He-Wolves of Siena beside them." Memories of our last battle against Lord Greco flooded through my mind. I shivered, and he pulled me back into his arms, resting his chin on top of my head as he stroked my hair.

He moved to kiss my forehead, my eyes, my cheeks, my lips for several long, searching moments. Right then, I wished we could stay together. Forever. Get married, if that was what it took. I just knew I couldn't stand to be torn from him again, that I wanted more time to be together. To walk, hand in hand, to talk, just talk, for hours. And to kiss. Kiss like this—

He abruptly released me. I stood there for a second, dazed, coming down from the temporary high. He shut the trapdoor, set the sconce to rights, and motioned for me to follow him upstairs. I trailed behind him, reluctant, still trying to think of an option other than his terrible plan, when we heard a shout from the wall.

Marcello groaned and grabbed my hand.

Lia met us at the door. "What is happening?"

"Attack," Marcello responded. He lifted Luca's sword, by the door, and carried it over to him. The man struggled to rise and sat there, his upper body propped on one elbow.

He grabbed hold of the sheath and pulled it closer, staring at Marcello. "Battle upon us?"

"More like a war, my friend. Firenze knows we're here, and Siena is racing to our aid. It shall be fierce."

Luca sighed and threw off the covers and let his legs swing to the ground.

"Nay!" Lia cried, moving toward him. "You must stay—"

Marcello grabbed her arm and pulled her to a stop. "Lia. You shall go with your sister. Now."

She wrenched her arm from his hand and stared back up at him, as furiously defiant as he was insistent. "I am not going anywhere without Luca."

Behind her, Luca chuckled.

"You are of no assistance," Marcello complained to him, still staring at Lia like she was a rattlesnake poised to strike.

"Forgive me, m'lord," he said. "We happen to be in love with two of the most stubborn women in all of Siena."

We all stilled. Even Marcello glanced at him. Love? Luca and Lia—in love?

"It's his fever talking," Lia said, brushing it off. "But still, I shall not abandon my *friend*, ill as he is, to face off an attack."

Your "friend." Right. Got it.

She moved over to the bed, grabbed his boots, and helped him slip them on, taking care to not look in our direction. When he rose, she was again by his side, helping to steady him, even though he probably outweighed her by forty pounds. "We go, Marcello," she said. "But we shall go together."

Her tenacity gave me strength too. "*Si*, Marcello, *adiamo insieme.* Let us make this journey together. I cannot bear to be parted from you again."

He sighed in exasperation and ran a hand through his hair, eyeballing all three of us. "Very well. But remember this moment," he said, shaking a finger in our direction. "This is your plan, not mine."

"And if it proves to be successful?" I asked, teasing him.

He relented and smiled. "Then, of course, it was my plan all along."

We left the room and hurried down to the tunnel entrance.

Are You there, God? Do You hear me? I said silently, even as I accepted my sheath and sword from Marcello and strapped it on. *Please give us a break here. And get us safely through this tunnel. Uhh… amen.*

I strapped a dagger to my calf, ignoring the knight in the corner who was staring at my bare leg as he perched on the edge of a chair. Marcello saw it too and barked an order at him. I smiled and grabbed several more short blades and tucked them into my belt. I felt *waaaay* better heading out with the guys with us, even if Luca was as sick as a dog. Leaving them behind would've made me throw up.

With us together, I had a sense of hope.

Or is that You…God?

Marcello gathered with the men in the courtyard and explained our plan.

"And what if Lady Gabriella is correct, that you have the plague?" asked one, eyeing Luca, then Marcello.

"At least we shall be on land that belongs to the enemy. May it spread back to those who sent it to us."

The men chuckled. One by one, they clasped arms with Marcello and nodded toward Luca. "Until another day," Marcello said. "I know you shall make Castello Forelli and all of Siena proud of her sons again this day. I pray that we shall all soon be reunited at the castello. Remember that you must be without symptoms for at least ten days before you return there. Understood?" He looked about the circle of remaining knights. One by one, they thumped their chests with a closed fist, promising to do as he bade. "For Siena!" Marcello said.

"For Siena!" they returned, so loudly that it scared me a little.

We could hear the roar of soldiers beyond our walls, like a rolling thunder, then the clattering of arrows atop the tiled roof. In seconds, we could smell smoke.

"Shall we depart, or shall we pour a cup of wine and sit by the fire?" Luca asked, wiping his forehead of sweat.

Marcello smiled. "I think we shall depart." Pietro tossed him a lit torch. He caught it and turned.

At the door, Giovanni handed me a second torch, wound and ready to be lit. "Take care, m'lady. We don't wish to fish you from Firenze's pools. There are many sharks in those waters."

I smiled back at him. "I'm fairly adept at swimming." I glanced down the tunnel, where Marcello's torch danced in the dark, with Luca and Lia following behind. "I must be off."

"I shall guard this entrance with my life. Make haste, m'lady," Giovanni said. And with that, smoke swirling down the hallway behind him, he shut the door.

I turned and hurried along the dark tunnel, glad for the light of Marcello's torch, for the smooth stones beneath my feet, and that we were away, free of the burning mansion behind us. Perhaps ten feet above, men fought and cried out, their voices muffled by earth and stone. Behind me, the darkness yawned.

At last I was behind Luca, his big boots already dragging across the stones. "Feeling well, Luca?"

"Like I was just born," he lied, panting.

"Uh-huh," I muttered.

The tunnel was so low hanging, the guys had to duck as they walked. Farther behind, in the deep, dancing shadows of the torch and my comrades before me, I kept bumping my head. When Luca did the same, he paused and rubbed his head. "The thing was carved from the earth by far shorter people than we."

"Indeed," I said.

He sighed and pressed forward. A couple minutes later, we met Marcello and Lia, who had stopped.

"Cave-in," Marcello explained.

It was a particularly creepy place to be standing. Above us, we could hear laughter, a leader among our enemy calling out orders, cries as they sustained return fire. As though we'd neared the surface. "It sounds like the battle that day I first came out of the tomb," I said lowly.

"Only a hundred times bigger, I'd wager," Luca said, leaning against the wall, panting, closing his eyes. He clearly felt horrible.

"No way through but through, that's what our dad always said," Lia muttered.

She looked to Marcello, and he stared back at her.

"We'll pass back the stones," Marcello said. "Gabriella, you must form them into a second wall, making it look like a cave-in behind us, so that if we are pursued, they shall come across it and believe we did not come this way."

I nodded. Smart plan. "*Capito.*" *I understand.*

"You rest for a bit," Lia said to Luca. "Sit. There."

He nodded.

No funny comment? My eyes met Lia's worried ones as he sank to the ground. He leaned his head back and was immediately breathing as deeply as if he were tucked into bed at his mother's house.

Marcello passed a stone to Lia, and she passed it to me. At first, I tossed them a way back, giving it that casual, caved-in look we were shooting for. About ten minutes later, my arms already aching, I began to be more methodical in my building method. We picked up the pace, hearing the enemy troops roar in excitement and then move forward, away from us, toward the villa. Clearly, they were making gains.

Luca was snoring now. I was glad he was getting rest—he'd need it for the journey to come. But man, did I wish we had his strong hands, arms, and back as part of our chain gang.

"We're through!" Marcello said, looking back, panting. At the top of his pile was a tiny hole. I found it oddly encouraging. *Desperate, Gabs?*

"We're about halfway to the ceiling," I said, looking back at the pyramidlike pile I was making behind us.

"All right. Raise that wall as fast as you can," he said.

With renewed energy, we continued our task, hearing the forces above again make headway toward the villa. How soon until they flooded inside the gates? Found our entryway? I peered down the tunnel with each stone, as if I might be able to suddenly see in the dark. I pictured Giovanni standing guard, unwilling to let anyone pass—but even he would eventually be overcome by a hundred of his enemy.

Lia had twenty-four arrows in her quiver. She could take out a few if I ducked, before they raised a shield before them and charged. I shivered at the thought.

We'd been working on it for over an hour, and the wall was shoulder high now. Just another fifteen or sixteen stones…Lia was slowing, Marcello waiting behind her instead of maintaining our previous rhythm. "C'mon, Lia. Keep it up. We have to hurry," I said in English.

"I'm doing all I can," she grumbled back at me. She handed me the next stone so hard I almost dropped it. Not on purpose, I knew. Her fingers were probably trembling like mine now, weak, untrustworthy.

Luca came to a few minutes later and forced himself to his feet. He studied the nearly complete pile and stretched out his hands for a rock. "Here, allow me to assist," he said with a grin.

I laughed. "You have," I said, panting, "the most uncanny timing."

He cocked a brow and smiled back, then turned around and asked Lia to stand aside. Mouth open in a pant, she wiped her forehead of sweat and nodded, backing up.

Quickly, Marcello tossed rocks past us and directly to Luca. He set them in place, finished blocking off the passageway and then added a second layer to strengthen it.

When he was done, he leaned back, looking so pale he was almost blue, and glistening with sweat in the fading light of the torch. "Thank you," I said, touching his arm. I knew how hard it had been on him. But seriously, I didn't know if Lia and I could've done any more.

A sound echoed down the long tunnel and made us all freeze in place.

Someone had tripped the door latch.

They were coming.

"Make haste," Marcello said, waving me forward, helping me over the pile. Now holding the torch, I scrambled awkwardly across it, then leaned back to help Lia across too. Thankfully, the tunnel ahead appeared empty, the way clear. Would they buy the cave-in behind us?

We weren't sticking around to find out. Luca came next, then Marcello, protecting us from our pursuers.

"Put the torch out!" Marcello growled.

I dropped it and stomped it to ashes. It had almost burned out anyway.

We hovered in the darkness, each listening hard. We heard a shout and then another, then the muffled sound of footfalls. Could they hear us, too? I tried to be as silent as I could as I hurried down the tunnel. Reaching out to feel the rough stones of the walls, running blind. How much farther? Would we find ourselves in the midst of an enemy camp when we emerged?

The men behind us fell abruptly silent. They must've reached the cave-in site. We pulled to a stop and glanced back, four mice fearful that our hole was about to be discovered by the great big cat. Their torchlight filtered through holes and cracks in the pile. We could hear the men talking, debating, then the sound of one stone falling on another.

The tunnel was surprisingly straight and uniform, and we could see the place our enemy lingered in the distance. At the top of the rocks, where it was but two stones thick, torchlight danced through the cracks.

"Stay completely still," Marcello whispered.

They moved another stone. No doubt they could see through to the other side. To us. "Bring the torch closer!" a voice said, echoing down the tunnel.

I couldn't bear to watch. To observe the moment of discovery. It was enough to listen. I closed my eyes. *Please, God, please, God, please, God…*

"He can't see this far," Luca whispered.

I hoped he was right. Because I felt completely exposed and vulnerable.

"There's another cave-in up ahead," said the man. "Not as high."

"They're not down there," said a second. "They've made their escape to Siena. *Above* ground."

"Back to the mansion!" cried another. Abruptly, the soldiers turned, and gradually, their torchlight faded. Relief flooded through me, making me feel suddenly weak, exhausted.

"It's okay, Gabs," Lia whispered after a moment, once she was sure they were gone, pulling me in for a hug. "Maybe we should just hide here. Until they're gone-gone."

"No," I said. "We have to move on. If Lord Greco takes down the villa, and yet doesn't find us within the wreckage, or on the road, escaping, he'll come back to this tunnel. We need out."

I blinked slowly, as if that might clear my vision and I'd be able to see. "Shall we light the other torch?" I whispered back to Marcello.

"Nay. Let us feel our way forward. We might have sore need of that torch later. I think we are nearly to the end."

"I hope so," I muttered, moving forward, tapping my foot in front of me like a blind woman's cane, my hands on the wall. The last thing we needed was to break a leg on our way out. It was slow going, but in another fifteen minutes, I could see a bit of daylight. That, or I was losing it, imagining things…

But no, there it was. The rectangular form, light on all four edges.

"A door," I said over my shoulder, picking up the pace, feeling more confident now, with the end in sight.

But that was just before I tripped.

And landed in a deep, cold pool.

CHAPTER 14

I went under and took in a bit of water before I could make sense of it. I rose to the top and coughed, gasping for air. Marcello's strong hand grabbed my shoulder, and then, having located me, took hold of my arm and yanked me to the rocky edge of the pool.

Lia was shushing me, freaked out by all the noise I was making. I tried to keep it down, but I couldn't help it. I had to breathe. So I coughed several more times, shivering in Marcello's arms, the rest of them tense in silence.

When I finally had a grip, Marcello leaned in and kissed my forehead. "I should have mentioned the water," he said. I could hear the tinge of laughter mixed with genuine regret in his voice.

"That would have been kind, yes," I sputtered.

"It was why the tunnel was built. To reach water supplies in case of attack."

"Ah, yes." It was logical. The tunnel had widened here, to give better access to the pool. I could sense it now by the way our voices echoed off the wall.

"No matter," he said. "We'll all get wet now. Just in far less dramatic fashion."

I clamped my lips shut, no longer in the mood to be teased. "Lead on, m'lord," I said tightly.

He squeezed my arm and bent to pull off his boots, and my shivering began anew without his body heat. I could hear him wading into the pool.

This would not be good for Luca, getting wet, sick as he was. I shook my head. *No way through but through.*

"It is as I remembered," Marcello whispered from the other side of the pool. His voice carried across the water, making it sound as if he were a foot away. I could see the silhouette of his head, neck, and shoulders against the daylight around the door. "Come over, but stay to the left. It's shallower."

Luca and Lia were making their way over, right in front of me, when I heard Luca collapse and go under. "Luca!" Lia cried, before she remembered herself.

I groaned as she splashed around. But I did not hear Luca emerge.

I slipped under the water and felt around, finding Lia's sodden skirts first, then, a glance of Luca's cold finger. I pressed forward, ignoring the cry of my lungs, and grabbed hold of his arm, yanking him to the surface.

It was his turn to cough, spitting out water as Lia and I dragged him across the rest of the pool, struggling to maintain our footing on the slippery rocks.

"Forgive me, m'ladies," he said, leaning back against the rocks on the far side as if he were sinking into a feather bed. Lia and I clung to him from either side, willing our body heat into him. "My head is tilting back and forth. I cannot get it to stop."

Dizzy. He is dizzy. His fever must be soaring…

With my eyes adjusting, I could see the dim forms of all three of my companions. I looked up to Marcello. He was leaning against the door, listening.

I held my breath a moment, trying to hear too, but between Luca's teeth chattering and moaning and Lia's panting, I couldn't make out anything. I waited, staring at Marcello.

He looked back in our direction. "Can we move him?" he asked lowly.

All three of us were shivering now. Luca passed out, and we struggled to hold him. "We must," I said between my own chattering teeth. "We must all get dry and warm. It is vital for Luca."

He paused, seemingly digesting my words. *Vital for Luca.*

"Can you manage him, between you?" He pulled his sword from its sheath.

"I think so," I said, looking over at Lia.

"If we can rouse him," she said.

She was right. There'd be no way we could drag his dead weight and move at more than a snail's pace. But Marcello had to be ready to defend us. "We'll do the best we can," I said to Lia, encouraging her.

She turned to Luca and shook him a little as Marcello lifted the crossbar from the door and set it aside. Luca didn't move.

"Luca," I said, slapping his cheeks gently until his eyes blinked open. "Come, friend. We'll get you someplace safe and warm."

With a few grunts and groans, we reached the door.

"We'll emerge in a small cave beside a bend in the river," Marcello said, opening the door an inch on creaking hinges and peering out. "The most difficult part will be to get from the cave to the tree line. A hundred yards. Then, a mile or so south, there are a series of grottos and caves. We can hide there until nightfall."

I nodded. "Let us lead. You take the big lug."

He grinned at me and lifted his head in assent. Then sheathing his sword, he glanced at Lia. "Draw an arrow. If anyone spots us, we'll count on you to silence his call."

She nodded and pulled an arrow from her quiver while Marcello wrapped Luca's arm across his shoulder. If need be, I knew he had the strength to carry his friend.

"'Tis a shame you two do not travel alone," Lia said. "In the clothes of the mansion's servants, you appear as none but loyal sons of Firenze. Our skirts shall draw their attention; surely there are no womenfolk this close to the lines."

His eyes moved back and forth as he thought through some-thing. "That's it," he said. "You two shall go ahead. Creep through the grass on your hands and knees if necessary. I shall follow behind, carrying Luca, as if we are Fiorentini loyalists and I am bringing a wounded man into camp. We shall cut over and into the trees to find you when we see the opportunity."

I nodded, finding hope, even as my heart stopped at the thought of separation. "But what if...what if they capture you? Figure out your true identity? What if they imprison you, haul you off to Firenze?"

"They shall never believe that a young lord of Siena would march directly into their camp."

"And if they do?"

He gave me another small smile. "Then my beloved lady shall have to come and rescue me."

"Us," Luca corrected him, slurring his words now, as if he were drunk. "Have to rescue *us*."

He adjusted Luca across his shoulders. "Stay with me, Luca," he said sternly.

"Can't get much closer, m'lord," Luca mumbled.

Marcello looked at me once more. "'Tis our only path, really. If we do not find you near the caves by sunup, you make your way back to the castello. Understand? We may be waylaid, but we'll find our way to you in time."

I nodded, feeling my stomach turn. I knew he'd sacrifice himself for me in an instant. Luca would too.

He gestured to Lia, and she crept forward with me following, sword drawn. The guys trailed behind us. At the edge of the cave, Lia peered around, staring for a long moment, then carefully drew back. "A contingent of ten or so men, arming a catapult," she said to me and Marcello. "Twelve more on horseback beside it. Twenty-four men in rows before them."

"Preparing another line of attack," Marcello said with a grunt. "Their focus will be on the Sienese beyond the villa. See any scouts?"

"Nay," Lia said, after a long moment of searching. "We could stay here until dark."

Marcello shook his head. "'Tis only a matter of an hour or two before they'll clearly see we're not among those who remain to fight. They'll make a second pass at the tunnel, and if they move a few stones…"

My eyes shifted from the door behind us to the trees ahead, guessing how long it would take us to cross the great expanse of knee-high autumn-brown prairie grass and at last reach the spare oaks. The sprawling trees would allow precious little cover. Beyond them was the deeper forest. That was where we had to go. In there, we could hide, at least.

I looked to Marcello. "We cannot outrun soldiers on horse-back."

"Nay. Move steadily, hunched over, and fall to the grass to catch your breath. Move carefully, so as not to attract attention."

"Leave me here," Luca grunted. "You should go with them, m'lord."

Marcello ignored him. "Go, Evangelia, Gabriella. *Go.*"

We did as he told us, falling to the shelter of the long, swaying grasses, catching our breath, then steadily rising and scurrying quickly up the hill. I kept waiting for singing arrows to come arcing down on us, but none came. Halfway across the field, I dared to think, *Can we actually make it? How can they possibly not see us?*

I glanced over my shoulder, finding it impossible not to look after Marcello and Luca. According to plan, they were moving straight up the hill. At the crest was a ring of white tents, Firenze's flag proudly flying from all twelve of them, and a tendril of a smoldering fire at its center. Seriously? Did they actually intend to enter it? He was not that crazy…I hoped.

But then I saw what was happening. Six soldiers were making their way down to them, hands on the hilts of their swords. Two more followed on horseback. Even among the noise of battle far below us, I could hear them barking at our guys.

Marcello and Luca were distracting them, running interference, keeping them from seeing us. *Idiotic, wonderful heroes.* "Hurry, Lia," I said.

We ran the rest of the way, pausing on the far side of ancient twin oaks, their red leaves chattering away above us. Lia caught sight of the men then. "They're pointing toward the battle," she said. "Making up their story."

"Let's hope it's a good one."

"Pray no one recognizes them."

"I will."

The words settled between us. As far as I knew, Lia was as much a praying type of girl as I was. And that wasn't much. But it seemed right, here. We were desperate. And desperate people prayed, right?

"Come on," I said. "We need to get deeper, find those caves Marcello was talking about." I ran forward, hoping our luck would hold and no one would spot us. From this angle, it'd be tough for the soldiers with Marcello and Luca to see us. But down below, at the front line…if they turned back toward camp, it wouldn't be hard. Our long, wet hair hung on our backs. Perhaps they would mistake us for peasant women, in our current garb, displaced from our homes by soldiers. But more worrisome was the thought that every man on the field wanted to collect the price on our heads—that they would see we were no peasant women at all.

We took no more breaks. I could sense that Lia's urgency matched mine. If we'd been spotted, we wanted to disappear as fast as possible, deep in the woods, where no one could find us. Find a defensible position, rest there. Then make our way to the caves.

Once in the comforting arms of the forest, we paused and caught our breath. I looked back and then did a double take. From this angle— "Lia, I know this place. You do too. We've been here before, uh…you know what I mean."

She turned around, and her eyes widened. "We're near the old river ruins," she said.

"Right," I said with a smile, trudging forward. "Where Mom and Dad brought us when we were little." The site, in our time, was overrun with tourists, since Etruscan tombs lined the limestone cliff for miles. *The River Necropolis*, I remembered. Some had elaborate carvings, noblewomen sanded away by time to blobs that resembled mermaids. Lions, lounging on their sides. Elsewhere, there were fluted columns. Tombs, square and tidy, but with not nearly the decoration necessary to hold my parents' attention for long. Besides, they had forever been looking for the *undiscovered* ruins, not those that were in the public domain.

Striding through the fallen leaves, I flashed back to that day with them. Laughing. Dad had played with us, hiding and making us find him, behind trees, inside the caves. He'd paid attention to us that rare day, calling us his "Etruscan Princesses." I rubbed my arms, feeling the chill of the tunnel pool all over again, even though my gown was rapidly drying. I looked up, around.

"I remember too," Lia said.

She waited until I reluctantly met her gaze. "It was one of the best days ever," I said simply.

She nodded, grief edging her baby blues like I knew it edged my own eyes. "What if…Gabi, what if we could go back in time and pull off before the present? What if we could pull off, get a message to Dad? Even see him? Save him?"

I sighed. She was voicing thoughts I hadn't dared to think through myself. I shook my head. "You're talking about massive confusion. Some possible rift in the time continuum. If we save Dad, what other things will it change? If that farmer didn't run him off the road, will he hit someone else? Will it just be another family mourning, instead of us?" I swallowed hard. "And if we save him, does all of this disappear? Maybe he would've convinced Mom to look elsewhere for the tumuli. Maybe they would not have discovered them at all. Which means—"

"No Luca," she said lowly, pulling to a stop. "No Marcello. But Dad…Gabi, Dad would be *alive*."

"Right." I looked her in the eye. "I mean, *maybe*." I trudged forward, suddenly aware that we'd been still for far too long. But my head swirled with thoughts of Dad, of saving him, of righting that horrible wrong. It sent my heart soaring. And yet the thought of never meeting Marcello, this all fading away like a brief dream…that made my heart sink. Even now, what was happening to him and Luca? Had they convinced the Fiorentini they were on their side? Was Luca being cared for by camp medics?

Lia paused suddenly and raised her hand. "*Horses*," she mouthed.

Despite the thunder of hoofbeats, we remained as still as deer as the troops passed by us, probably a quarter mile distant. There had to be a hundred or more.

"If they turn their attention to finding us, we're dead," she said. "But I'm betting they don't know how vast the necropolis is." She looked away and ducked under a branch. "I bet these trees cover most of it still, and superstition keeps them out."

"I hope you're right," I said, following behind her.

The wind blew, sending a cascade of leaves to the ground, and we both shivered. "The caves, Lia. Let's get to the caves. And pray Marcello and Luca can find us." We hurried forward. In the distance, the battle continued on, and the sun was growing low in the sky. Would they fight all night? I knew no man cared to fight by the light of a quarter moon. It was too easy to take out your own men.

"There," she said after a few more minutes, nodding upward. Just barely visible above the crest of the trees was an old tomb carved out of the rock.

Narrow, disintegrating steps zigzagged downward beneath it, mostly hidden by the oaks that lined the cliff. We could see them clearly only as we drew nearer. "Think they'll hold?" I asked.

"It's worth a try," she said. "At least from above, we'll have a bit more sun for warmth, as well as a view to see what's going on. Maybe we can spot the guys coming our way."

"Or the enemy coming to get us."

"Don't be so negative," she said. She slipped her bow across her shoulder and climbed to the base of the stairs. Tentatively, she tried one and then the next. On the third, it crumbled, but not all the way.

"I'd hate it if one gave way up there," I said, looking twenty feet above us.

"Positive thoughts, Gabs," she hissed, continuing her trek. But I noticed she had a grip on a stair three above her toehold with each one. Just in case.

At the tree line, she paused and peeked outward. "It's perfect," she said, looking down at me. "Come."

Yeah, I thought. *Perfect for you.* I wasn't just a few inches taller than my sister; I also had a good twenty pounds on her. What she had crossed easily might give way under me.

"Gabs, *come on.*"

"All *right.*" I sighed and began to climb. Only one stair gave way in the first fifteen. With fifteen more to go, I glanced up and saw Lia's wide, frightened eyes above me. She gestured with them to my lower right. She reminded me of a cartoon character, with large blue arrows pointing out her alarm.

Carefully, I turned my head. I was hidden, mostly, by the canopy of the tree. But in a slight gap among the trees, I could see the head of a horse. My eyes scanned forward, searching for another peephole.

There. The man was squatting, his fingers running through the leaves.

A tracker.

"Over here, m'lord. They came through here," he called over his shoulder.

Two more came up behind the tracker, walking their horses. I caught sight of dark, black hair, and then he was gone. Lord Greco? Then a third man.

A gust of wind came up and a hundred leaves went with it. I felt as exposed as if I was watching my skirt unravel, thread by thread.

"This way?" Greco said below me, ahead of the tracker now, clearly identifiable now by his voice. "Be they witches, capable of disappearing into the cliff itself?"

I closed my eyes as they neared the base, wishing I *were* capable of sinking into the limestone behind me. Another few feet and they'd see the stairs, and atop them…me.

I forced my eyes open. I had to be ready. I dared to let go of the stair and pull a dagger from the back of my waistband. I knew that above me, Lia was already drawing an arrow across her bow. But for her to shoot, she'd have to expose herself.

Lord Rodolfo Greco's mouth dropped open as he spied me there.

I had no choice; I scurried up the stairs and, in my rush, tore away two steps.

Lord Greco's laughter was a low, melodic sound. Pleasant, almost, if I didn't know that it came from a man who wanted to see us dead.

Lia showed herself then, swiftly shooting the man beside Lord Greco, who had stupidly edged forward. Lord Greco stepped back beneath the tree canopy, well aware of the lethal nature of Lia's aim. I heard the sickening strike of her second arrow as I reached the top, my fingernails filling with dirt as I clawed my way up and over the edge.

Below me, a man gasped and belatedly cried out, like a baby just winding up for a good cry. A fourth man.

Lord Greco seemed to ignore his friends, he was so focused on us. "What will you do up there?" he called. "It is just as well. Perhaps I'll leave you there until I'm certain you don't have the plague that shielded you from me before."

We remained silent, simply staring at each other, trying to figure out our options.

What options? We're treed. Raccoons with a hound dog below us.

He waited a minute before calling out again. "Rest assured, you shall not escape that cave, ladies. At some point, you shall be mine." He turned and said something to another man.

He was sending for help. Eventually, they'd have enough troops and resources to bring ladders. Or come from above and rappel down on ropes. I eyed Lia's quiver. Twenty-two arrows left.

"We have to get out of here," I said.

She nodded, clearly already thinking the same thing. We had minutes, at most.

"Ready?" I asked.

CHAPTER 15

"Ready as I'll ever be," she returned.

I edged to the stairs. "Lord Greco, we surrender," I said. I took a step and then another, expecting a dagger or arrow to come winging my way. Or were we worth more alive than dead? Marcello's warning rang through my head like an alarm bell—*Fight. To the death, if you must.*

"Do you show any symptoms of plague?" he called, still hiding beneath the branches of the trees.

"None, as yet."

Lia was behind me, already on the stairs.

"Throw down your weapons!" he demanded. "At once."

"But—"

"Disarm!" he demanded, edging into view, an arrow across his bow. He was pointing it at Lia.

I didn't think. From fifteen steps up, I leaped to the trees, knowing it would distract him. I heard Lia's arrow race past me just before I hit the branches. Three small limbs cushioned the brunt of my fall, thankfully, but then gave way. A large one beneath them slowed my descent. I folded around it, swung with my momentum and fell feet-first now. I reached out, grasping for a branch, anything, feeling the tug of my hair as a clump pulled out of my scalp, then deep scratches at my leg, face, arm.

At the very last, my fingers found a branch, and I held tight. I was hanging there, face to face with Lord Greco five feet away, his arrow pointing in my direction. "A gift from the heavens," he said with a low laugh, "my prize to claim." He pulled back on the bow-string and adjusted his aim.

I dropped from the branch, turning as I fell, and rolled away through the leaves. His arrow hit the ground, inches behind my leg—he was obviously trying to wing me—then another near my shoulder. But then I had the trunk of the tree to shield me.

I grabbed one of the daggers from my waistband, so glad they'd stayed put, and aimed at him. Lia was down the stairs now, taking her shot. It narrowly missed him.

He was good. His intuition uncanny. I let out a growl of frustration. He should've been dead five times over, facing Lia.

I threw the dagger, and it stuck in the tree, not three inches from his head.

I groaned. "Come on, Lia!" I cried, realizing, too late, that I spoke in English.

She came tearing through the wood, still uphill from me, and I turned and ran with her. We were decent runners, going for jogs most mornings from Mom's archaeological site. *Hopefully Lord Fancypants always has his running done for him,* I thought. He had the advantage of running straight after us. We were weaving, conscious that he might still try to wing us with his own arrow. And, oh yeah, we had long, damp skirts on. Totally unfair.

But we have the advantage of sheer terror, I thought, a grim smile spreading across my face as I panted.

Lia shot me a look, wondering how on earth I could be smiling.

Hey, I'm thinking positively, I thought back at her.

She just looked confused, for some reason. Our sister telepathy had never been particularly good.

We ran over a mile, losing sight of Lord Greco somewhere afterward. He must have dropped back for reinforcements.

At last she pulled me to a stop, leaning down on her knees, panting. We could hear them. Horses.

"They don't have dogs," I said, gasping for breath. "At least there's that."

"Yeah, but a hundred men, combing these hills for us?" she said. "It'll still do the trick."

The sun was casting the last of its warm orange light on the cliffs above us. I stared at them, then down below, trying to get a sense of where we were. "Aren't those passageways around here? The ones the Etruscans cut into the cliff?"

"Yes!" she said, her eyes widening in excitement.

"Come on," I said, grabbing her hand and resuming our run.

Fifty yards farther, we came across the tomb that we remembered from our childhood visit. Massive fluted columns. Statues, not quite as ravaged by time as I remembered, their features more distinct. We could hear the horses churning down the road below us. They passed us, obviously aiming to cut us off, circle around, close in on all sides.

At last, we came across it. Up top, we could see the break in the stone. But down below, it was totally choked by brush.

"Well, hello there," I said, "you big, beautiful overgrown passageway." I looked over to Lia. "Let's confuse 'em a little."

She knew what I meant. We ran forward, as if we were still on our path, making sure we disturbed lots of leaves. Then, thirty yards ahead, we carefully climbed atop the stones of the tombs and leap-frogged back to the passageway. I pressed inward, ignoring the branches scratching my cheeks, pulling at my hair. Lia made her own way in from the edge.

"Don't leave any footprints," I said.

"Or disturb the leaves," she returned.

We turned, periodically, to pat branches back into place, or cover our trail with rocks.

We were through the dense foliage, between the moss-covered, curving banks of the ancient walls, when we heard them. It was dark in the twenty-foot tall chasm, giving us hope. If they were forced to search via torchlight, it might be even harder to find trace of us. They'd go beyond, thinking that we were faster than they thought, confident that we were on the front side of the cliff, perhaps hidden away in another cave.

"This is good," I said to Lia, taking her hand. "Really good."

"Yes," she said, nodding. "Except for one thing."

"What?" I asked as we hurried forward, careful to not kick a stone that might send a telltale alarm back to the Creep-Fest back yonder.

"We're going deeper." She gestured ahead.

She didn't mean deeper into the passageway. We both knew it would emerge up top, on the ancient site of an Etruscan city.

She meant deeper into Firenze's territory.

"We're just taking the scenic route," I said to her lightly. But I was certain she heard my voice break oddly. I was having a hard time catching my breath, my heart was pounding so hard.

I was going away from Marcello. From Mom. And closer to the enemy than ever.

"They won't expect us to do this," Lia whispered, squeezing my hand. I realized we'd been holding hands for several minutes now, like two little girls trying to draw comfort from each other. But I didn't let go.

"No, they won't," I said lowly, as we reached the top of the passageway and the vast flat of the ruined city. Here and there, the indentation of roads and the slight rise of foundations could still be seen. "The Ladies Betarrini have a few tricks left." I turned to face her and pulled her into my arms. "I love you, Lia. If anything happens—"

"Don't say it," she said, clinging to me, then repeated, "Don't say it," anger edging her tone. She stepped away and shook a finger at me. "You promised me, Gabi. Remember? I didn't want to come back here. I was too afraid because of what happened last time—"

"And look," I said, pulling her forward and to the edge of the trees. "If it wasn't for me, you wouldn't have found out what love was like." We had to keep moving. Just in case...

She blew out a dismissive breath, and I sighed in relief. I'd distracted her. "Love? Serious *like*, maybe, but I barely know him."

I raised a brow. "What's not to like? He's funny. You love funny guys. And handsome, in that California-dude look you're into. And loyal. Not to mention clever and strong. He's way better than that guy in Boulder who always texts you."

"Well, yeah…but you can hardly compare them. Their lives are so different—"

"So are ours, with these guys. Marcello. Luca. They're men, Lia. Not boys. It takes guys at home another ten years to have the maturity that these guys have."

She pulled her hand from mine. "Yeah. They *have* to grow up fast here. People want to *kill* you all the time."

I nodded. She had me there.

"Besides, Luca…"

She was thinking about him—how sick he was when we left them. Battling a foe far fiercer than another soldier. The Black Plague. "Luca will beat it." I patted her shoulder. "He's strong, Lia, really strong."

She paused and pulled me to a stop again. I turned to face her. "What?"

"Marcello and Luca will not find us among the caves, down below."

"No," I said slowly. "They'll see Lord Greco's men combing the face of those cliffs and know two things: one, that they've lost our trail; and two, that we're making our way to Castello Forelli as planned."

"Via the scenic route," she said with a small smile.

"Via the scenic route," I agreed, slipping my arm through the crook of hers.

We slept on the floor of a shallow cave for several hours, then resumed our trek before daybreak, searching for a main road. I wished we'd paid more attention when Mom had pointed out the old Roman roads over the years. Chances were, there was one around here somewhere, most likely still in use. The Romans had been as good at crafting roads as the Etruscans had been at tombs, setting their massive stones at the right angle to make them endure the long-term effects of weather and traffic. I remembered that much—the perfect, angled lines, the ruts in the stones where wheel after wheel had worn them down.

We emerged on a mountain ridge and, shielding our eyes, looked to the valley below us.

"The road," she said.

"Not like we can hop on that one," I returned. Hundreds of troops were moving toward Siena in uniform lines. Peasants went the other way, on either side of the road, fleeing the carnage behind them, heading toward the sanctuary of Firenze. "Guess the battle is still raging."

"How'd the two of us set all of *that* in motion?" she asked, looking at me, really looking at me. She reached up and pulled a leaf from my hair, then another. "You're not looking so hot, Gabi."

"Neither are you," I said, tucking her hair behind her ear.

We both bent and broke twigs from a nearby bush and attempted to gather our hair into a bun. We shoved the twigs through and they held—for the moment, anyway. "Better?" I asked.

"Yeah, except for the gash across your cheek."

"Battle scars. We can tell anyone we meet that we're fleeing the front lines, and be telling the truth."

She smiled. "How're those ribs?"

"They hurt like crazy, every time I take a breath," I said. When we'd lain down for the night, I'd discovered it at last. A broken rib or two from my insane leap into the trees. The adrenaline from our escape must've masked the pain for hours. Kind of like when moms are able to lift cars to save children pinned beneath. Superhuman kind of stuff. Sad that it was over. Now I had to deal with regular-human kind of pain. "I'd kill for an Advil. Or five."

"Let's look for some foxglove," she said. "Remember how last year, Mom made us that tea every time we got a headache?"

"Little late in the season for foxglove."

"You never know," she said, raising a brow.

"Right, right," I said. "Thinking positively."

Now that we had the road in sight, we moved parallel to it, searching for a good spot to try to cross unseen, to the eastern side—where we could then head south and avoid Lord Greco's search. We walked six, maybe seven miles that day. But there was never a letup in the stream of soldiers.

"It's almost night. We'll find a crossing spot soon," Lia tried.

"Maybe." Down below us was a vineyard, its straight rows of vines curving along crossbars. "Let's go down here."

We picked our way down a small, dried-up gulley. Here and there were pools of stagnant water. While our throats were parched, we dared not drink from them. We were Colorado girls. Our dad had taken us camping once or twice. We knew a breeding ground for giardia when we saw one.

We held strong, but when we caught sight of the well in the empty yard, we raced down to it. Lia hauled up the bucket and set it with trembling hands atop the edge. She cupped her hands and sucked in the water. I was right behind her, splashing it in my face in the effort to get more of it down my throat at once.

"My well will go dry if every fleeing villager that comes through here helps themselves," said a woman at the door of the house. She wore no weapon, but the threat in her voice said we'd better watch out. She was as tall as my grandma—a good foot shorter than I—but she sounded equally as tough.

Lia glanced at me.

"We beg your pardon, Signora," I said with a slight nod. "But we have been on the road all day, without water. We could not stop ourselves. Might we…repay you with a bit of work?" I glanced around. "I see your vines still bear their fruit."

"Husband conscripted into the ranks," she said, nodding toward the highway, still below us. "He may be gone days, even weeks."

I swallowed hard. So it happened on the other side of the line too. Soldiers, taken from their homes, never to be seen again. At least in our day and age they had dog tags, a means to identify them, send word home to loved ones. It was so like Signora Giannini's story, but this lady was twice her age.

And now her fruit rotted on the vine. Her means of living, her future, her way to get through the winter…

She sighed and padded out to the nearest vine, then looked to us. "I am Signora Reggello." She came over and lifted my hand, saw the calluses there, and gave a grunt of approval, then glanced at the cuts on my face, my arms, the sword sheath I wore over my shoulder. Then she went to Lia and did the same. "You are uncommon peasant women, but do not tell me your names. I am too old to bear the burden of secrets."

I glanced at Lia and back to the old woman. "Our men are gone too," I said. "When the men are gone, women must do what they must to survive, no?"

She studied me a long moment, then nodded her small, gray head. She gestured out to the vines. "Most of it is too far gone to save. But with your help we could bring in the last of it before it too, turns."

"We're fairly good with a vinekeeper's knife," I said, smiling at Lia, remembering that day—only about a week ago?—when we beat Luca and Marcello so soundly harvesting the Giannini vines.

"Glad to hear it," she said, tossing up her hand as she turned, as if she truly didn't care. "First we eat, sleep. Work come morning."

Lia grinned at me, threw her hands up, and followed the old, squat woman into the small building.

CHAPTER 16

I don't know if it was the comfort of the woman's tidy, warm cottage or the thick pasta she'd fed us, or if it was a witness to how totally wiped out we were, but Lia and I slept so soundly in front of the fire, we didn't even hear the horsemen until they were right outside.

As the sounds registered in my ear, sending a jolt to my heart, I shook Lia and put a finger to my lips. I tossed aside the blanket and crawled to the shutters. From the lower corner, I dared to nudge one aside and peek out.

Lord Greco was there with twelve knights, talking with Signore Reggello.

Lia peered over my shoulder. "Dang it, that didn't take long."

I looked around the one-room cottage, desperate to find a hiding place, but there was nowhere but beneath the bed—way too obvious. Lord Greco was pointing to the shed, demanding knights search it. He sent two more toward the cottage, despite the woman's complaint. His expression told me he didn't really expect to find us here. He was merely looking everywhere he could.

"Gabs," Lia whispered, hurrying over to the bed even as she shouldered her bow. She stepped up and jumped to grab the rafter above, swung her leg, and curled up to the top.

I didn't know if I'd have time to climb it in time, or if my ribs could handle Cirque du Soleil stunts at that point, but I had to at least try. I ran, sprang from the bed, and did the same as my sister. I'd just rolled on top of the rafter, closing my eyes and gritting my teeth against the scream of pain that threatened to burst from my lungs, when the first knight came in, followed closely by our hostess. A second was right on her heels, hovering in the doorway. Slowly, steadily, I pulled my skirt up and out of their line of vision, clenching it in my fist. It was the only move I dared make.

The first man went to the blanket spread out before the fire. It was the tracker. He bent, lifted and smelled it. What? Was he a bloodhound or something? He turned to Signora Reggello. *"Ha avuto ospiti stanotte?" You had guests last night?*

At his words, the other knight moved fully into the room.

"Nay," the woman said. "The nights are getting colder, and my husband has been conscripted into Firenze's troops. I sleep better there."

He walked over to her, closer to me and Lia.

Please don't look up…please, please, please don't look up…

Then he bent down and smelled her. Seriously. He took a big whiff like he was checking out supper on the stove. It was totally creepy. Because I know he was comparing what he'd smelled on the blankets—us—to her. *He knew.*

"Search the rest of the cottage," he ordered the second knight. Then he dragged the woman by the arm out to Lord Greco.

The second knight nosed around, tossing aside the blanket and pillow on the bed, peering underneath it. Then, with an eye toward the door, he snitched a half loaf of bread from the table, took a bite, shoved the rest under his tunic, and went outside, leaving the door open.

We could hear Signora Reggello arguing with Lord Greco outside. I looked up at Lia. If our hostess was in trouble, we'd have no choice but to come to her rescue.

"You gave shelter to two women last night," he ground out. "Tell me the truth now, or it shall not go well for you."

"Yes, all right, yes!"

"Why did you not tell us this immediately?"

She remained silent a moment.

"Why? Are you a traitor?"

"Nay! My own husband serves alongside you and these men! I did not know they were Sienese. They appeared only as women in need, without menfolk to guard them. Pretty girls like that..." Her voice trailed off, but the implication was clear.

"You believed we hunted them for pleasure," he said evenly. "Where did they go? When?" I didn't have to see him to know he was probably shaking her or getting in her face.

"I know not! I went to milk the cow, and when I returned, they were gone and you were riding up."

"The truth, now."

"That is the truth! I swear it!"

I tensed, getting ready to swing down as the fear in her voice increased. "Please, m'lord, spare a loyal woman. Please."

I changed my handhold, thinking through how I could get down and cause the least amount of pain.

"It was only when they promised me assistance with my vineyard that I gave them shelter. Would you not have done the same, were you in my position? Even now, the grapes rot upon our vines."

He sighed. "Do you swear to send word to me if you catch sight of these women again?"

"I swear it, m'lord. I swear it."

I could almost hear his sigh of frustration. He laid plans to send two men to the south, two to the north, and two back to the east, from where we'd come. "The rest of us and I shall divide and check each villein's face," he said. He thought we had merged into the crowds along the western road.

"They shan't be difficult to spot," said a knight. "They'll be the only two beauties heading *toward* Siena!"

The others laughed, but I did not hear Lord Greco's low, melodic voice join in.

"They are far more elusive than we anticipated," said a knight. "May I suggest an addition to the bounty upon their heads? I, for one, find this cat-and-mouse game…stirring."

Judging from their response, the others seemed to like that idea. A shiver ran down my back as Marcello's warning again ran through my head.

"Nay," Lord Greco said sternly. "Your reward shall be in glory and gold, as discussed. I have far greater plans for the Ladies Betarrini. They shall be of extreme value to us in our negotiations with Siena."

His troops quieted.

"Anything?" Lord Greco asked, obviously speaking to one of the men.

"Nay," the man returned. *The tracker.* He'd been off, trying to find our trail again. "The road is quite rocky here, impossible to find their path. Our only chance is to find them among the people."

Lord Greco turned his attention back to the old woman. "Did you give them clothing? What were they wearing?"

"Nay. They left with the same clothes upon their backs that they arrived in. Plain gowns, white blouses. Very dirty. Nothing noble about them."

"And their hair?"

"Falling down like young girls'," she said. "Like they hadn't had a comb through it in days."

"They still had their weapons with them?"

"Yes, m'lord. One with a sword at her back, one with a bow."

That was all they needed. They set off. But Lord Greco lingered. "Remember your oath, signora," he said.

"If I catch sight of them, I shall run to the road and give word to a soldier," she said.

I eyed Lia. Soon Signora Reggello would be back. I didn't want to kill her. So what? Tie her up and leave her? She might die of dehydration before someone found her. There were a hundred vineyards and farms around here. Maybe a neighbor would check on her...

The rest of the men rode off, and the woman returned to the cottage. She paused beneath us. "The bats in my belfry may come down now."

I studied her, silent in my shock.

"But don't let me see you," she said.

I smiled, understanding after a second. She'd promised to run for help if she *caught sight* of us. I nodded to Lia, and she swung down and I followed. It hurt more coming down. Or maybe since I wasn't rushing, quite so scared, I felt it more.

"If you knew we were in your rafters, why did you not hand us over to them?" I asked her back.

"It is not my way to betray those in need," she said, bending to set a stick upon the smoldering fire. "And you, clearly, have more than your share of enemies."

"But your husband—he fights for Firenze."

"As he should," she said with a nod. "But that is none of your affair. It would go on even if the Ladies Betarrini had not helped capture Castello Paratore." She waved dismissively toward the window. "Women are naught but pawns in the affairs of men and war. We must tend to our sisters." She glanced over her shoulder, in our direction, but stopped short of actually looking at us. "You shall change into my husband's clothing. Disguise yourselves as boys. Bind your chests, wear a hood. And get across the border as soon as possible."

She stood, went to a chest, and pulled out two threadbare tunics, shirts, and tights. It was fortunate for us that they were clean. And that Signore Reggello was taller than his wife. Quickly, we stripped and took the bandages that the old woman handed over her shoulder.

"Man, Gabi, that's gotta hurt," Lia said, unwrapping the bloody bands from my torso—a medieval version of a bra.

"Yeah, a bit."

I glanced down and saw the blue and green bruising across the lower right of my ribcage for the first time. The blood had come from a gash on my chest. Another branch. My sister began winding a new, fresh strip around me.

"I'll do it tightly. It'll be good to support those ribs—and take you down to a B-cup."

I returned her smile.

"Do you have any foxglove tea?" Lia asked over her shoulder as she tucked the end of the rags in at my waist.

"I might have a bit. I'll put some on over the fire. There's some porridge here too."

"Grazie, Signora."

We finished binding Lia's chest and put on the shirts, keeping the tights up with ropes, tied at the waist. We slipped into the tunics and then tried the boots. They fit me, but there was only one pair. Lia shrugged. "Let's hope no one looks at my feet."

"As long as we carry weapons, they'll ignore your girly slippers."

"I hope," she repeated.

I turned to face the old woman's back. "We owe you a great deal, Signora." I glanced at Lia. "We cannot very well take to the road now, as Lord Greco searches it. I suggest we give you a day's work in the vineyard, as we agreed, spend the night, and set off come morn. If that is an acceptable risk to you, that is."

She raised her head, shocked that we weren't fleeing immediately. "What if you are spotted?"

"What's to see?" I asked with a grin. "Naught but two peasant workers, boys, among your vines. And in a day's time, I wager we could get every decent grape to a wagon. Don't you agree, Evangelia?"

"At the same pace but with twice the finesse as menfolk," she returned.

"I'd be most grateful to you," said the old woman, her voice thick with emotion. "With what we could bring in, I might make it through the winter without needing to sell the cow."

I paused. Never in my life had I not had a glass of milk if I asked for it. Or food, for that matter. The longest I'd ever had to wait for a meal was a couple of hours when I was "starving." The way she spoke, with her crop mostly gone, I envisioned cold winter days stretching out with nothing to eat. The cow provided milk and cream, to use, drink, or trade for other food. She had to keep the cow. I knew it, understood the importance of such a thing, for the first time. What if her husband never came home from this battle? What if what she had on the farm was all she would ever have?

"Come," I said to Lia, now determined. "We shall work on the far side of the land," I said to our hostess. "Far from your line of vision."

By noon we'd finished half the vines. It was painful to pass by the clusters of collapsed orbs that had once been fat and promising grapes but now were nothing but spoiling raisins. It was like finding piles of dollars shredded to bits. So much waste....

I stood and shielded my eyes, staring down at the relentless columns of men that moved toward Siena. Was Siena sending equal numbers to meet them? This was swiftly moving to all-out war. Fortunately, few looked in our direction. To them, we were but peasants gleaning from the vines, picking off the last of the harvest.

"For the crows," Signora Reggello called out above us, setting a board down atop the edge of the well.

We smiled at each other and trudged to the top, first taking deep drinks of water and then inhaling the cheese and freshly baked bread. We sloshed it all down with a mouthful of wine from the jug—she would've considered it an insult if we hadn't—and then returned to the vines. As evening came on, swiftly becoming chilly, the stream of soldiers down below slowed to a trickle. We'd not caught sight of Lord Greco all day. By now, he was probably at the front. Maybe he considered us lost, our trail cold, his potential glory evaporated. Maybe he'd finally found something better to do. I hoped. He and that tracker dude freaked me out. They were way too dedicated to finding us. What had he meant, anyway? *Far greater plans…extreme value to us in our negotiations with Siena…*

Those had been some loaded words, all right. I wasn't sure what he meant, but I was pretty sure I didn't want to find out.

"Gabs," Lia hissed. I looked up and saw what had alarmed her. A finely dressed lord and six men were coming up the farm road on horseback.

I adjusted my hood. Lia had braided my hair and tied it with a triple knot, but I was still worried it'd come out.

The men stopped at the top of the hill before the cottage, and the old woman went to meet them. She talked with them for a long time, gesturing angrily to the vines. Then she sighed and looked to us. "Boys!" she called. "Come at once, grandchildren."

I glanced at Lia and she at me. We ducked our heads and trudged up the hill, trying to walk like guys.

"You have been conscripted, boys," the old woman said, as soon as we were near. "With the Lord's blessing, you shall see this battle through and return to me within a fortnight. Fetch your weapons. I shall get some provisions for you."

The nobleman sighed heavily. I could feel his eyes move over us, assessing, and he snorted in derision. "Why is that we can only find scrawny recruits in these hills? How old are you?"

He was talking to Lia.

"Fifteen, m'lord," she said, as low as she could, still staring at the ground. I saw, then, that she'd ditched her slippers and was barefoot.

"Fifteen, and still with the voice of a girl," he said.

"But decent with a bow and an arrow," she defended, clenching her fists like he had offended her.

At home, she had always gotten parts in the school plays. She was rockin' this role, I thought admiringly.

The lord laughed. "And your brother? He's skinny too, but at least he has some height on him. And boots."

"He doesn't say much," Lia said. "But you don't want to come against his sword."

I could feel the lord's smile upon me. "Well, I beg your pardon," he said to the woman. "It seems I rushed to judgment on your sons. If they are as good as they say, they shall do honor to your name."

"I prefer they come home alive, m'lord," she said, as any worried mother might. "Look after them."

We just might pull this off—

He sniffed, as if her demands were wearing thin. "Well, hasten upon your way, boys. Fetch your weapons and join us on the road. We shall be waiting. We have some Sienese dogs to slay on the morrow."

We went inside, and Lia sat down, hard, on the edge of the bed. She was trembling. I paced back and forth.

The old woman came inside and stared at the fire, still apparently trying to keep her word. "'Tis a blessing from above. They'll take you as close as you'd ever get on your own, to the border. You are as good as the stories say, with your weapons?"

"We hold our own," I said.

"Good. Then enter the battle and run, run as fast as you can, for home. You will be but a long day's walk from Castello Forelli."

I walked over to her, and she closed her eyes. I took her hands, bent, and kissed both her cheeks. "Grazie, signora," I said with a smile. *"Non dimenticherò mai."* I *wouldn't* ever forget her. She was one of the bravest women I'd ever met.

"We owe you so much," Lia said, bending to kiss her too.

The woman waved at us as if she thought we were silly. "You brought in my crop," she said. "When you could have run. It is I who am grateful. Go, now, with God. Back to your own people."

I turned and left the cottage, attaching my sword as I walked, Lia at my heels. *My own people.* Mom. Marcello. I longed for them, longed to be home at Castello Forelli.

Fortino came to mind, and then Romana. With two days left before their wedding, would they press on? Or had Fortino been called to battle too?

How had he not been? Hadn't Marcello said he was a tactical mastermind? It had been his plan to take Castello Paratore. And now Marcello was likely missing. How could Fortino not return, prepare for battle now that he was healthy? He had to be there already.

Man, Romana was going to be seriously ticked at me if I'd ruined her wedding. In Italia in this era, it wasn't so much about the ceremony—that was a small affair. But their version of a feast for a daughter of the Nine would put a Beverly Hills reception to shame, dollar for dollar.

Knowing how she'd treated me before, when she'd been engaged to Marcello, I knew somehow she'd see it as all my fault. I was sure of it.

I smiled. That was all right. It gave me more time to make sure she'd be good to Fortino. Be a real bride for him. Not some conniving, secretive wench just trying to get out from under Daddy's arm and make a name for herself. Fortino deserved more. He deserved love. So far, I'd seen a certain fondness, like she'd held for Marcello. But love? I didn't know that for sure.

"Gabi," Lia said. "Quit walking like a girl."

I pulled up a little, remembering, and looked to the lord and his men, still a hundred yards away. I ducked my head and changed my gait to a more lumbering, long-stepped rhythm. "Think they noticed?"

"No. But we have to watch it."

"Right." We walked on. "Lia, if they figure out we're girls, we immediately fight and run, got it?"

"Got it." She didn't hesitate. She'd probably heard Greco's men discussing their plans for us—what they'd consider a *real* reward—as clearly as I had. And if we were caught here, now, Lord Greco wasn't around to stop them with his bigger plans.

CHAPTER 17

I was glad that Signora Reggello had given us two capes, worn as they were, with their wide hoods. It struck me, then, that Lia probably wore the woman's, and I, the man's. There was no way the man had had two extra, not judging by their scant possessions. Most of the peasants around us wore them, especially with the cool autumn night. What would the old woman do without hers? If we lived through this, somehow, I had to send her a replacement.

Two knights rode up and teased us about being only big enough to spar with the Sienese children but then, in big-brother fashion, warned us to stay clear of Sienese knights. We nodded and trudged along. In time, they left us, and the nobleman in charge pulled up beside Lia. "No boots?" he grunted.

"Nay, m'lord," she said.

He blew out his breath in exasperation, mumbling about his impossible task, turning farmers into soldiers, and moved forward to the next group of conscripted men. In the distance we could see a vast number of tents and numerous campfires. Apparently, that was where we would spend the night.

The coming dark comforted me. It would help disguise us, and if these men were snoring, they wouldn't be looking at us. We just had to steer clear of the fires and keep our heads down.

"Lia," I said lowly. "Maybe we can again come to the aid of our people."

She dared to lift her head and glance at me. I quickly looked to the ground, and she followed suit. "If we can get near enough to those in command," I whispered, "we can find out their plan for tomorrow. Then…"

I made a circular gesture with my hand, not daring to say more as two knights approached us again.

Then, we could make our way to the Sienese, tell them of Firenze's plans, and help them turn the tide.

If the Fiorentini didn't kill us first.

I thought back to our battle against the Paratore knights. At least in that battle, the men wore either the Forelli gold or the Paratore crimson. How in the heck were we supposed to know who was who in this war? Thousands of us would look just like Lia and me.… We'd be as likely to die upon the sword of one side as the other, once we were intermingled.

I shivered and wrapped my arms around myself.

Belatedly, I remembered the knight beside me.

"You there, halt," he said.

"Me, sir?" I said, putting a fist to my chest.

"You. Show yourself."

I took a half breath. "I cannot, sir. My head, 'tis deformed, since childbirth," I said in a voice barely louder than a whisper. I kept my head stubbornly down, as if ashamed. "Should the others see me, sir…I might not get my chance to honor my father's name." I shook my head as if that was an intolerable thought.

He hesitated and seemed to think over my story. "Very well, then," he said at last. "See that you do."

When he was ten paces off, Lia nudged me. "You do Dad proud every day, Gabs," she whispered. "And I, for one, think your head is lovely. Even if your nose does lean to one side."

I laughed under my breath. "He'd be proud of you, too, Lia. Both of us."

"Mom must be going crazy with worry."

I sobered, thinking of Mom and her concern. I could picture her pacing the castle floors, wondering. I worried she had not made it back at all. She was no good with a bow or a sword. Her chief weapon had always been her brain. Which was good—but right now, I thought, fingering the rope of my sheath, I was glad for the heavy steel at my back.

"She knows we're strong," Lia said, reading my thoughts. "We'll be with her soon enough."

"But we cannot enter the castello. Not for another week or so, until we know we aren't sick."

It was her turn to fall silent. Where was Luca? Was he suffering? Sweating through the feverish dreams? Were there more buboes on his body? For most, the plague claimed and conquered its prey within four days, five tops. He'd been sick now for…I counted back. Three. Three days. Two since we'd seen him and Marcello.

Thoughts of Marcello made me almost sick with longing. Physically sick. What was wrong with me? I was so crazy in love it surprised me still. I'd never felt anything like it…and practically all I could think of was being with him again. I sighed, acknowledging it. This was no high school crush, this thing between Marcello and me. It was big. *Love.* Nothing compared. I wished he were here, to plan with me, talk it out. Reassure me. I put my hand to my chest, feeling my heart actually hurt with the need for him. If only I could feel his hand in mine, his arms around me.

"Gabs, your hand," Lia warned lowly.

I dropped it, remembering myself. *Marcello, where are you? Can you hear me?* I willed my thoughts to him, as if they could pass through the air. If only we had been able to remain together…how much different I would feel with him here, beside me… *We're heading back to the castello. Remember? That's what you told us. Please, please be on your way too. Meet us there, my love. Meet us there.*

We reached the edges of the camp as night fell. I never thought I'd be happy to be entering a camp, but my crazy lovesickness made me glad for the distraction. Here, there were makeshift tents, little more than blankets perched precariously on branches to fend off some of the chilly evening breeze. At the center were the more elaborate, regal multicolored tents with Firenze's flag flying from the top of each, visible in the flickering light of the fires.

Few but the commanders' tents seemed occupied, with everyone gathering around massive bonfires that climbed twenty feet in the sky. They were celebrating. Doing their man-thing, beasting up before battle. We saw men to our right painting their faces with mud. Others with stripes—laughing and shouting. They might as well be boys at Boulder High, jumping up for chest bumps, I thought.

I looked to my left as we neared the center of camp and glimpsed a couple of lords in their tent—this one a deep crimson color with fringe across the top of the doorway. Was this the big boss? The real guy in charge? Two noblemen were poring over a curling parchment map on a table as we passed. One glanced up at me, and I hurriedly looked to the ground.

I didn't know them. But then I laughed at myself. The only nobleman of Firenze I knew was Lord Greco, and he was still searching the road for us. I smiled. Never would he think that we'd dare to be here, among his men. It was perfect. Really, really perfect.

"You boys!"

Okay, almost perfect.

Lia nudged me, and we went to stand before the nobleman who'd dragged us from the vineyard. We paused before him.

"You've been assigned to assist the cooks."

Kitchen duty? I frowned. "Nay, m'lord," I said. "We must see battle come morn. Please," I added awkwardly.

He grabbed my hand and lifted it to the firelight. "Your hands are not strong enough to wield the sword upon your back."

"You might well be surprised," Lia said, lifting her head, apparently forgetting herself. Fortunately, her back was to the fire, her face in deep shadow. "Give me a target. Now. In the dark. If I don't hit it, we shall report to the cooks without complaint."

The nobleman pulled back a little. "Very well," he said tiredly. He waved around. "Surprise me."

Lia searched for a suitable target. Remembering the light, she didn't turn too far in one direction or another.

I sighed in relief. One clear look at her pretty face, and our hoax would be totally over.

"Is that your tent?" she asked, gesturing toward a structure, three over. She'd matched the color of his tunic to it.

"Yes."

"The flag at the top? Do you have another?"

"I do, but—"

No! Don't do it!

She didn't hear my silent plea. In two seconds she had an arrow atop her bow and the string pulled back, taking aim. Men paused around us, watching.

Her arrow flew toward the flag flapping in the breeze, one moment illuminated by the fire, the next in utter darkness. What if it passed by just as the wind—

But no. The arrow pierced the flag and dragged it down to the tent ceiling like a downed duck. The men beside us cheered and thumped Lia on the back. But we froze.

Because she may as well have screamed…that's how many people were looking our way.

I could feel the heat of the men's gaze on us. Now the nobleman was torn between being pleased with her skills and being ticked off about his flag. That wouldn't go over well with his boys, to see a flag pierced by an arrow before the day's battle had even begun. They might consider it an omen or something. I bit my lip and stared at the ground, fighting back an insane urge to laugh.

"Where did you learn such archery skills?" he asked.

"Piercing pigeons nibbling at my grandmother's vines," she said evenly.

"Very well. See that you pierce some of our enemy on the morrow."

"Yes, m'lord."

"Follow the line for your bowl of stew, and see that you bed down for the night over there, with the others." He pointed a threatening finger at us. "No revelry for my troops this night. Only rest. Understood?"

We nodded and moved, trying not to rush and give away our desire to escape him. We stood in line for half an hour to receive our big ladle of watery stew, then sat down to eat it. It was bland, tasteless, but we made ourselves eat it anyway, knowing we'd need the strength. I covertly stared across the fire, counting the men within my line of vision. There were more than a hundred in this circle, and there were nine others like it—with more men beyond in makeshift camps. Somehow we'd landed in a group of pros, mercenaries eager to enter another fight. More than a thousand here…

My heart stopped for a second and then pounded painfully.

What if this wasn't the only camp? How many more men fought for Firenze?

"Wait here," I murmured to Lia. I rose, stretched, and ambled toward the latrines. Just before I reached them, I veered left and moved behind the noblemen's tents, then between two, testing the boundaries. No one stopped me.

Lia fell in step beside me. I sighed, seeing her bare feet beside mine. "I told you to stay back there," I said lowly.

"You need me," she returned.

We passed the crimson tent, the color eerily reminding me of the Paratores. But Lord Paratore was vanquished. Released from

Siena's prison, yes, in exchange for a hundred of Siena's. But without a home. Honor. Or ears.

Marcello believed it likely he was ostracized from noble company, even banished from Firenze-held lands.

Unless…

I paused at the empty tent doorway, where I'd seen two nobles leaning over a map. It still sat there, but there was no one else in sight.

"*Gabi.*"

"Go to the side, between the tents," I whispered over my shoulder. "Keep watch."

I was inside, blinking in surprise at my own stupid bravery. *Focus, Gabi, focus.* Two candles burned on a side table beside a narrow bed. I turned and released the rope that held the tent door to one side. It swung across the empty space and stilled, giving me a crazy sense of safety. I grabbed the candles and went to the map.

The first thing I saw in the corner made me want to throw up. *Prepared for Lord Cosmo Paratore.*

He was here. Somehow, he was here.

He'd marshaled enough support to come, undoubtedly to try to regain his name, if not his land. I didn't know those two guys who'd been in here earlier, but it wouldn't take much for Lord Paratore to identify me or Lia, disguised or not.

I shuddered, remembering his accusation. *They're not who they say they are!* And my order, to cut off his ears…

Gabi, this is important. It was my own voice but deep and demanding. Different, somehow. And yet known.

I focused on Paratore's pen and corked ink well on the desk. He'd been here, writing. I shook my head as if I could shake out the scary memories of the man as easily as water from my ears.

I reached out trembling hands and leaned down on the table to force myself to study the map, feeling the seconds pass with each pound of my heart. Clearly, I was looking at Siena's and Florence's territories. I could see the jagged line of the border. I could see the Roman road we had traveled to get here, the camp, marked with an indigo-inked star. "Firenze's finest," I muttered.

Across the valley from us was an indigo square, just between the border and Castello Paratore and Castello Forelli. There, the border line had been changed, hatched out, moved to denote the lands won that night last summer. Along the border, there were four others. Sienese troops assembling, I guessed.

I frowned and my eyes returned to Castello Paratore and Castello Forelli. Except on this map, Castello Forelli had been renamed Castello *Rossi*. And lands far beyond Forelli borders had been shaded in and labeled Rossi too.

Was it an error? A shiver of foreboding ran down my back.

My frown deepened as I forced my eyes beyond the name.

There were five squares.

There were seven stars. Three more were among them, drawn with a finer line and a date: *21 Sept.*

September twenty-first. I counted back, trying to figure out what day it was now.

The twentieth, best I could guess. So, if I was reading this right, four thousand more soldiers would be on the border come tomorrow.

Men passed by, laughing and shouting. I straightened, easing a dagger from the back of my roped waistband. But they moved on, and I forced myself to take a deep breath and study the map again.

Arrows pointed to the two stars on either end and swept around, through Umbria and Lazio—the traitorous neighbors—coming around and behind Siena's men. These were dated *22 Sept.*

Was Siena prepared for this onslaught? How could they know what was soon upon them?

I frowned at the map, trying to make better sense of it. Four of the stars were in deep forest; apparently they intended to sneak through the trees. Could a thousand men at a time truly remain hidden? With scouts out?

I knew these hills, and her forest, knew how dense the trees could be in places. *Yeah*, I reluctantly admitted, *it's possible.* If they didn't light fires. Which they might just be dedicated enough to do.

My eyes went back to the lighter-colored stars. The twenty-first. September twenty-second, the following day.

Fortino and Romana's wedding date.

The last day of the temporary peace treaty. The day all of Siena had been poised to celebrate and rejoice.

A symbolic moment to take back what Firenze and Paratore believed was stolen from them. And by the looks of this map, much more…They were gunning for five castles on the outer borders, Castello Forelli among them. Did they have aid from within? Was Lord Rossi truly a traitor?

I heard voices coming my way. This time straight on.

Lia whistled the first few notes of a top-ten hit from the twenty-first century. Hurriedly, I grabbed a candle and tried to set it back on the side table, but it was flimsy, and collapsed. The candle tipped toward the side of the tent, a brown spot appearing almost instantly. Flame caught and raced upward.

They were at the door. I had no choice but to cut my way out.

I used my dagger to jab into the back of the tent, then dragged it down. It stuck on a seam, only a foot long when I heard a man shout. "You there—thief!" He paused. "Fire! *Fire!*" he screamed.

I glanced back and met his eyes.

He stared at me. Paratore.

Belatedly, I turned away. I was sure my clothes confused him, but he'd seen me, looked into my eyes. I rammed the knife down, through the seam and dived through, wondering if he would grab my ankles as I did so.

But the fire was spreading too fast, already licking down the back of the tent too, keeping him away.

"Stop them!" Lord Paratore cried. "Out back! Stop them!"

Lia pulled me the rest of the way out, her eyes wide. We rushed away. "What'd you do?" she said with a groan.

"I couldn't help it, I—"

"Stop!" cried a man behind us, three, almost four tents away now. "You two, halt!"

We looked at each other. It wasn't like we were going to be able to outrun him. He'd call down the entire camp on us. Slowly, we turned. It was one of the noblemen from the tent, one who had been there earlier. I could tell from the tunic.

"Let me see your hands!"

We put them out before him. I scanned the crowd behind him. Others were being searched. Most stared at the burning tents, the peasants laughing behind their hands.

"Lift up your tunics. Let me see your waistbands."

He wanted to see if we were the Paratore thieves, assuming we'd taken something. But it wouldn't be a good thing, us lifting our tunics. He might figure out we had hips.

"Fire! Fire!" cried a man, running past us. It was spreading among the tents. Hurriedly, other noblemen and servants were madly collapsing their tents. "Go for water! Down by the river!"

"Do it now!" said the nobleman, drawing his sword. "Let me see your belt!"

I glanced at Lia and nodded once. She turned to him and lifted her tunic, higher than he expected, giving him an eyeful of her flat stomach, a wisp of a belly button, and the graceful curve of hips.

It had the desired effect. His sword tipped to the ground, and his mouth went slightly agape. She stared him in the face, then grinned.

At that moment, I kicked his sword to the ground. He turned in a daze toward me. I pulled back and belted him with my closed fist.

The pain shrieked through my arm, shoulder, neck, and up into my head.

But he spun and went down, just like in the movies.

Others were pausing, looking our way in the odd, flickering light of the tents on fire. Beyond them, Lord Paratore plowed forward, shoving people aside, looking left, just turning toward us…and I could see the red, raw skin where his ear had been.

"Run," I said to Lia. Her hood was already off, her blond hair streaming behind her. Men stepped aside as we charged toward them, mouths open in surprise.

"You fools!" Paratore cried. "Do you not see the enemies right before you? Catch those two! They are the *Ladies Betarrini!*"

CHAPTER 18

"Well, that's not good," I panted, hearing our name in the air behind us as if it had grown wings and was flying around the camp, shrieking its repetition to everyone it passed. We were the symbol of defeat. The reason they were all here. And now the sole focus of a thousand men.

We jumped from camp and into the woods, holding hands so we didn't lose each other in the dark. We held our other hands out, guarding against branches that slowed us down, desperately seeking a path. And taking a beating while we did so.

"Here they come," Lia grunted.

I glanced back. The forest was alive with torches, more arriving by the second.

"Burn them out!" bellowed Paratore.

"Is he insane?" Lia asked in a whisper. "He intends to burn down the forest to kill us?"

"Yeah."

"Here," she said. "Come on." She yanked me to the right, and my tights ripped on a thorny bush.

"Lia. This is my only pair."

She ignored my weak joke and we rushed on. We found our stride and tore down the path as fast as we could, one in front of the other now. After a while, freaked that they'd find the path too, we cut right and moved through the trees again. Slowly, we were making our way to the border.

I thought. Unless we were getting totally turned around in the woods.

Which was possible, since we were operating by gut instinct and in the total dark. For the thousandth time, I wished I had my cell and its compass app. Or GPS. *Yeah, that'd be helpful...*

We hit a patch of boulders and immediately started climbing them. Up top, we paused. We could see torches coming our way, but fewer of them. They'd divided up; obviously they didn't know where we were.

"Which way is south?" I asked Lia, looking up. Here, away from the fires and torchlight, we were again under the blanket of a thousand stars. The Milky Way was more like the Creamy Way in Toscana; you could see her millions of glittering stars so clearly. Stargazing was so good here, in fact, that it made it harder to pick out the major constellations. Fortunately, Mom and Dad had always been big on us getting to know the night skies when we were little, dragging us out in the dark for meteor showers. But that'd been a few years...

"Big Dipper," she said, speaking behind me. "See it?"

I turned and studied the sky with her. "Got it. So if that's the North Star off the end, then south is...this way."

I turned to my right, fighting the feeling that it was the wrong direction. "Right? This is south?" I picked my way down a boulder, tapping my foot out, reaching for the next.

"Right," she said.

The assurance in her voice calmed my fears a bit. Lia had always had a better sense of direction than I.

We were halfway down the rock face—this side twice as high as the other, obviously some sort of cliff descending into a valley—when we heard voices above, not thirty feet away. They'd caught up to us, impossibly fast. Or we'd been too slow, picking our way down, trying to avoid a total freefall.

We stilled. I squeezed Lia's hand and let her go so we could each slip into a crevice in the rocks.

"They came through here, m'lord," said a man, looking down the cliff.

Lord Greco's tracker. So they'd joined the party too. *Super.*

"Right here," said the tracker. "They moved through these boulders and down."

Man, I hate that dude. What? Can he see a pebble out of place?

Torchlight grew long around us, but we remained in shadow. I found myself thanking God that there was a large boulder directly above us, giving us a bit of overhang.

"Do you truly believe they made it down there?"

"They've proven fairly versatile in their capabilities among the rocks and forests, m'lord," he said. He was coming down.

"True enough. They head toward Sienese lands."

"We shall cut them off before they reach it."

That was enough for me. Lia, too, I guess, since she was rising up and drawing an arrow.

"There they are!" cried Lord Greco. "Over here!" he shouted. "Here!"

I groaned inside but began scrambling down the rocks, too fast, scraping my palms and forearms, landing painfully hard on the rock below me when I slid. "Come on, Lia!" I demanded.

"I can hold them off," she said over her shoulder. "You go."

"No," I said, alarmed at her words. "We go together. Come. Come, *now*."

She shot one more arrow, and up above, I saw a knight crumple.

"Can't you get that tracker dude?" I asked, when she reached me. "It'd be handy to get him off our tail."

"Uh, *yeah*," she said, and we slid down to the next rock. "But he's good. He seems to anticipate my shots."

"Like any good hunter with his prey," I said. "That's just super fantastic."

We slid down the next rock, and then the next. But when we hit that one, our combined weight seemed to shake it loose from the cliffside and it gave way, striking the next, which dislodged it. "Look out!" I cried.

We were in a rockslide. *How far to bottom?* I thought, longing for the base to meet our feet. To be sliding, unable to see…How high was this crazy hill? Or were we on a mountain?

I grunted as I hit my injured ribs on another rock.

I didn't need the stars in the sky. They were dancing in my head, then. Really. I always thought it was just in cartoons, but no—

We hit bottom. Pain ran up my ankles, calves, thighs. I felt a burning tear in the back of my right thigh and collapsed all the way to the ground.

I gasped for breath. "Lia? You okay?" I managed to ask.

"Yeah," she said, rising. "Other than my feet and hands getting all torn up. Come on. At least we're ahead of them now. They won't want to take our express route." I could tell from the direction of her voice that she was looking up. "But there are more probably coming around the hill," she said. "We've gotta hurry."

I forced myself to rise on my good leg. Tentatively, I tried my other. I gasped.

"Gabs…"

I panted, trying to avoid my sudden desire to cry and not stop. "It's not good, Lia. When we hit—something happened to my leg. The big muscle in back of my right thigh."

"Your hamstring?" I could hear the panic in her voice.

"Yeah. Not so good when you're trying to outrun the bad guys, huh?"

"C'mon," she said, sliding under my right arm. "Try and keep your weight off of it."

We limped on for five minutes, now on a small road that seemed to circle the base of the hill. As much as we were making decent time on it, we knew that if those that pursued us were on it too, we'd soon be overtaken. I heard a horse whinny, and Lia looked back over her shoulder.

We dashed into the woods again, but it was slow going. She had to let go of me, the trees were so dense. I was hopping and making too much noise. She cried out once in a while, her bare feet getting cut up by pinecones and sticks and thorns. When we reached a creek, still running a couple inches deep, I sat down and looked up at her. "It's no use," I said.

"What?" she asked, turning to face me.

"This is where we split—"

"No, Gabi. No."

I reached out and took her shoulders. "Listen to me. Listen!"

"No. C'mon. We can't wait here. They'll be here any minute!"

"Exactly."

She stilled.

"What I saw in that tent...we have to get word to Fortino, Lia. They have twice the men that Siena anticipates. I'm sure of it. Tell them thousands are hidden, deep in the forest. They plan to send thousands around on two flanks, through Umbria and Lazio. They intend to strike on Fortino's wedding day—and take Paratore's castle back, along with all the other outlying castles. And tell him...tell him that I saw a map that had renamed Castello Forelli as Castello *Rossi*." He could figure out what that meant and what to do about it.

"This is not our fight, Gabi," she said, gripping my arms and shaking me back to the present.

"It is now," I said. "There's only *one* way to change Castello Forelli into Castello Rossi—and Mom will be right in the middle of it."

She was quiet. We'd seen firsthand what came down when a castle changed ownership. I'd almost died during our last castle takeover.

"You run down this creek," I went on. "Keep your feet in the water as much as possible. That'll throw off the tracker. With luck, it will lead you to that river that winds between the castles, beneath the tombs."

"And you?"

"I'll stay here and distract them."

"Distract them? *Dis*—Gabi, they'll *kill* you."

I swallowed hard. "No. They won't. Remember? We're worth more alive than dead."

I could feel her peering through the dark, trying to see my face. "But, Gabs, Marcello said that—"

"I know what he said," I bit out. "Now go! Please! Find Marcello, Luca. Rally the men. And come and find me, as soon as you can. Wherever I am. I'll be waiting. You understand me? I'll be waiting. I'm counting on you, just as Siena now counts on you."

She paused. We could hear the men, again drawing near. "Go, Lia," I said, my voice cracking.

Lia was crying now too. "I'll come for you, Gabi. I promise."

She hugged me then, hard. Clung to me.

"Go," I said through my tears.

"I'll do as you say," she said. "But I won't leave you just yet." She pushed away from me and ran.

"What?" I asked.

But she did not respond. I heard the clatter of the rocks on the far side of the stream and then she was in the trees. I lost sight of her dim form.

They were upon me. Horsemen, coming out of the forest on a wide path we had not been as fortunate to find. I turned, trying to hide my bad leg, drawing my sword.

Their torchlight caught, surrounded, held me.

Three knights stared at me, as if wondering if their eyes deceived them. One opened his mouth, finding his tongue, and was about to shout, when Lia's arrow came whizzing out of the forest on the far side and sliced through his neck. He gurgled and fell, as the other two edged away, trying to find the source of the arrow.

Another one took an arrow to the shoulder. It hit with such force that he toppled backward over the hind end of his horse.

The third shouted for help, edging his horse around and into the trees. Lia's arrow stuck in the trunk of one directly before him. "Over here! They're here!" he yelled.

I grabbed madly for the reins of one of the horses as it came by, pulling it up short, crying out when I was dragged a few feet, the pain rolling through me in waves. I could hear the others coming and thought about mounting, racing away. But I knew in an instant that my leg would not allow me to hold on. I'd confuse the mare with my unbalanced hold. "Lia!" I called. "Come! Take the horse! Go!"

She paused and then ran from the wood, a hundred feet downstream from me, and I slapped the horse's flank, sending her to my sister. Lia was atop the mare in seconds. We could hear the others now, a collective roar. A hundred men.

"Go with God," I said, watching with satisfaction as she tore off down the creek. *Please, God, be with her,* I prayed silently.

At least her bare feet wouldn't suffer more abuse, I thought.

The third horseman came galloping past me before I remembered he was still there, in pursuit of Lia, still carrying a torch.

I moved without thought, drawing my last dagger from my waistband, aiming with my left, like a rifleman taking his target through the crosshairs. I let the dagger fly, visualizing it circling, end over end, toward his back. Willing it to catch up to him before he was out of range…

He cried out, dropped the torch to the ground, where it sputtered and sizzled on the water's edge. Then he fell to the creek, obviously dead. His horse reared up.

I limped toward it, using my sword as a sort of cane.

But it was no use. In seconds, they were there—thirty or more coming—running down either bank, surrounding me.

Cheering, jeering, leering.

They closed the circle and began closing in, their eyes on my sword.

As I circled, trying to keep them at bay like a cat surrounded by a pack of dogs, I could see that they understood that I was hurt. Weak. Vulnerable.

It seemed to make them meaner. Fed their lust for death, like a shark smelling blood in the water.

I was so scared I almost peed my pants.

And that made me angry. "Yes!" I cried saucily, gesturing for them to come closer. "Draw near so that I might slice your fat throats!" My eyes widened and I smiled. "The closer you are to one another, the easier target you shall make for my sister."

That put them off a bit. Some stared at me, seeing if I was bluffing. Others were looking around, pulling back a step, studying the woods.

"These two knights took arrows!" cried a man from the back. "She's here, somewhere, the archer!"

"She is not here, you fools," Lord Paratore cried from the outer edges of the growing mob. Obviously, losing the outside of his ears had not impacted his hearing. He was shoving aside men, raking his way inward toward me, as if pushing aside piles of autumn leaves.

Men fell on either side, shouted, grew silent when they saw who it was.

He paused at the edge of the circle and looked me up and down. "If Lady Evangelia Betarrini were here," he said, never releasing me with his eyes, "many more of you would be taking arrows to the gut." He stepped forward, watching me, smirking when he saw I was favoring my left leg. "Ahh, here is the reason you divided. One She-Wolf came up lame, no?"

I could see he'd decided on his path of attack. I pushed back my hair, over my shoulder, out of my way, lifting my sword. I tried to ignore the gruesome nubs of his ears, wondering if he'd take mine as payback.

He never paused as he approached, drawing his sword as if settling in for a friendly spar. I managed to block his first blow, feeling the pain radiate down my arms and shoulders as I held him back. But his fury fueled his movements, and he focused on forcing me to my right leg, again and again. With four, maybe five strikes, my sword went skittering away over the rounded creek stones. The men cheered.

I closed my eyes, waiting for what would come next.

He grabbed hold of my hair, winding it in his fist, and I cried out, reaching up.

He pulled my face close to his. I could smell the rot of his teeth, saw again where the Sienese had knocked some of them out. "Where is your sister?" he bit out, word by word.

"I know not."

He let go of my hair and slapped me, hard, with the back of his hand. Then hauled me up again by the hair, pulling my head

back until I could feel his breath on my throat. "Where…is…your…
sister?" he screamed. He knew what I'd seen on that map; he feared
she was off to do exactly as I had told her. *Tell Fortino. Warn Siena.*

I let a smile begin to spread across my face, feeling a little hysterical, distant.

"Deep in the wood," I said. "Across the creek. Look for her, won't
you, m'lord? She'd love to sink an arrow into your neck."

"M'lord," called a knight. "One man down, dagger in his back.
But the two that took arrows—one of their horses is missing."

Paratore pulled me closer. "She had better not reach Siena, or I
shall slice the skin from your beautiful body myself," he whispered
in my ear. He tossed me aside, and I fell to the rocks. The pain from
my thigh and ribs shook me so fiercely, I thought I might throw up.

"Fifty of you, down this creek bed. See that you find Lady
Evangelia Betarrini and bring her back in chains, or don't come back
at all. She seeks to warn Siena of our attack."

I tried to rise, but Paratore put a boot to my back and shoved
me down. If I was going to throw up, I hoped I could hold it until I
could do so all over him.

"Twenty more of you take to the woods, just to be certain she is
not intending to make her way under the cover of trees. We all know
how wolves like the shadows of the forest."

Men chuckled. Troops set off at once. I closed my eyes, hearing
the thunderous sound of all those horses, their sole task to capture
my sister. *Hurry, Lia…*

He was behind me, stepping down hard, keeping me from
breathing. The pain was so great from my ribs, I cried out with the
last bit of air in my lungs. He was untying the tunic at my back. He

lifted me up, leaving the vintner's old tunic on the stones before me, leaving me covered with nothing but my thin shirt and the strips of cloth Lia had wound around my torso that morning. I faltered, hunched over, gasping for air.

He motioned for two knights to come forward. "Hold her arms."

I focused on finding my breath as he studied his gloved hands. "Do you know," he said, turning toward me and cocking his head, "that 'tis illegal in Firenze for a woman to dress as a man?"

"How fortunate for me," I shot back, "that my loyalties lie with Siena."

He stared back into my eyes. "Ahh, but you are not in *Siena*," he said. He took hold of the neckline of my shirt and ripped it down the center. Cold air rushed across my torso. He smiled and then backed away, lifting a hand behind him at me, as if I were a bit of evidence for a prosecuting attorney. "This is what becomes of women who are allowed to set their feminine side aside and act as men!"

The men growled their dismay. Again, Marcello's words of warning came echoing through my mind. *Fight—*

Paratore turned. "Mayhap this wench need only be reminded what it is to be created *female*," he said, spitting the last word in my face. He paused and eyed me up and down, studying the knot of rope that held my tights up. *Please, God, no…*

"That is quite enough, Lord Paratore," said Lord Greco, now shoving his way into the inner circle. "Lady Betarrini is my charge. The lords of Firenze asked *me* to fetch her and her sister."

"And yet it is *I* who has captured her," Paratore said, stepping between me and Lord Greco.

Lord Greco stared at Paratore, not rising to his bait. "You sent men after her sister?"

"Fifty. They will return with her before sunup."

Lord Greco looked to the tracker at his side and lifted his chin in the direction of the creek. "Go and make certain that is the way of it." The tracker set off to do his master's bidding. I sensed Paratore bristle.

Fantastic. Caught between two dudes in a serious turf war. Could this night get any better?

"I shall make it known that it was you and your men who brought Lady Gabriella Betarrini to bay." He moved around Lord Paratore and gruffly took hold of my arm. "The lords of Firenze will be most grateful."

Paratore glanced back at me and eyed me up and down again, considering. At last, he spit out, "'Tis the eve of battle. I've already expended far too much of my strength on this wench."

I didn't know what freaked me out more. The idea of being at the mercy of Lord Paratore—or that they planned to attack Siena tomorrow. *Tomorrow.* Had I counted the days wrong?

Paratore wrenched Greco's hand from my arm, and I tensed, waiting for him to grab me back, or for a blow. But Paratore only came close, staring down at me. Men hooted and called. Slowly, a smile lifted the corners of his mouth. I glanced to the side, away from his horrid teeth and ear holes. "You'll go with him now, She-Wolf," he said, his breath washing down the side of my cheek. "But after we deal this deathblow to Siena and those who serve her, I shall come and claim you as my rightful bounty. I shall teach you what it means to be a woman in my keep."

Defiant, I dragged my eyes up to meet his.

He studied me. "Yes," he said, nodding. "It shall be a pleasure to see that spirit beaten from your eyes. You'll remember my dungeon, and the devices there…" He circled me, letting me remember the horrible contraptions he'd threatened Lia with. "You shall not escape me as your sister once did. And far greater will be the joy of taking Marcello Forelli's woman as my own."

"You shall never have me."

He gave me a closed-lip, sly smile. "Won't I? Don't be so certain, She-Wolf." He wrapped an arm around me and then pulled me to him, making me gasp with pain. I pushed against him, struggling to get away, but he held me effortlessly. He grabbed one wrist, turned it, and pushed it up, behind my back, stilling my struggle at once.

The men cheered again, closing in, enjoying this spectacle.

"I shall hunt down Fortino and cut his throat. Relieve Lady Rossi of her bridal duties, so that she can come to Firenze, where she shall be received as a queen."

I drew back. So Romana was in on it?

"Lord Paratore," Lord Greco cut in, but Paratore ignored him, leaning in toward me.

"But I shall allow Marcello to live. I want him to know what it is to be without his home. And even better, to *know* that you are in *my* keep. To cut your ears from your head. Or mayhap your nose."

"Lord *Paratore*," said Lord Greco, stepping in again. "Release her to me."

Lord Paratore abruptly let me go and carefully set my hand upon Lord Greco's arm, as if we were at a ball and Lord Greco was merely my next dance partner. Which in a crazy way, I suppose he was…

"Do not pine for me, She-Wolf," he called, hands lifted as he backed away from me.

The men laughed and then turned to follow him. All but twelve, apparently Lord Greco's men.

I was shaking, feeling weak. I glanced up at him. "I suppose I ought to be grateful to you," I said. Maybe I could wiggle my way into his heart. Make him like me. Help me out. Or at least weaken his resolve—

"Ah, no," he said, sweeping his cape from his shoulders and gently wrapping it around mine. Carefully, kindly he tied it at my neck, as if I were a child on my way out to school, then met my gaze. "While I am not the vindictive, lecherous cad that Lord Paratore is, you'll find that I have far greater ambitions. And that, my friend, can make me quite ruthless."

I swallowed. He was really handsome. I mean, really, really handsome. Making me think it wouldn't be hard to pretend—pretend that I was attracted to him. But there was no warmth in his watchful gaze, and his words had sent a cold shudder of fear through me, slamming down on any hope like a gate across a castle door.

Marcello had not feared Lord Paratore when he warned me—I was pretty sure he didn't even think Paratore was part of the mix. He had assumed Paratore was exiled, long gone.

He had feared that others in Firenze would capture me.

Men like Lord Greco.

And I was not eager to find out why.

CHAPTER 19

It was well past midnight when we returned to camp, me riding behind Lord Greco. He positioned guards on the outside of all four sides of the tent. I glanced to my left, considering my chances at escape, but when I glanced back to the right, Lord Greco stared down at me with a look that said *don't even think about it.*

Sighing, I preceded him into his tent, and with a low-toned word, he sent a servant off to fetch bandages and hot water.

He laid out a clean shirt and another pair of leggings across the bed. "Forgive me, m'lady," he said with a small smile. "I didn't think to pack a gown for you."

"It will be well," I said. I'd be swimming in his clothes, but at least they were clean.

He ducked his head and stared at me. "Are you able to manage changing? The camp physician should be here any moment…"

"Yes," I said quickly. "I shall manage."

He picked up the clothes and nodded to a makeshift screen across the floor, little more than a blanket hanging over a stretched rope, in the corner. "Forgive me, m'lady, but I must keep my eyes on you at all times." He lifted a brow. "Given that you have experience in slipping through the backs of tents. You shall find reasonable modesty there."

Glaring at him, I grabbed the shirt and leggings from his hands and turned to limp over to the screen. There, I untied his cape and set it to one side, then eased my tattered shirt from my shoulders. I looked down at my bandages, dirty, bloody, knowing that I'd done more damage to my ribs this evening. I glanced at Lord Greco over the blanket's edge, making sure he was staying put; he stared dolefully back into my eyes, the only part of me he could see.

I quickly glanced down, untied the rope at my waist and let the ragged, filthy leggings fall. Gingerly, I turned my right leg outward, trying to see the back of my leg. Already, the bruising was stretching across the span of it and down toward my knee. *Hammy. The ol' hamstring. Yessiree, I really did it this time. But at least it's not a slice to my gut again. Now that was bad…*

"Lady Betarrini," he said.

I peeked over the blanket, and he gestured toward a tall, spidery man beside him. "The doctor is here to see to you. If you wish for him to examine your leg, you can come out in the shirt alone. I shall turn my back."

I hesitated, even as he turned. "I thought you had to keep your eyes on me at all times."

"You wish for me to watch?"

"Nay!"

He smiled over his shoulder and then turned fully away again. "Even you would not be brave nor foolish enough to flee into a camp full of soldiers in naught but a shirt."

He had me there. I sighed and then edged around the screen.

The doctor gave me a kindly, fatherly look. "Come closer to the light, m'lady, if you please. Here, to this chair."

I limped over to him, and he studied me from head to toe, viewing me in the detached manner of a medical professional. He took my hands and turned them palm up, frowning over the deep gouges there and along my left arm. He let go of them and lifted my hair, finding the cut on my forehead, the other at the top right of my chest. "Turn, please."

I did so and he squatted behind me, his knees cracking as he did so. I flinched when he touched my leg with cold, thin fingers.

"Forgive me, my dear. Now this might hurt a bit more. Hold onto that post, please."

I nodded and tried not to scream as he dug his thumbs in and ran them down the length of my thigh, apparently feeling for a tear. He took hold of my ankle and slowly made me flex my knee, and I cried out. I gripped the post so hard I thought I might leave dents in the wood. Lord Greco was before me in an instant, covering my hands with his, frowning in concern. Confused by the empathy I saw on his face, I studied him, but then the doctor's hands were examining my hurt leg again. I bit my lip as I screamed, trying to keep it to myself. And failing.

The doctor rose. "I am done," he said to me. He looked to Lord Greco. "Injured muscle," he said. "It shall take some time to heal, but I do not believe it is torn. We must bandage it tightly, and she must rest."

"No dancing," Lord Greco said to me, his furrowed brow lifting in the center.

"Oh, and there was that ball I had hoped to attend," I returned.

Lord Greco gave me a small smile. He admired me. I felt it. It ignited a tiny hope in my heart.

"Please, m'lord, turn away again as I examine the lady's ribs."

Lord Greco immediately did as he was told. I studied his broad back as the doctor methodically unwound the strips from my torso, trying to ignore the humiliation of the moment. Rodolfo Greco. He and Marcello had been friends as boys. He was taller than Marcello by a couple of inches. But they had similar backs, strength through the shoulders, arms.

I covered my breasts as the last of the bandage slipped away. The doctor turned me toward the light and gently ran his cold fingers along one rib and then another, then still another. "Broken, two of them," he muttered. "With more severely bruised." He looked into my eyes and let Lord Greco's shirt fall to cover my torso like a nightshirt again. "The Lord kept you from death. Had those ribs moved much more, they might have punctured a lung."

"God be praised," I said numbly.

"Along with his saints," said the doctor, nodding. "I shall wash your scrapes and cuts, and bind them. Then I shall bind your ribs and thigh. Give you something for the pain"—he arched an admiring brow—"which must be considerable. That should keep you until morn." He took me by the elbow and ushered me over to Lord Greco's narrow bed. There he did as he had said, seeing to all my needs in a max of twenty minutes. At the end, he slipped some powder from a parchment packet and leaves from a small box into a cup of hot water. He let it steep for a minute, then strained out the leaves and handed it to me. "Drink it down. It shall help you sleep."

I hesitated. The last time I'd taken medicine a doctor had given me, I'd very nearly lost my life.

He straightened and looked over to Lord Greco.

"Drink it," Lord Greco said, staring at me, hard.

Reluctantly, I brought it to my lips and smelled. It didn't have any of the cut-grass smell the poison had held. It smelled of spearmint and flowers. I sipped, rolling it over my tongue.

"It is what he says it is, m'lady," Lord Greco said with a sigh.

"I shall return come daybreak," said the doctor.

"'Tis but hours away," Greco said.

The doctor nodded. "Once the battle begins, I shall not have time to see to her."

"'Tis well. We shall be away on the morrow, en route to Firenze." He glanced back at me, as I drained the cup, and then to the doctor. "No signs of the plague on her?"

The tall, thin man's eyes narrowed, and then he shook his head. "Nay. You should have warned me, m'lord, that you suspected it."

"Thank you, Doctor," he said, ignoring the man's complaint. They walked to the tent flap, and Lord Greco paused to speak to the knights outside.

Tomorrow. He meant to take me to the city tomorrow. My eyes drifted to the southern wall of the tent. *Marcello...*

Greco was before me, then. How'd he do that? He moved as swiftly and stealthily as a cat! My head felt groggy, like I'd had too much wine. The medicine...

"Lie down," he said gently.

I frowned. Did he mean to—

"Nay, m'lady," he said, reading the fear in my eyes. "We are both in need of rest. Trust me. Lie down. On your back."

I hardly had a choice, with him hovering over me. I lowered myself, suspiciously staring up at him. Crazily there were three of him now. All three Lord Grecos moved to the bottom of the cot and unfolded the heavy blanket, pulling it up and over me. They really weren't looking at me with anything more than the eyes of a friend. *Maybe they're gay…*

I closed my eyes, knowing it was the drug making me think there were three when there was only one. I was so terribly tired. So terribly, horribly, mind-blowingly weary.

I peeked just in time to see him—thankfully back to one person—throw out a second blanket beside the cot, sit down on it, and then put out his hand. "Your right hand, please."

Frowning sleepily, I reached out my hand. He took it and tied a thin rope around my wrist, tight enough that there was no way I'd get it off without a knife, and yet still with enough room to give my fingers circulation. "This way," he said, tying the other end of the three-foot rope to his right wrist, "I shall know if you even try to roll over in your sleep."

"Excellent. I always wanted a watchdog."

"Every She-Wolf deserves one," he returned evenly. He finished his task and stretched out beside me.

I thought of trying to wait him out, wait until he was snoring to work on the knots that held my wrist. But as I listened to his slow, rhythmic breathing, watched the rise and fall of his shoulder in the candlelight, I knew that this night, there was no fight left in me.

CHAPTER 20

It was my throbbing head and ribs that woke me first, as dawn lit the outside, changing the color of the tent from plum to lavender. Kind of a girly color for a knight, I thought. *Maybe he really is gay.*

As if he sensed me looking at him, Lord Greco's eyes squinted shut and then opened wide, staring directly at me. Our gaze held for a long moment.

It was then I knew he was no ally. No friend. He tended to me, did not harm me, because I was worth something. The fatted calf on my way to slaughter.

"What shall be your reward for delivering me to Firenze?"

"Far more than you can imagine," he said, sitting and untying his end of the small rope that bound us together.

"The Forellis," I began. "You know them. They have significant means. I could—"

He lifted a finger to his lips, gently shushing me. He shook his head and rose to untie my wrist. "This is a matter of honor. Though I once considered Marcello Forelli a friend, my loyalties will forever be with Firenze." He finished and turned from me, walking to the basin and pouring water into it.

Outside, I could hear the commanders calling their troops into order, the *clop, clop* of horses, passing by. Today they would attack Siena.

Had Lia reached Castello Forelli in time? Would they have chance to send for reinforcements? Would the castello be taken, and my mother with it? Paratore would probably be there, if Castello Forelli fell. He would not be kind to the prisoners he took. I'd seen what he did with prisoners, myself, when he had Lia in his dungeon, when he very nearly had me. And if he got Mom…I shook my head. I had to stop it—

"'Tis out of your hands, m'lady. You are a mighty and worthy adversary," Lord Greco said with a nod of deference, "but you are one woman. You cannot save a city. Not this day."

I stared back at him, wanting to scream at him, convince him he was wrong. But inside I felt hollow, empty. Marcello and Luca were gone, perhaps prisoners themselves. Today, Siena might fall. Had I done this? Set into motion a course of action that would change history?

No way through but through, my father's voice said to me. *Do the next thing, Gabriella, and then the next, and then the next.* I swallowed and said, "So what is to become of me?"

"That is for the elders to decide," he said, staring back into my eyes. "You are the sworn enemy of Firenze. Your way shall not be easy." He went to the trunk of clothes and began rummaging through them, then paused. "Unless…"

I waited a second, letting his word hang in the air. "*Unless?*"

"Unless you have something they want."

"Such as?" I asked with a frown.

"Access." He dragged his fingers casually across the metal edge of the fine red mahogany trunk.

I stared back at him. What kind of access were they after?

"Not into Castello Forelli," he said gently. "As formidable as she is, she cannot withstand the attack to come, not without others to come to her aid. And they shall not. We've seen to it that she shall be cut off from any reinforcements."

I didn't flinch. I was proud of myself for that.

He found a shirt and rose, slowly meeting my gaze. "I speak of Siena," he said.

"Siena," I repeated.

"Yes. You are very nearly kin to Lady Rossi," he said. "You've been in their palazzo several times."

"Twice, in the traitors' palazzo," I said, testing out my theory.

My heart pounded as he came over and looked down at me, like a patronizing older brother. "I prefer to see them as people capitalizing on uncommon opportunity. Siena's days are short. The wise shall side with us, aid us. Lord Rossi is one of them. We shall breach Siena's walls within a week, two at the most. But she is well fortified. You know this. You've been there."

Fortified, yes. But there were ways…I thought of the secret tunnel. The one that ran from Palazzo Pubblico to the apartment inside Palazzo Rossi.

He squatted before me and brushed my hair over my shoulder. I edged away from his touch. He smiled and then nodded. "Yes. You're seeing it now, again, in your mind. You're a clever woman.

A warrior. You know the way from the Palazzo Rossi into Palazzo Pubblico."

"I know no such thing," I said.

"You are a decent liar," he said evenly, unperturbed. "But you'd need to be excellent, m'lady, to fool me."

I waited him out. For as much as he claimed to know me, to have me figured out, I knew, deep down, that it was just a part of his game.

"There is another tunnel, leading from Palazzo Pubblico, to the outer walls. An escape route that might be of some use." He shook his head. "The door cannot be opened from the outside, but those who wish to do so could open it from within." He rose and paced for a bit. "I know it is a great deal to ask," he said, his chin in his hand. "But in Firenze, to avoid death, you shall have to convince our people that you are our heroine, not Siena's."

"And how would I do that?"

"Gather the Nine, under the guise of giving them information you've gained while in enemy territory. They shall come—for you. Once we have the Nine in one room, we shall relieve eight—those not following the path of greatest wisdom—of their duties."

I took a breath. "You mean kill them."

He stared back into my eyes.

"Why me?" I whispered. "Lord Rossi has many men. Why not have him do this? If all you're after is mutiny—"

"Lord Rossi's allegiances must be hidden. If he is found to be a traitor, it shall only make the Sienese more furious. But if the *She-Wolf* kills all of the Nine but him, and urges submission to Firenze, and Lord Rossi stands behind her, the Sienese shall stumble." He paused. "To them, m'lady, you are Siena. Their hope. Their future. It is a kindness, in a way. Lead them to submission, and a great many shall be saved."

A *kindness*. He was smooth. Deadly smooth.

"And…and if I do *not* choose to lure the Nine to their deaths? If I do not wish to betray my people?"

"Then you shall die, after a prolonged period of agony." He turned, threw some clothes into the trunk, and gazed over at me. "Either path shall be difficult. The choice is yours," he said, shaking his head, "and yours alone. You can consider it on the road today."

He walked to the edge of the tent. "The doctor shall be here in a moment to see to you. After that, you shall have a bath."

Whatever, I thought dismissively. I had much bigger things to worry about than whether or not I smelled good.

Someone blew a horn outside, making me jump. Men were on the march.

Lord Greco gave me a sad smile. "Today, Siena begins to crumble. She may fall fast or she may fall slowly, but she shall fall."

Says you. I kept my lips clamped shut.

"'Tis time to rethink your loyalties, consider your future." He waved about the tent. "All swords and knives and anything sharp have been removed. All sides are guarded by knights. Do not attempt escape."

He left, then. I paced for a time, in my lame, limping fashion, trying to figure a way out, a plan. But came up with nothing. His men had literally stripped the tent of everything but the bed. I was just considering breaking it apart, to use a piece of wood as some sort of weapon, when the doctor arrived.

He studied me, reading too many of my thoughts, judging from his raised brow. Without a word, he gestured for me to show him my palms. He studied every scratch and cut, apparently looking for infection. Satisfied, he unwound my thigh and chest bandages.

There was a new green hue to my bruises today. Hadn't seen that before. The one at the back of my leg now stretched all the way down to my calf. "I cannot do anything more for you but rebind you," he said. "I shall return after you see to your bath."

Two men brought in a heavy round wooden tub, like the bottom half of a wine cask. They set it behind the screen, brought in several buckets of water, and then ducked out, never looking my direction. Favoring my left leg, I knelt in the cold water, bending to wet down my hair. I found a cake of soap in a net to the side and lathered up, rinsed, and rose, shivering. There was no towel. I hurriedly slipped on Lord Greco's big shirt and yanked on the leggings. They came to my chest, so I rolled them down and tied them with the rope.

I turned around the corner of the screen and gasped. Once again, he'd crept in without me knowing. Lord Greco stared at me, his eyes falling from my wet curls to the damp shirt…for the first time letting me know he thought I was something more than a sack of potatoes to deliver. *Not gay.*

I crossed my arms and stared back at him, tensing in defense.

He turned and spoke over his shoulder. "The doctor shall be back in moments. As soon as your wounds are bound, we shall set off."

"Oh. Good?" Was that the required response?

He nodded to a trencher, a wooden platter, near the entrance. "Break your fast," he directed. "We shall not eat again until we enter the city."

I went over to the makeshift table and picked up the bread, still warm. I ate it and then the wedge of cheese. Last, I drank down the cup of cold water, just as the doctor returned.

He did his number on me and gave me a bit more pain powder for the road. I accepted it but was determined not to take any of it. I preferred the knifelike pain at my ribs and thigh to feeling like I was a drugged up and out of control. When he finished binding my chest and leg, he straightened and looked at me with sad eyes. I frowned, knowing that him feeling sorry for me could not be a good thing.

"Will they kill me in Firenze?"

"I don't believe so," he said with a slow shake of his head, and his eyes become more sorrowful still. "But you might wish they had. You must rethink your loyalties, m'lady. 'Tis the only way."

"Loyalty is not loyalty unless one clings to it in the face of adversity. No?"

He stared back into my eyes and, seeing he wasn't going to sway me, gathered his things and left the tent without another word. The flap was open, and I could see him talking to his tracker.

I came out, and a knight grabbed my arm.

I shook him off. *Man, relax, dude.* "I shall go no farther."

"See that you don't," he growled.

Lord Greco was frowning, making angry gestures as he berated the helpless-looking tracker.

I smiled, feeling a twinge of hope, the first of the day.

They hadn't found Lia. She had made it. *Please, Lord,* I prayed silently. *See her all the way to safety. Help her warn Siena. Save Siena. Please.*

Lord Greco glanced in our direction, caught sight of me, and then shouted at the knights, "Get her inside! She is not to be out here."

We set off an hour later, four knights in Greco purple leading the way, Lord Greco on a dark brown gelding, me on another gelding— flanked by two knights—and six more behind us. The journey was made longer by the sickeningly huge number of men who still journeyed south to the front lines, streaming past us on either side. With each group that arrived, Lord Greco called out, "I present to you, Lady Gabriella Betarrini! Tell everyone that if one She-Wolf of Siena can be captured, then so can the other! They are mortal after all."

The men laughed and jeered. Greco's knights kept them from grabbing me, or stoning me, as some tried to do. He was using me as some kind of crazy inspiration, a symbol of Siena's impending defeat. Was that what I would do for all of Firenze? Stir them up, get them ready to take on Siena?

There was no way that Siena could fend off such numbers, not when she was so ill-prepared.

Not that these were the finest specimens of warriors. Many carried nothing but a pitchfork or axe over their shoulders. But I knew that victory often was claimed by the side with the most men willing to die. At least that was what my world history teacher had said to us. And so they went, why? For land? Honor? Glory? Spoils of war? What?

What could be worth it? I doubted the women they left behind would consider it worthwhile, should they be left widowed, alone, struggling to feed themselves and their children. Sure, men got the glory and honor. But women were abandoned to try and pull the pieces together. I thought of Mom, carrying on without Dad. But that was different, a different time. Still hard, for sure. But at least she had education, a way to make a living. These women...my eyes trailed up the hills, toward a vineyard much like that of the old woman who'd helped us.

These women were left to watch hope itself wither on their vines. Helpless to stop it.

I stilled even as my gelding carried me forward.

You are not helpless, said my father's voice. Was it Dad's...or God's?

Yeah, right, Gabs. Now God's speaking to you. Getting a little full of yourself, aren't you?

But then it came again. Unmistakable. *You are strong, Gabriella. Smart. You'll survive this. Find your way.*

It sounded like Dad, in my mind. Memory of my father's voice comforted me. I had to go with that, that he was speaking to me, reaching out to me, even if only through my memories of what he *might've* said. For the thousandth time, I wished he were here. He'd know what to do. Because right then, I felt like just a kid, really, in shoes way too big for my feet.

Dad, it's too much.

Not too much for one of my girls.

If only you were here—

You have what you need. Within. Draw deep, Gabriella. Search your heart. Use your mind. You'll find it. You are not alone.

His voice faded then, and I closed my eyes, clinging to the memory, wishing I could sit down across the kitchen table from him and talk. Make him listen, really listen rather than read his latest copy of the *Oxford Journal of Archaeology* and nod while I went on. There was so much I wanted to ask him yet. So much I never had a chance to ask.

"What pains you so?" Lord Greco had fallen back, taking the position to my right for a moment.

I blinked rapidly and decided to use truth as my weapon. "Memory of my father. He died recently."

Lord Greco crossed himself and stared at the road for a time before looking my way again. "It is what set your path to Italia, from Normandy? Three women, alone?"

Yeah, in some ways. I nodded once.

"I do not believe you are from Normandy."

"Oh?" I asked.

"I heard English upon your tongue, back in the woods."

I paused for a moment. No doubt this guy had already spoken with Lord Rossi, who suspected the same. And Lord Paratore...

Lia and Mom and I had figured out our story—should this come up again. "We spent the majority of our years in England, where we learned to speak and read. Your own Tuscan is my second language," I said, meeting his eyes. I shrugged. "I admit, my French is not as it should be. *Parlez-vous français?*"

"Nay," he said, staring at me as if he knew I wasn't telling him the truth.

But I didn't care. I owed him nothing.

By midafternoon, we crested a hill and could see Firenze down in the valley, but she looked nothing like what I knew. Countless towers dotted her cityscape, as they had in Siena, but there was no huge red-domed church or campanile—the bell tower. *They must've been built later.* It felt like going home and finding out your favorite rooms had been torn out.

"Here is where you shall relinquish your mount," Lord Greco said, looking back at me.

I frowned as the knights beside me dismounted and came up on either side. One reached up and lifted me down. I looked at Lord Greco as they tied a length of rope to my bound hands and then roughly removed my boots, but he kept his back to me.

When they were done, they remounted, leaving me on the ground between them. "All is in order, m'lord," said one knight, handing the end of the rope to him.

They intended to walk me the rest of the way into town, like an animal on a leash. The She-Wolf of Siena, captured.

Fine, I thought, defiantly staring back at him as he looked down at me, winding the end of the rope around his forearm.

"Get on with it!" I snapped.

"As you wish, m'lady," he said, turning at once. The rope was shorter than I realized and I lurched forward, crying out, my side feeling like it had been ripped open. The knights beside me laughed, but Lord Greco did not. He didn't turn either. Why? Did he feel guilty? Like the jerk he was for treating me this way? *You should*, I thought venomously. *I hope you and your men die in the battle. Every last one of you.*

I shivered. I'd never wished anyone dead in my whole life. Well, other than Lord Paratore…

Mom wouldn't like my hatred. She'd always taught us to love everyone, that war was misery and never resolved anything for long. That humankind's greatest hope was peace. But she hadn't experienced stuff like what was coming down now, here. I winced as I stepped on a sharp rock, then another, but bit my lip to keep from calling out. I kept my eyes on the road in front of me, picking my way forward while keeping some slack in the rope. I did pretty well for the first mile. But around the second I tripped and fell. Lord Greco allowed me to drag for ten feet before he wearily pulled up and let me regain my feet.

I swallowed hard. Now the tops of my feet were cut up, bleeding. I wanted to yell at him, scream, cry, but instead I put my shoulders back and waited for him to resume our walk. People were coming toward us, from the city gates, wanting to know what a woman, with hair down around her shoulders, was doing, bound and dragged behind Lord Greco's horse. And in men's clothing, to boot.

They recognized him with cries of greeting, celebration. Apparently, Lord Greco was some sort of big deal in this town.

"Lady Gabriella Betarrini!" cried the knights, announcing our arrival. "The pride of Siena, now m'lord's prisoner!"

The first piece of spoiled fruit surprised me. I gasped at the impact to my shoulder, and at first, thought I had been injured, was bleeding. But then another hit me on the back, still another my head, the juice and seeds dripping down to the stones beside my bloody feet. The crowds were gathering, growing thicker.

Not exactly the flowers I got in Siena, I thought.

But then someone threw a stone. It hit my arm, and I cried out in spite of myself.

Lord Greco looked back and frowned. "Nay!" he demanded, holding his hand up. "I have been charged with bringing this woman to the *grandi.* If they sentence her to stoning, so be it. But you shall not do so without approval!"

The crowd booed and hissed, and I felt a shudder of fear go through me. I was hated here. Really hated. For what? They didn't know me! All I had done was fall in love with a son of Siena! And help my sister escape an evil lord. I hadn't done anything that any of them might not have done in my place, had the tables been turned…

I tripped again, and the crowd laughed, then more rotten food came flying. I smelled the vinegar, the mold. I quickly found my feet and ducked between the rump of Lord Greco's horse and the nearest knight's. "Go," I said to my captor.

He eyed me. "There is another way, Gabriella—"

"Get on with it!" I shouted, his use of my first name irritating me. It was irrational, I admitted to myself. A million people called me Gabriella, Gabi, Gabs…but not *this* man. He was not allowed to sound like he *knew* me. And I wanted him to remember my title, to show me a shadow of civility, even if I was wearing his clothes and was covered in spoiled juice. I wanted him to remember this injustice, that I had been tied to *his* horse, so that when I had the opportunity, when I regained my sword and my strength…

He met my gaze without faltering. He knew what I was saying with my eyes, read the hatred there. Then he turned and pulled me forward again, through the city gates. People were running in from every street and alleyway, shoving others aside in an effort to see me. The barrage stopped then, perhaps not allowed inside the city, I thought, but the jeering kept on.

"So the Sienese adorn their women in the fruits of the past year?"

"Is she a man or a woman? I cannot tell!"

"Where is your fearsome sword, girl?"

"The She-Wolf bleeds!"

"Behold, the pride of Siena! Today, she is ours!"

We turned a corner and then another, making our way deeper and deeper into the city until we emerged on the enormous Piazza della Signoria, with the city hall modeled after Siena's own. Back when the two had been sister cities, not such bitter enemies. Maybe back when Marcello and Rodolfo had been buds.

The men dismounted, and I glanced over my shoulder. The crowds had all come here, celebrating my capture as if their home team had just won the World Cup or something. But they looked upon me with hatred, panting with a crazy kind of anticipation in their eyes.

It hit me then.

They were waiting.

Waiting for me to be turned over to them.

For what? What exactly was the sentence for an enemy of the Commune di Firenze?

CHAPTER 24

"Tell us, m'lady," said Lord Greco, hands behind his back as he paced before me. "Have you thought again about our offer?" Beyond him were eleven men sitting in high-backed, ornately carved chairs. Siena's ruling body was the Nine. In Firenze, I was facing their counterparts.

And it turned out that Lord Greco was one of 'em.

Perfect, just perfect. One of the lords had actually gone out just to hunt me and Lia down. I sighed. *You really know how to make friends and enemies, Gabs.*

They'd given Lord Greco words of praise for bringing me to them. But they chastised him for losing my sister, "allowing" her to return to the safety of the Sienese and quite possibly warn them.

"It matters little," Lord Greco said, brushing off their concerns. He stared down at me, spying my small, defiant smile. "Even if Evangelia reaches Siena, our men will soon be upon them all."

He cocked his head, hands on his hips, and said to me again, "Will you agree to gather the Nine in Siena?"

I slid my eyes up to meet his. "Never."

He slapped me then, surprising me. I turned, took a half step back, but kept my feet. *What's with him?* He was remarkably different toward me here, in sight of the city and her lords. Meaner. Slowly, carefully I stood straight again. "So it is true," I said. "The men of Firenze must always resort to violence." My eyes flicked up to Lord Greco's. "My father always told me that a man who would strike a woman is no sort of man at all."

"Your father," he said evenly, leaning down, "taught you to be more of a man than woman. You do not know your place."

"My place," I returned, "is to defend all I know that is right and true. Ever since I arrived in Toscana, it has been *your* men who forced me to raise my sword, my sister to raise her arrows, to *defend* ourselves. It has been Firenze's subjects who pursue us, attack us, abuse us." I glared at him. "Siena has done nothing but show us kindness after kindness."

He glared back. "Many men loyal to Firenze have died at the end of your sword, your sister's arrow."

"*Forgive* me for not relinquishing my sword and allowing myself to be slaughtered as a woman ought. *Forgive* me for helping to free my sister from the *dungeon* of Lord Paratore and then attempting to make certain he could never imprison, torture, or threaten another of us again. *Forgive* me for not dying at the hands of your venomous doctor, sent to poison me." I glanced at Lord Foraboschi, who hovered in the background with a few other nobles, looking askance at my outburst. I shook my head with a sarcastic little laugh. "You ask far too much, m'lord, from me. From any woman, any woman with a pinch of courage in her heart." I thumped my chest. "*That* is what my father taught me. Courage. Standing up for what is right. For *who* is right. And in this case, it is *clearly* my Sienese sisters and brothers."

He sighed, straightened, and then placed chin in hand, staring at me.

"The She-Wolf of Siena has a sharp tongue," said one of the others behind him.

"Indeed," said Lord Greco, still studying me.

Abruptly, the rest of the men stood. Lord Greco bowed and stood to my side, so that all of them might look at me. "Daughter of Siena," said the man at the center, apparently the main guy. "You shall find that we are not as unmerciful as you seem to think."

He walked toward me, and Lord Greco grabbed hold of my arm from one side, his knight taking the other. *What? Do they think I'll deck this guy or what?* I wasn't an idiot.

The man was short, no taller than my chest, reminding me of Lord Rossi with his steady, methodical mannerisms. But when he looked into my eyes, I saw that while he was small, he was as tough as a terrier with a cornered rat. "You are the one that saved Lord Fortino Forelli? You are the one whom Sir Marcello Forelli loves, are you not?"

I stared over his head at the wall beyond him. I would not be a part of selling out Marcello or Fortino. I would not.

"She is, Lord Barbato," Lord Greco said at last.

Lord Barbato peered up into my face. "What do you believe the brothers Forelli might give us in exchange for your freedom? Might they relinquish Castello Paratore and Castello Forelli? Might they swear their allegiance to us?"

I let out a breath through my nose, just barely keeping it from a snort. What scheme led them to believe they could conquer the castle, her men? Whatever their plans, I knew no man within the Forelli household would ever aid them. "Never." I looked down into his eyes. *"Never."*

He smiled, then. "I am not so certain." He reached out and touched a strand of my hair. "Even in such disarray, my dear, you are quite becoming. I can see why Sir Marcello is smitten, why you and your sister have stolen the heart of every man in Siena."

I tried to wrench away, but the men at my side kept me in place.

"What would the Forellis do," Lord Barbato said slowly, "if Marcello Forelli's intended had but days left to live?" He smiled. His teeth were small but straight and white. "Lord Forelli is likely dismayed at his own interrupted nuptials, this day. With greater disruptions ahead." The men shared a laugh.

Yuk it up, fellas. I'm all LOL myself.

Lord Barbato turned back to me. "Would Sir Marcello come for you?"

I refused to give him the satisfaction of a response.

He glanced back over at the other men, then up at Lord Greco. "Would a man in love not do anything he could to save his woman?"

Barbato interlaced his fingers and turned them out, cracking them. "We offer a truce. We do not have to conquer Siena, though we have the power to do so. No, we can be magnanimous neighbors, offering a celebration as proof of our good intentions. Our desire for *unity*." He paced back and forth, tapping his chin, nodding to himself, then he looked to me. "We are not the villains you make us out to be," he said. "We would relish a lasting peace with our neighbors.

But we shall have Castello Forelli and Castello Paratore, as well as other castles on the northern border—if not Siena herself—before this battle is done. The Forellis would be wise to go the way of the Rossis."

So. There it was. Another confirmation that the Rossis were in on it.

He turned away from me, strode to his seat, and stared back. "Bathe and dress her in the finest wedding gown the dressmakers can create. Braid flowers into her hair. Then send this message to her beloved: 'Lady Betarrini awaits you, Sir Marcello Forelli, in a cage at the Firenze city gates, a lovely bridal bird, seeking her groom. If you can meet her bride price. But she has limited time, for she shall have no food or water. If you do not arrive in time, she shall perish in her cage.'"

"Lord Barbato," said Lord Greco at my side. "She could convince the Nine to gather within Siena, I am certain of it. And we could follow through on our original plan, avoiding much bloodshed on both sides."

Lord Barbato flicked out his hand dismissively. "Look at her, Lord Greco. Into her eyes. She has no intention of aiding our cause. We shall follow our alternative plan. Without the seven castle outposts, they shall be crippled, in disarray. I believe we shall find the Nine far more amenable to negotiation once we have them in hand. Siena shall become our sister city once again, eager to do as we ask rather than defy us at every turn. We can take the other five. I am confident that shall be done in a week's time. 'Tis Castello Paratore and Castello Forelli that must be breached, or they shall stand for months, giving Siena far too much time to rally her support."

The others were nodding.

"And if Sir Forelli does not capitulate?" asked Lord Greco. "What if he does not come to claim his bride? Or Lord Forelli forbids it?"

"Then the road becomes more difficult," Lord Barbato said casually, picking at a hangnail. He glanced up. "Lady Betarrini shall die, her corpse shriveling and decaying in the cage." He gave me a look that sent shivers up my spine.

"That was never our—" Lord Greco tried.

"Lady Betarrini will become an entirely new symbol for Siena," Lord Barbato said, rising. "All shall see what becomes of those who dare to defy Firenze. Weakness exposed. Love, unrequited. Desire, unmet. Life itself, coming to a perilous end."

I was taken to Lord Greco's home, a palazzo on a hill in the heart of the city. There was a fine garden and fountain in back. The knights brought me to a grand hall, and I collapsed on the warm stones in front of a blazing fire, shivering in spite of it. My mind was swirling, trying to figure a way out without betraying Siena.

Lord Greco did not remain with me. He hadn't said a word to me all the way to the mansion, even when I begged him to let me go.

An army of female servants entered a half hour after we arrived, and the knights disappeared outside the doors, closing them firmly behind them. I knew they stood right outside, at the ready. Even if I managed to escape the room, could I make it to the edge of Firenze unseen?

I was undressed without ceremony and given a thorough bath, and clean bandages were wound around my feet, thigh, and ribs. The maids remained eerily silent, as if they knew they were contributing to my murder. A light, delicately woven underdress, reminding me of butterfly wings, swept down over my body. It had the lightest lace I'd ever seen at both the sleeve and bottom hem. Under it, I wore pantaloons in a similar fabric.

Then came the heavy, teal-blue colored silk gown, wide at the shoulder, beaded across the entire bodice. Had I chosen my own wedding dress, it might well have been this one, I thought sadly, running my hands over the beads that cascaded from the neckline to about my belly button. It clung to my hips, then fell heavily to the floor in deep, regal folds. It was the gown of a princess. *Except I would want it in ivory rather than the medieval bridal blue—*

What are you thinking *Gabriella?* I chastised myself. *Are you totally insane?* I wasn't ready to get married! But then, more than that, I wasn't really game for this whole dying-in-a-cage-as-a-symbol thing either…It wasn't the way I was going to go out, not if I could help it. *Figure it out. There must be a way to escape. There must!*

They could not get the delicate slippers onto my feet, heavily bandaged as they were. They debated among themselves if they should unbind my feet in order to put proper shoes on me. One argued that no one would see them. "Until she's up in her cage," said another. I remained silent as they unbound my bloody feet and placed the slippers on them, ignoring the tears that slipped down my cheeks from the pain.

They attacked my hair next, weaving one braid after another, forcing it into submission, along with more strands of beads, until at the end, they pinned all the braids into a knot at the nape of my neck.

A delicate ring of beads, a crown of sorts, was settled atop my head and pinned in place. The women backed off, *ooing* and *ahhing* over their own work, nodding in satisfaction. *Traitors*, I thought, glaring at them. *Selling me out, a woman, your sister, daughter, friend...*

"You will let me die in that cage," I sputtered, feeling regal in the gown, strangely powerful. "This is no fairy tale! This is war! And I am but a pawn in their game!"

"And, by far, the most beautiful pawn I've ever seen," said a voice from the other side of the room.

I twisted to see him. Lord Greco. Leaning against the far wall. How long had he been there?

The servants scurried out as if to avoid the crossfire about to come.

He shook his head. "Lady Gabriella Betarrini, it is no wonder you have captured Sir Forelli's heart. You are stirring in so many ways. Truly, you have the countenance of a queen in such finery."

I clenched handfuls of my skirt as he neared. "M'lord, you must intervene. Please. I beseech you. You cannot let this horrible thing unfold."

He was walking around me, checking me out. Furious, I waited until he came around and lifted my chin. "Are you quite finished? I am no prized calf to be considered from all sides!"

He gave me a gentle smile. "How I wish I had weeks to explore that mind of yours, Gabriella."

I paused. Again, with my first name. Should I play up to him? Flirt? So that I might find my escape route? I let my eyes fall to the floor, as if I was suddenly shy under his attentions, wondering if I really had the guts to play it out. He was plainly interested. But he was also frightfully clever, seeming to see through me.

No, I'm not going there. I can't. It felt too wrong. Unfaithful to Marcello, even if it was only a ploy.

I raised my eyes to meet his, again defiant.

He let out a little breathy laugh, as if this pleased him, and eyed the closed doors. We were alone in the vast room. He offered his arm. "M'lady."

Seeing no choice, I took it, wondering where he was taking me. He led me over to the towering windows opposite the doors and unlatched one, then another, opening the onyx panes, allowing the cool evening air to wash over me. I hadn't realized until then that I was feeling a bit faint. But he'd seen it. Known it. I took in a deep breath, then another.

What he did next surprised me. From beneath the edge of his tunic, he brought out a cloth sack. He untied it swiftly, handing me a small loaf of bread and then a wax-covered round of cheese. "Eat. Quickly. It shall be your last meal in some time."

I hesitated only a moment. Then I had half of it down in a couple minutes. "Why are you doing this?" I asked, mouth full, taking a goblet of water from his hand, studying him in the soft evening light that streamed through the windows.

"All is not as it seems," he said simply. He urged me to take another drink and then refilled the goblet while I chewed the rest of the bread and cheese.

"Oh?" I repeated. "You are not the specter of death, come to usher me to my hideous end?"

"Do I appear as such?" he asked, quirking a smile at me from the side. "Drink," he urged, lifting the goblet to my lips. "Truly, it might be your last for days."

I frowned as I gulped it down, already feeling the thirst to come. I drained it, and he refilled it again, but I stood still, stubbornly waiting.

He stared into my eyes, then sighed and rolled up one sleeve.

On his left arm, right beneath the crook of his elbow, was a triangular tattoo.

Identical to one I'd seen on Marcello's arm.

Our eyes met. I drew back, trying to make sense of it when I heard the boots of what sounded like a squadron of knights approaching through the marble hallway outside the great hall.

Hurriedly, he rolled the sleeve back down. "Drink, Gabriella. What is to come shall not be pleasant for you. But you are not alone. Remember that. You are not alone."

CHAPTER 22

When I was led back into the vast piazza later that same day, the city was in full festival mode. Bonfires burned across the plaza. Musicians led the processional, as if I were truly a bride on her way to meet her groom. Again and again I searched for an escape route but saw none. There were simply too many people, people acting as if they were celebrating me but who were truly celebrating my public humiliation.

"The She-Wolf of Siena, conquered!"

"How could a bride so pretty be so fierce with the sword?"

"Where is your intended now, Bride of Siena?"

"Will your bride price be met?"

They taunted and laughed. But at least now no one threw spoiled fruit or stones. I walked beside Lord Greco, my arm atop his, drawing strength from him, visualizing the tattoo beneath his shirt, wondering what it meant. It comforted me that he was somehow inexplicably tied to Marcello—even if he laughed along with those in the crowd.

Marcello. Has word yet reached you? Do you know what they intend?

Even if I tried, I could not imagine the Forellis without their castle, living anywhere but that precious corner of the republic. What would happen to them? If they lost their home, as well as their means of making a living? I shook my head. I could not be a part of that, regardless of the cost.

The crowd was parting before me, throwing flower petals at my feet, but they were dead, shriveled blooms crackling beneath each footfall. Each step pained me—the new slippers chafed my tender, bruised, and cut soles, and the strained muscle in my thigh throbbed. But the people laughed, thinking I reacted to the piles of crunchy petals.

Freaks, I thought. *Who keeps piles of dead petals, anyway?* What kind of crazy ceremony called for such a thing?

We turned a corner into the piazza, and I saw, a hundred feet away, a cage of branches that curved from the top and were secured at the bottom. Dead, shriveled flowers on vines wound through the branches above. My eyes followed the rope, which held it aloft, to the center of a grand arch, fifty feet high, part of a wall that extended to the edge of the piazza. I swallowed hard.

Did they really intend to lift me to the top of that? What if I fell?

Lord Greco felt my hesitation and looked down at me with sad eyes. He pulled me forward, and the crowd parted farther until I could see that on either side were the rest of the grandi.

They stood, somber and waiting. Lord Greco waited until a knight opened the cage door, then he turned to me and waved me inside, as if he were offering me the finest carriage possible.

The crowd erupted in laughter.

I shook my head. "Nay. Please, nay. There must be another route," I said to the men beside Lord Barbato, looking from one to the next, leaving my eyes on Lord Greco the longest. "This is hardly civilized. What if I were one of your daughters?" I cried. "Your sister?" I said to Lord Greco.

His arms came around me then, and he bodily lifted me inside. I nearly blacked out from the pain as he pressed into my bruised and broken ribs—on purpose? How could he be so cruel? *I am so confused…*

He shut the door as I turned and tried to block it, in full panic now. The cage was barely bigger than my body.

Lord Greco would not look me in the eye as a knight tied it shut, and the rest of the men circled the cage.

"Lady Betarrini," said Lord Barbato, directly at my door. "You are hereby sentenced to the cage until your groom comes to claim you, with the required dowry in hand, be it before or after your death. May his way be hastened."

I gripped the branches that formed the door and stared at him. "May Castello Forelli lead the way to Firenze's defeat," I said, "and may your soul rot in the pit of Hades."

He stared at me coldly and gestured with his hand for his men to haul me up.

The rope was immediately taut, and I felt the cage tilt and lift. I hurriedly set my feet on two of five branches at the bottom, feeling a shiver of fear race up my back when they creaked, as if groaning in complaint from my weight.

Lord Greco gripped the edge and swung it, making me lean far in the opposite direction. I spun, even as the knights above continued to haul me upward, and I thought I might vomit all across the jeering crowd beneath me.

I almost wanted to. *Would serve 'em right…*

But I held it down. I needed every ounce of carb and protein and liquid inside me, if I was to survive what was ahead of me.

At the top, the cage continued to twist in the wind. I shifted my feet, trying to find a position that didn't make my cut-up soles burn so badly. Above me, I saw that the rope went through two doors and wrapped around a winch atop the wall. A guard locked it down and then shut the trapdoors, sealing me off.

This can't be happening. Dimly, I remembered some movie in which the city's prisoners had been caged and left to rot along the main road into and out of a city. I knew punishment was severe and often barbaric in this era. But this? Surely they wouldn't allow me to die here in this cage! Someone, somewhere, would show me mercy in time. It was all for show. A parade of sorts. Right?

If they had cell phones, they'd be taking shots of me and sending them to Marcello, goading him, mocking us. Unfortunately for me, it might take a day to find Marcello with word—assuming he was near Castello Forelli or on the front lines. But what if he was elsewhere, nursing Luca? Still in hiding? I counted back. Luca had been ill for four days now. Was he rallying? Improving? Or dead?

Lia. Lia and my mother would receive the word, even if Marcello or Fortino were not within reach. Together, they'd find some way to come to my aid. We'd been given gold, in Siena. Maybe they could use some of that to hire some mercenaries to help come bust me loose.

I looked down. *Who am I kidding?* The people of Firenze seemed pretty committed to this whole hostage deal. They danced and feasted—even with so many men off to the battle, the square was packed. The festivities became louder, more raucous, as the wine set in and the hours ticked by. It was the only good part about my high perch—they couldn't reach me. I shivered in the cold evening autumn breeze, wishing my bridal gown was a high-necked one, and at last, I gingerly sank to the bottom, trying to give my poor feet a break.

The cage was so narrow, I had to sit with my knees to my chest. But I discovered that the generous folds of fabric from my skirts and train could be utilized as a sort of padding for my rear end, when adjusted right. The crowd pointed and laughed when I sat down, as if I had just admitted defeat or something.

I ignored them and looked up to the sky, the stars dim against the glow of the fires beneath me. I tried to ignore the fact that I was already thirsty, tried to forget the feel of Lord Greco's cold goblet at my lips. I leaned my forehead against a limb and found him again among the throngs beneath me, near the rest of the lords, dancing with a pretty woman. I didn't know what his connection to Marcello was—what that tattoo was about—but he obviously wasn't riding hard to meet him. He wasn't squiring himself away in some secret place, talking with knights who might dare to come to my rescue.

Then, as if he sensed my stare, he turned in the dance and glanced up at me.

I looked away, back to the stars. He had probably played me the fool. Showed me the tattoo to give me false hope, encourage me to go quietly to my doom. Somewhere, someway, he and Marcello had been close enough as friends to have received the same mark on their arms. Perhaps that friendship was long over.

The smell of meat cooking over the fires had been drifting up toward me all evening, but now my stomach rumbled. Just the idea of not having another meal made me feel more anxious. *Think of the Hunger Pledge, Gabs,* I told myself, remembering a time sophomore year when a group of us raised money for the poor by going without food for twenty-four hours. *Just pretend you're doing that again.*

But at least then, I'd had water. And no one was having a barbecue in my backyard…

I dozed off as the fires died down and the square emptied. Only nine or ten revelers remained, so drunk they could not make it home, sleeping where they fell, or in corners of the piazza, leaning against the buildings. I awakened a few hours later, my breath fogging in clouds before my face. I was shivering uncontrollably.

Even worse was my shrieking bladder. I heard a guard on the wall above me and saw the light of his flickering torch. "Sir!" I called, trying to get my teeth to stop chattering. He ignored me at first. But when I kept calling, he finally moved over to the wall, directly above me by about fifteen feet, and peered through the trap doors. "I…I need to relieve myself."

He rolled his eyes. "So be about it then."

I paused, his words sinking in. Even for this—*this*—there was not to be some semblance of…of…civility?

He walked off, taking up his position again. The square was already coming alive, workmen there to clear the debris of the fires, getting ready for the morning market. *It's only going to get worse, Gabi.* Quickly, I lifted myself to my feet, letting the feeling come back to my legs with the pin-prickles of blood flow, then gathered my skirts, shoved down my pantaloons and squatted.

I concentrated on the agony of my hamstring as I ignored the laughter and surprised shouts of two men below, and above me, the low chuckle of the guard. As soon as I was done, I hurriedly lifted my pantaloons, let the skirts fall and resumed the process of stretching out my sore legs, trying to push aside the humiliation.

I clutched two branches before me and stared out to the east, taking comfort in the pink glow, the first bits of sunrise, appearing there. In an hour, it would be far warmer. I stretched my fingers, which looked weirdly white, wondering if September was too early to get a case of frostbite.

You are not alone, Lord Greco had said.

But the words came back to me in my father's voice.

You are not alone, he repeated.

I feel alone. Never have I felt lonelier.

You are not. You are seen. Known. Remembered.

Fab. Can someone who remembers me get me out of this mess?

There was no more voice in my head, warming my heart.

There was only the cold morning.

The morning passed by like a version of medieval C-Span, cameras rolling 24-7. And I was the camerawoman, watching fishmongers and produce sellers and butchers and cloth merchants set up tents and peddle their wares. Bargain, barter, bicker.

They all greeted me as they arrived and departed, as if making some rude comment was a key to a locked entrance.

I ignored them and then thought of smart things to retort. Long after they were gone, of course. Already, my weary, dehydrated brain wasn't working so well.

Come early afternoon, the market closed, and most everyone returned to their homes for a hot meal and an afternoon siesta. Only a few continued to walk the square, and again I was confronted by the smells of cooking sauces, sausage sizzling above fires, the yeasty odor of bread. I closed my eyes and leaned in the corner of my cage, hoping for some sleep of my own. At least when I was sleeping, I could forget my parched throat and empty belly.

I awakened to the crowds of evening, walking among their friends, gathering in huddles to share news of the battle not thirty miles to our south. I leaned to the side, hoping to hear what was happening, but could not make out more than a word or two. My eyes traveled over the people, obviously more of the aristocracy at this hour, although I didn't see Lord Barbato and his peeps. Women were in fine gowns and jewelry; men wore exquisite tunics. They were the rich and powerful, apparently able to buy freedom to stay back from the battle for their husbands and sons. There were soldiers among them, drinking, cavorting, dressed in the matching tunics of their overlords. Was the battle going so well that they could send some home to the mother city?

I closed my eyes in pain at the thought.

They acted as if their own men were not dying now, lying in trenches or dry riverbeds, bleeding, suffering. Here in the plaza, they laughed and flirted and occasionally made a joke at my expense. In those moments, they would look up at me as a group, seemingly holding their breath. I'd look away, weary of such games, and then hear their laughter.

My hunger abated, reaching that place at last when you just feel empty but don't have that insane desire to fix it and fix it *right now*. Hunger I could live with, I decided, other than the nagging headache residue it left behind. But I was so thirsty now that my tongue felt thick and dry in my mouth, as if it were a lump of dead flesh. My lips were cracking.

At least I don't have to pee, I thought dully as the sun set and the chill of night crept near again. I forced myself to rise and stretch my aching legs, staring to the south, where I could see smoke rising to the sky. A castle on fire? A forest? *Marcello, where are you?*

More than twenty-four hours had passed. I wanted to scream, rip the limbs open at the top of the cage and climb up the rope. But the rope disappeared between two doors, doors I'd never seen open after the guard peered through. I assumed they were for molten lead or hot oil, the remnants of an old city wall. Now it was merely decorative, a lookout point for guards, a place to hold the city's trophies.

Like me.

CHAPTER 23

Thirty-six hours, I thought dimly. The market was in full swing by the time I forced myself to my feet, clawing my way awkwardly up the branches of my cage. Again, pain shot through my limbs as the blood began to flow to my feet. I hung there against the branches, clenching my teeth to keep from screaming. When the pain abated, I opened weary eyes on the people beneath me.

Whereas my tongue felt like a lump of dead flesh yesterday, today it felt shriveled, even odder in my mouth. Four nuns were walking toward me. I could not help myself. Even though I'd sworn I would not stoop to such measures. The idea of a drink, just a sip—

"Please! Sisters!" I cried, my voice monstrous and garbled, foreign to my own ears. "A bit of water! Only a bit of water!"

The one in front paused but did not look up. Her companion bent and said a word in her ear, and they immediately went on their way.

With frustration, I felt tears rise to my eyes. *Dry as the desert, Gabi, and you're going to waste what you've got left on tears? Seriously?*

But I couldn't help it. I was trembling and weak, feeling not at all like myself. Tears streamed down my face. If I could only have some water, just a cup full, how much better I'd feel!

I wept as if I was the only woman who had ever suffered such horror, ever. Then I cried over my weakness, knowing that others had suffered far worse. *Come on, Gabi, get a grip. Get a grip!*

As the piazza emptied for siesta that afternoon, I sank back to my corner perch and fell into a sketchy, dream-filled sleep, waking again and again, and yet not able to stay alert either.

You are not alone.

I opened my eyes then and turned to my right, trying to get my eyes to focus in the fading afternoon light. Who was there, below me?

Lord Greco. He waited until a pair of women passed by, then with his foot, he casually traced the shape of a triangle.

I closed my eyes and opened my mouth, with the dim idea of calling out to him, to beg for water, but he had moved on through the arch and out of my line of vision. Slowly, I rolled my head to the left, looking down the street in that direction, but he wasn't there either.

Could someone speak when dying of dehydration? When her tongue refused to cooperate? When one small movement made her dizzy?

He wanted me to remember the triangle tattoo, I decided, dragging my eyes up into the pale, washed out sunset. Why? So that I knew not everyone in this city was my sworn enemy? That he'd look after my body, after I died? See me properly buried rather than left here as Barbato threatened?

What was the point?

I could tell already that, come morning, I would not be able to rise. I was too weak, my arms and legs feeling like sticks of butter in a hot kitchen. Worse, I was getting to the place that I didn't care.

That can't be good, I thought distantly, assessing myself as if I was my own nurse.

But really, wouldn't it be easier to let go, give in, rather than fight? These people were not going to show me mercy.

I had only a day left in me, anyway. People could survive a long time without food. But without water? I knew it was impossible. I'd seen enough *Man vs. Wild* to know that. People set adrift upon the sea. Plane crashes in the desert. Lots of time on the food front. But liquid? Seventy-two hours, tops. Then the internal organs started shutting down. Once your kidneys went, you were totally messed up.

Forty-eight hours, I thought, watching as stars began to emerge in the darkening sky, drifting again, as if I were in one of those life rafts.

I had a day left in me, then I'd be dead.

Dead like my dad. With my dad?

With him? Somewhere? Heaven? For the first time that day, I felt a jolt of hope. Peace.

Lia would have Mom.

And I'd have Dad.

Forever.

CHAPTER 24

I was dreaming of battle. I heard a man cry out then fall silent.

But then, oddly, nothing but the cooing of two doves in their muddy nest to my upper left. I opened my eyes, blinking—they felt so dry it was like my eyelids were scraping across them. I could see the dim shape of the arch above me, a black monster against a smattering of stars. But then the two small doors opened, and I could see the shape of two heads peering down at me.

The *tap, tap* of boots approaching rang through the plaza, and the heads disappeared. Beneath me, a group of twelve guards came into view, carrying torches. They looked up at me and then forward again as they moved to the other side of the piazza in their nightly formation.

Nothing had alarmed the guard. All seemed normal to them. I looked up again, wondering if I had dreamed that two sets of eyes peered down at me. But no, they were there again.

"Gabriella, 'tis I," came a low voice.

Marcello?

My heart leaped. *Impossible.*

I was hallucinating. But I didn't care if it was only a dream. I'd gladly give in to this one.

"Do not move, beloved," Marcello said.

No worries there, I thought. I couldn't even force myself to speak.

"Has she lost consciousness?"

Who was he speaking to? Another responded. I couldn't make out the words, but I knew the voice. Lord Greco.

"Bring her up. I'll ride down with the cage, release her at the bottom."

"You may have to carry her, when you do."

"Lucky for us the city sleeps and the guard has passed."

They began cranking on the winch. I winced at every click of the wheel—to me it was as loud as if it were a church bell ringing across the square. I let my head fall to the side, searching the cobblestones below for any sign of alarm.

They shared another word above me, then Marcello climbed down the rope. I wanted to reach up to him, touch him, but my strength was gone. "Mar…cello," I whispered.

He stared down at me, his handsome face now visible in the faint light of a torch far below us. "Lower us down," he said, speaking to Lord Greco but still staring at me as if I were dying in his arms, like that fateful night I almost succumbed to the poison. "I came as quickly as I could," he said.

We lurched, and I gasped, feeling what I had now dreaded for two days—falling. But we came quickly to a stop again. Marcello looked up and then nodded. We resumed our descent, this time more steadily.

Distantly, I worried that he might fall, but he appeared as strong as ever.

I saw the torches the night watchmen carried, along the far wall, before Marcello did. But I didn't have the strength to try to warn him. They paused, obviously catching sight of my lowering cage and the form atop it, and hovered, staring across the acres of cobblestone, as if to make certain their eyes did not deceive them in the dark. My eyes met Marcello's, and I let my head fall to the right, trying to point with my head, but he did not get it.

The bells rang then. "The prisoner! Someone attempts to free her! Knights to arms!"

Marcello swore under his breath, jumped to the ground before my cage hit it, and worked furiously at the knot that held the door shut.

I let my head roll right again, watching the knights run toward us as though I were watching a movie unfold.

"Gabriella," he said urgently, "can you move?"

I tried—really put my mind to it—but was only able to lift one hand.

"It's all right," he said grimly, finally drawing back and ramming the knot with his sword, taking out a branch at the same time. He threw open the door and dragged me out, then lifted me into his arms. I looked past his shoulder to the knights, now just twenty feet away, heard the singing of arrows flying toward them, and watched the first two fall. The others charged on, two remaining behind with their fallen comrades.

They all shouted.

So much shouting. It rang through my head like a pained echo in a deep canyon.

But then we were through the arch, Marcello hurrying as fast as he could, with my dead weight in his arms. Behind us, I could see two archers dressed from head to toe in black, fending off those who pursued us. Was one Lia?

"She shall catch up," Marcello grunted, reading my mind. "Do not fret."

He turned a corner, then paused and whipped around the corner again, his back to the wall, panting.

I could hear them then, another group of guards, coming our way at a dead run. Marcello glanced around, looking for a place to hide, then set me abruptly on the ground as the boots drew nearer. He yanked a skin from his belt loop and hurriedly uncorked the mouth of it, pouring some precious water into my mouth. Then he set it on my belly, rose and drew his sword at the same time, turning around the corner to strike the first knight in the midsection, the second at the shoulder.

His archers were there, then, taking more down in rapid succession.

I thought I heard Lia's voice, then Luca's, but I couldn't be sure. There was a distinct possibility that I was imagining all of this, I assessed distantly. Hallucinating.

In minutes, I was back in Marcello's arms, with no signs of pursuit, even with the bells of alarm still ringing in the plaza. We slowed and dipped into a covered alley, arches crisscrossing above us. Marcello lowered me to the ground again and gave me more to drink. I felt the water run through me like rain through sand— I could actually *feel* it flowing through me—making me believe it all might be real. My body screamed for more. "Easy, easy," he said soothingly. "Not too fast."

Lia and Luca pulled off their black robes, and I saw that my sister was in a pretty gown, Luca in a nice tunic. "Just four young people out past curfew," Marcello said with a wink.

"With the Bride of Siena in our midst," Lia said, staring down at me in consternation. "That dress won't draw any attention." She knelt beside me. "Are you injured, Gabi?"

I shook my head. "In need of food and water," I said, my voice still croaky but at least working again.

"Your thigh, ribs?"

"Still as they were," I said. The headache was back, throttling my brain from one side to the other, as if complaining that the meager amount of water was not enough. It made me forget about my other ailments.

"Can we make the river?" Luca asked Marcello, peeking around the corner. For the first time, I got a good look at him. I squinched my eyes up tight, and then opened them again, staring at him, wondering if I was seeing things. He'd been so sick, and now he seemed—

He whipped back. "Hide," he growled.

We pressed against the wall as a contingent of knights came trotting past. More bells were ringing. We had to get out, now, before the entire city awakened and took to arms.

They made it sound like Firenze was being attacked, not like a trapped girl sought to escape her cage.

"Come," Marcello said, helping me to my feet. "Better?" he asked, looking at me with his sad, handsome eyes.

"A bit," I lied, blinking wide eyes against the searing pain in my head.

"Good girl. Can you run?"

"That…might be a bit much to ask."

"I'll hold her from one side, you the other," Lia said. "We'll make better time."

Marcello immediately did as she asked. Luca went to the door, arrow drawn, and then nodded, pointing, encouraging us onward.

We moved out, toward the river, I decided, getting my bearings again.

Two blocks from it, we heard another group of knights approach at a steady run.

We again huddled in the deep recesses of a tunnel, hearts hammering in our chests as they passed by. Marcello grunted. "Rodolfo has pointed them in the wrong direction. But take care, the entire city is liable to be peering out their windows, aiming to see what the fuss is all about."

We moved out, hurrying along as best we could, Marcello and Lia dragging me between them.

When we finally reached the river, Marcello pulled up short and quickly lifted me in his arms. "Laugh," he directed. "Giggle. Pretend you've been deep in the sops."

He lifted me higher. "Where is my threshold?" he said, stumbling backward as if drunk. "'Tis around here somewhere!"

"Just another groom anxious for his marriage bed!" cried Luca behind us.

Lia burst out in hysterical giggles.

I saw them, then. Four men, commoners, but with axes on their shoulders, staring at us, half in irritation, half in amusement.

"Good gentlemen," Marcello said, as I curved my face into his neck like a blushing, embarrassed bride. "Too much wine, I confess. And those bells! The bells! They have me all confused. Would you be so kind as to point out Calle Lorenzo?"

We paused before them, and Lia and Luca kept giggling behind us.

"'Tis but three more blocks, Sir," said one man at last.

"Good man, good man," Marcello slurred. "Now go and see what that fuss is about, will you? Sounds like all of Firenze is afire."

They set off beyond us, running again, and we hurried forward—me between Lia and Marcello—but then dodged left at the next street, toward the river docks not far from Ponte Vecchio.

Marcello quietly gave a whistle, and another came in response. In seconds, a large skiff drew alongside the dock. Marcello tossed a small bag of coins to a dockman, who appeared to be dozing in the corner. His only movement was to reach out, grab hold of the coins, and hurriedly tuck them inside his coat.

Marcello picked me up and handed me to Luca, who had climbed aboard.

"Luca," I breathed, so glad to see him on his feet, his strength regained. My eyes had not been deceiving me.

"Ahh, m'lady," he whispered happily, setting me in the front of the skiff. "This what they're selling now in the markets of Firenze?" he asked Marcello, reaching for Lia. "Beautiful women ready for their wedding day?" He held on to Lia until she smiled and squirmed away.

"Apparently they have so many, they're free for the taking," Marcello returned. "Come, let us be away."

Luca was already plunging his pole down into the dark waters, easing us away from the dock. I could feel the pull of the current, hear the lapping like a gentle lullaby, dulling the constant pricks of my headache.

Marcello handed me the skin of water. "Slowly, beloved. Slowly," he reminded me in a whisper. "I'll give you a bit to eat once we're safe."

Once we're safe. I remembered how vast Firenze was. There were miles of river ahead of us yet, a couple of bridges, and a guardhouse at the edge of the city, before we were clear.

He turned to Lia. "Evangelia, ready your bow," he said, pushing down on a pole at the back of the skiff, directing us into the center of the river, away from either bank, where it was darkest.

He and Luca dug in with their poles, and when it grew too deep, they reached for long paddles.

I looked to the left as we drifted, closer to the piazza and the wall where I had been perched. The city had more torches alight here, their light reaching toward us in craggy waves on the water, as if they meant to betray us.

"Trouble ahead," Luca said over his shoulder.

A group of knights had spotted us.

CHAPTER 25

"You there! Come ashore!" demanded the head knight, stepping down onto the dock and shielding his eyes for a better view of us.

We could see him fairly well among the torches his men held high. But we had to be little more than a dim form on the black river to him. I frowned down at my gown and tried to make myself lie more flat at the bottom of the low-sided skiff, ignoring the cold puddle of water seeping into my skirts.

Lia knelt next to me, her bow at her side, arrow in hand, ready.

"Come! Now!" the man demanded as we drifted past him, not fifty feet from his dock.

"Nay, m'lord!" Marcello called, regret in his voice. "We cannot. We've been sent by the grandi of Firenze to deliver precious cargo to the front. And we must make haste. The Sienese have breached the gates and even now flood across the Rubaconte."

The captain faltered and gazed upriver. Given the activity behind him, I could tell that the alarm had reached this part of the city. More and more torches were lit ahead, making it appear that something indeed might be transpiring up there.

He peered at us as we eased down the river. "You men alone?"

"Only a dock wench to help us pass the time," said Luca with a laugh.

I could feel Lia shaking her head, even in the dark.

And I could feel Luca's grin.

"Well, be on the lookout for the Lady Betarrini," the captain said uneasily. "The foul dogs have freed her and escaped!"

Marcello sputtered, as if shocked by the news. "Indeed! I'll kill any man myself who dares steal our prize!"

I bit down on my lip, wanting to laugh at his double meaning, even as my heart continued to pound.

The knight gestured for his men to enter a skiff. "I must send my men to check your cargo," he said apologetically. "Protocol and all."

"Understood. As long as they do not force us to tarry upon our mission."

"They shall not," the man promised.

I peered over the edge and watched the knights load into their skiff.

"Do you know how to swim?" Marcello whispered to me.

"Yes."

"She'll sink like a stone in that heavy gown," Luca warned, eyeing the skiff with the knights leaving the dock.

"All she must do is stay hidden and hold on. We have little choice," Marcello said grimly. "Forgive me, love."

"No, you're right," I said. There really was no option; it was our only chance. I only hoped I had the strength to hold onto the edge.

Marcello handed me a knife. "Move quickly. Mayhap you can shed some of that fabric before they're upon us. We'll buy you a little time." He turned and dug into the water with his oar. Luca did the same.

Across from me, Lia unpinned her hair and tossed it about, playing the part of a dock maid. I turned and handed her the knife. She took off the short train first, leaving a ragged edge. Then I took out a length from either side. Yards of fabric were at my feet.

"You there!" called the knight behind us. "Pull up!" We could clearly see them, with a lamp held aloft, but we knew we were likely still little more than a dark form on the water.

"Ah, yes sir, right away sir," Luca called over his shoulder. Turning to me, he said, "Time for an evening dip, m'lady. We don't wish them to find the treasured contraband aboard."

I didn't wait. Anticipating the cold only made it worse. I lay down on my stomach at the edge and then slipped over the side, peeking from the far side of the skiff as I made my way, hand over hand, to the front. We were moving at a quick enough pace that the teal gown was apt to spread out, making it more visible than ever. The only way to go unseen would be to let my body float beneath the shallow-bottomed skiff, effectively hiding it. I reached the front and felt my knees bump against the bottom.

"Excellent." Marcello dared to kneel and kiss my forehead when they were but twenty feet behind us. "Most beautiful mermaid I've ever come across."

"You must not sail a great deal," I whispered back with a smile.

"I could sail the seven seas and never find another like you, Gabriella." Casually, he wrapped the fabric we'd cut away around an anchoring stone and let it slip into the water beside me. Then he covered my fingers with the edge of his cape and rose to greet the men on the other skiff, now coming alongside ours.

I lowered my head as deep as I could, just keeping my nose and ears above water.

The water was perhaps sixty degrees, and I was already shivering. Given my hunger and weakness, I didn't know how long I could hang on. *But Marcello knows,* I thought, trying to comfort myself. *He'll hurry them along as fast as he can.*

One knight clambered aboard and paused, now within my view. "Never seen you on the docks, woman," he said to Lia. "Do you serve at the tavern near the bridge?"

"Nay," she said, with a hint of flirtation. "I favor another."

"Lord Calidori's inn," Luca put in.

"Ahh. I shall have to relinquish some of my coin in that establishment, on occasion." He leered at Lia and turned toward Marcello. "Sir, I need to see your papers for transit of cargo. Or a letter of passage?"

"Yes, about that," Marcello said. "You see, we have no official papers. Our sole mission is to deliver this lovely lady to the front, to a Lord Paratore. Apparently, he won a key battle today, and the grandi of Firenze wish to reward him. Unofficially, of course."

The knight guffawed, and so did the men behind him.

"I see," he said, his two words heavy with meaning. I could just imagine him leering over at Lia again. "He shall be most gratified. Nothing like a victory on the battlefield and a woman to warm a man's bed come night."

"Indeed." I could hear the tightness in Marcello's voice. Could the soldier hear it?

"I still need to have your name, sir."

"Sir Antonio Fernandini," Marcello said, "of Umbria."

The knight paused. "Forgive me, Sir. Since we have not yet met, I need to see your letter of passage, at the very least. As you heard, there has been an escape this night—"

"Does this look like the bride who was put into your cage?"

The knight paused and then laughed. "Lady Betarrini was a lady, every inch of her. This one is clearly a harlot in a lady's gown."

"Well, then…"

"Forgive me," said the knight with a small laugh. "I shall not keep you any longer."

I waited, but did not feel the rock of the skiff, telling me the enemy had unloaded. Everyone was quiet. He'd edged out of my view so I couldn't see what kept him from moving.

Come on, I urged silently. My hands ached with the cold; my entire body was trembling.

"Is there something wrong, sir?" Marcello asked.

I wanted to peek over the edge so badly. But I made myself stay down, out of sight.

"This bow and quiver of arrows. To whom does it belong?"

"Me, sir," Luca said. "Though I've yet to pierce a Sienese scoundrel myself."

The knight paused again. I glanced up at Marcello's back. Was he tensing?

"Why, this is a bead." Beads. From the bodice of my gown. They must have popped off when we cut the fabric—or when I slipped over the edge. I tensed. From the direction of his voice, I guessed he'd picked it up from the bottom of the skiff. "And here is another. From your gown, miss?" He looked over at Lia, obviously took in her unadorned skirts, and then looked to Marcello again. His voice grew more strident. "There was another lady this day, in a gown heavy with beading. All of Firenze spoke of the gown's magnificence."

Marcello laughed. "Well, as you can clearly see, we have no ladies in beaded gowns present," he said. "Though I'd welcome a maid of my own this cold night."

The knight of Firenze did not laugh. I could tell from the reflection on the water that the other two were now standing in their own skiff.

I closed my eyes in frustration then looked to the side, trying to get my bearings. We were nearly clear of the last bridge outside of town. So close…*so close!*

"It is them!" the knight cried. He pulled his sword, as did the four others directly after him. "'Tis Lady Evangelia Betarrini, and I'd wager this is Sir Marcello Forelli," he said over his shoulder. "Knights to arms!" he screamed into the dark sky. "Knights to arms!"

"Now that will not do," Luca said, leaping forward, his sword clanging against the interloper's. The skiff rocked crazily, and I gasped, nearly losing my grip. "You offend me, not knowing my name too."

Marcello left my line of vision, entering the fray. Someone fell into the water between our skiffs, and the boat rocked again. Lia shrieked and then yelled. I heard the thrum of her bow and a cry from the other skiff.

Marcello and the first knight fell down at the front end of the skiff, rolling from one side to the other. I heard Marcello grunt, and they rolled again, this time with the enemy knight atop him, hands around his neck. I hovered in the water, wondering if I should stay hidden or leap up, help Marcello—when the knight's eyes widened, spying me there.

It was the opening Marcello needed. He plunged a dagger into the man's neck. Blood spurted down, into my eyes, and in horror, I pushed down, intending to just wash off, so I could see again. But at that moment, the skiff rocked precariously again, and I lost my grip.

I was under the skiff, riding along in the current.

For a long moment, I wondered if this would be it. If I would drown here, in the waters of the river Arno.

But then the boat was no longer on top of me. I rose, gasping for air, and felt a strong hand grab my forearm. "There you are, m'lady," Luca said, hauling me halfway over the edge, before turning to meet another knight's strike, punching him in the face and then, when he hovered at the edge, shoving him backward into the water.

Lia crawled over to me, then helped me all the way into the skiff.

Men were running along the river's edge, holding torches high. Light danced across the water to us.

"Well, that's not good," Luca said.

"Truly?" Marcello said, panting. "'Tis not good to have half of Firenze alerted that we are here?"

"Nay," Luca said, tucking a thumb in his belt. "If we are to properly free Lady Betarrini, then *all* of Firenze must be chasing us. *That* is the makings of legend."

Marcello reached down and waited until I placed my frigid fingers into his. He bent down and kissed my knuckles. "I believe Gabriella has endured quite enough to give the bards sufficient yeast for their bloated tales."

Luca shrugged as if he didn't want to argue it. I knew that he was just kidding around, back to his normal cocky self. It strengthened me, to see him well again. It gave me hope that I might be too, sometime soon.

But my eyes moved to the next bridge, just ahead of us. Men were running across it, even now, getting ready to meet us. Would I never be free of this cursed city? I'd always liked Firenze, in my old life. Michelangelo's *David*, the bronze doors of the Baptistery, the passageways beneath the magnificent brick dome…but right then, I decided it'd be fine with me if I never saw the place again.

"Get me home to Siena," I said to Marcello through chattering teeth.

He stared down at me. "I shall, Gabriella. Trust me."

I looked back up into his eyes. The guy had no doubt braved several battles, crossed a heavily fortified border, breached an enemy city wall, and found a way to get me this far. If there was anyone I could trust, it was him. "I do," I said, my teeth chattering.

He reached for his cape and wound it around my shoulders. "One more battle," he said, kissing my forehead. "Then we'll be free of this city so intent on keeping you."

He turned and studied the bridge again. We could see fifteen torches, more on their way. "We need a bit of distraction, Evangelia," he said. "Flaming arrows might do the trick."

She smiled and immediately moved to the front of the skiff. In short order, she'd torn off some of her underskirts and wound them around the tip of her arrow.

Luca reached for the lantern we'd scored from the guys who tried to intercept us, and opened the door so that she could light the first. "Take into account the added weight," he said, as she pulled it away, the flame licking upward.

"Indeed," she said. She glanced toward the bridge, gauging the distance, seemingly able to ignore the flame, growing, licking terribly close to her bowstring.

If that reaches the sinew—

But then it was away, arcing up and onto the roof. It hit and clattered down between the tiles.

"Good, but the next two need to hit something flammable," Marcello said. "We must put this lantern out. In seconds, they'll be firing back upon us."

Luca was already wrapping the next arrow. Lia bent to light it, and Luca wrapped another.

We were getting close enough that we could hear the men downstream, above the wash of the river. Two fired arrows at us; one hit the back of the skiff, the other to our left side. "Snuff it out," Marcello said again in a growl.

"Just a moment," Lia mumbled, sending the arrow flying, already reaching for the next.

Marcello and I watched as the last sputtered and seemed to go out, even as it reached its intended target—a thatched roof. But then three seconds later, a flame grew where it rested. "You did it, Lia!" I cried.

"This shall be," she said, releasing the third flaming arrow, "even more true."

It hit the opposite side, nestling into the reeds of another thatched roof.

Men began to cry out, abandoning their posts now to go and fight the fire.

"One more," she said.

Three arrows sliced down, right beside us. All three went into the water, but they missed the skiff by inches.

"Last one," Marcello said, letting her light it.

We were but fifty feet from the bridge, which was coming fast, since the river narrowed here.

Lia fired, and the fourth arrow went into an open window. Immediately, we could see light dancing inside.

"You have done well, Evangelia," Marcello said. "Now all three of you, prepare to be boarded." Thinking better of putting out the lantern, he set it upon the other skiff, and together, he and Luca gave it a mighty shove, then did their best to put distance between it and us. With some luck, our enemies would think the other skiff carried us. He turned toward me. "Do you have the strength to wield a sword?"

"And a dagger, m'lord," I returned, even though my teeth still chattered. There was no way I was going to enter this fight unarmed…

He grinned and handed me both, courtesy of the dead Firenze knights. "What do you say we take the battle to them?"

"Wh-what?"

"Do you trust me, Gabriella?"

"I do, but—"

But he was already over with Luca and Lia, telling them in a whisper what was about to come down.

Atop the bridge, twenty feet away and fifteen feet above us, people battled two major flames, and a third was growing, seemingly undiscovered as yet. We could hear the confusion in their voices.

They escape! Water! We need water! Stop them! Seize them! Fire! They approach! There they are! Arrows away, you fools!

The other skiff drew their fire for a bit, until the torchlight finally reached both boats, and it was clear none of us was upon the other. We sensed the mob above move toward us, even as we finally entered the relative protection of the great stone arches.

Fire! Over here! They're beneath the bridge! Here they come! Ready yourselves!

Marcello grabbed hold of me at the waist, and even in the deep shadows, I could see that there was a narrow dock beside the arches, with a steep stair stretching upward to the bottom of a shop. Cargo dock. We landed hard upon it, with Luca and Lia right behind us.

I sank to the stair while the three of them turned and lifted the edge of the skiff. In a second, they had it tipped and let it loose.

Where are they? Do you see them? The scoundrels! Bring water! Do they swim? Keep alert! They may be in the water!

We were underneath a trapdoor that opened onto the bridge. No one was directly above us, by the sound of it. A rope appeared hanging from the arch to our left, and a man came sliding down it, yelling.

"Evangelia—" Luca began.

But her arrow had already pierced our attacker's neck, and he fell to the top of the skiff, dead.

"Have I told you how much I think of your sister?" Luca asked with a grin. Marcello was through the cargo door and reached down to help me up. Lia came next, then Luca. We stood in the center of a tiny shop atop the bridge.

Outside, we could hear the melee.

There they are! They've overturned! One is dead! No, that's our man! A woman screamed. *Where are they? Fire! You fools, leave them to drown and come and douse this fire before all is lost!*

I pulled Marcello's dark cape closer, trying to cover every bit of the luxurious gown I could. He reached back, took my hand, and then dived out the door, running decidedly to the left.

Lia put her hand on my shoulder, clearly determined to not get separated.

It was a crazy scene. The bridge had been overbuilt, with two- and even three-story houses, side by side, all the way across it. On the bottom level were shops, with homes above. Men, women, and children ran, fleeing the flames. Knights dashed along the edge, searching the dark, roiling waters for us. Men swore and shouted orders. Women screamed. Children cried.

"That way!" Marcello said anxiously, thumping a man on the shoulder and pointing beyond us. "They've cleared the bridge!"

The man ran on, never looking back at us.

He's brilliant, I thought, staring up at the silhouette of Marcello's curly hair as he led us forward. Had we cleared the other side of the bridge on the skiff, they would have pierced our backs with arrows.

This was our only way. And in the confusion, it looked like we just might make it out. Everyone seemed either preoccupied by the fires or looking for us in the water.

That was my thought.

Right before a troop of six massive knights stopped fifteen feet from us, swords drawn.

CHAPTER 26

"Surrender," said the captain, a man who looked like he'd been spending his whole life at Gold's Gym. "You are surrounded."

I glanced back. He wasn't faking it. Six more behind us. Both groups were about twenty feet away.

No convincing these dudes that they had the wrong foursome. *No way through but through…*

"Evangelia…" Luca said.

But she was already down on one knee, taking down two knights with two rapid strokes across her bow.

Every knight still on his feet charged.

Marcello glanced at Luca over my head. "Back to the water?"

"I think it's best, yes," he said.

They grabbed my hands and pulled, yanking me to the wall, only a short distance from men who still searched the dark waters for us. "Dive far and deep," Marcello growled. He bent, forming a stirrup with his hand, his eyes on the men, coming fast behind us. I did not hesitate. Besides, ten against four was hardly a fair fight—and that wasn't even counting the rest of the city's faithful, all hoping to pierce us with their swords, arrows, or daggers.

My launch was totally lame, however, since I instinctively put my right foot in his hands, forgetting my injury, and I faltered as I felt my hamstring tighten. Fortunately, Marcello used my momentum and sent me flying as best he could.

I glimpsed Lia, already ahead of me, diving toward the water as people screamed, spotting us. I hoped our men were right behind us, but I knew I had to stay under as long as possible. *Far and deep.*

The water felt curiously warm this time. *Maybe 'cause I'm so dang cold…hypothermic. Definitely in hypothermia territory. Hypothermia-city. Hypothermaroma.* Now I was making stupid internal jokes. I really had to be losing it.

I put my hands forward and pulled, drifting with the current, and imagined an arrow piercing my back. Dimly I wondered if I would even rise to the surface once I was hit, or if in the act of drowning, I would simply take one last breath, filling my lungs with water, and then sink to the bottom, my gown catching on the stones below, forever one with the Arno.

I could not stay under any longer. I kicked and pulsed upward, knowing I needed air, despite the risk. Frowning, I tried to kick again. The dress, while it was much lighter than it had been, was still a sodden weight, clinging with frustrating dedication to my legs. I seemed to be sinking rather than making any progress. I opened my eyes, hoping to catch a glimpse of the surface, know how far I had to go to make it. But all was dark, so dark.

A hand grasped my hair, and I winced, pulled away. But then I knew it was a friend, searching for me in the inky waters. I reached up and grabbed hold of it. Male. Marcello? Luca?

We broke the surface, and I coughed and sputtered, splashing as I tried to stay above water. Without the skiff to hold on to, the gown continued to be like an anchor, trying to pull me to my death.

"Shh, I have you," Marcello said, an arm around my chest, easing me backward onto his. I could barely make out the forms of Lia and Luca, a few feet away, swimming with us. "Almost to shore. Be at peace."

Be at peace. Sure. I've about died a hundred times over in the last week. And you're wanting me to hush and be a good girl.

I wanted to lash out at him. Scream. Weep. Laugh. All at once.

Yeah, I was pretty much losing it.

I opted for crying as we reached the rocks on the far side of the river. Then I was mad, because crying made me feel weak and lame.

He cradled me close, against him, pulling me half out of the water. Then he leaned over me, pressing me back between two giant boulders, underneath him, kissing my face and my eyes, as if trying to soothe me. What was he *doing?* Making a move on me when I was half frozen and half dead? Among rocks that smelled of rotting grass and fish and worse? I pushed against him.

He grabbed my wrist and leaned closer. "Shh, Gabriella, shh. Please," he whispered. "I shall get you home, I promise. But *please…* They approach."

I quieted, my weeping and crazy hiccups seeming loud in my ears, despite the rush of the water past us. I was *so* losing it.

We could hear the beat of horse hooves on a cobblestone road above us. Two men trailed behind, torches raised, searching the rocks.

For us.

Where were Lia and Luca?

The riders came closer, hovering horribly near us for a long moment. I was still crying, unable to stop now, my broken, choppy breath like silent screams in the night.

I shut my eyes tight, tucking my head into the crook of Marcello's neck and collarbone, clinging to his shirt. I wanted to melt into him, summon his strength and resolve, remember myself again.

A group of horses clattered to a stop above us. "Anything?" barked a man.

"Nothing, m'lord. They've either swum onward or drowned."

"Continue your search. We must not stop until we have them in hand or find their wretched corpses."

"Yes, sir." The torches moved on, beyond us. I choked on my own spit, trying to stay quiet, and then gasped.

One torch returned, hovering. Marcello tensed above me, my rock, my shield. I imagined him leaping from the shore, tackling the knight above us, like some defending angel of the river.

But then, after a call from downriver, the man and his torch moved on.

I gave in to my sobs. "Forgive me, Marcello. Forgive me."

"Nay, shh. It is I who needs forgiveness. If it were not for me you would not be here, suffering—"

"Nay," I said, reaching up and kissing his jaw, his cheeks, his lips, holding his head between my hands. "If it were not for you, I would be in that cage inside Firenze's walls, dead, be it from the cold or from thirst." I wished I could see him, but it was too dark.

"Come, beloved," he said, taking my hand and helping me up.

We crawled up and through the rocks. I sighed in relief as Luca and Lia's whispered calls reached us from the shelter of the trees on the opposite side of the road. There was a break among the groups of soldiers searching along the Arno's banks. We had to hurry if we didn't want to be seen.

I limped across the road beside Marcello, feeling every bit of my exhaustion. "I know of a place where we can rest until morn," Marcello said in my ear, the trees closing in around us like a welcome blanket. "With daylight, you shall remember your strength." Then, no doubt tiring of my slow, belabored pace, he swept me into his arms.

I leaned my forehead against his chest as he walked, steady and sure.

Luca was ahead of us, Lia behind. In that moment, I felt hope, peace. I wanted to freeze time, to feel this—my friend, my sister, and my love all around me, and, for a few seconds at least, not in grave danger. Firenze, though it was but a half mile distant, felt much farther.

We moved deeper into the forest, Marcello clearly aware of where he was going. I didn't know if it was my desire to stay forever there, in that moment, or my exhaustion, or both, but in a few more steps, I could not keep sleep from claiming me.

I awakened on a pile of clean-smelling straw, Lia's arm draped over my waist. Her breathing was soft and steady, her lithe body warm and welcome against my back.

Luca snored in the corner, leaning against the far wall, his hands wrapped around his sword. I looked around and found Marcello, standing in the open doorway, the rich, golden sunlight of dawn filtering around him. He was looking out, watching, but he seemed at ease, peaceful. Beyond him, the wind stirred, and oak leaves fell. He took a deep breath and closed his eyes, then tucked his head, as if thinking.

I smiled. He had come for me. Saved me. How many times would this man save my life? And I his? I hoped we were getting to the end of having to go to such lengths. Surely, our luck couldn't hold out forever.

Luck? Or God? It seemed as if something, or Someone, wanted us alive. If I were just a lucky girl I would have won the lottery or something.

Maybe I had, I thought, staring dreamily at Marcello.

He glanced over at me then, as if sensing my gaze, and gave me a soft smile, like I was some sort of vision about to disappear with the wind. He cocked his head, his smile growing, and came over to me, gently lifting Lia's arm and helping me rise. He settled her arm so carefully, so sweetly, that I fell a little bit more in love with him right then and there.

He led me over to the doorway, and I looked out over a tiny farm, not much more than the ruins of a half-collapsed stone cottage and this small stable, still intact. He pulled me into his arms, and I leaned in against his chest, wrapping my arms around his broad back, pure muscle beneath his shirt. "Ahh, Gabriella," he said, holding me more tightly. "How I feared I would never see you again."

"And I you," I said, feeling his steady pulse against my cheek. It reminded me that I was not dreaming; this was real. *Thank You, God. Thank You, thank You.*

We stared out into the woods for a few minutes, content to simply be in each other's arms. But then I had to ask. "We are still in Firenze's territory, are we not?"

"We are," he said.

"How did you know of this place?" I asked.

He paused, then reached up above us.

I saw it, then. The dark, chiseled form of a triangle.

"What is that? I saw it on—"

He lifted a finger to his lips. "Say no more. We are brothers, sworn to silence. Our bond goes deep."

I frowned, trying to figure out what he was saying, and stared up into his face, as if there might be more clues lingering there. "A bond beyond loyalty to the grandi of Firenze," I said.

"Or the Nine," he said unapologetically. "It was forged long ago."

Some sort of club, I decided. A brotherhood. "How many?" I dared to ask.

"One over there," he said, nodding toward Luca, as his cousin and friend snorted, started to wake, then let his head fall back against the wall with a dull thud. His snoring resumed.

I smiled. "Of course."

"The others," Marcello said, pulling me close again and looking out, "are much more distant. It is by the grace of God that you were taken by one."

"But why take me at all?" I asked, frowning and pushing slightly away. "He captured me, Marcello, at the grandi's behest. He wanted to use me so they could *assassinate* the Nine. And he threw me into that cursed cage in order to take your castle and force you to swear your allegiance to Firenze." If Greco was a friend, who needed enemies? How could Marcello be excusing him?

Marcello sighed. "As a Sienese sympathizer, Rodolfo is at great risk. And yet he knew if he didn't bring you to the grandi, Paratore would. Your only chance was with him. And his only chance was to play the role expected of him. He sent me word even before the grandi sent me their missive."

I thought back, as I stared into the trees, to how Lord Greco had treated me. While he'd been a jerk at times, I had been way better off with him than I would've been with Lord Paratore. Greco had to play a role, be convincing to everyone around him.

"Rodolfo was charged with finding you and bringing you back to Firenze. And when you stumbled into their camp, dared to discover their plans…Put yourself in his place, Gabriella. What choice did he have? His intention was to use you against Siena as a weapon, convince me—or you—to betray the Nine, not see you killed."

"He honestly believed I might betray the Nine?"

Marcello nodded. "We argued over it ourselves, at Lord Rossi's. He tried to convince me it was the only way to avoid the bloodshed to come."

"But you would not agree."

"Of course not. There are other paths toward peace."

"Greco killed some of our men. Outside Villa Orci. He was there, Marcello. How can you get past that?"

Marcello looked into the distance. "It is a hard path, when a man has divided loyalties. He had to convince the grandi of his loyalties. And now, he is in great danger. If his duplicity is discovered…"

His words trailed off. I didn't know what to say. I remembered Rodolfo's face beside Marcello's on the bridge above my cage. Marcello had said that he was helping lead away the soldiers who pursued us. We probably owed him our lives.

Thoughts of the soldiers reminded me of the battles yet to come. "You must return to Siena? To aid your brother in the fight?"

He took my neck in his hands, tenderly, and nodded, staring into my eyes. "Yes. We must make haste. I came, despite my brother's wishes."

I became still. "Fortino forbade you to come?"

He met my gaze. "He thought it suicide. Believed we could negotiate your freedom. But from Rodolfo's message, I knew there wouldn't be time. I couldn't convince Fortino, so I left."

I took that in. Fortino had been willing to risk my death. But if it came down to saving him or saving Lia, wouldn't I make the same decision?

"All of Siena wanted you freed," he said. "Your suffering was truly felt by all. Had I not gone to you, the republic would never have forgiven me." He gave me a small smile.

"Lia got there in time? To warn Fortino? Siena?"

"Indeed. Because of her, Fortino and the Sienese met the Fiorentini at the border, in time to reinforce our troops already there. When we left, Castello Forelli and Paratore were still in Sienese hands. Those to the west…" He shook his head. "We still have not heard."

"And my mother?"

"Reportedly wild with concern, but holding up." A slow smile spread across his face, and he cocked a brow. "It is easy to see where the She-Wolves of Siena get their strength. I dared not send her word of our plan, or she would have insisted on coming with us."

I returned his smile. "And you? How did you escape the Fiorentini?"

"Luca was far too ill to travel far. We spent two nights in their hospital, masquerading as knights of Firenze, before he was well enough to escape."

"It was you who were reluctant to leave their fine wine and bread," Luca tossed out, rising and rubbing his head as if attempting to wake himself. He picked straw off his sleeve.

"Ah yes, I have already forgotten. It was I who wished to tarry in the company of our enemy," Marcello said, a sarcastic glint in his eye. "Even though I was half mad with concern for my beloved."

"We made it across the border," Luca said, coming closer while giving Lia—still sleeping—a lingering, loving look, "and, as soon as we met up with the Sienese, learned of your capture. We found Evangelia and immediately set out toward Firenze."

I gave Luca a grateful smile and then looked up at Marcello. "Can she continue to stand? Castello Forelli?"

"She shall stand," Marcello said. "Siena has rallied her troops. Had not Evangelia alerted our side to the enemy's intent, it might have gone far differently."

"Castello Paratore may be lost," Luca said.

"We do not know that," Marcello said, obviously irritated by his words.

Luca lifted his hands and brows and took a step away.

I kept my thoughts to myself. If Castello Paratore fell back into Firenze's hands, so be it. As long as Castello Forelli and her inhabitants were safe, I, for one, could live with it.

I hesitated. "Marcello, what of Lord Rossi? Romana? How did Fortino take the word that his future wife and father-in-law are traitors to Siena?"

He turned and stared at the doorway, as if visualizing his brother, miles away. "I am not certain he knows. He had been called upon to lead troops a good distance west of the castle, where the fighting has been fierce. But when he does find out about the Rossis' treachery"— he looked down, then over to me—"it may well destroy him."

CHAPTER 27

Luca proudly returned after an hour, with three grouse hanging from his belt. I was like a madwoman, ripping the feathers from the first bird, seriously considering eating it raw, when Marcello set me aside with a pile of almonds and some edible roots, then skewered the birds and placed them above the fire to roast.

"You do not fear that someone will smell our fire and come to see who is cooking?" I asked.

"We are safe, Gabriella," he said, lowering his head with a look that said *trust me.*

We spent the day eating, drinking, laughing, and sharing all we had learned. I slept on and off, hardly able to keep my eyes open in the process of coming down from my stress-o-rama life. Marcello kept me close, his arm around me, and when we sat down I leaned back against his chest, his legs around me. Between my weariness and the comfort that was him, I was out again for hours. That proved a good thing, since I later learned we were to make it back to our side of the battle line by traveling under cover of darkness.

"How does your leg fare?" Marcello asked, cocking his head to watch as I walked.

"It improves daily. But it is hardly whole."

"And your ribs?" Lia asked. She was carving an arrow from a stick as Luca was showing her how to do.

"In a similar state."

"And she's without a sword again," Luca said, gesturing at me with a smile. "Mayhap that She-Wolf wishes to do battle with her pretty teeth alone."

"If any man of Firenze stands between us and getting back to our mother," I said, nodding, "they shall see I am willing to use my teeth."

He and Marcello laughed, while I shared a meaningful look with Lia. Mom had to be going insane, not knowing where we were or even if we were alive or dead. She'd been through enough with Dad. We had to get to her or at least get her word.

"She'll have heard that I was near Castello Forelli," Lia said lowly to me.

"And then you went charging back to retrieve me," I returned.

"She had better become accustomed to living with concern," Marcello said, lifting a brow. "You two seem to attract danger like moths to a flame."

"Mm, I believe it might be the most delicious thing about them, don't you agree?" Luca said with delight. "Aside from their startling beauty, of course," he added, winking at Lia. He smiled as he handed me a bit of cold meat, the remains of our morning meal, then lifted a morsel to my sister.

She set aside her arrow and took it from him, returning his flirty smile.

He laughed under his breath and looked around at us. "I could spend my entire life alongside you three and die a happy man."

"No," Lia said, her smile fading. She stepped forward and poked him in the chest, driving him backward. "I do not wish to ever, ever, *ever* hear you say such words again. Do you understand me?"

He bumped up against the back wall and frowned down at her. He threw up his hands. "What words? 'Entire life'? 'Alongside you'?"

"Nay! No words of dying. Death." She whipped around and pointed her finger at me and Marcello. "From any of you."

I gave her a tender smile, waiting for her to catch up with herself, realize she was making a scene because of some weird reaction-slash-phobia spawned by Dad's death, when Luca reached out and grabbed her around the waist. She clawed at his hands, trying to escape, but then she was shrieking in laughter as he tickled her and tackled her to the straw.

Luca sat back and looked down at Lia. "Do I appear as a specter to you, m'lady?"

"Nay," she said, sitting up beside him. "You are very much alive. And I aim to keep you that way."

"Ahh, 'tis up to you, now? To protect a knight of Siena?"

"Si, 'tis up to me," she said softly.

Marcello pulled me around the corner and out into the yard, giving them a moment of privacy. He smiled as I grinned. "It pleases you," he said, nodding toward the open stable door.

I lifted a brow. "Does it not please you?"

"It is beyond pleasure," he said, taking me into his arms, "to not only know love, but also to know that those I love know it too."

My eyes widened with hope. "Do you believe it? Truly? That it is love?"

He shrugged. "I know 'tis for Luca. What of your sister?"

I shook my head. "I know not. Never before has she had strong feelings for a man."

Marcello grinned. "Well if there's one thing Luca does for a person, it's elicit strong feelings."

We set off as dusk gave way to dark, passing the forest border and then making our way through a valley, stealing from farm to farm. We had rubbed dirt into every possible inch of the gown, but the silk still had a luminescent quality to it that made me feel like a glow-worm at night.

And I still had nothing but a dagger to hold on to. I longed for the comfort of my sheath, the steady weight of my broadsword at my back. While the straps had chafed my shoulders, grown heavy after a long day out, forming a lump of protest in the muscles, I would have taken that any day to this feeling of nakedness, vulnerability, traveling without a weapon.

Because the closer I got to home, the more intent I was to never be taken away again. I longed for the comfort of Castello Forelli's high, grand walls. The warmth of the great hall, her men gathering and laughing, eating and drinking within. I even missed my cold, high-ceilinged, nunnerylike room, with the long hallway outside that led me so often to Marcello. *Get us home,*

Lord, I found myself praying as we hurried along a path. *Just get us home. Somehow.*

I thought about what Luca said, about dying happy if he could be with us forever. And of that concept itself, *dying happy*. Had Dad died happy? Not wanting to die, obviously, but content, fulfilled, knowing he'd done his best?

And was that why I was latching on to this place, Castello Forelli, as home? Here, there was nothing to reflect Dad, bring up memories of him. Here there was a reprieve from the sadness. The thought of it made me feel both thankful and guilty.

In some way over the last few days, between starvation, and thirst, and narrow escape from those wishing to kill me, I started to think about the life beyond. The forever place. Heaven.

Is it real, God? Heaven? Or just something we make up so we can deal?

I didn't know if it was a fable, a collective dream that we all willingly fell into, but deep down I knew that the thought of heaven, a place where Dad was now, where I would be someday—along with Mom and Lia and Luca and Marcello, in time—was not something to fear. It was a comfort. A dream I wanted to keep believing in.

We slept the following day in a shallow cave, stacked together like sardines in a can, one of the men in front of Lia and me, the other ten feet away, on guard. We had narrowly missed a long line of Fiorentini soldiers who were wearily making their way north, hauling wounded,

dying, dead. I decided it was their grim task that kept them from seeing us, plain in the morning light. But then, they did not expect the
enemy here, so far from the border; even Sienese soldiers would have
left them alone, in the odd code of honor among those at war. They
were, in effect, retreating.

It gave us hope. Had Siena turned more than this stream of men
back?

We set off come nightfall and skirted a vast camp of Fiorentini
knights. One glimpse brought back unpleasant memories for Lia and
me. We would've run, but my leg couldn't tolerate it, and Lia was
sticking closer than ever, constantly holding my hand.

Marcello and Luca seemed to know this land now, walking
steadily along a stream for a time, then rounding a hill and heading
directly south. "We are just north of Castello Paratore," Marcello
said. "In but half an hour, we should be able to see her, and beyond
her to Castello Forelli."

We hurried the rest of the way, ducking beneath a stone bridge
as a patrol of six knights crossed it. I was glad the creek bed was dry.
The whole soggy dress thing? Yeah, I was totally over that.

Marcello paused when they had passed. Luca and Lia looked
back at us, questioning his hesitation. "What is it?" I asked in a
whisper.

He shook his head, barely visible in the narrow moonlight.
"They were not on alert," he returned. "They fear no spies or enemies
about."

A shiver of fear ran down my back. *Mom.*

Knights of Firenze not on alert? So close to the border? Only
having gained significant territory would put them so at ease…and

we were within reach of Castello Forelli's. I tried to give him a comforting smile, but it probably came off more as a flash of teeth in the dim moonlight. "They are most likely fools, or drunk, or thinking as we are—only of home," I offered. "Besides, we are still on the wrong side of the border, right? A quarter mile farther, and we'll see Firenze's men on guard…"

He rose, but I could feel his lingering concern. We quickened our pace: Hunched over, rushing, we reached a cliff that descended to the river, the river that ran between the two castles. We crawled through the bramble to the edge of the rock and looked out.

There, a stone's throw from us, was Castello Paratore.

I frowned. Crimson flags again flew from her parapets, lit by torches.

Worse was what I could see beyond it.

Castello Forelli. *No. No, no, no.*

Her entire front wall was collapsed. Fires blazed within.

"Mom," Lia cried, her voice garbled. She was on her feet in seconds, and Luca chased after her.

I stared over at Marcello, just making out his profile, knowing there was no way I could catch up to Lia.

And when he turned his face to me, my heart stopped.

CHAPTER 28

Disbelief. Fury. Sorrow. Agony, as if he felt the castello's devastation physically, himself.

"I thought…I believed…" I said stupidly, staring back out, "she was impenetrable."

"Obviously not," he bit out, shoving himself to his feet. "The Rossis somehow saw to that." He barely paused to help me up before running down the goat path Lia and Luca had made their way down moments before.

"Marcello, wait," I called in a stage whisper, conscious of the noise he was making in his rush.

He stopped, reluctantly, and waited for me to reach him. He sighed heavily. "Forgive me," he said, offering his hand. "But please, we must make haste."

"To do what?" I asked, pulling him back when he started off again.

"I know not!" he grumbled. I gave in, trotting behind him in my lurching, limping way, until we reached the bottom of the canyon— and Luca and Lia, who were arguing face-to-face in a whisper.

"Evangelia, she is not there!" Luca said, obviously repeating himself, holding on to her arm when she tried to go again. "None of our people are there! We can only pray to God that they fled and reached safety before the castle was breached. What we need to do now is find out what has happened. Who lives. And where."

She angrily shook off his hand, as if he was the reason for this new pain.

I put a hand to my head. All along I had forced myself to imagine that Mom was back here, safe. Home. In our home away from home. Waiting on us. Worried about us. But never, I thought guiltily, had I worried *for* her. *Too obsessed with your own situation…*

"Come on. We must make it to a Sienese camp and find out exactly what has transpired," Marcello said, pulling me into motion again. I could hear Luca and Lia follow behind. We crept along the shore of the riverbed, where we could easily duck into cover among the trees and brush if necessary, but also where we could cross the most ground in the least amount of time.

We put some distance between us and Castello Forelli, fighting every desire within us to rush toward it, make certain our eyes had not deceived us. But no, through the trees, above the parapets, well lit by triumphant torches, were the crimson flags of the evil, conniving, lecherous, murderous jerk.

I shoulda killed Paratore when I had a chance. Not that I regretted gaining the prisoners' freedom. But I should have tried harder, found a way. Because never had I hated another human being more than I hated Paratore in that moment.

As we set off running again, one thought brought me up short.

Lia looked back at me, a question in the cock of her head.

"Lia," I said, fear flooding me like a dive into a frozen pond.

"What?"

"What if…what if *he* has Mom?"

She turned from me and ran harder than before. A few times, I thought I had lost them. But Luca—when he wasn't trying to keep Marcello from diving headlong into a battle he could not win—circled around to collect me. We caught up, finding both Marcello and Lia pacing like wild cats caged just off the savannah.

After a couple of miles, we crested a hill and saw the Sienese encampment just below us. Marcello seemed to make himself stop, wait for me, despite his agitation. The closer we got, the more I was convinced that Paratore had Mom, had everyone I'd ever cared about in the castle, in fact…Cook, Giacinta, Fortino…

We hurried down the hill, and a scout gave out a warning cry. "Who goes there?"

"'Tis I, Sir Marcello Forelli," he called back. "I bring with me Luca Forelli and the Ladies Betarrini!"

The scout repeated the report, and the camp erupted with activity.

Twelve knights rode out to meet us, the men dismounting and clasping both Marcello and Luca's arms, before bowing, with shy grins, to us. We were ushered into camp amid their praises.

"Saints be praised!"

"Alive, despite the reports!"

"Bet they are smarting, letting you four slip from their gates."

More came out to greet us, and we realized that the camp held not only knights, but also women and children, people from the villages and farms about us, as well as the servants from Castello Forelli.

Refugees. I looked from face to face, returning smiles, but anxiously seeking the one I wanted to see most: Mom.

Giovanni was there, then, in front, greeting the men, grinning over at us. I noticed he held his shoulder stiffly, as if he'd been injured—from Villa Orci? But then he bent his head and discussed the fall of the castle with Marcello. Marcello wrapped his arm around his friend's good shoulder, and they walked a few feet away, followed by Luca. I pressed closer, wanting to hear. "Words cannot be uttered that would bespeak my sorrow over it, m'lord," Giovanni said, shaking his head. "We did all we could."

Marcello waved down his apology, but his tone was dull. "From the looks of her, you faced a catapult. Not many men can succeed against such an attack."

"We might have withstood it." He hesitated a moment. "But there were traitors within the gates, m'lord, those loyal to Lord Rossi. They made a way and, in tandem with the enemy, struck fast at our men inside a mere hour after we'd heard from Lady Evangelia," he said, nodding in her direction as she joined our smaller group. "There was simply no time to rout them. Had we had more...everyone fought so bravely, I—"

"I know," Marcello said, nodding. "I know. What news have you of my brother?"

A darker shadow crossed Giovanni's portly face. He shook his head. "We'd sent him word of the Rossis' duplicity. Fortino was attempting to make his way back here this morning when he and his men were surrounded and suffered severe attack."

Marcello swallowed hard, his Adam's apple bobbing. "Is he—?"

Giovanni shook his head. "I know not. Try as we might, we have not been able to obtain word. There are so many injured, m'lord, so many dead…"

"And Lady Rossi? Lord Rossi? Where are they?"

"Presumably still in Siena, m'lord."

Marcello frowned.

"Giovanni, what of our mother?" I asked, glancing back at Lia. I couldn't bear to wait another moment.

"Your mother?" His face broke out in another big smile, and he shook his head. "We now know where the She-Wolves of Siena get their fighting prowess. She took out five or more men as we fought our way free of the enemy. And she's been a godsend in the camp, taking her healing to—"

"Wait. M-my mother?" Lia sputtered. "She's here? She *fought* in the battle?"

"Your mother," Giovanni repeated with a gentle smile.

"But she wields neither sword nor bow," I said. Did he have her confused with someone else? Mom had always bowed out of our swordplay and archery lessons with Dad. She'd called herself a pacifist.

"Nay, I do not wield either sword or bow," Mom said from a few feet away, her long fingers wrapped around the hilt of a staff that was as tall as she was.

"Mom!" Lia cried, rushing to her waiting arms. I limped after her and fell into their shared embrace.

"Oh, girls, my girls, how glad I am that you are back with me, safe." She backed up and touched my face, then Lia's, then returned to me. "You are whole? Unharmed?"

"Nothing that won't heal in time," I said. "And you?"

"I'll be fine," she said, moving a hand to her arm. She'd been injured. How badly?

I shook my head and reached for her staff, checking out the scary-looking points on either end, the weight of it. I looked over to her. "I thought you said you could never hurt another living thing."

She gave me a small smile. "There is something about having your daughter abducted, your other daughter racing to save her, that makes a woman willing to inflict harm." She shook her head. "I did not enjoy it, but every man I removed, I saw as one fewer between us." She pulled us into her embrace again. "Oh, girls, I don't know what I would've done had anything happened to you."

"Thank God we are *all* well," I said, thinking over the words only after they were out of my mouth. I studied Mom's face. She seemed so broken, vulnerable, *open*. Looking at me and Lia like…I didn't know. She was just different, new somehow. But then, facing death did that for a person. It made them appreciate life in a whole new way.

My heart was full, my sense of gratitude almost moving me to tears. And I did believe God had something to do with it. There had been so many opportunities for us to fail, turn the wrong way, be captured again, die. Clearly, our Maker had something else in mind for our future. And I, for one, was overcome. I reached out to wrap an arm around Mom and Lia, and with Marcello and Luca nearby, my heart swelled.

So many ways it could have gone wrong…My mind moved to Paratore. "Mom, tell me about the night Castello Forelli fell."

We sat down on a log and looked out over the men as Mom spoke.

"The men fought hard, sending arrows into the forest every time an enemy knight dared to show his face. But they knew there was only one way into the castello." She paused to glance at me. "They knew if no one was letting them in, they had to break down the gates. The archers were merely distractions. The catapult was firing by morning, massive boulders that battered the gates. At the same time, fifteen men inside turned on us, killing many of our men before we realized that we had traitors within our ranks. Pietro had sent for reinforcements the day before, but Siena was in need of assistance on all sides, including fortifications at the front. There was no way to fend off those who attacked us, from within and without."

"How did you escape with your lives?" I asked. Knowing Paratore, he had probably envisioned total devastation. If Marcello and I returned, it would be to every one of our loved ones dead. He was hardly known for acts of mercy, especially when he was so bent on revenge.

"Pietro," Mom said, nodding over to the man. "He and his men held a line so that every one of the castle's people could escape."

"But it wasn't free and clear for you."

"Nay," she said, shaking her head and staring at a nearby torch as if remembering that night all over again. "There were so many. And they did not wish us to escape. So bloody…again and again I saw men die. Again and again I narrowly escaped. It was there that I was forced to either fight or die. As your mother," she said, "I seemed to be a particularly attractive target."

I gave her a sad smile. "Sorry about that."

She reached out and squeezed my shoulder and Lia's, too. "Such is the burden I must bear, having raised two heroines and, therefore, enemies." She shook her head. "I could not be more proud of you."

"Who taught you to use this?" I asked, picking up the staff.

"Once you were gone, I could not spend all my time in the library. I was going nuts. And after I got word that you'd been exposed to the plague, I had this terrible sense of foreboding, fear. I wasn't sleeping at all. So I asked the men to choose a weapon for me. Given my height, this apparently was a good choice."

She took it from me and dug one end into the dirt between her feet, then passed it back and forth in her hands.

"Your weapon will become like a second skin," I said, simply. "Whenever I'm without my sword, I feel naked. Which I am right now. Any idea where I might get another?"

Mom looked toward the center of camp. "That tent"—she pointed—"is the armory. You'll find what you need there."

My eyes went down twenty or more tents to the spot. It was fairly uniform and impressive for a camp that had been thrown together by an army in retreat. "And is there a tent where a girl could ditch a wedding gown and find something more suitable for the battlefield?"

"Meant to ask you about that—"

"I'll tell you later," I said hurriedly. I didn't want to think about what could've happened if Marcello hadn't arrived when he had.

"There is a tent near the armory where you might be able to find some men's clothes and make do," she said, studying my face as if she could make out the story in the lines around my eyes.

"Thanks." I nodded. "I'll be right back, okay?"

"Okay," she said, reluctantly letting go of my shoulder.

"Fetch me a new quiver of arrows and an extra bowstring, will you?" Lia said. "I want to stay here with Mom."

I walked down to the center of the tents, nodding and smiling as people—my people—recognized me and called out greetings or reached out to shake my hand. While the soldiers of Firenze were but a mile away, I felt safe here, among my own. I knew, instinctively, that every last one of them would fight to the death to save me and my sister, and now my mother. And I would do the same for them.

Seeing a man emerge from a tent, a new cape over his arm, I opted to start there. Suddenly, I could not wait to strip the remnants of the dreadful bridal gown from me, as if I might free myself of all the horrific memories it carried at the same time.

Giacinta looked up at me when I entered. She cried out, rushing into my arms. "M'lady, how we feared for you!"

"And I you," I said.

"Saints be praised," she said, clasping her hands before her, "You're home. Well, as close as you can get to it for now."

"For now," I agreed. "You escaped unharmed?"

"Right as rain," she said proudly. "Though I owe my good fortune to your mother. She saved me not once, but twice, from being carried off by Paratore's men."

I raised a brow in surprise, still trying to envision my mother in battle. "I am glad," I said.

"As am I, obviously. Now," she said, standing back to look me over. "I imagine you seek something to wear." She leaned over and fingered the silk of my sleeve. "Heavens. Did they try to force you into marriage, m'lady?"

"Do not ask," I said. "Please. What would you suggest? I understand that you have more men's clothes than women's."

Giacinta turned and went through one pile, then another. I saw that some had blood upon them, others holes and gashes. Stripped from the dead, I figured, stifling a shiver that ran down my back. It made sense, though; the dead were no longer in need of clothing. And men returning from battle…their clothes were in rags.

Giacinta lifted a cape. "Black will have to do," she said. "Now, if only we had a gown or two."

"Do not fret," I said. "Just a clean pair of leggings and a tunic will suit me fine. Best for riding and fighting anyway."

Giacinta frowned over at me. "Oh, no, m'lady. You must remain here, where 'tis safe. We just got you back!"

I gave her a small smile and ignored her concern. "Leggings, Giacinta? Any leggings without holes this big?" I asked, lifting up a pair with a hole the size of a dinner plate in the rear.

She giggled and dug again, then lifted a pair. "Here! Oh, and look!" She pulled a lovely tunic from the pile. It was huge, but it was green, with gold thread embroidered through it, clearly once belonging to one of the Forelli knights. A knight, now dead.

I took it from her, feeling the full weight of the somber gift.

"Here's a shirt for beneath it," she said, lifting the puffy sleeved garment for my inspection. "Only a bit dirty," she said, spotting the smudge at the top right shoulder.

"It is perfect," I said. "Thank you." I gathered the clothing and moved to the tent door, then realized I did not know where I could change. "Giacinta, do you think you could assist me in changing in here?"

"But of course, m'lady," she said, with an immediate bob of her head. "Just let me speak to a knight outside, so that he might take temporary duty and keep anyone from entering."

I nodded. While she was away, I dug through a pile of boots but couldn't find a matched pair. The process depressed me, made me think of so many men, dead on the battlefield, among the broken stones of the castello…

"There, we're ready now," Giacinta said softly, as if sensing my mood. "Shall I help you off with that gown?"

"Please," I said. Did my tone betray my anxiety? I wished I could take a deep, hot bath, but I doubted that was a possibility here, this night.

She unbuttoned the back and then helped me ease off the tight sleeves. I stepped out of it and then pulled the underdress off. Giacinta gasped, seeing the bruising across my back that had spread from my ribs. "M'lady—"

She caught herself, and I didn't jump to explain. I didn't wish to remember those moments behind me; I preferred to contemplate what lay ahead.

I stepped out of the pantaloons and could feel the heat of her stare on my leg, but again, I resisted the urge to explain. It was what it was, and I was past it. Or wanted to be, anyway.

I yanked on the leggings, and she handed me a fine leather belt. "Much nicer than the rope I wore last," I said with a smile, running my finger over the finely treated material. "It's almost…feminine."

She smiled and then lifted the shirt up and over my head. It slipped down over me, and I was thankful it did not carry with it the odor of the man who once wore it. Then the tunic was over my shoulders, reaching almost to my knees. Its previous owner had to have been a very large man. I mentally went through the knights I had known, the biggest among them, trying to figure out who it might be who had died.

"Best not to think of it, m'lady," Giacinta said, reading my face.

"Agreed," I said.

She let the cape spread between her hands and wound it over my shoulders. "That will help keep the autumn chill from you."

"Indeed." I turned and, after briefly considering going barefoot, put on the cursed bridal slippers again.

"May I do your hair for you before you leave, m'lady?" she asked.

"That," I said with a sigh, "would be lovely. It's been intolerable ever since I left the castello." Other than the updo those servant women had created…

She gestured to a chair and returned with a horsehair brush. She began at the bottom and moved up my hair, pulling out the countless tangles and knots. My hair told the story of where I'd been, among the swirl of the river Arno, running through the forest. Quietly, she set aside a bit of ribbon embedded with beads, a piece of hay, tiny branches, leaves, even a couple of small rocks. I laughed inside, wondering how Lia could have let me travel all the way here looking like Medusa with a head full of snakes.

"Was it quite awful, m'lady? What you endured?"

"In turns," I said. "At times horrific. Other times miraculous."

She stepped back and gave me a sad smile. "Well, I am glad that the Lord saw fit to bestow the miracle of your return upon us."

I paused. Had anyone ever considered me a miracle? Just by being present?

She shook her head. "Forgive me, m'lady. But I have no pins and no hair net."

"That is all right, Giacinta. Just a quick braid?"

She nodded and set to work, quickly pulling my hair into a tight braid, tying it with a leather band, and setting it over my shoulder. She came around me. "Pretty as a princess. You and your sister will give the men hope, being among us again."

"Thank you, Giacinta."

"Pleasure, m'lady," she said with a curtsy.

I moved out of the tent, and the knight outside gave me a bow. "Lady Betarrini."

"Thank you for guarding us."

He bowed again and then strode away, joining two knights who awaited him and studied me with curiosity. I did not know them. They must've hailed from a nearby town or Siena itself.

I moved to the next tent and slipped inside, introducing myself to the man who was keeping the armory, a Sir Pezzati. He was about fifty years old, with a white beard trimmed close to a handsome face and bits of gray at his temples. He smiled at me. "I arrived at the castello after you had departed. Had the pleasure of seeing to your mother's final training with the staff."

I considered him a bit longer. "Then I am grateful to you, sir. Because of that weapon and her training, she lived to see our return."

"No gratitude necessary," he said, suddenly a bit gruff. He checked out my shoulders, as if sizing me up. "Forgive me, m'lady. 'Tis well with you that I do this?"

"Indeed," I said. "Go to it. You know what I seek?"

He grinned. "Everyone in the land knows of the Ladies Betarrini. And you, being Lady *Gabriella* Betarrini, must be in search of a short broadsword and sheath."

I smiled. "I lost mine some time ago. I would feel much better with them at my back again."

"Well, I can imagine," he said. He walked around me, still taking measurements with his eyes but in a fatherly sort of way. He moved off to a table in the corner and fished out a sheath with shoulder straps, then to another, tossing aside sword after sword, seeking just the right one. "Ahh, there," he said, lifting a fine blade into the air.

I joined him at the table and took it from him, feeling the heft of it. I backed up and did a figure eight with my wrist, feeling the flow of the sword, then lifted it to look down the length, against the light. It was straight, true, trustworthy. "It'll do nicely," I said.

He lifted the shoulder straps for me, and I slipped it on, then slid the sword into it. I took a deep breath, almost feeling like it was my first real breath in a while.

"Daggers, too, I assume—"

His voice trailed off, and I looked to see what had distracted him.

Marcello stood near the tent flap, staring at me with fury in his eyes. "A minute, sir, with the lady," he said, demanding rather than asking, never looking fully in the man's direction.

Sir Pezzati immediately departed.

I frowned back. "What is it?"

"You are arming yourself."

"Which is wise in the midst of a war, is it not?" I turned toward the table of daggers, wondering why I was feeling so defensive. And why he was feeling so…offensive.

"Your battle is over, Gabriella," he said, coming over to me. I kept my back to him, wondering when he became my boss. He reached around, took a dagger from my hand, and set it down.

"Marcello, you will soon be away to look for Fortino. I shall go with you."

"Nay. You shall flee, deeper south, far away from the battle."

I turned to face him, and my braid flopped over my shoulder. "If you go, I go too. We will bring strength to our men, hope. If Marcello Forelli can free his beloved from the very center of Firenze, how much more can he do at the front? Firenze must be quaking in their boots at this very moment, fearing your return. And mine," I said, tapping my chest.

He sighed and wrapped a hand around the back of my neck, then lowered his forehead to rest against mine. "I must go alone, beloved. And I must know that you are safe, so I can concentrate on my brother."

"I can help you, Marcello. Lia and I can—"

"Nay," he said, leaning down to cover my lips with his.

I allowed it a moment, having missed our stolen moments. But as good as it felt, I was not really in the mood for kissing. Not if he was thinking about heading off without me. I pushed him gently back and turned to collect several daggers and tuck them into my belt. I went over to the table filled with sheaths again, ignoring his sigh of frustration, and chose another leg sheath for a fourth blade, to be worn at the calf.

Once I'd fastened it on, I turned to face him, arms folded. "You can take me with you, or I shall simply follow. And you know what happens when we get separated."

He shook his head. "Even you are not so foolish that you would again risk being taken by the enemy."

"I will if it means I am aiding you and Fortino!"

"Gabriella!" he barked, running his fingers into his hair and staring at me with wide eyes. "Do you know what I've heard? Do you know what the enemy's intent is? Do you?"

I frowned. "Nay," I whispered.

His lips clamped together, and he turned away, shaking his head slowly, as if trying to get a grip. "Never mind," he said, putting out a hand to the side. "Just choose to trust me."

I sighed and moved over to him to take his hand. "Marcello, tell me. What is this new threat against you?"

"Not against me," he said, staring at me as if knowledge of it tortured him. "Against you. Your escape—Gabriella." He shook his head. "It has infuriated them, to the point of distraction. The new bounty offered for your head would buy any man a thousand acres, cattle, a home."

I stared back at him numbly. "My head. Literally. Meaning, they only need show up with my head to collect their prize." I swallowed quickly, not wanting him to see, feel my fear.

"I do not know if we can keep you safe, even deeper to our south. Enemies shall track you wherever you go. We must get you home. Somehow. If only there was some way—"

"Home?" I asked blankly. Castello Forelli was decimated, overthrown…"Siena, you mean?"

"*Home*," he said softly. "To Normandy."

I stared back at him, unable to believe what I was hearing. After all we'd endured, made it through…did he not clearly see that we were meant to be together? Forever? I shook my head. He was willing to give up on us, on love, to keep me alive. It was both infuriating and amazing at the same time.

He gave me a barely perceptible nod, misery in his eyes. "Do you see now?"

I smiled suddenly. "Yes."

"Why are you smiling?" he asked, looking irritated.

"Because, it's perfect, really. They want my head. And who will be most eager of all to capture it? Paratore. We can deal with him once and for all."

He shook his head, clearly disliking my tone.

I stared over to the flame of the torch and then back to him. "How do you catch a bear, Marcello?"

His frown deepened. He refused to play my game.

"With bait," I answered for him. "And a very big trap."

CHAPTER 29

"Absolutely not," Marcello said, walking between the tents. Men and women parted before us, eyes wide, wanting to look away but rubbernecking at us in spite of themselves.

"Marcello, simply listen. It was your idea to begin with. You have yet to hear my entire plan! The tombs are on that little knoll, between the two castellos. If we can draw them all in there, surround them, you can reclaim both again for Siena."

"Come," he growled, grabbing my arm and yanking me into a tent.

"Ow!" I said, pulling it from his grasp and frowning at him.

He ignored my complaint. "So you wish to be at the center of them *all*," he said, "surrounded. By every last Fiorentini knight. And then you make your *escape*. I hear you, Gabriella, as loud as church bells. Are you so eager to be rid of me now that you'd gladly risk death?"

"Rid of you? 'Tis you who seem anxious to be rid of me."

He gave me a helpless stare. "Only to keep you safe. Only for that."

I stepped toward him, reaching out, wanting to apologize, ease the pain behind his eyes. "We shall leave, but only as before. With the intention of return. In a month's time, when all is safe." I paced away, but then frowned. Why wasn't he going for this? My mom, my sister, and I would be well, safe, while he secured the territory for our return. Did he not get it? "I simply provide bait for your trap. I'll be out of the fray while you trap the bear and reclaim the land that is rightfully yours."

"'Tis *not* perfect." He shook his head. He looked down at me, misery in his eyes. "I cannot, Gabriella. Do not ask it of me. If we were certain you could reach the tumuli, I'd consider it. But to get you there…it'd be a miracle if you made it."

"Think of it. Castello Forelli fell because the traitors surprised our men, attacking from the inside. Where is the last place the men of Firenze expect me to be? Fighting from the *inside*, the center of battle."

He rubbed the back of his neck. "Risking your life—I'd rather die myself, a hundred times over."

I snorted, hardly ladylike, but he was ticking me off. "Ah, so it's all right for you to risk your life, but I cannot? What you feel—" I said, reaching out to lay a hand on his chest. "Marcello, I feel the same. I cannot lose you. I cannot. And if we are in danger, if Firenze wins this battle, you will be imprisoned or worse." It was my turn to shake my head. "Nay, that is intolerable for *me*."

He stared down at me for a long moment and then wrapped me in his arms. I relaxed and melted into his embrace. He kissed my forehead, then moved down my cheek to my lips, kissing me for a long time, deeply, searchingly, as if he were trying to memorize me—

I read his intent a second too late. He'd interwoven his fingers in my right hand. Swiftly, he turned my wrist and twisted it to my back. "Ouch! Marcello, what are you *doing?*"

"Forgive me, beloved, but I do this to make a point. Press me, and I shall see no other recourse but to leave you behind, tied to a post and under guard."

I frowned up at him in shock. "You would not."

"I would," he said, frowning back. "To keep you safe. To keep you alive."

"Sir Forelli!" called a man outside. "Sir Forelli!"

Marcello gave me one last, long stare and then let me go. I regretted not kicking him in the shin with everything I had in me. Of all the outrageous—

"Sir Forelli!" Pietro called, opening the tent flap. "Come!"

Marcello left with him. They ran down the line of tents to the edge of camp. I hobbled along behind. Men were surging around me, shrugging into breastplates and shoulder guards, urgently preparing for battle.

"Gabriella! Gabi!" Lia cried, shoving her way through to me. "What is it?"

"I don't know," I said. "Where's Mom?" But then I saw her, making her way over to us, staff in hand. She looked regal. Like a queen. Calm. Unafraid.

Together, we reached the top of the hill. Across the valley was the back wall of Castello Forelli, and before her was line after line of soldiers bearing the flag of Firenze.

Lia blew the air out of her cheeks and casually pulled her bow from her shoulder. "Do they mean to attack? Because we do not—"

A trumpet sounded, and the men across from us cheered, their voices eerily following their actions by a second's delay.

"Knights in formation!" Marcello bellowed. Men all around us quickened their pace.

But my eyes remained on the enemies across from us. They parted at the center, and we heard laughter, triumphant cries. A man stumbled forward, hands tied before him. He was naked, gruesomely bloody. Who was it? A prisoner? My stomach clenched inside as a man reached out to whip the prisoner's back, sending him to the dirt.

"Who is it?" Mom asked, stepping up beside me.

But then I saw Marcello take a step, falter, bring a hand to his chest.

No, it can't...please, no. No!

It was Fortino.

Men on our side shouted and cursed, eager to charge, to free one of their lords. Others held them back, waiting on Marcello's orders.

Paratore trotted down the hill, past Fortino—who now lay unmoving—and on toward us, flag bearers on either side of him. He waited halfway down the hill, unwilling to go any farther. *Blasted, cursed, wretched excuse of a man...*

Two knights rode up, Marcello's mount between them. He was atop it in seconds. He searched the crowd until he found me. "Gabriella, you must get out of sight. Are you mad?"

All eyes moved to me.

I nodded, no fight left in me, and turned to go.

Luca walked beside us, and I knew then that he'd been assigned guard duty. I glanced over my shoulder. Before the men closed ranks again, I saw Marcello turn and ride low and hard to the valley floor. To his brother.

Luca relayed to us what was coming down, as we remained well hidden behind ten rows of soldiers. "Marcello has dismounted. He's talking to Paratore now."

He frowned and watched for another few moments. Some of our men shouted and groaned.

"What? What's happening?" I said.

"Paratore is turning, leaving." He looked hard at me. "And they're taking Fortino with them." He pried his way through the men, apparently to find out more. In his agitation, he left us behind. I glanced at Mom and Lia, fighting the urge to claw my way to the front myself. "What's happening?" I asked the tallest. "Can you see?"

"Sir Marcello returns," he said distractedly.

"Why does he not call for the attack?" cried a man. They were anxious for vengeance, so soon after the capture of Castello Forelli and her surrounding lands. Many of them were farmers and shepherds on those hills, but in this moment, they were unified as *knights*. The men surged, moved as a group, chanting, shouting. *"A morte Firenze!" Death to Firenze!*

They quieted as Marcello drew near. "Men of Siena," he called, "they have taken Lord Fortino Forelli prisoner, demanding a trade price that m'lord himself refused, regardless of his ill health."

"What?" called a man.

"What did they want?" called another.

"Immediate surrender and retreat."

The men cried out in complaint and then grumbled, the sound like a wave crashing and then washing over a shore.

"We shall battle them in hours," he said, "and fight to win my brother Fortino's freedom, as well as the land that belongs to us. Are you with me?"

The crowd shouted their assent, radiating the fury that had fueled men in battle since the dawn of time. Lips curled back, muscles rippled, weapons were raised. After a moment, they parted, and Marcello came through, followed by Luca, Pietro, and Giovanni. Marcello took my hand and continued to stride forward, down the hill to our tents. I ran to keep up with him.

"Marcello, I—"

He held up a hand to shush me. "Please, m'love. A moment."

Mom, Lia, Luca, Pietro, Giovanni, and I followed him into his tent, which held nothing but a bedroll and a few clothing items, as well as some maps, open on a table. My mother and sister hovered by the flaps of the doorway, while the men moved to either side of Marcello, arms folded in front of their chests. We waited as Marcello paced back and forth, his eyes moving constantly. In the last twelve hours, he had lost his home and now perhaps his brother. He rubbed a hand through his hair and then squeezed the back of his neck, as if it might force the right plan to his mind.

"He's not dead yet," I said quietly. "Do not give up on him, Marcello."

He frowned at me. "Do you not see? I must." He paused and looked up to the top of the tent, his face awash in anguish. "If you could've seen him, Gabriella…" He put his hands over his mouth and took a deep breath, then turned to us. He stared at me for a moment, started to speak, and then abruptly shut his mouth.

"They wanted more than surrender and retreat," I guessed. "They wanted us, too."

"As expected," he said, meeting my gaze, misery in his eyes. He looked to my mom and sister. "All three of you now." Mom looked a little pale. "What's worse is that Paratore has a very good idea you are here, now, with us. You must be away in all haste, for—"

"M'lord," Luca said from the doorway. "Rider, coming hard."

Marcello stepped up beside him and opened the other flap so that the scout could enter. The young man, little older than I, looked nervously around at us and then back to Marcello. "M'lord, there is word of three separate armies on the move toward Siena."

"Three?" Marcello said. "From whence have they come?"

"Umbria, m'lord."

"What does that mean?" I whispered to Giovanni. "How many men?"

"Fifteen hundred. Mayhap more."

"And they shall arrive at Siena's gates…" Marcello led.

"By sundown, on the morrow, m'lord."

"She may be able to withstand such a force, but they'll be looking to us to aid them," Marcello said to Luca.

Luca nodded once.

"M'lord," I said, my heart picking up its pace. "What if they don't intend to try and breach Siena's gates? What if they arrive as a fearsome show of force, merely to push the Sienese into surrender?"

The men frowned at me, not understanding.

"What if," I went on, "word has not reached Siena about the Rossis' treachery? What if...Lord Rossi, Romana, are calling the Nine together, even now? To see through what we would not? Betraying the Council of Nine. Murdering all but one."

Marcello searched the ground, thinking it through. It had been days since Lia had arrived with word, but the focus had been on turning the tide of the Fiorentini armies back from the border, defending the castles. Giovanni had not been certain that word had reached Siena...only Fortino.

"Send two scouts," he said to Luca at last. "Our fastest riders. To warn the Nine. And tell them that we will be there on the morrow." His tone was firm, furious, but his eyes held fear.

And that scared me more than anything.

CHAPTER 30

At sunset, I found Marcello on a hill above camp, looking toward Castello Forelli. I slipped my arms around his waist and leaned my head against his back, between his shoulder blades. "I am sorry, my love. For all you have endured this day." Would Fortino even survive another night of captivity, as ill as Marcello had described?

He remained quiet but placed his hands over mine.

"I am thankful that you were spared," he said, turning to face me. "That you're here, with me." He leaned his forehead down to touch mine and pulled me closer, eyes closed. "If only we did not so soon have to part..." We stood there a moment, sharing the grief, the fear.

"I wish I could ease your pain. After we lost my father..." My voice broke, and I took a halting breath. "I'm here. Ready to love you. Support you. Come what may."

He pulled back a little, his eyes pools of torture. "Only one thing would ease the pain in my heart this night."

"What? Anything. *Anything.*"

"To do what I have longed to do—claim you as my own. Thoughts of losing you, when I've as much as lost Fortino..." He closed his eyes in anguish, turned, and knelt before me. "Gabriella Betarrini, please honor me by becoming my bride."

"Marcello," I sputtered, searching for the words. "We are to part within hours."

He remained on his knees, staring up at me.

"Do you not see?" I said. "If I promise you forever, then my mother and sister must remain here forever too."

"I shall make a home for you all," he said, rising and taking my cheek in his warm hand. I closed my eyes against the glory of him. Even displaced, frightened, grieving, he was a force. A man. I had trouble breathing. "Somehow. Somewhere I will take care of all of you. Do you not trust me?"

"'Tis not a matter of trust," I said softly. "'Tis a matter of choice. If it were only me, I'd say yes this very moment. But for my family... You must understand, we would be leaving much behind."

"But welcoming much here," he said. "True?"

"True," I said mournfully. I sighed and stared back up at him, helpless. "Forgive me, Marcello. But I cannot accept your offer of marriage." Were these words really coming out of my mouth? And yet I could not stop them—I knew they were the right words. "Not yet," I continued. "Not until Lia and my mother agree to remain."

He gave me a tiny nod. "I understand, Gabriella," he said. Then he bent and set a tender, soft, lingering kiss upon my lips, as if he was saying good-bye. Forever. Tears rolled down my cheeks again as I struggled to understand what was happening.

He dropped my hands, then turned and walked down the hill alone, pain radiating from the defeated curve of his shoulders.

With each step he took, I felt a tiny bit of me die too. *I've made a mistake. This is wrong!* It took everything in me to remain where I was, to not go tearing after him to agree to his proposal and wake up in the morning as his bride.

But I'd be waking up alone for days to come, with him off to battle. My sister and mom stuck here whether they liked it or not. I couldn't do it.

Not yet.

At sunup, I watched as Marcello clasped arms with Luca. Then he called out orders to all men to pack up and be ready in fifteen minutes' time, with three days' supplies on their backs. "And see to it that you pack both bread and dried meat with you, if you have not yet," he shouted. "A hungry man is a dead man."

They cleared out, fast. But I remained, waiting for him to see me, face me.

At last his eyes settled on me. They moved from sorrow to determination. He stepped forward and took my hands. "Gabriella, you must promise me."

"What, love?"

"As soon as you are ready, my six most trusted men shall escort you and your family southward, beyond the reach of any man loyal to Firenze. I have a friend—"

"Nay." I squeezed his hands. "Take us with you. We will help you fight, help you galvanize the Sienese in case—"

"Think about it, Gabriella. For every man you take down, four more will be bent on reaching you, capturing you, or worse. You said it yourself. You are bait to the bear. And my men will feel they must defend you, rather than press forward. *I* will feel that way."

I opened my mouth to argue but then decided I had to agree with him. We would be more of a distraction than an asset. I took a step away and put a hand to my face. I hated having him leave, like this, with so much yet to be resolved between us. "How long? Until we might be reunited?"

He shook his head. "Our men weary of the battle, as do those of Firenze. With the outposts gone, the attention has turned to Siena herself. If we were in time to warn the Nine..." He took a deep breath. "The tide turns this week, one way or the other. We cannot stay at this impasse for much longer."

"So then, you shall come and retrieve us when it is done?"

He nodded. "As soon as I see their backs, I will come for you." He stepped forward and took my hands. "Promise me you will stay with Luca and the others."

"I promise." The last thing the guy needed was to worry about me. I wanted him to come back alive. And to do that, he'd need to be focused, able to concentrate.

I lifted my face to his, and he gave me a soft, fleeting kiss. "Until the day of our reunion, Gabriella."

"Until that day," I returned. "Come back to me, Marcello Forelli."

"I shall do my best." He backed away slowly, as if reluctant to leave me. "Wait on Luca and the others to escort you," he emphasized, narrowing his eyes. "Go nowhere without their escort, do you understand? Keep Luca with you at all times."

I nodded, not particularly fond of his bossy demands, or that he was going into battle without his best men beside him, but knowing it had to go his way. He loved me. And since I had to go and fall for a full-on knight—possibly the future Lord Forelli if Fortino didn't survive his injuries—I had to bend a little toward the whole lady-to-be-protected thing. At least for now.

And this parting was so much better than last night's, I was ready to accept pretty much anything. *Just bring us back together, God. Give us a chance.*

I waited there, and Mom and Lia joined me. We followed behind the knights as they moved to the horses, where hundreds of men on foot waited. Marcello turned, took my face between both his hands and kissed me swiftly but soundly.

The men laughed and shouted their approval.

Then he was atop his gelding, riding before the mounted men, shouting instructions for what was to come. Laying out their goals—to intercept the new forces, before those men reached Siena's city gates. "We take down those men," he said, his horse prancing beneath him, "and Paratore's forces too, away from our home. Once we destroy them, we will find my brother and free him. Then we shall return for our own. Mark my words. Be it this week or this year, Castello Forelli shall return to us. And she shall be rebuilt, stronger than ever before."

The men cheered.

"For Lord Fortino Forelli!" he shouted, lifting his sword to the sky.

"Lord Forelli!" shouted the men in response.

"For Siena!" Marcello cried.

"For Siena!" the men thundered.

"May God Himself watch over us. Come, men. Let us be about it."

With one last, lingering glance toward me, Marcello turned and moved down the hill at a pace that would not leave the men on foot in the dust nor alert Paratore's scouts that they were departing. They'd left the tents as we'd found them, with several bonfires blazing.

Luca and I lingered, watching. I glanced over at him, sensing his hesitation. "What is it?" I said. "Hate to miss a battle?"

"Indeed," he said, flashing me a smile. But I couldn't miss that it was somewhat subdued.

"You never know," I said, nudging him with my hip. "You said yourself that the Ladies Betarrini tend to draw action."

"There is that," he said, his smile widening.

I walked ahead of him and then glanced back when he fell behind again, his brow knit in puzzlement, as if he was trying to figure something out. We entered camp and sat down next to Lia in a corner, slightly away from the other five men who were to accompany us south: Pietro, Giovanni, and three others I didn't know very well—Valente, Alonzo, and Santino. We dug into bowls of bland porridge in rich cream.

"Think they could ever go Atkins on us?" Lia asked in a whisper.

I giggled. "They enjoy their meat, but they'd wither and die without their carbs," I returned.

"So would I, really," she said. "Not that I would miss this slop. But Cook's pasta? Mm, yeah."

I nodded and shoved another biteful in my mouth. It wasn't great, but at least it'd stave off the hunger thing for a while.

"You okay?" Lia asked. "I mean, without Marcello and all."

"As okay as I can be," I said. "It's kind of like a piece of me has been torn from my body, you know?"

She nodded, looking at me with understanding eyes. "You ready? I mean, really ready? To stay here forever? What if *this* was our life, day in and day out? Always in the middle of a battle. Fighting for our lives—or those we love."

Mom sat down beside us, bowl in hand.

I looked at them both and shrugged. "I don't know. I kind of think this fighting might settle down a bit, in time. And really, isn't it better than flopping down in front of a TV and watching someone else's story? I feel more...*alive* here, now, than I ever did at home."

Mom was staring at her porridge. "So you'd leave everything you had ahead of you? College? A career? Your friends?"

"You two are all that really matter to me," I said. "My friends would be okay. And the best kind of education is all around us, don't you think? I'm thinkin' a girl could do pretty well in business, with or without a man. Especially a girl with a little Norman knowledge."

She smiled. I knew she would be reluctant to give up on the life she had lived with Dad. She really had the most to go home to—she was on the brink of a major discovery, the unpacking of the Etruscan Mother Lode back in Radda in Chianti. The thing that was going to make all the years of sacrifice and distraction worthwhile.

Mom held my gaze and seemed to know what I was thinking. She sighed. "Gabriella, Evangelia, these next steps…they're yours to take. You two are my life. I know that our career took so much of your dad and me from you…And losing him…" Her voice cracked, and she rubbed her mouth, trying to get a grip. She looked up at us after a long moment. "What I'm trying to say is that if you're staying, I want to too. There is nothing more important to me than you two. Nearly losing you…" Tears sprang to her eyes, and she smiled. "As long as I'm with you, I'll be good."

We stared back at her, stunned. She was really ready to give it all up? Everything she'd worked so hard to obtain? Right when it was within reach?

Whoa, talk about a rift in the space/time continuum…

I looked over at Lia. "What about you?"

She looked back at me reluctantly. "I don't know, Gabs. I just don't know."

I sighed and nodded. But a spark of hope glowed inside me. There was a definite *maybe* in her eyes. I'd talk about it more with her in the days to come. She could pursue her art here as well as she could at home, right? Maybe she was destined to be a world-class fresco artist, or the Michelangina that predated Michelangelo.

We rose and went to rinse our wooden bowls in a larger tub, then went to our tent to collect the few things we still had.

"I had one thought," Mom said, laying an uncertain hand on the center pole.

"What?" I asked, wondering why she was acting so hesitant.

"Is it possible…"

"What, Mom?"

"What if we could get back…before…"

"Before?" Lia asked.

"Before your father died. What if we could go back, but not quite so far—"

"And save him," I whispered.

"We wondered about it too," Lia said, slowly, wringing her hands, puzzling over the options. "But if we stop at that point in time, do we even remember that he is about to die? Since, really, it wouldn't have happened for us? We only know how this works from one end to the other. Our present time and here. If we change history, find Dad, warn him, then does Mom ever find the tumuli site?"

"We could write ourselves a note, everything pertinent," Mom said. "In case that memory is erased."

I shook my head. "I don't know. Trying to pull off at a certain time is tricky. Even getting back here…I was off by months. It's just so fast. And heading home—we might end up a hundred years early, not a couple hundred days."

Mom nodded, her eyes shifting back and forth, trying to think it out.

"But let's say it worked, somehow," Lia said excitedly, still focused on the potential. "We get to Dad…but if we don't get to the tumuli again, is history erased? Does Gabi remember Marcello? Or is that gone too?"

"Or do I remember that part because I lived it now, back here?" I rubbed my temples. It was enough to make my brain hurt.

"I don't know," Mom said, looking down, nudging her toe in the loose dirt. "Forgive me for even suggesting it. It's probably impossible. A crazy idea."

"No. It's not," I said. I went to her, and we hugged. "Getting Dad back?" I shook my head. "That'd be crazy-insane *good*."

I looked over at Lia as she melted into Mom's embrace too. "Stellar good," she said.

Mom gave us both a squeeze and sighed. "We'll think it through more together. All right?"

But as we left the tent, I had the sure feeling that this wasn't something we *could* figure out. The best we could do would be Best Case and Worse Case Scenarios. Educated guesses.

Because that time tunnel made no sense, really. No sense at all.

CHAPTER 31

We were a couple miles into our journey, each step that took me farther from Marcello feeling terribly wrong, like I was tearing apart inside, bit by bit. I tried to concentrate on good thoughts. Like that my thigh and ribs felt better today. Every lurch of the horse no longer sent pain radiating through my body. And that I could even use my right leg a little to guide the horse.

We reached the crest of a hill. This part of the republic was quiet, untouched. No battle had ever been fought here or nearby. The only evidence of the broader trauma was that each village we passed was abandoned, her women and children fleeing until it was all over, her men on the front lines. It was eerie, in a way, like walking through ghost towns.

Luca pulled up and frowned. I followed his line of vision. Our scout had ridden ahead, just to make certain no surprise lay in wait. This time it seemed to take forever for the scout to return, but when he did, he was as sweaty as his horse, panting for breath.

"What is it?" Luca growled.

"Trap…Sir Marcello."

"What?" Luca barked.

"Two contingents…closing in…from north and west side. Joining Paratore's. Chasing down Sir Marcello's." His eyes flicked over us. "The knight I met had suffered grievous wounds. The Rossis have fled the city. Siena has suffered a breach to her western wall, Lord Rossi's doing…"

Luca frowned. "We are aware of Lord Rossi's treachery. But why come after Marcello now? What do they care about him when they have the chance to conquer Siena herself?"

The scout did not know.

My heart leaped into triple time. "They want him killed," I mumbled, putting it together. I pictured the grandi in my mind, Lord Rossi, Lord Foraboschi. "If the Nine have been killed… They knew Fortino was as good as dead. They intend to murder any nobleman with the stature to take their place."

Luca nodded, following my logic. "Siena shall surrender, mayhap never rally at all. We shall all fall under Fiorentini jurisdiction, as they wish." Luca looked back to the scout. "How is that these troops in pursuit of Marcello slipped by our other lines of defense?"

The man dismounted at last, as did we, and accepted a drink from one of the other knights. "They came through Umbria, as the others did. They're rested, Sir, and riding hard."

Luca grimaced. Even I could figure out why such news was difficult. Our own men had been fighting for six days, existing on meager rations and poor sleeping conditions. And they were about to be surrounded by men in much finer form.

I looked at Lia. "What is the one thing Firenze would want more than Marcello's head?"

"Those of the She-Wolves of Siena," she returned. She'd seen it for herself in Firenze; the mad chase, the desire to capture us. We had to be at least one hundred percent more enticing than a lord turned out of his castle, no matter what his castle had meant all along.

Luca grimaced and looked up at the sky.

"There is a way to resolve this," I said to Mom and Lia. I could feel Luca's eyes on me. "We show ourselves. Bait them. Draw enough away that Marcello and the others have a fair chance in battle."

It would pull some of the heat off Siena, give them a chance too...

"And then make our way home."

"Home?" Luca sputtered. "The castello is hardly defensible, and there's the small matter of enemy soldiers still occupying the..." His words trailed off as he understood the look on my face. "Ah." He grimaced and glanced over to Lia, then back to me. "Home."

"Gabriella, the armies of Firenze now hold the castellos on either side of *that* valley," Mom said, shaking her head. *There's No Way*, her eyes said. *Not yet.*

I raised my hand and nodded. "It is a grave risk. It shall be a fierce fight. But I can do no other than this." I looked her in the eye. "I cannot stand by and watch my man die. Not when I can do something about it."

Mom's lips clamped together. She knew what I was saying. *This is a death we can help stop. Wouldn't you do the same thing for Dad? Isn't it what you want to do, even now?*

She nodded once. "I am with you, Gabriella. To the end, wherever it takes us."

"As am I," Lia said, repositioning her bow on her shoulder.

Luca shook his head. "I swore to Marcello that I'd keep you three safe."

"Would you rather apologize later to his face…or to his gravestone?" I said.

Luca laughed under his breath and shook his head. "I guess we are in then too." He eyed the men, one at a time. "We follow them, every step of the way. There is a hidden point of escape for them, between Castellos Paratore and Forelli. It will be our duty to see them there."

"By my life," said Pietro.

"And mine," added Giovanni.

The others piled their hands on top, and I was last. I looked around the circle of men, brothers more than friends, handpicked by Marcello. Loyal, regardless of the cost. "To the end," I said.

We rode hard to reach a place in which we could show ourselves and yet have half a chance of escape. At the back of the abandoned village were the remains of ancient generations, caves carved into the cliffs above. The sun was high in the sky when we paused by a well in a village and shared a loaf of bread and a bit of cheese. We drank deeply from the bucket, the water cold and sweet.

Giovanni arrived, having ridden ahead to scout the land. "About a half hour out," he said. "They're coming fast."

"Rested," Luca said casually. "We remember."

"There are over four hundred in that first contingent, sir," he pressed. "With the other two groups numbering over a thousand. But with fewer horses."

"Fine odds, fine odds," Luca said, cocking his head like this was the most perfect plan possible rather than a signature on our death warrants. "Well," he said, rubbing his hands together, "let us draw in the four hundred, and the rest are bound to follow."

"Done," Lia said, standing back. She'd used a white chalky rock to finish her quick sketch on the first building they would reach.

I came around and looked at it, as did the others. I giggled. She'd depicted two wolves standing on their hind legs, one with a sword, one with a bow and arrow. Between them was a flag of Siena. "All right," I said. "Let us take up our positions."

"No matter what happens," Luca said, pointing at each of us, "everyone able is on their horses, two minutes after the men arrive. We'll be counting it out, together. One-thousand-one, one-thousand-two…At one hundred twenty, you *move*. Understood?" He shook his head in warning. "We ride with or without you. Make certain you are *with* us."

He drew the map in the sand at our feet one more time. "Everyone understands our plan? If we get separated, your only chance is to catch up with us, ahead. We toy with them here, for a bit. Get them properly riled, and then we run our horses to the north wood. There, we shall take the Santa Fiora Road to Gaiole, then on toward Castello Forelli, keeping to the side paths and off the main

road to avoid Fiorentini troops. God willing, we will get the ladies
properly hidden in the woods by nightfall."

"God willing," I muttered.

"Truth be told," Giovanni said, "I preferred our last battle. Better
to pretend to be shot by Lady Gabriella than to be really shot at by
the dogs of Firenze."

Luca and I shared a smile with him, remembering that night we
had claimed Castello Paratore. Tonight, all I hoped for was survival.
For all of us.

He erased the map in the sand, and we ran for our positions,
climbing a narrow path up the cliff and settling into seven separate
perches. Mom, Lia, and I were together at the center, closest to the
horses, ground-tied just ten yards behind us.

The enemies on horses came then, shortly after we settled in.
We could see the foot soldiers not a half mile in the distance. The
first group paused at Lia's picture, gesturing toward it and looking
furiously about.

"Now," I said. Casually, slowly, we stood, the three of us, taking
on the same pose as the drawing. Mom held the flag of Siena atop
her staff.

As it caught the wind, the first of them saw us. They pointed,
shouted, and stared, as if they were seeing things. "'Tis a decoy!"
echoed up a young nobleman's voice. "Those are not the Ladies
Betarrini! They are naught but villagers, sent here to distract us."
But then Lia and two of our men fired upon them, each taking out
multiple men in rapid succession.

The enemy soldiers scattered, taking cover, shouting. Those on
foot, hearing their alarm, were coming at a dead run now. The sight

of their mass, stirring up dust on the autumn-dried road, made my heart kick into serious gear.

"Seven down, three hundred and ninety-three to go," Luca said.

Lia aimed, shifted, and waited, watching one man peek out, time and time again. She let her arrow fly, anticipating his next peek at us, and it pierced his eye.

"Okay, that's just going to make 'em mad," I said.

"Three hundred and ninety-two," she said to Luca, tossing her braid over her shoulder and taking aim again.

"Saints in heaven," he said to me, rolling his eyes, "how much deeper in love can I yet fall?"

I smiled. "A good bit yet, I'd wager." I glanced at Mom. "How many seconds do we have left?"

"Ninety-four, ninety-three," she muttered, staring down at the men, now scattering, trying to make their way toward our cliff. Others were taking off on their horses, coming up and around either side, as we assumed they would.

"A bit faster than we anticipated," I said to Luca, motioning to the horsemen with my chin.

"Yes. But it will still take them four more minutes to get up here," he replied.

"Giving us a two-and-a-half-minute lead, eh? Generous."

"You, m'lady, directed my plan. I believe the word was *bait*."

I lifted a rock, aimed, and threw it at a man a hundred yards beneath me. It missed him when he dodged away at the last second, eyes wide with surprise. Then I threw a second at another, with similar results. "A bear can smell bait from a mile away. He does not need have it in his teeth."

"Down, Gabi!" Mom said.

I ducked just as the first arrows came sailing toward us.

"Oh, no you *don't*," Lia muttered in English, rising again and shooting in one fluid motion. She took out an archer on horseback, and he fell from his saddle. Our horses stirred behind us, agitated by the sounds of those below them.

The other archers shot five more men, and I winged a guy with a rock before Mom got to the end of her countdown. We could see the cloud of the riders to our east. The western side was rockier, and therefore there was no telltale cloud in that direction, but I assumed they were coming too.

"Time to go," I muttered, running toward my horse.

We were mounted and ready to go when Giovanni topped the cliff, limping, an arrow in his leg. He waved at us, scowling. "Off with you!" he cried.

"Go on," Pietro said to Luca. "I'll fetch him."

"Nay," Luca growled. "You're with us. We need you. He's a good man, a fine knight. He'll catch up."

"Let me go to him, Luca," I said, eyeing Giovanni's painful lope toward his horse.

"You shall not. We stick to our plan." Luca whipped my horse's flank and then Lia's, too, sending us lurching ahead. "Go! Go!"

We tore off across the plain, meeting the road and turning north, the dim line of the woods a haze in the far distance. I fretted about Giovanni. With his previous shoulder injury and now an arrow in his leg, he would find it as hard to ride as I was finding it now, as my thigh tired. But if anyone had remained with Giovanni, he would likely die as well.

May it be fast and merciful, I prayed. *Fast and merciful for any of us who die this day.*

But as I rode, I didn't have death in mind. Not today, anyway. No, I wanted life. Marcello. Love. *Help us, God. Help us...*

CHAPTER 32

We looked like a small tribe of Indians chased by the entire U.S. Cavalry. And Giovanni was falling behind, nearly in reach of the enemy's archer's arrows. "C'mon," I muttered, looking forward again, conscious that at this speed, I had to steer my horse or we might go tumbling on the rocky road.

We were forced to slow just short of the woods, to pick our way down a twenty-foot bank and across a massive floodplain, now dry. It was unnerving, hearing those who chased us draw nearer, but we took comfort in the fact that the same landscape would slow their pursuit.

"Make haste!" Luca cried to me, Mom, and the two men who rode behind us as our rear flank. Lia was beside him.

Mom and I reached the far bank, and our horses churned upward. We dared to pause and glance back. There, across the dry riverbed, was Giovanni, barely slowing his horse.

The look on Luca's face made him appear as if he'd been kicked in the gut. We all felt it. Giovanni would be captured or killed within minutes.

"May I give him half a chance, Luca?" Lia asked. "Only a minute's lead…He'll die here, in this riverbed, without aid."

"I'll stay and assist," Valente said.

"Let's be about it," Luca said, his mouth thinning into a grim line.

She handed her reins to him, slid off her horse, and stood
between the men.

Luca looked to the other men. "Go, as fast as you can. We shall
meet at the village. If Evangelia and I are not there two minutes after
you arrive, carry on. Do you understand me?"

"We shall not leave you and Lia behind," I said. "If we are to
stand and fight, we shall stand together."

Luca shook his head. "We do not intend to stand anywhere.
Remember? This is all about keeping them," he said, motioning over
his shoulder, "from reaching Marcello and our men."

"Go, Gabi," Lia muttered, taking aim across the riverbed at the
opposite bank. Our enemies would be there at any moment, and
Giovanni was only a third of the way across. "We will be right behind
you."

I looked at Mom as the three men assigned to our care turned
back, waiting on us.

The first men of Firenze arrived on the far side, a cacophony as
men screamed to *hold, pause, halt.* Several horses tumbled down the
bank, rolling. I shuddered as the sound of bones cracking echoed
across the riverbed.

Lia and Valente shot their first arrows.

"Go!" Luca demanded.

With one last glance at Lia, Mom nodded, and we surged into
motion, pounding down the narrow road that led us into the shade

of the woods. There were brief spots of sunlight when we charged beneath giant oaks that had already lost their leaves. Then sudden dark when the trees again closed in above us, making it hard to see, with our eyes constantly adjusting.

So I wasn't really surprised when Mom's horse stumbled in a mud hole and went down, throwing her. She flew through the air and into the woods. We all pulled up, circling around. "Mom!" I cried. "Mom!"

She lurched to her feet, brushing the leaves off her arms. "I'm all right," she said, "just a little shaken."

My relief crashed against my horror at the sight of her mare's broken leg. "No," I moaned. It was impossible. A horse with two riders would never be able to outrun those who pursued us.

Pietro was off his gelding in a moment. "M'lady, take mine," he said.

"Nay," she said, shaking her head.

But he took her waist in his hands and roughly tossed her up into the saddle, then strode over to her horse to grab her staff. He trotted over to her and handed it up. "Be off with you. All of you. I shall hide here and slow them down as much as I can. And those who will be coming after Sir Luca and Lady Evangelia as well."

"Pietro, I——" I whispered.

"To the end, m'lady," he said with a nod. His eyes did not break from mine. "See that you get to it, that you save Marcello and Fortino, as well as yourselves, and I shall consider my life well spent."

Inside, my heart again screamed at me to stay, to fight with him, but my mind understood that it would do no one any good if we all died here. And unless we escaped, we *would* all die this day. I looked at the other two men and Mom, then back to Pietro. "I shall remember you forever."

He smiled and covered his heart. "To be remembered forever by one of the Ladies Betarrini is an honor I shall cherish with my dying breath."

I turned from him then, before I changed my mind again. Our two escorts, Alonzo and Santino, churned down the road ahead of us, cutting the path. We hunched over, urging our horses faster. In half a mile the woods became more spread out, oaks among grassy hills. Down below us, through the meandering valley cut by hill after hill, was the tiny village of Chianciani, where we'd meet up with Luca and Lia.

Where are they? I thought. With the delay after Mom's fall, I half-expected them to be directly behind us. I again dared to peer under my arm as I rode hard, never breaking pace.

My heartbeat picked up when I saw the other riders, first with joy, thinking it was Lia, Luca, and the other men. But it sank when I figured out that there were too many and spotted the crest of Firenze on the leader's breastplate. I looked under my other arm and did a quick count.

Eight, and rapidly gaining on us. They'd sent their fastest riders ahead to hunt us down. "Riders behind us!" I shouted. One by one, the men and my mother glanced back. We urged our horses faster, but they were tiring, having already given us everything they had. I dared to again look at the men behind us, now dividing, intending to flank us, only a hundred paces away.

Where were Luca and Lia? Were they dead? Or had these riders come around from another road? If something had happened to Lia, there was no sense in pressing on. Even if I made it to the tombs, there would be no escape for me or Mom without Lia's hand on that print too.

I looked back. Seventy-five paces. "Press on!" I called.

Ahead of us, Alonzo and Santino shared a look and then divided, easing their pace enough to let us fall to the inside, protecting the side of us that would be exposed first to those who pursued us. But the road was too narrow for us to ride four abreast. I looked at Mom. "I'll meet you at the village! Up ahead, at the bottom of the valley!"

She nodded, and at a group of trees ahead, she and Santino went left and I went right, Alonzo beside me.

As we curved, I saw that four men were but twenty-five paces away. Holding the reins with my left hand, glad the horse seemed to know where he was going and how urgent it was, I slipped a dagger from the back of my belt and bit down on it, tasting the metal against my tongue. The sword would be useless until I was on the ground and fighting them, which, by the looks of things, would not be long.

A man drew his sword and charged toward Alonzo as if he intended to crash his horse directly into my knight's. When he was ten feet away, his eyes solely on Alonzo, I took the dagger from between my teeth, timed the swaying, churning motion of my horse to make sure my aim was true and then sent it flying at him.

It struck him in the throat.

His eyes widened in surprise, and he immediately dropped his reins and sat up, his hands going to the knife. The three others surged past him, looking at us with deadly intent in their eyes.

I waggled my eyebrows at Alonzo and the shy man grinned. "Thank you for that, m'lady."

"Mayhap we can pick the others off in kind," I said. We steered around another clump of trees and I dared to look for Mom. The men who pursued them were getting perilously close too. Santino had drawn his sword.

"Take care, m'lady," Alonzo said. "No two shall die the same way."

"Let us stand and fight, then," I said. "Take them down, then go to my mother's aid." I looked beyond his shoulder. "Another one, coming fast."

My knight gave me another look, considering. "We stand when we have but two left. Agreed?"

"Agreed."

He reached for a chain at the side of his saddle, slowly, staring ahead as if he didn't know the rider was coming for him with sword drawn. I forced myself to look ahead too, not wishing to give him away. I was sure we could both hear the lathered horse nearly upon us. At the last possible moment, Alonzo turned and threw the chain. I could see, then, that it had small balls on either end, sending it like a long, twirling stick at our attacker.

The chain sank, right before it hit the knight. He grinned in victory for but half a second and lifted his sword, preparing to strike, when the chain wrapped around his horse's leg, immediately sending both rider and horse tumbling down. The way he fell…he wasn't going to rise.

"Two left," I muttered. I pulled up and rounded the next tree. The men behind us looked surprised and divided, one chasing me in a broad loop, the other after Alonzo.

I jumped to the ground and pulled my sword, rolling my neck, preparing for the blow to come. He was about my size, but with an intensity that freaked me out. His horse churned toward me, and I counted, timing his approach, getting ready to deflect his blow, wondering if I'd have time, then, to turn and at least hit his leg before he was past me.

Five, four, three, two…one. It was harder than I remembered. Deflecting a blow from above. I staggered back, wondering if I had been a fool to go to the ground. The height gave the horseman a definite advantage. But there had been no way I was going to take him on while we were both seated. It was too difficult to gauge how the horses would react. I preferred solid ground beneath my feet, even if I still felt like I was riding—kind of like getting your land legs once you were off a boat.

I left the tip of my sword in the ground, resting, while the knight slipped from his horse. He paused and removed his helmet, dropping it casually to one side as he walked steadily back toward me.

It was Captain Rossi. Romana's cousin. I fought for breath, stunned.

"I want to see every bit of this," he said, sneering. "I want to remember every moment of the day I killed *Lady* Gabriella Betarrini."

I gathered myself, remaining still, wanting him to think I was weak, injured in some way. "You would kill a woman?"

"A woman like you," he roared, lifting his sword in a circle and bringing it swiftly after me.

I shifted, and it swung past me, missing me by inches. If I could tire him a bit, it would help me to best him. *Get 'im good and mad.*

"That was a sorry effort," I goaded. "Can you not do better than that?"

He growled, turned, and brought down the sword like a saw blade. I narrowly turned in time. But as he swung around, so did I, blocking his next blow and staring into his eyes. "'Tis not my death that you shall remember this day."

"Nay?" He lifted his sword and met mine again and again.

"Nay. Your last thoughts shall be of your own death." I whipped around and aimed low, for his legs.

He yowled when I sliced his thigh. I ignored the sudden remembrance of my own aching leg, turning and bringing my sword around again, one-handed.

He blocked my strike and sneered in my face. "The lady must—"

With my left hand, I rammed my dagger into his gut, just under the edge of his breastplate, and waited for the knowledge of his impending doom to register in his hateful eyes.

He dropped his sword and closed his hands around my neck, pushing me back.

Surprised, I took a fumbling step and then fell, him on top of me.

I didn't get him right, deep enough, I thought. Still he pressed his thumbs into my throat, murder in his eyes.

My own eyes were becoming narrowing tunnels of black when I felt him rock atop me, then roll away. I sat up, gasping, rubbing my throat, wondering if he had collapsed my windpipe.

Luca leaned down into my line of vision and smiled, clasping my hand and helping me up. "So the Rossis are rotten from core to peel," he said. "Be you well, m'lady?"

I didn't know where he'd come from, but relief flooded through me at the sight of his smiling eyes. "Fine, fine," I lied with a gasp, glancing over at the captain's lifeless form, waving Luca off even while wishing I could lean on him. "Giovanni?"

He shook his head sadly.

I absorbed that for a sec, suddenly realizing how close to the edge we were. My mother, Lia, the other men were bound to be in need of help. "Go."

He turned and ran, and I hobbled after him, trying to get my eyes to focus again and my breathing back to normal.

Luca passed Lia as she let an arrow fly. It sliced into the shoulder of a knight circling my mother, and he staggered to the side.

Mom didn't hesitate. She brought up the edge of her staff and rammed the knight in the face, then turned the long stick around and rammed the pointed end into his gut.

"Whoa," Lia said as I reached her.

"I know," I said, wrapping an arm around her shoulders, still panting. We hobbled toward her, my leg suddenly aching like crazy. "Our mom is some kind of freakin' warrior queen."

"Luca," she whispered, breaking away from me and running down the hill. I saw him then, fighting two knights, bending crazily backward in a moment to avoid one's strike, then rolling to avoid the second's.

I lurched down the hill after Lia, my right thigh again demanding favor. But by the time I reached them, Lia had taken down one knight, Luca the other. Mom and Santino came over to us. Alonzo rode toward us, three horses' reins in hand.

Valente was on the ground, a gash across his head and a broadening circle of blood at his belly. I felt for a pulse. He was gone.

"More coming!" cried Alonzo, handing us the reins.

I glanced to the ridge—a mile distant—and frowned as I saw the hundreds of men there, poised to rush us, crush us. "Okay, maybe this whole bait thing wasn't my best idea," I muttered in English. We were only halfway to the tomb, and the sun was getting lower in the sky.

Luca and Santino lifted me and Mom into our saddles. Lia was already atop her own horse. Luca grabbed Santino's arm, and the man swung around and up, behind his captain. His horse was a quarter-mile distant—fortunately right by the road we had to take—drinking from a creek. We all turned and charged forward, well aware of the cloud of men not far behind us.

We'd lost three of the six men we'd set off with—Giovanni, Pietro, Valente. But we still had Luca, Alonzo and Santino beside us. I glanced back and allowed myself a small smile of satisfaction. At least the plan was working. Hundreds of men were now after us, rather than after Marcello, cascading into the valley like water into a funnel. My man would be free to carry out his own plan this day; perhaps he was even on the offensive now, working to defeat those who dared to attack his noble city or hold his brother.

Outside the village, we captured Santino's horse at the small creek bed. We had no choice but to allow the horses to drink for a full minute. We hurriedly filled our skins and drank from the stream too, all the while watching the men coming closer and closer.

"Their mounts will be in similar shape," Luca said. "They will have to stop too."

"You hope," I said, mounting while my gelding still drank. The others did the same. Unable to bear the pressure any longer, I yanked my horse's reins upward, forcing him back to the road. In seconds, we were galloping in pairs toward our next cover—the woods that filled the valley leading to Castello Paratore and Castello Forelli.

To our southwest, we could see clouds of smoke rising in the sky, but none were close to Siena. *Probably a few villages getting torched by the bad guys*, I thought. I welcomed the cool of the woods as we hit the crossroads of the old Roman road that ran between Siena and Firenze, and the cobblestone path that ran down our familiar valley. We pulled up and circled, oak leaves scattering around us, wanting to make certain that the men knew exactly where we were going.

We did not want them to give up on us. Not yet.

CHAPTER 33

"'Tis a thorough enough look, m'lord?" Lia muttered to Luca.

We all felt her unease. The men were close enough that we could make out sideburns and beards. But they hesitated, recognizing the significance of the crossroads, and there seemed to be some debate going on between their leaders. Would we be enough of a draw to keep them coming? Or would they turn and join in the assault on Siena? And therefore, Marcello?

Too late, I recognized the inevitable.

They divided.

There goes my career as a military genius.

A hundred still came our way, many of them on horseback. But I felt sick inside as we set off, knowing that more than a thousand now marched toward Siena. My only hope was that we had distracted them long enough that they would have to camp for the night before joining their comrades. *Forgive me, Marcello,* I thought. *My plan failed.*

Would there be enough men to defeat those already inside? To turn away those that still came?

We rounded the corner at full gallop, and things got even better. We nearly collided with Lord Paratore and his men.

They were as surprised as we were, dividing narrowly to let our horses race between their two-by-two parade. It took me about twelve pairs before I decided my eyes had not tricked me—we really were in a very special version of misery. "Really? Paratore, of all people? A little help, God?" I muttered in prayer.

But then we were fighting our way out, on serious defense. I swung my sword around, messy in my technique, trying to keep my seat atop the horse and in a bit of—*okay, total*—panic. I could sense Lord Paratore pushing his way toward us, hear the grate of his voice among the shouts and screams and grunts and groans of battle.

Only the narrow road and towering trees kept us from immediate capture, since few had direct access to us. Paratore led a hundred men, and our delay had allowed those who pursued us to catch up.

Surrounded. A hundred before us, a hundred behind. We had to take to the woods. *Have. To. Get. To. The. Woods.*

I slid from my mount and pulled the horse in a circle, driving the two nearest knights back. I dived away, somersaulting down the small bank and then leaping to my feet and hobbling through the trees. Now my leg was seriously killing me, not to mention my ribs. I heard the crack of a tree branch behind me and ran faster, pressing through the vine maples and small white pines, desperately searching for a place to hide and figure out how to get back to help Lia and Mom and the rest.

That was when I was grabbed from behind, and someone's hand clasped over my mouth. I struggled, but he had my arms pinned to my side, my sword hanging uselessly from my hand.

"Simply couldn't tolerate our separation?" he asked, half laughing, half furious.

I frowned and stilled, and he let me turn in his arms.

Marcello.

He lifted a finger to his lips. "We have been sent to surprise those who expected to surprise us," he said in a whisper. "And rescue my brother. Wait here," he commanded with a frown, pointing at the base of the tree. His head whipped around, toward the road. Men were coming, looking for me, maybe for the others, too.

Without pause he took hold of my shoulders and shoved me down to the base of the trunk and pointed a finger in my face. "Truly," he growled. "Do not try me further."

"Yes, m'lord," I said, smiling up at him. "I didn't leave Luca's side," I said defensively. "He's here someplace."

He shook his head in exasperation at me, then turned and lifted an arm. Out of the woods crept a wave of Sienese loyalists, hundreds of them. My heart surged with hope. They were all dressed in brown and black, their faces smudged with dirt to help them blend in. A good hundred advanced with bows in their hands, an arrow drawn on each string.

Lia broke through a patch of vine maples then, pausing and blinking slowly when she saw the men approaching. Then she rolled and came to her knees and drew her last arrow across her bow. A man tossed her a new quiver as he passed her, still waiting for more to come through.

Luca was there then, running through the thick brush as if he was tearing through waist-deep water. His face froze and then lit up as he recognized comrades around us.

At last Mom burst through the trees, but two knights were right behind her, gaining on her. Luca dived onto the closest, pounding him with his fist when they rolled to a stop. But the other grabbed her and wrenched her around.

Slowly, three Sienese archers within six feet of them stood erect, all arrows pointing at the enemy's head, neck, and heart. He stilled, blinked with wide eyes, then raised his arms in surrender. Mom picked up a tree branch and whirled, whacking him in the face.

I laughed under my breath.

But then the rest were through the trees, reaching us. The men waited until a good number appeared, then let the arrows fly, taking nearly all of them down. Only five were missed. Men with swords were next to rise, among the archers. They made short work of those who had survived as the next wave arrived, and again the archers took most of them out.

Shouts were heard. Paratore bellowed an order to attack. But I could hear from my position that the men were scattering, afraid, confused. Horse hooves clattered away. A few brave troops dared to wade into the forest, only to meet their death. "Welcome to guerilla warfare, boys," I muttered.

I saw Marcello's back as he and half of his men ran to cut off those who sought escape to the south. Luca ran with the other half in the opposite direction.

They would never get home to Firenze nor live to attack another of Siena's loyal people, nor even home to Castello Paratore. Not if our guys had anything to say about it.

I smiled as Mom and Lia drew near. Then I limped over to them to wrap them both in my arms. "We must go," I forced myself to whisper, hearing the groans of the injured among the brush and shoving down a shiver of fear. Marcello had wanted us to stay here, knowing that we were relatively safe. But we had to go now. It would be our only opportunity to slip away, to reach the tomb portal, now just a mile distant. For once, no one was thinking about the Ladies Betarrini.

I ran ahead of them, finding a deer path and following it as the sun set, sending neon rays of orange through the trees as if they were pointing our way home. I wanted to stand and argue, convince Mom and Lia that we belonged here, in Toscana, now. But ever since Mom had suggested we might be able to go back and try to save Dad…as much as I wanted to remain, I knew we had no choice.

We had to try.

I took one last look back to the forest, hoping I might see Marcello again. Wave. Give him some hint at least. "Come on," Lia said. "I've got you covered."

I followed behind her. "What do you mean?"

"I'll show you at the tomb," she said, bending beneath a branch.

We trudged onward, tense with suspicion at every turn. We could hear the roar of battle on the wind, but it was difficult to discern whether it was coming from our north or our south. Perhaps it was both.

At last, we reached the creek, little more than a trickle during the drought of autumn, and began our ascent of the hill that led to the tombs. With each step I took I became more aware of the war that raged inside of me. One side of me longed to fall among the rocks and cling there, to stay here, with Marcello, never to be pulled away. The other side of me could do nothing but push forward. *Dad. Dad!* Was it possible? Were we fools to even think it possible?

Marcello will feel horrible when he discovers I am gone…will he believe I'm gone forever? Unable to convince my mother and sister to stay in this century? And what would transpire in our absence? Weeks, months. Battles for the castellos, Siena.

"It's bigger than you are, Gabriella," Mom said, laying a hand on my shoulder. "Do not try to think it all out right now. Only the next step."

"But Marcello," I said, stepping up onto the next boulder. "What if something happens to him…"

"Something *will* happen to him, whether you are here or not. Something is forever happening to all of us."

I nodded and looked down at the rock, then over to Castello Forelli, wanting one last look.

A guard stared back at me. He wore the emblem of Firenze across his chest. Lia stepped beside me and followed my gaze. "Way to go, sis. Had to raise one more alarm, didn't you?"

"I know, right?" I said, shaking my head. We turned and scurried up the rest of the path as shouts reverberated across the valley and an alarm bell began to clang behind us.

We reached the top of the hill and turned. Now Castello Paratore was in view, and with all the noise the boys were making at Castello Forelli, I knew they were on full alert, her parapets loaded with knights peering through the fading light to figure out what was going on. They spotted us, pointing, yelling.

"C'mon," Lia said, dragging me forward. Mom was ignoring it all, already a hundred paces ahead of us, her own mind clearly on one thing. *Dad.*

We edged out of view from Castello Paratore and entered the small meadow with the tombs, domes sticking out of the heavy grass and twining vines of the forest. Mom ran to Tomb Two and turned to face us. We could hear the creak of Castello Paratore's gates opening, then the distinct noise of knights in battle.

I frowned. "I have to look," I said to them. "I have to know what's going on! Get ready, I'll be there in a sec." I ignored their cries of complaint and hobbled up the path and around the corner that would give me the clearest view of our enemy's castle.

They'd opened the gates to come after us. But they had failed to recognize Sienese forces in the woods, waiting for just such an opportunity. They battled at the wall, between the gates. "Go, boys, go," I whispered. If they could capture Castello Paratore again, it would only be a matter of time before Castello Forelli was back in Sienese hands.

But some men were climbing the path below me, heading up to our meadow. "Time to go," I muttered, turning and rushing back to the tomb as fast as I could.

Mom waited for me at the mouth of the tomb and followed me in.

"I have it all set," Lia said. She was barely visible in the tomb. "I've left a note for Marcello and Luca."

"You have? What does it say?"

She hesitated. "It says, 'Wait for us. We are coming back.'"

"We are? You really want to do that? Both of you? To come back here?"

"If we get your dad," Mom said, slipping her hand over my shoulder. "And even if we don't. If this is where your heart is, both your hearts, then I want to be here too."

I turned back toward Lia. "And you? I thought you wanted your life back. Your real life."

"This…" She paused to take a breath. "Somehow, it's become my real life. I've caught your medieval bug. I want to be here."

"Medieval bug or a medieval hottie."

She shrugged. "Maybe I'll come back and figure it out." She poked me in the chest. "But next time, let's go for a few less near-death experiences, all right?"

"All right," I agreed, willing to say anything in that moment in exchange for what she was promising. "If only I could say good-bye…"

"It'll be minutes for us. Weeks or months for them," she chastised me. But her use of *us* and *them* was not lost on me. Oh yeah, she was finally falling for Luca. As hard as I'd fallen for Marcello.

We could hear voices outside the tomb. They were upon us. We had to leave.

"Trust me, Gabs," she said in a hushed voice, pulling me closer to the wall. "Marcello Forelli will be waiting for you."

We moved toward the handprints and reached up.

"All the way home," Lia whispered. "Then we'll figure out our next step."

Mom grabbed hold of our shoulders.

And then we were gone, cascading back to the future.

CHAPTER 34

We hit the end of the time tunnel, and this time, it felt like we'd hit a brick wall, running at full speed. We rammed forward and then fell back on the floor, on top of Mom, all three of us gasping and groaning.

"Shh, shh," Mom tried, remembering before we did the new danger at hand.

Dr. Manero.

How long had we been gone? Five, six minutes?

She crawled forward, peered around for a moment and then backed into the tomb again and stood.

"All right, so now we touch our handprints—just for a few seconds—and we'll be back a year, maybe two, and we can find Dad," Lia said.

"A few seconds? Wouldn't that take us back to, like, before we're born?"

"Let's think about it. How long do you think the whole journey takes?" Mom said.

I shook my head. "It's hard to tell. We get into that warpy-stretchy place and it feels like I'm not breathing, like time is standing still, not whipping by a century-a-second."

"I think it's about twenty seconds," Mom said, eyes narrowed. She had her Science Voice on. All analytical, all of a sudden.

It comforted me. Because I couldn't figure it out. It was like a nightmare of a story problem. With life-and-death, love-or-loss kind of stakes.

"If it takes twenty seconds to cascade through six centuries…"

"Six hundred and seventy years, give or take," Lia corrected.

"Then ten seconds to go through three hundred and thirty-five… five seconds to go through a hundred and sixteen…two seconds to go through fifty-odd years." She looked up at me and Lia. "We're a hair's breath away from your dad," she whispered.

I shivered. Could we really be that close?

"It'll take but a touch to send us back five years."

"Can we even match the prints and get back off that fast?" I asked.

"We have to try," Lia said.

"Where were you five years ago, Mom?"

Her face fell. "Capua."

I frowned too. That far south…the other side of Rome. It'd take us a day to get there, find him—if we could find him—and return. I shook my head. "I can't. Mom, I can't! That would take too long. Marcello will have waited *years* before I get back. Maybe he'll have given up on me, married someone else."

"You'll get back before that happens," Lia cut in.

"Maybe not, Lia." I covered my aching eyes and leaned my head against the wall. It was too much to figure out, too hard…

Mom paced, chin in hand, thinking. She looked over at us. "Two years ago, we were in the next valley. Remember? We thought *this* place might be there."

"We won't have a car to get there," Lia said slowly.

Mom looked at me with an expression that said *Don't Lose Hope.*

"Mom," I said. "We'll have to climb out of this valley—without that old guy who brought us here guiding us—and hitchhike over there. We'll have to find Dad, if he's there at all, explain it to him and bring him back…"

"Your dad will have the Jeep, Gabi."

"But it'll take *hours*. Do you know what that means for Marcello? For Luca?"

"Years," Lia whispered.

I put my hand on my head. "And it was 1342 when we left. Do you know where *years* puts us?"

"In the middle of the Black Plague when we return."

"We just have to pull off before then. He'll leave us a sign. You asked him to do so, right?" I said to Lia. "In the note?"

"Yes," she said with a nod. "It'll be there, Gabi. We'll know. Even easier than before."

"You think."

"No, Gabs, I know. He'll be ten times more anxious than you to get back together. Because he's living without you, right now. Days going by for him while it's just minutes for us. It'll be there."

"Remember why we came back at all, Gabi? For your dad." Mom moved toward me, touched my arm, and then ran her hand down to mine. "Gabriella, please. *Please.*"

It was a horrible decision. Was I taking a course that would save one man I loved but cost me the other?

But we were here, now. And Dad's death impacted all three of us. Marcello could figure out why we'd left. Would he think that the portal had somehow ceased to work? Or worse, that I had simply decided not to return to him?

I gasped around the lump in my throat. The decision weighed upon my chest like an anchor in deep seas, dragging me backward, down. Each word, each step was an agony of effort. I put my fist to my mouth and looked at Mom. "Okay. But we have to move fast, Mom. Really fast."

Lia pulled a scroll from a pocket in her gown. "I've written it out. So we remember. We might forget everything when we go. Two years ago, we didn't know about this place. We didn't know what would happen to Dad."

"We didn't know Marcello. Or Luca." I swallowed hard. Would I forget all that had happened? Forget what I felt for the man? This everything-in-me pull back to him? If I forgot him, would I go at all?

"You won't forget," Mom said, resting her hand on my shoulder. She shook her head. "This," she said, gesturing toward the handprints, "is some sort of time-space continuum. If we remember Marcello and Luca and all now, we'll remember it when we stop two years back."

"You're sure."

"I'm sure. Trust me, Gabriella."

Trust her. Trust Marcello. Trust God. Everyone demanded I trust them! I kinda liked it better when I just had to trust myself.

We heard voices outside. "All right," I whispered. "Let's do this." I looked at Lia. "The fastest touch possible."

We practiced a few times, counting, on and off, a tap that had to be perfectly timed.

"One, two, *three*."

We staggered backward, and Mom steadied us. The only light came in from above, through the tomb raider's hole.

We'd done it. Gone back. But how far?

"Quick," I said, bending to give a foothold to Mom. She reached the top and, with her legs swinging wildly, curved up and over. It was then that I thought about us all in medieval gear and groaned. How much harder would it be to snag a ride in these getups? "Come on, Lia," I snapped, reaching down for her foot.

She ignored my irritation and held on to my shoulders before reaching for Mom's hands. Soon, she was turned around and reaching down for me, with Mom holding on to her. I backed up, ran and jumped, just barely connecting to her hands.

As I swung, Lia grinned down at me and began to giggle. "We're like a circus act," she said, laughing so hard her grip began to loosen.

"Don't laugh!" I said. "You'll drop me! Pull, Mom, pull!"

Lia edged upward, pulling me with her. At the top, ten feet from the ground, I struggled to get over the edge, but then Lia and Mom both grabbed my belt and dragged me up and over.

Outside the curve of the tomb, we looked around. There was nothing but the sounds of nature. No people in sight.

"It's summer," Mom said with a smile of satisfaction.

"The question is, which summer?" Lia asked.

"Last year. Maybe the one before. You girls were on and off those handprints lightning fast. It was perfect."

"You remember the way," I said to her, ignoring her praise.

"I remember everything. Don't you?"

I thought about it a sec. She was right, I decided with relief. It was all still with me. Every memory from past and future.

"Come on," she said, offering me a hand. "I'll lead the way."

We pushed through the forest and picked our way down the face of those boulders as fast as we could. "See?" she said, showing me the ancient paving stones that our guide had once pointed out to us. "This is the right way."

"Got it. Go," I said, not wanting to waste a second.

We pressed on and eventually hit the old gravel road where we'd originally met the landowner. It was a good two miles back to the highway, but we set off, jogging as fast as we could. It was then that I realized that neither my thigh nor ribs hurt any longer.

"It heals for sure, that tunnel," I said to Mom in a pant. "My injuries…they're gone. Just like last time with the poison."

"It's good to know," she said, eyeing me. "If we're going back to the era of the Black Plague."

She did not need to say more. But as we ran, I wondered what we'd do if one or more of us contracted the awful disease. I thought of bringing Marcello back here, to the present, and how there was something timeless about him.

Yeah, he was pretty much a stud in any year. *Wait for me, Marcello,* I thought, hoping that somehow, some way, he might know my thoughts. *Tell him, God. Tell him to wait for me.*

When we spotted Castello Forelli we came to a dead stop, hands on knees, panting. Because it was no longer in ruins. A good number of the walls were intact. All five towers still stood.

Which was good, of course. But the first two words in my head were *oh no*.

Because we'd changed history. Castello Forelli, no longer in ruins as we'd seen it in at the very beginning. Someone—Marcello? Paratore?—had rebuilt the tumbled wall. It had been inhabited for centuries, judging from the good condition.

And because of that, it was now a tourist draw. There was a parking lot to our right, where there had once been nothing but road and woods. A ticket booth had been erected at the front, just outside the massive gates, gates that had been rebuilt recently but looked like they'd been carefully redone to historical specifications. I ran forward, compelled, drawn.

Mom stopped at the ticket booth.

"Siete qui oggi per lavorare?" the young man asked idly, looking us up and down. *You are here to work today?* Lia and I shared a glance. Maybe their volunteers dressed in medieval costumes.

"Indeed," Mom said, readily picking up on the excuse. "But we have an emergency. Our car has broken down in the next valley. Is there anyone who can drive us and haul it back?"

I looked inside, to where grass now grew across the courtyard. The keep and Great Hall were still in place, but the doors leading to each corridor were new. Perhaps they'd rotted away too much for the historians to figure out what they once looked like. Or maybe at some point, they'd just been replaced with the more durable steel that graced each doorframe now.

I looked back in agitation at Mom, who was still talking with the ticket dude. Precious minutes were passing. Weeks.

I bent over and cried out. "My…my stomach!"

Mom stared at me a moment, then leaped on it. She came over to me and wrapped an arm around my shoulders. "Appendicitis?" she asked.

I nodded. "I think so."

She'd caught on—the nearest medical care was in the next valley. The guy might be able to ignore a request to pick up a broken-down car, but an ailing girl? Nah. He'd have to act.

Ticket Dude, frowning, picked up the phone and called someone, speaking in quick, hushed tones. Lia came over to me and held my arm. I groaned and bent over again.

"Careful," Lia whispered. "You're supposed to have appendicitis; you're not about to have a baby."

I grimaced and turned away so the guy wouldn't see my smile. She was right. Appendicitis would create a steadier, building kind of pain. I modified my act.

"I can take you. I just need to wait for my replacement."

I groaned and bent over again.

He frowned, then came out the side door and shifted his weight, back and forth, anxiously looking toward the castello, to where his help must be coming from.

"Please," I said, reaching out to him. "Can we not go now? Please."

He gave the castello one last look and then gestured over to a tiny vehicle, barely larger than a Smart Car. Lia and I climbed in the back, our knees practically at our ears, and Mom and he climbed into the front. As he started the car, I cried out again, *"Sbrigati!" Hurry.*

Much to my satisfaction he sped out of the parking lot. Climbing the road and turning onto the highway within fifteen minutes.

"Gabriella, stay with us," Mom said in Italian. She looked at Lia. "Is she thinking straight?" Then to me again, "What year is it?"

Man, she was smart, my mom. "Uh," I said, gritting my teeth against the pretend pain. I guessed a year, five back.

Our driver snorted. "Is she simpleminded or feverish? You can see right now the year...." He pointed to his cell phone on the dash. It had the date as his screensaver.

I leaned back with a sigh of relief as Lia squeezed my hand in excitement. We'd done it. Or God had. We'd gone back two years. And it was summer.

Come on, Dad. Be there. Be where you're supposed to be. Not filing paperwork in Firenze or Siena or Roma. Be there, be there, be there, please...be there.

In another fifteen minutes, we reached the next valley. "Turn here!" Mom said, gesturing toward an upcoming dirt road to the left with a *Societa Archeologico dell' Italia* sign on a tree. "I think this site has a doctor on campus."

"There is a doctor at the clinic, just ahead."

"Turn here!" all three of us yelled, just as it was becoming too late.

The guy slammed on his brakes and barely made the turn, frowning at us like we were crazy. With agonizingly slow speed, he found a spot in the dirt parking lot. "Can you wait here a moment?" Mom asked the driver.

He rolled his eyes and complained that he needed to get back, but she gave him a pleading look that no man, regardless of age, could deny.

Mom ran along, ignoring the calls and greetings of others around her, recognizing her, wondering about her strange gown. People we knew well—scientists, university students, volunteers— looked at us as if they wanted to greet us but were afraid to say something. Because, of course, we'd grown into young women since they'd seen us, the *day before* for most of them. *Talk about growing up overnight....*

I stopped abruptly. Could it be that we'd come face-to-face with ourselves? Our younger selves? I glanced around warily. *That'd seriously creep me out.*

"Have you seen Dr. Betarrini?" Mom asked one.

"He's around here someplace…"

"Phoebe, have you seen my husband around?" she asked the next, her anxious movements betraying her casual tone.

Phoebe shook her head and looked my mom over.

"He's over here!" called Jack, another colleague of my parents. He gave my mom a curious look too and hooked his thumb over his shoulder.

It was then that a man straightened behind him and looked over at us, his eyes slowly focusing on us, recognizing us. Sort of. Mom, anyway. But he was looking at me and Lia, as if he was trying to decide if he was in the middle of a crazy daydream or if two young women who looked just like his daughters, but older and dressed weird, were really standing fifteen paces from him.

We, of course, were totally stuck. Overwhelmed. Tongue-tied. And scared as all get-out.

"Oh. My. Gosh," Lia said. "Is it real?" she asked, tears already in her eyes.

But I was moving, along with Mom, toward him.

Running now.

Dad.

Dad. Dad! Dad!

We flew into his arms, and he stepped back, laughing, surprised, wondering what the heck was going on. Lia came then and wrapped her arms around all of us, laughing, crying too.

He leaned back, his face a mask of confusion. "Whoa, whoa, what's going on here?" He took my face in his hands, then Lia's. He glanced at Mom and down at her gown. "What's with the medieval wench getup?"

Mom smiled through her tears and pulled him closer, reached up and touched his face, as if she were trying to memorize every wrinkle and pore. "Oh, Ben…You have no idea how good it is to see you."

Tears were streaming down my face and Lia's. We reached in to hug him with Mom again.

"All right, all right," he said, half exasperated with us, half bewildered. "Who is going to tell me what's going on here?"

"Come with us," Mom said, pulling him along. I stayed glued to his side, under his arm, trying to believe this was really happening.

I helped Mom propel him forward. "We'll explain on the way, Dad. Please."

"N-now?" he sputtered. "We're about to—"

"Right now," Mom said, accepting no argument. "Do you have a car?"

"*We* have a car," he said slowly, speaking to her as if she was losing it. "Remember?"

So Mom had been right about the vehicle. The Jeep we'd had that year. It barely ran. Hopefully it was a good day. Because on bad days it had left us stranded, over and over again. We'd had to steer while Mom and Dad pushed it to get it started, then we'd move aside so they could jump in and take the wheel.

"Come on," she said, pulling at his hand. She looked apologetically to their colleagues. "Wrap camp for the day," she said. "This might take a while."

We ran back to the parking lot. The Ticket Dude lifted his hands as if to say, "What's the deal?" when we ran past him and got into the Jeep. He made an angry gesture and peeled out of the parking lot.

"It running okay today?" I asked, anxiously looking after Ticket Dude.

"Uh...*yeah*. You were in it this morning, remember?" Dad said.

"Not quite. Get in and start driving," Mom said, sliding into the passenger seat as Lia and I swung into the back.

"There's something weird going on here," he said, glancing back at us. "I know I haven't really been paying attention to the girls this summer, Adri, but when did they grow up? Overnight? Is it the clothes? What's with the costumes?" He stared at us, trying to sort out what had to be the most confusing day of his whole life. He shook his head and frowned, looking from me to Lia and back again. "Nah, it's more than that. I mean look at you!"

I was torn between wanting him to just keep talking, unable to keep my eyes from him, and wanting to scream at him to drive.

"I'll tell you what's happened, Ben," Mom said. "But please, drive while we talk."

"Okay," he said, turning the key. But the engine wouldn't start, of course. Lia and I glanced at each other, hopped out and began pushing the vehicle down the hill. In a few seconds, the engine caught and we hopped into the back.

"That's new," he said, gesturing back at us and looking to Mom. "Last I remember, that was our job."

"There are quite a few new things I need to tell you about," Mom said as we bumped over the dirt road, following behind the kid from the ticket booth.

"Please pass him, Dad," I said.

"Are we in a hurry?"

"Yes!" we all cried together.

He clamped his lips shut. And passed the ticket guy on the highway.

"How long you figure we've been here?" I asked Lia.

"Counting the minutes at the very end, bouncing back here, I'm thinking it's been a good hour, maybe an hour and a half."

Mom told Dad what she could as he drove, finally reaching the road that ran past Castello Forelli and to the edge of the tomb field. We noticed she didn't tell him the biggest thing. That he'd died. That we'd come back to save him. Was she afraid it would change that outcome somehow?

To his credit, Dad didn't stop or demand that he take us all to see a psychiatrist. In his place, I might've done that. We passed Castello Forelli, and Dad didn't pause. Apparently, in his world, it had been there all along.

But he seemed reluctant as we ducked through the trees and climbed the boulders, as if he might be dreaming, that his dream-wife and dream-daughters were taking him on a journey he wasn't really ready to take.

"Come on, Ben," Mom said, gesturing back to him. "This is where I found it."

He climbed up the last boulder. "That's what I don't get, Adri. Where was I?" But his attention was then on the tumuli before them. He reached up and ran his hands through his thick brown, curly hair, so like mine. And his face broke out in excitement. "Adri! Adri! We found it!" He hooted and shook his head in disbelief as Lia and I dragged him forward. "It was so close, all along! We were so close!"

"Yes," she said, smiling at him tenderly, staring at him in wonder. "How I longed for you, for this moment."

"Can you talk about it on the other side?" I muttered, pushing them toward Tomb Two.

"Other side?" he asked. "You intend...we are going back? In time?"

"Yes," I said. "I have to, Dad."

"First we'll go to the future, by two years. Then back. That's how it works," Lia said. "We have to kinda bounce from one end to the other. I think."

Mom gestured behind her. "If you think this is the archaeological discovery of our lives," she said, "wait until you see Italia in all her medieval glory."

"You realize this makes no sense, whatsoever, Adri. This is totally unlike you. Maybe you three stumbled into some bad mushrooms when you were collecting herbs or something?"

Mom took his hands in hers and looked into his eyes. "Believe me, Ben. I know what you're thinking, feeling. How crazy this all sounds…But it's important you come with us. Can you trust me?" She glanced back at us and then to him again. "Trust us?"

He hesitated a moment longer. "I'm willing to suspend disbelief for a bit. Test a theory." He squinted at her. "We can make this leap? All of us? Safely?"

Lia and I looked at each other. We'd hardly been safe, considering all the battles and escapes we'd endured. But this was life. *Life,* more full and vital and exciting than we'd ever known. And we wanted more of it.

Mom was still trying to figure out how to promise him that it was safe. That was a laugh.

"All I can tell you is that the girls have made the journey twice already," she said at last. "And that we must go too. In a way, Ben, we travel not to the past, but to our future." She looked over at us. "We'll be together, come what may. And that, I've found, is the best thing of all."

Lia and I stepped closer. I held out my hand. "I like that, Mom. 'Together, come what may.'"

"Together," Lia said, putting her long fingers on mine.

"Together," Mom added, placing hers on top of Lia's.

We looked to Dad, waiting. He smiled at us, each one of us, and then gently put a big, warm hand beneath my own, and his other on top of Mom's. The gesture made a lump form in my throat. I couldn't look at Mom or Lia, knowing that I'd cry if I did.

"I don't know exactly what's happening here, or why," he said. "But I know this…if my three girls are going somewhere, so am I."

... a little more ...

When a delightful concert comes to an end,

the orchestra might offer an encore.

When a fine meal comes to an end,

it's always nice to savor a bit of dessert.

When a great story comes to an end,

we think you may want to linger.

And so, we offer ...

AfterWords—just a little something more after you

have finished a David C Cook novel.

We invite you to stay awhile in the story.

Thanks for reading!

Turn the page for ...

- **A Chat with Lisa Bergren**
- **Discussion Questions**
- **Historical and Factual Notes**
- **Facebook Fan Site**
- **Acknowledgments**

A CHAT WITH LISA BERGREN

Q. I understand that you listen to soundtracks as you write.

A. Yes. It makes me feel like I'm watching a movie unfold instead of just pounding away at the keys. For this series, I've been listening to *I Am Legend,* the Chronicles of Narnia soundtracks, *Gladiator, The DaVinci Code,* and a mix of medieval songs my husband found for me.

Q. Tell me about working at the library.

A. I wrote most of this book in our local library. I got almost obsessive-compulsive about it. I had My Chair. And My Table. And My Footstool. An outlet close by. Thankfully, I only rarely came across someone else sitting in My Chair. Because when I did, I just sat really close to them until they finally gave up and went away.

Q. Why write at the library? Not at home?

A. It's weird, huh? For the first time in fifteen years, I have an empty house on school days. But all that space and silence just makes me want to fritter away the day rather than get anything serious accomplished. I'm sucked into Twitter and Facebook and email far too easily. I had to separate myself—go to the library, and never, ever,

ever log on to the Internet. I'd slip on my headphones and disappear into medieval Italy for hours at a time. It was perfect.

Q. You'll go back there to complete Torrent?

A. Oh, yeah. Obsessive-compulsive now, remember?

Q. What impact did your focus group have on these books?

A. They saved me, over and over, from looking like the Dweeb Mom trying to speak to Teen Culture. There is an example right there—they'd never let a word like *dweeb* slip into Gabi or Lia's speech. Moreover, I was encouraged when they fell in love with these characters with me. And they've been a good sounding board for me when I'm trying to figure out a particular plot or character problem. I loved hearing their feedback on the River of Time Series Facebook page or via my surveys.

Q. What happens next for the characters in the series?

A. Can't tell ya. It's between me, God, and the librarians.

DISCUSSION QUESTIONS

1. Growing up, most of us were taught to go the extra mile in peacemaking and getting along with others. But in this *Us or Them* medieval world, Gabi and Lia come up against this decision over and over again. What would it take to make you draw a line in the sand and refuse to budge? Would it be a societal trend, physical survival, or what? Describe.

2. Gabi goes through extreme physical and emotional trauma in this book. When she's in the cage in Firenze, there is a very real possibility that she might die. Have you ever been on the edge of death? If so, describe. What did you learn about life that you want to remember? If you haven't experienced this, what do you think it would teach you?

3. Would you ever date two different brothers at different times? How about two guy friends? Why or why not?

4. Do you ever wish arranged marriages were still done today? Discuss the pros and cons.

5. Many lives are lost in the battle for borders, property, and power in this book. What land would you fight for? Your family property? Your state? Your country? Other countries? If you wouldn't fight for any land, describe your thoughts on that.

6. When Gabi is in the cage, she hears a voice she identifies as her father's, but she's not entirely sure and isn't thinking clearly … it might be God's. Who do you think it was? Discuss.

7. If you were in Gabi's shoes, how would you convince your mom and sibling to stay with you? What would be the good parts about living in that era versus living in today's culture?

8. In the end, Gabi risks her relationship with Marcello in order to try and go back and save her dad. Would you have done the same? Why or why not?

9. How would losing a parent change your family? If you have lost a parent, describe what has transpired for your family.

10. What do you think will happen in book three, *Torrent?*

HISTORICAL AND FACTUAL NOTES

I used a good number of research materials to give this series its backbone. A full bibliography can be found in *Waterfall*. While I like to base my novels on historical fact and stick as close to it as I can, I'm a novelist and compelled to write the best, most dramatic story possible. Therefore, I feel free to take liberties! Here are some things to note:

While Siena and Firenze were constantly at odds and often battled, and the lords within them oft battled one another, there was no such "war" as depicted in this book. Significant battles occurred over the centuries. But it wasn't until 1555 that Firenze really took on Siena and forced her to swear allegiance.

Also there were outbreaks of various forms of illness and plague—something every city was worried about—but it wasn't until 1348 that the worst wave of the Black Death ravaged the population of Europe, taking a third of Siena's population alone. I'm assuming there were smaller, earlier waves of illness.

At one point, Gabi and Lia escape through a passageway among an Etruscan necropolis. This locale was inspired by a real place: Sovana, far from where the bulk of this story is set—in the south of Tuscany. The rounded tumuli I've described were inspired by those in Cerveteri, near Rome, but the "igloo" aspect was a figment of my imagination. Most Etruscan tombs are square or rectangular.

I hope you forgive me for playing around with facts and history to best serve the story. Such a power trip, this author gig!

Join other readers and Lisa on the "River of Time Series" Facebook page. There, you'll find information about the books, discussion with other fans, and contest and prize information.

Use this QR code to join the River of Time Facebook page.

Acknowledgments

Thanks to the publishing team that is bringing this series to life: Dan Rich, Don Pape, Terry Behimer, Ingrid Beck, Traci DePree, Caitlyn York, Amy Kiechlin Konyndyk, Sarah Schultz, Karen Athen, Karen Stoller, Jeane Wynn, Jeremy Potter, and Marilyn Largent, among many others. Also thanks to my agent, Steve Laube, for cheering me on in new directions (after a few careful, thoughtful questions). And blessings on the heads of David Carlson, who designed these gorgeous covers, and Christine Canterra, who made sure the Italian translations between the covers made sense.

My River of Time Tribe girls, who read this manuscript (and *Waterfall,* and soon, *Torrent!*) gave me excellent feedback that I could incorporate. Thanks, girls. I appreciate each one of you.

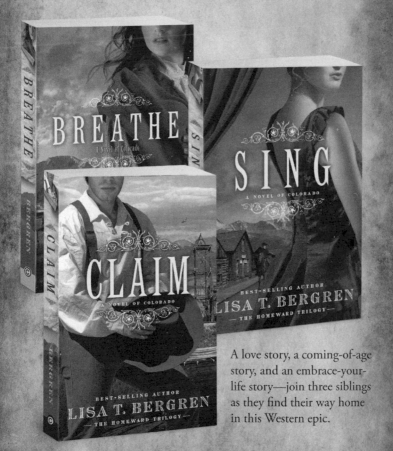